Effortless

S.C. Stephens

Edited by Debra L. Stang
Cover photo © iStockphoto.com/Manuel Gutjahr

ISBN-13: 978-1469982991
ISBN-10: 1469982994

Thank you to all of the fans who enjoyed
Thoughtless and asked for a sequel!

And a special thank you to Monica, Nicky,
Becky, Jenny, Natalie and everyone else who
helped me get this story published!

Chapter 1 – My Boyfriend, the Rock Star

According to the channel four weatherman, it was the hottest summer on record in Seattle. Since I'd only been there a little over a year, I took the kind man's word for it. As I was jostled, smashed into, and bumped up against, I felt the afternoon heat in the clammy skin of every person that touched me. It was revolting to have strangers rubbing up against my body. It was even more revolting when some of those people decided that being crammed together like sardines gave them the freedom to invade my personal space. I'd smacked more hands off my butt in that one afternoon than in the entire time I'd worked at Pete's bar.

Sweat poured down the back of my t-shirt, and I momentarily cursed my fashion choice. As I glanced up at the cloudless, azure sky, the midday sun hit me square in the eye, blinding me. I rolled up the short sleeves of my midnight black shirt, then went to work tying a knot above my bellybutton, just like MaryAnn from Gilligan's Island.

But then I smiled, remembering why I was wearing it and what I was doing in this crowd of sweaty bodies. As I stared past the few rows of glistening people in front of me to an empty stage, I was overcome with nervous energy. Not for me. No, all my nerves were for my boyfriend. Today was his and his band's big day. In anticipation, I bounced on my feet as I waited for him to bound up onto that stage. I knew he was going to rush to that microphone at any moment, and the waiting crowd was going to let out an ear-splitting scream.

I couldn't wait.

Hands next to me grabbed my bare arms. "Can you believe it, Kiera? Our boys are playing Bumbershoot!"

I looked over at my best friend, my coworker and my confidante—Jenny. Her face wasn't pouring with sweat like mine; she looked gloriously dewy. The spark of excitement lighting up her eyes was identical to mine though. Her boyfriend was also playing at the Seattle Music Festival for the first time.

Squealing in my growing eagerness, I clutched her arms in return. "I know! I can't believe Matt actually booked them here." I shook my head, impressed that my boyfriend was performing in the same venue that Bob Dylan would be playing at later tonight. Hole and Mary J. Blige were scheduled to perform in the next couple of days.

Jenny looked over when some stranger collided into her; he seemed completely stoned. Glancing back at me, her blonde ponytail lightly flicking my face, she shrugged. "Evan says he worked really hard to get them this spot. And it's prime! Saturday afternoon on a perfect summer's day, smashed right in-between two great acts. It doesn't get any better than that."

She tilted her head up to the sky. The sun's rays glinted off the white lettering on her matching black t-shirt, a t-shirt glorifying the full name of our favorite band—Douchebags—although, they shortened it to D-Bags, for marketing purposes.

I nodded when her face returned to mine. "Oh, I know, Kellan said he--"

A sudden eruption of sound disrupted my conversation and my eyes automatically darted to the stage. Smiling broadly, I watched what had the raucous crowd's complete attention. Our D-Bags had finally decided to grace the crowd with their presence.

The assemblage before the outdoor stage started jumping and hollering as Matt and Griffin hopped on stage. Matt was his normal, contained self, acknowledging the fan fest with a small smile and a slight wave. He quietly walked to his microphone and strapped on his guitar. I hollered for him, but the cacophony of noise drowned out my voice, and the guitarist didn't hear me. His light blue eyes scanned the crowd nervously as he adjusted the strap on his shoulder.

On the opposite end of the spectrum, Griffin, Matt's attention-seeking horn dog of a cousin, ran up and down the stage, smacking people's hands and pumping his fist in the air. His pale eyes scanned the crowd, and although I wasn't yelling for him, he actually heard me. Spotting Jenny and I back a ways from the front, he pointed at us. Then he lifted his fingers up to his mouth in a V shape and did suggestive things with his tongue that made my cheeks flame hotter than the steamy sunshine I was standing in. I immediately averted my eyes.

Several people around Jenny and I laughed and looked at us. My embarrassment tripled. Jenny beside me saucily exclaimed, "Ewww, Griffin!" then started laughing with the crowd. I shook my head, wishing my sister, Anna, wasn't at her photo shoot for the Hooters calendar today, so she could, maybe, attempt to keep her pseudo-boyfriend in line.

Evan entered during the middle of that display, and seeing Griffin sexually harass us, looked over our way. He smiled and waved, blowing a kiss to Jenny. She snatched it in the air and blew one back. His smile expanded, but once he acknowledged us, he twisted to take in the scene, and his dark eyes seemed awed by what he saw. I laughed at the look, happy that the good-spirited man was taking a second to enjoy his success.

Then the screams grew so loud my ears started ringing. I actually cringed in pain. The girls beside me, looking all of fourteen, started clutching each other and chanting, "Oh my God, there he is. Oh my God, he's so hot. Oh my God, oh my God, oh my God!"

I grinned and shook my head, amused at how my rocker boyfriend could affect people. Of course, I completely understood. Lord knows he had completely affected me in the beginning. Still did. Just watching him confidently strut onto the stage, the stage he owned with every fiber of his being, my body tingled for him.

Kellan slowly walked up to his microphone. Or perhaps it was a regular pace and my mind was operating in slow-motion. For whatever reason, it seemed to take him forever to get to his destination. He raised one hand, waving to the electrified crowd clamoring for him, and he ran the other back through his thick, bed-head hair. The heat and sweat made the sandy-brown mess stick out even more haphazardly; he looked completely edible.

I bit my lip as he sauntered to his microphone stand. He scanned the crowd as he adjusted the height of the stand. I knew from experience just what the front row was feeling as those midnight-blue bedroom eyes washed over them. Kellan had a way of looking at you that made you feel like no one else existed in the world, even if a crowd was around you. Add that to the sexy half-smile on his face, and you got a man who could ignite you with just a glance. He was igniting me now, and he hadn't even spotted me yet.

As his face turned away, hopefully searching for me out in the masses, I studied his jaw line—strong, masculine, so freakin' sexy it hurt. The girls behind me obviously thought so too. From among the shrieking, I clearly heard, "That is going home with me tonight," and, "God, that man is completely fuckable." I resisted the urge to turn and tell them that he was mine and instead, focused my gaze on him. I knew I shouldn't be jealous or irritated by his fans, but their remarks were a lot less cute than the previous comments from the pubescent girls.

As Kellan's eyes finished inspecting the first half of the crowd, they shifted over my way. Like magic, he spotted us instantly. Jenny waved, then whistled with her fingers in her mouth. I flushed and smiled as those amazingly intense eyes locked on mine. He nodded at me and mouthed, "I love you."

The idiotic girls behind me started moaning that he'd said it to them. I again ignored my desire to tell them that he was mine. It wouldn't change their feelings towards him one tiny little bit, and it would only create endless questions about our personal life. Questions I did not want to discuss with complete and total strangers. I'd put up with enough of that at school before Kellan and I had even started dating.

Instead, I discreetly mouthed that I love him too and gave him a couple of thumbs up. He laughed at my move and shook his head in amusement, clearly confident that he'd completely kick ass on stage. And he would. If anything, Kellan had spent his whole life preparing himself for this moment by playing small bars and clubs in L.A. and Seattle.

Slinging a guitar over his shoulder, he wrapped his hand around the microphone. The screams intensified when it became obvious that he was going to speak. Over the sound system, I heard his warm laugh, then, "Hello, Seattle!" The girls around me jumped and screamed his name. I laughed and tried to move away from some of the more excitable girls, but with nowhere to go, I only ended up colliding into a couple of guys in front of me.

I was muttering apologies when they glared back at me as Kellan's voice hit me again. "We're the D-Bags...in case you didn't know..." he paused for another long screaming session, "...and we've got something for you...if you want it."

He raised an eyebrow and gave some of the women in the front row a look that was a little lascivious for my taste. But I knew it was an act. While his face clearly said, *screw me later*, that wasn't what was in his heart. I was in his heart. Heck, I was tattooed over his heart. Well, my name was, anyway. I smiled, enjoying the fact that not a single woman here was aware of his hidden art. Well, besides Jenny.

He held up a finger to quiet the crowd. They surprisingly responded. "Do you want it?" he asked suggestively. The throng jubilantly indicated that they did. Jenny was hollering her answer through her hands, so I joined in.

I noticed Matt shaking his head, smiling as he flexed his hand. Evan was now sitting in front of his drums, moving his body to an unheard beat and spinning a stick in his hands. As Kellan eyed the crowd, I watched Griffin try to get a couple of girls to lift their shirts. I didn't keep looking to see if they did.

Kellan brought his hand up to his ear. "Well, if you want it, I'm gonna have to hear you ask for it." The audience hooted and hollered and the girls behind me made more obscene suggestions, but I didn't care. I no longer cared about any of them, because Kellan was looking straight at me and the pure joy I saw on his face was enough to make all of the audacious women, indecent men, and sweaty strangers, completely worth it.

It was like watching his soul come alive as he smiled down at me. He loved this. Aside from me, it was the one thing that Kellan really lived for. He acted like it didn't matter, that he did it just because it was something to do in the evenings, but after spending so much time with him, I was beginning to understand that that was just one of his coping mechanisms. A part of him feared that this would get snatched away from him. He hadn't grown up under the best of circumstances. Quite the opposite. He'd had a horror story childhood that would have left most people running straight for booze and drugs. But Kellan had found music, and music, along with a seriously healthy sexual appetite, had saved him from a life of mind-numbing addictions.

Kellan flicked his wrist behind him, and Evan, waiting for his cue, immediately began to play.

The song was fast, catchy, and even though I've heard it a bazillion times, I started jumping up and down with excitement. There was just something electrifying about the crushing, noisy bodies rubbing against me, the deafening vibrations of the amplified music, and the hot sun beating away on all of us. It gave me a rush. I could only imagine what Kellan was feeling.

His voice cut through the music, perfectly on time. No matter what he was feeling *off* the stage, Kellan was a professional *on* the stage. The countless practices and small shows around the area had paid off well; his voice was spectacular. A high-pitched, feminine squeal surged throughout the crowd as his voice drifted throughout the arena. He was singing an older song, a D-Bag classic, and several people around me were singing along. Since I'd watched Kellan write songs before, it was awe-inspiring to witness his lyrics being repeated back to him, especially in a crowd this size.

He beamed as he strummed and sang. A distractingly sexy half-smile was on his lips. It never failed to amaze me that he could play his guitar and sing at the same time. Me? I could barely do just one of those things. Jenny waved her hands in the air and cheered for her man. I did the same, happy that I could come out and support him today—support them all today. Well, maybe not Griffin.

The song ended with a thunderous reaction from the crowd, even impressing the guys directly in front of me. I was ecstatic for Kellan and the boys. They deserved the success. Kellan put his guitar away for the next song, and popped the microphone off its stand. This stage was wider than Pete's, and with more room to walk around, Kellan also had more room to flirt. Moving into the next song, his eyes seduced the crowd in ways that I was only used to them seducing me.

It annoyed me a little, but I let it go. He was just excited to be here, eager to play. He'd slipped back into the aggressively sexy guy that I'd first seen on stage. The salacious behavior had seemed over-the-top to me on that very first glance that I'd had of him, but the audience here was eating it up. Hands were stretching out to him from everywhere, even from rows behind me. I wasn't quite sure what those women expected him to do. Stage dive? I furrowed my brow, hoping he didn't do that. He could get hurt…or fondled to death.

As he propped a foot on a speaker and leaned out to grab a fan, I idly wondered why that one? Did he like her hair? Was she the most excited one in that section? Did she have the biggest…voice? Shaking my head at my insecurities, I pushed them out of my mind. He had so many things to concentrate on up there, he probably wasn't thinking at all. Just reacting to a fan asking for more attention. And they could certainly touch him. I wasn't such a jealous harpy that I couldn't handle a few caresses. Within reason, of course.

And Kellan was good with keeping most of his flirtations on the stage. He would never look or act that way in our daily life. You wouldn't even know he was practically a rock star when he wasn't performing. Really, he seemed a little lazy to the untrained eye. But I knew his mind was always busy, even if he was just slinging back cold ones at the bar.

As the temperature increased throughout their set, I wondered if Kellan might strip down. It wasn't a preposterous notion; he'd done it before while singing on stage. A couple of times, from what I'd heard. He was wiping off the sweat with the lower half of his shirt whenever he got the chance, pulling it up to reveal his gloriously defined abdomen. With the eruption of screams when he did that, I was sure the crowd would approve if he chose to remove it all together. The bulk of them, anyway.

I wasn't sure how I felt about women ogling my boyfriend in that way. I wasn't sure how I felt about his tattoo being exposed, either. That idea almost bothered me more. But after a quick wipe, he always let his plain, white t-shirt fall back into place. I preferred to believe that he liked keeping his tattoo a cherished secret, shared only by the two of us. And it should be. Even though it was on his body, it was incredibly personal for each of us. It kept him connected to me while we were apart. It also helped seal us when we reunited.

Once their allotted time was over, the band members each gave small bows and Kellan thanked the crowd for listening. He was happier than I'd ever seen him as he backed away from the stand. His eyes flicked down to mine in the crowd. No, I was wrong before. The look he was giving me now was the happiest look I'd ever seen on him.

The crowd around us started shifting, some staying to watch the next show, while others left to check out another venue. Bumbershoot had dozens of artists playing at any given time, from the big names to the locals like the D-Bags. After attending the show last year with them, when Kellan and I were merely friends, well, as much of friends as we'd ever been, it was a little surreal to see their name on the lineup posters. I'd snagged about three dozen of those posters as mementoes.

Giggling, Jenny locked her arm with mine and pulled me towards the side of the stage. The guys were alternating between acknowledging the fans and unplugging their stuff. Kellan grabbed his prized guitar, and with a smile and a nod at me, ducked behind the stage. Jenny and I approached a metal railing fencing off the backstage area from the rest of the populace. And if the fence wasn't enough of a warning, a couple of yellow-shirted security guards were there to shoo people away.

Waiting in the spot where I knew Kellan would eventually appear, I, for a moment, wished I was adventurous enough to sneak behind the fence. I wanted to go to Kellan and give him the huge congratulatory hug that was bursting my prideful stomach apart. But it was off-limits to normal folks, and I didn't want to cause a scene by getting busted by the burly guys who put Pete's bouncer to shame.

I sighed as I watched Evan and Matt disappear from the stage, while Griffin leaned over to suck face with some blonde before he, too, vanished. I again wished my sister was here. Anna was hot, by most men's standards, and she could get into places closed off to ordinary girls like me.

After what seemed like an eternity, Kellan came out, sans guitar and the rest of the guys. Rushing up to me, he leapt over the metal rail. The security guards glanced at him, but they were more interested in keeping people out, not in. A small scream erupted from the knot of people also waiting for their rock-god, but he headed directly for me.

His arms were immediately around me, sweeping me into a hug. With his exuberance, I thought he might sling me over his shoulder and twirl me around. If I hadn't been sure that he'd also smack my bottom a few times, turning my face beet-red, I might have let him do it. But I'd prefer it if those sorts of things occurred in a more private setting. And Jenny and I weren't the only girls waiting around back here for the band.

So, giggling as he lifted me up, I made sure to sling my arms firmly around his neck so he couldn't get too carried away. His smell hit me instantly. That undeniable aroma that was purely him. Clean, manly, seductive…it was a scent that lingered with me, even in my dreams.

Kellan laughed and squeezed me tight, the air compressing from my lungs until he set me down again. Pulling back, his impossibly blue eyes glowed at me. "That was so much fun! I'm so glad you were here…did you like it?"

His eyes sparkled in a shaft of sunlight as he grabbed my shoulders and squatted down to look me square in the eye. I giggled more at his question. Really? Of course I liked it, I loved watching him perform. His expression was so sweet, his joy child-like…almost innocent. Cupping his warm cheeks, I nodded. "I loved it. You guys were amazing! I'm so proud of you, Kellan."

His face beamed at my praise, then he seemed to notice something that he hadn't before. His fingers around my arms pushed me back a little and his eyes traveled down my chest. I swear I felt the heat increase in a straight line down my body by his gaze alone. Stopping at my exposed navel, his lips twisted devilishly and he peeked up at me from under his so-long-it-wasn't-fair eyelashes. The smoldering desire in his eyes was enough to quicken my breath. Kellan's innocent moments never lasted very long.

"I like your shirt."

His voice was melted sex. Yes, melted…sex.

I flushed all over. He could still make me feel like he was looking at me for the first time, not the thousandth time. He still gave me butterflies.

Just as I was about to come up with some response to his comment, Kellan was attacked. Not literally, but female hands did grab his arms and twist him around. Laughing adorably, he let go of my shoulders and basked in the affections of his fans. Some of them looked at me with raised eyebrows, but then ignored me. That was fine. I'd rather not be in Kellan's spotlight, if I could help it.

While Kellan signed autographs and had his picture snapped with cell phones, I shook my head at the surreal situation before me. I constantly forgot that he was a little famous. I mean, I was used to the girls at Pete's, but this wasn't Pete's. Watching that popularity follow him to such a public venue was kind of hard to wrap my head around. As I watched, the next girl in the crowd clamoring for him to notice her pulled down her tank top to expose the cups of her bra. She begged him to sign her chest. He glanced back at me really quick, but then he did it…and there was plenty of room to sign his full name, if you know what I mean.

My cheeks flamed hot, and I felt a knot of tension in my stomach. Yeah, I tried to be cool about his lifestyle, but his face in her chest while he signed away with a sharpie was a little much. As were her hands on his ass. Just as I thought to shove the vixen away, a firm hand rested on my shoulder.

"He loves you, Kiera. He's just playing."

I looked over my shoulder at Evan. He'd come out from behind the metal fence while I'd been preoccupied with watching Kellan. Kellan could do that to me— make me oblivious to the world. My habit of getting so wrapped up in him that everything else around me blurred into the background was sort of a weak point in me. I was working on it.

Evan grinned at Kellan as he slung his tattooed arm around Jenny's waist. The perky blonde gazed up at Evan with adoration. Being the front man, and drop-dead gorgeous besides, meant Kellan drew a lot more attention than the other guys, but Evan certainly had his followers, too. They were behind him now, waiting for the sweet teddy bear of a man to disengage from his girlfriend.

His warm brown eyes glanced down at me as he pointed his other tattooed arm at my boyfriend. "It's sort of his job, you know, to keep the fans wanting more."

I glanced over at Kellan, now smashed in-between two girls kissing his cheeks while a third forever captured the moment with her camera. I was certain the photo would be on the Internet within hours. I sighed. At least he drew the line at them kissing him on the lips since he'd become my boyfriend. He didn't used to. And yes, those pictures were on the Internet too.

Looking back up at Evan, I shrugged. "I know…I just wish he wasn't so good at it." My voice came out a little sullenly and Evan chuckled, clapping my shoulder as he finally twisted to acknowledge his fans.

With Jenny by his side, Evan signed autographs and made playful small talk with complete strangers. Jenny did, too. Standing back from the mayhem, I marveled at how comfortable they both looked. Me? I'd rather die than make multiple introductions over and over again.

My eyes darted to Kellan's broad back. A woman had her hand resting inappropriately low on his backside. I quickly averted my eyes. There was no point fueling my jealousy by watching. Instead, I glanced over at where Matt had quietly joined the fray. He looked just as uncomfortable as I felt. He enjoyed playing, being on the stage, and creating and making music. That was where his passion lay, not in the people-pleasing part. But he nodded politely, posing for a couple of pictures and signing a couple of t-shirts.

Attached to Matt's arm was his equally quiet girlfriend, Rachel. She was a beautiful mix of Latin and Asian with bronze skin and deep brown hair. She held the hand of her spiky, blond boyfriend, not looking jealous by the attention he received, but not looking like she wanted to partake in the socializing either. Not one for crowds, Rachel had watched the show from the lawn nearby. She was reticent and far more bashful than I…which was saying a lot. Rachel was Jenny's roommate. She and Matt had started seeing each other last spring, around the same time Kellan and I had officially become an item. The low-key pair was still going strong. Their personalities blended very well. They were adorable together.

The last D-Bag to stroll into the waiting crowd was not so adorable. I rolled my eyes as Griffin sauntered into my line of sight, his hands fondling anything that he could. Some girls smacked him, others giggled. He always returned to the giggling ones. His form of signing autographs usually involved tongue. It turned my stomach, watching him. Honestly, I didn't get what my sister saw.

Matt's near-identical released a girl he'd just deep-throated and swung his head around, looking for more prey. Unfortunately, his horny eyes fell on me. His thin lips twisting into a familiar curl, he started walking over my way. I instinctively started backing up. Griffin was one person that I liked to keep some distance from. He had a tendency to be a little…grabby. Tucking his chin-length blond hair behind his ears, he threw his hands out to the side, conveniently brushing against a fan's breast as he did.

"Kiera, my future lover! I'm thrilled you came to check me out." His hand went down to his cargo shorts and cupped his…stuff. "Did you like what you saw?" he asked, tilting his head.

Wanting to gag, I twisted to leave. Close enough to grab me, he sidled up and snatched my hand. I thought he was going to place my palm on his junk, and my eyes widened in horror. Suddenly, my fingers were torn away from his. Stepping between us, Kellan shoved Griffin's shoulder back. "Fuck off, Griffin," he muttered, shaking his head and rolling his eyes.

The bassist shrugged and found some other girl to touch him. I breathed a sigh of relief and sank into Kellan's side. "Thanks."

Chuckling, Kellan kissed my head. "No problem. I know how much you love conversing with Griffin." I cringed as Kellan waved goodbye to some of the lingering fans who were possibly hoping he'd stay behind and chat with them all day.

No, Griffin was about my least favorite person to talk to.

Rotating us around, his arm firmly attached to my waist, Kellan started walking us away from the private area and back to the main part of the park. Almost subconsciously, like they'd follow him anywhere without giving it a second thought, his band members started trailing after him. Looking back, I watched Matt and Evan strolling along with their arms around their girls. Griffin strolled along with his hand scratching his privates. In a way, they did follow Kellan anywhere. When his parents had died, Kellan had ditched everything to come up here, and they'd all followed him without a moment's hesitation. They'd been here ever since.

Fixing my focus back on the man beside me, I slung my other arm around his waist, cinching him tight. I couldn't imagine what that day must have been like for him. It was true that Kellan had good reason to hate his parents; they were abusive, cold-hearted bastards, blaming Kellan for all of the miseries in their lives, but still…they were his family. The only close family he had. Their death had deeply affected him.

He was only nineteen when they died. Tired of their abuse, Kellan ran away to Los Angeles right after high school. Right after the graduation ceremony, from the way he told the story. He didn't tell them he was leaving and they didn't bother searching for him. Kellan told me once that when he finally called them a few months after his disappearance, to tell them of his whereabouts and to let them know he was, at the very least, still alive, their response had been apathetic. It was as if they'd completed their jobs and he could live or die on his own. It was a miracle Kellan wasn't completely messed up.

Jerks.

It took Griffin coming up and clapping Kellan on the back to snap me out of my dark thoughts. With Matt and Rachel behind him, he pointed to a band playing in the distance. I could hear the heavy rock beat in the sweltering air. "We're gonna go check out some of the other bands. Comin'?"

Kellan looked back at Evan and Jenny, but they were happily gazing at each other, too absorbed in their own quiet conversation to hear the discussion through the multitude of bodies walking back and forth around our group; a few females passing by looked at the four guys like they seemed familiar, but none of them stopped for more than a couple of seconds.

Looking down at me, Kellan started to ask me what I wanted to do. My body answered for me. My stomach growled so loud that even Jenny broke away from her tender moment to laugh. I closed my eyes for a moment while I felt Kellan's body chuckling softly at me. Cracking just one eye open, I attempted to glare at him. He found that even funnier and laughed a little harder.

Glancing up at Griffin, Kellan shook his head. "I think we'll get something to eat first." Smacking Griffin's back, he added, "We'll catch up with you later."

After watching the physically similar cousins walk off, melding into the crowd around them, Kellan smiled down at me. "Should we get some food in you, noisy?"

I smirked and rolled my eyes, but then his lips were on mine and I couldn't have cared less that he was teasing me. With his hand brushing over my cheek as he ran his fingers through the hair above my ear, his warm lips expertly leading mine as he forced a small space between our mouths, and the tip of his tongue flicking out to briefly touch mine, I didn't care about much of anything anymore.

My hand reached up to securely tighten in his hair. I tried to angle him so his gently probing tongue was all over mine. All over my body would be nice, too. Chuckling, he broke free from my mouth. Just that brief intimacy had my heart racing, my breath quickening. It took so little for him to turn me on.

Grinning crookedly, he tilted his head. "Do you need a minute?" he whispered, raising an eyebrow.

Gathering my senses, I smacked his chest and started to storm off. Wasn't I just thinking earlier that I needed to work on not letting Kellan completely absorb me? Hmmm, I had a feeling I'd be working on that one for a while. Feeling a little dazed, I headed off to where I thought the food was. Laughing a little harder, Kellan grabbed my elbow and twisted me in the other direction.

Smiling in that seductive, devilish way that he could, he nodded his head at the concrete path, opposite of where I was going. "Food's that way." His smile widening, he added, "Unless you had something else in mind?" I instantly pictured finding a secluded spot in this massive campus and letting that tongue do…all sorts of marvelous, wondrous things to me. My breath hitched.

Shaking the steamy thoughts out of my head, I started marching up the path towards the one craving I was willing to cave into here. I was not about to indulge in public sex with my rock star boyfriend. As much as he would like that, I did have some self-control.

Still chuckling, still amused by me, Kellan easily caught up and slung his arm back around my waist. Smiling down at me as Evan and Jenny fell into step behind us, he murmured, "So adorable. What am I going to do with you?"

By the time we reached the pizza stands, I'd thought of at least a half-dozen things he could do to me.

Once we were all full of food and music, and enough memories to cement this day into our brains forever, we all rendezvoused back at the staging area so the band could collect their instruments. Except Evan. Due to the cumbersome nature of drums, all the bands used the same set. The big acts were the only exception to the rule, as they preferred to use their own drums.

With guitar cases slung over their backs, our group garnered more attention than before. Despite a designated park exit for band members, Griffin, being Griffin, insisted on heading out the main gate. Out of all of them, Griffin enjoyed the limelight the most. He was already living up his fifteen minutes.

Stopping to sign more autographs and take more pictures with fans, it seemed to take forever to get to the parking lot. But eventually, we did. Jenny gave me a quick hug and informed me that she'd see me at work tomorrow. Evan also gave me a huge bear hug, and jokingly told me that he, too, would see me at work tomorrow.

Smiling at them, I waved goodbye as they headed off together in Jenny's car, probably on their way to Pete's, as it was a work night for Jenny. I'd taken the night off, so I could spend the evening with Kellan. Because of their afternoon gig at Bumbershoot, Kellan and the guys were taking the evening off from performing at the bar. Not that that would stop the rest of them from spending the night there anyway. They could never be peeled away from Pete's for long.

I congratulated Matt as I gave him a loose, one-armed hug. He wasn't as overtly affectionate as Evan, and I tried to respect the level of endearment that he was comfortable with. Smiling shyly at me, he thanked me for coming, while Rachel merely smiled and waved goodbye as she and Matt put away Matt and Griffin's instruments and hopped into Griffin's Vanagon.

Griffin, perhaps noticing that I was doling out hugs to D-Bags, decided that he wanted to be a D-Bag, too. Checking his breath in his palm, he started striding towards me. I put my hand out to stop him, but I think it was Kellan clearing his throat, quite loudly, that gave him pause. Rolling his eyes, Griffin waved his fingers instead. "We're going to Pete's. Catch you guys later."

Kellan laughed and clapped him on the back before twisting to open the door of his sleek muscle car. A 1969 Chevelle Malibu from what Kellan had repeatedly told me. Shiny black with chrome all over, it was possibly the only possession, aside from his guitars, that Kellan cared about. He'd found the car cheap in L.A. and spent a considerable amount of time that first summer of his newfound freedom restoring it. It was his pride and joy…and he hadn't allowed me to drive it ever since the one time that I'd stolen it.

Sliding into the leather bench seat, he glanced over at me as I slid in too. "Your place or mine?" he asked, exaggerating the huskiness in his voice.

I laughed as I leaned over to kiss him. Still trying to keep our relationship on an even keel, instead of bursting right into the red-hot zone that we so easily could dip into, Kellan and I were still living apart, still taking things slow. "Mine," I breathed, trying to be as sexy as he was, but, probably failing horribly. Although, he did bite his lip as he looked at my face. Flushing instantly, I sat back and tucked a loose lock of hair behind my ear. "Anna's gonna be late tonight, so we'll have the place to ourselves."

His grin widened as he started the car, the hearty engine roaring to life, its growl as sexy as Kellan's smile. Feeling the heat on my cheeks, I shook my head and added, "School is starting soon, so I should start going through my stuff."

That wasn't really what I wanted to do tonight, but his intense gaze was rousing my body up, and I hated how much he could see himself affecting me. I wished I could be more subtle around him.

Twisting his lip, he seemed to contain a laugh. "Uh-huh, school stuff. All right. I'm great at…school stuff." His mouth breaking out into a heart-stopping grin, he pulled his car away from the place he'd just completely rocked.

Chapter 2 – Peace

Twenty minutes later, we pulled into the parking area of the apartment that I shared with Anna. Kellan still wore a fantastic smile on his lips as he shut the car off. I knew he was still on an adrenaline high from being on stage. While I could think of no greater torture than being the center of attention in front of hundreds of complete strangers, not to mention singing in front of them, Kellan lived for it.

He was grinning ear to ear, humming one of his songs, as he met me in front of his car. Smiling up at him, I looped my arm through his. I had no desire to live his life, but I would happily bathe in the aftereffects of it. Our path to each other had been a harrowing experience; his joy now brought me joy. I'd much rather see a delighted smile on his face than tears in his eyes.

After opening the door dramatically, he led me into my tiny two-bedroom place. Although it was postage-stamp small, it did have a pretty spectacular view of Lake Union. Following him through the door, I sighed tiredly and switched the light on. Removing my purse from around my body, I set it on a small table while Kellan shut the door. Mere seconds later, my body was jerked forward and then slammed back into the front door.

I gasped. Kellan's body pressed against me, his lips hungrily attacking mine. Without a thought, my fingers snuck up into his hair, twisting around the long strands. My heart surged forward so fast I thought I might collapse to the floor. Kellan's firm grip around me wouldn't have allowed that, though. Every inch of him, from his chest to his chiseled stomach to his sensuous hips, was flush against mine, pressing into me like he wished we could be closer.

As the fire in me started to heighten, the arousal I felt for him burned away every other thought in my head. My breath quickened. His breath between our hungry kisses, our light tongue flicks, was fast as well. Then his hand traveled over my bottom, curving around my thigh to the back of my knee. Shifting us slightly, he grabbed my leg and wrapped it around his hip. Lining us up perfectly, his aroused body pressed into mine, just where I needed it.

Groaning, I tightened my hands in his hair and firmly attached my lips to his. A sultry noise escaped his throat, rumbling through his body as our mouths moved together intently. It stoked the fire already within me to a boiling point. I needed him. All of him. Now.

Arching against the door, I broke away from his glorious mouth. "Kellan," I moaned out, instantly grateful my sister was not here, "...bedroom..."

His lips traveled down my throat, his tongue flicking every erogenous zone on the way down. I groaned again, rubbing myself against him, trying to dull the ache. A chuckle left his mouth as the tip of his tongue traced my collarbone. He was enjoying this, enjoying the way he was teasing me. Pushing his shoulders back, I frowned at him. He cocked an eyebrow at me, the edge of his lip curving up in a similar manner. It was so incredibly hot, especially with the desire smoldering in his eyes. No one could do bedroom eyes like Kellan could.

Then his demeanor completely changed. Smiling playfully, he let go of my leg that was hitched up his side. Cocking his head as he watched me struggling to breathe like a normal person, he took a step back. "Are you ever going to move back in with me?" he asked, his thumb coming up to trace the line his tongue was sliding down earlier.

I blinked at his sudden change of direction, my head feeling sluggish as I fought against my desire to push him back into the living room and take him on the monstrously ugly orange couch. I was pretty sure he'd let me. Wondering if he'd really just asked about us living together again, I took a side step away from him. It was also a side step toward the hall, toward my bedroom, and the smolder in his eyes came back a little.

Smiling impishly, he nodded his head that way. "Because I really hate having sex on a futon." Winking, he added, "Not that I won't, though."

Smirking at him, I reached out and grabbed his hand. "You're the one that kicked me out," I said, managing to keep my voice light, even though the memory was a painful one.

Backing us towards the hall, I watched a flash of pain wash over his face. It was gone instantly though. Shrugging, he laughed. "Well, it sounded like a good idea at the time."

My hallway was a short one. Anna had the larger room at the farthest end. Our tiny, shower-only bathroom was in the middle, followed by my room which was closest to the door. Kellan's place wasn't all that much bigger, but it seemed like a mansion in comparison.

Stopping in front of my bedroom door, I put my other hand on his chest. "No, it was a good idea." My hand traveled up his neck to cup his cheek; he leaned into my touch. "You and I needed space. We needed to get our heads on straight."

He smiled a little, then sighed. "Well, now that they are...why don't you come back?" His voice lowering, he stepped into my body and wrapped his arms around my waist. "I know we've taken things slow, but I still want to move forward...with you."

I swallowed at the warmth in his voice, the love in his eyes... I wanted that too, I really did, but, I was trying to be a stronger person. My own person. And I knew that if I moved back in with him, he'd be my world again. I'd drown in him.

Smiling encouragingly, I ran my fingers back through his hair. The serious look in his eyes softened as I caressed him. In as reassuring of a voice as I could muster, I whispered, "I think it's better if we keep waiting." Switching my hand to run my thumb over his cheek, I added, "I've sort of come into my own, being with my sister. I don't want to fall right back into needing a man to feel...complete."

I bit my lip, hoping he wasn't offended. His insanely blue eyes inspected my face, taking in every feature. Inhaling deeply, he squeezed me a bit tighter. "What if I'm the one that needs you?" His face was completely, heartbreakingly serious. Shrugging, his lips broke into a tiny smile. "I hate sleeping alone."

Even though he'd said he hated *sleeping* alone, I knew it was more than that. Kellan hated *being* alone. Oddly enough, it was something we had in common. But knowing we needed the separation, I threw on a bright smile. "You'll be all right."

His tiny smile curved into a disgruntled one and I laughed. Slinging both of my arms around his neck, I told him, "Besides, we almost always end up sleeping together anyway."

I flushed bright red after I said it, realizing how suggestive it sounded. He grinned at me adorably, reaching behind me to open my bedroom door. Laughing at my comment, he shook his head. "Exactly." Pushing my door open, his eyes came back to mine, playful now. "Think of the gas money we'd save." He walked me backwards into my room. "And rent, you wouldn't have to pay that, living with me. You could work less, concentrate on school more."

He smiled and shrugged, like it all made perfect sense. And logically, it did. Emotionally, though, my instincts told me that we were in a good place now, and maybe we shouldn't mess with that. Freeing one hand to flick on my light, I sighed. "I like my life, Kellan. I finally feel...well rounded."

As he closed my door with his foot, his hands slinked down to cup my backside. Smiling devilishly, he murmured, "Yes, I know, very well-rounded." I smacked him on the shoulder as he chuckled. Then he sighed, pulling my body flush to his and kissing me softly. "Fine."

I melted into his lips, savoring the taste of him, all wrapped up in the smell of him. Pulling apart, he kicked off his shoes with his toes and frowned at my lumpy futon. "But that seriously sucks. Can I at least buy you a decent bed?"

Smiling as I stepped out of my flip-flops, I grabbed his hand and pulled him towards the bed he hated. He was right, it was lumpy, with a heavy bar in the middle that dug into your back, but it was a large one and there was plenty of room on it to...roll around. Backing up to the edge of the futon, I grabbed the bottom of Kellan's t-shirt. "Of course. You can even help me break it in."

His seductive grin in place, he helped my fingers remove his clothing. "Hmmm...you may have sold me on this idea."

Laughing, I ran my hands down the wondrously etched lines in his chest. His breath hitched when my fingers traced the black ink of my name swirled over his heart. Nothing in this world was as beautiful to me as that tattoo, except the man bearing it.

"Anything that ends with sex sells you," I giggled.

Kellan playfully pushed my shoulder back, and I sat down on the bed that sagged a little in the spot that was technically the "sitting" area when the futon was folded up. Scooting into the center of the bed, the hard support bar apparent under my body, I felt heat rush through me as Kellan leaned over the edge of the mattress. His eyes peering up at me, he huskily murmured, "True."

My breath hitched as I watched him crawl over to me on his hands and knees. Leaning over me as my breath became embarrassingly fast, his eyes scoured the length of me. Feeling the pure sex appeal radiating from him, I swallowed. It amazed and mystified me that this man was mine, any time I wanted him. It was still a little miraculous to me that out of all of the women in the world that he could be with, he continued to choose me. I still didn't see why.

Smiling as his lips came down to mine and my hands traveled back up that smooth, perfect chest, I whispered, "Whore."

He laughed in my mouth as his body settled beside mine. "Tease," he breathed, his hand coming up to run through my hair.

I laughed at the terms that we'd once used to hurt each other with now being used as affectionate phrases. That was how it was with Kellan; cold one minute, red-hot the next. Going slow was how we were working on keeping our relationship consistent. Kellan didn't seem at all concerned that we'd burn out, but I sometimes worried about it. After all, he could have anybody. Even if he was experiencing something profound with me that he'd never had before—a true, deep to his core love—my greatest fear was that now that he'd been opened up to love, he could find it again with someone else if he wanted to.

God, I hated that thought.

Pushing back my doubts, I concentrated on what I knew with certainty. Right now, Kellan wanted me. Right now, Kellan loved me and only me. And at this very moment, my sister was not expected home for hours.

Dressed only in his worn denims that hugged him so perfectly, his sculpted chest above me as he leaned over my body, Kellan worked his mouth softly against mine as the fingers of his free hand spun around a dark lock of my hair.

My fingers were busy as well. They moved up to his wonderfully messy head of hair. It was so much fun to bunch it around my fingers, and I couldn't resist giving it a light tug. He grinned against my lips. Then my fingers trailed down his neck, enjoying the lean muscles, and the light pulse of his veins under his skin. From there they decided to swoop up and over his shoulder blades, lingering for a moment on the tensing and relaxing muscles as he played with my hair. Their only natural course after that was straight down his back. My lucky fingers delightedly roamed the smooth, lean expanse of skin on its way down to his waistband. Of course, halfway there, they decided to head back up to those shoulder blades and retrace the path down to his waist. But this time, I lightly scraped my nails across his flesh instead of using the softer, gentler finger pads.

"Don't tease me," he muttered as he sucked on my lower lip.

I laughed lightly as I remembered harshly digging through that perfect skin once before...in an espresso stand, no less. I felt my face heat as blood rushed to my cheeks. It had been sort of an embarrassing moment for me. Kellan pulled back from our kiss to look over my features, probably noticing my flushed cheeks and understanding my expression. His finger ran along my cheek before sweeping over my lips. "Do you have any idea what that did to me, when you scratched me?"

His lip twisted devilishly at the memory while my blush surely deepened. Not being able to speak, I merely shook my head. He smiled wider and leaned over to my ear. "I think that's what made me come."

My eyes closed for a second at hearing him say it, and I chuckled despite myself. "I didn't realize you were so kinky," I whispered.

He laughed out loud. "You're the one that cut me."

I giggled again, feeling my embarrassment slide from me with the laughter. "You're the one that liked it."

He kissed my chin gently before pulling back with a raised eyebrow. "You didn't enjoy doing that?"

I bit my lip and looked away from the cocky look of self-assurance on his face. Of course I'd liked it. My body had been just as satisfied by the experience as his. A bit of guilt washed through me. I did feel bad for hurting him, for drawing blood. That was a little more than was called for.

Surprising him, I shoved his shoulders back. He grunted and said, "Hey," as he tried to crawl back over me. Laughing, I kept him away with one hand while I squirmed out from where I was partly entangled in his legs. Before he could complain or manhandle me back into place, I straddled his hips.

As he was facing sideways, he started to flip onto his back. I could tell by the huge grin lighting up his face that Kellan assumed this was heading towards intimacy. He was turned on by the idea of me forcefully taking the top position. But then again, Kellan was always turned on. I laughed harder as I shoved his shoulder down, keeping his chest on the mattress.

Once I was firmly seated on his lower spine, he twisted his neck to look back at me. "What are you doing?"

My hands played over the expanse of pristine flesh before me while I answered him, a little huskily. "Well, I do feel guilty about hurting you…"

He twisted around a little more as his lips smirked at me. "I did mention that you made me come, right?"

I felt that flush return at hearing him say that word again—come. It wasn't even a dirty word, really, but hearing it pass his lips reminded me of toe-curling, blood-boiling, life-altering moments of ecstasy. Just hearing him say the word made me want him even more. Smiling, I pushed back that feeling…for now.

"I want to make sure you're not…damaged."

I traced my hands up his back, leaning over him so my hair brushed his skin. It delighted me to notice him shiver when my long locks stroked his back. His eyes flicked over my face and his voice dropped. "I only have one scar that can be attributed to you."

His eyes rested on mine and my breath caught at the love I saw in that gaze. I didn't think I would ever get used to seeing how much he adored me. It made all the flirting I had witnessed earlier irrelevant. None of those fan girls would ever receive that look from him. Nor would they ever have this level of intimacy with him. Not anymore. Evan was right, he played with them, but his heart was mine.

I nodded, surprised at how my eyes were misting. My mind replayed the memory he was referring to and I bit my lip. It was ages ago that he'd taken a knife wound while trying to defend my honor. It was one of the most amazing and horrifying moments of bravery that anyone had ever shown me. It amazed me that he'd stood up for me and horrified me that he'd been hurt. My fingers traveled down his ribs, touching the mattress as I curled them around his body. I leaned over and kissed the edge of the scar where I felt the roughness cutting into that once smooth skin. He sucked in a breath, his stomach clenching as my lips moved over the old wound.

I smiled and pressed kisses across his back as I thought of another wound he'd been inflicted with because of me. True, this one didn't have an external scar (the fracture was reset without surgery), but I knew the damage that lay beneath the surface. My hands ran up his arms, squeezing the left one, broken many months ago, during a fight with my former boyfriend, Denny.

I leaned forward and kissed that arm, and his eyes softened as he watched me. I knew he understood my gesture. "I adore you for all your scars," I whispered as I leaned over and gave him a soft kiss on the lips.

His hand came up to grip my head, keeping me ensnared in the loving softness of his kiss. He deepened it, and the fire of anticipation coursed through me when his tongue brushed over mine. My breath sped up and I leaned into the kiss for a moment before I stopped myself.

Skillfully, I pulled away from his hand trapping me to his mouth. With a playful scowl I smacked his shoulder. "You stop that. I'm not done with my inspection."

He sighed and rolled his eyes. "Well, can you hurry up? So I can make love to you and not this awful mattress?" He pressed his hips against the bed beneath him for emphasis, and I laughed. Laughing himself, he muttered, "We could switch positions when you're done?"

Ignoring that, I sat back on my seat at the base of his spine and turned all of my attention to his glorious back. He seemed fine. There were definitely no thin trails of puckered flesh from me tearing into him. I leaned forward to kiss his skin and then I noticed it. It was faint, so faint that you wouldn't have noticed the scar unless you were literally an inch from his skin, like I was, but it was there. Thin, white streaks ran down his back, right where I'd raked him. I smiled inwardly that a part of our crazy, intense night was still with him, maybe forever. As much as I hated that I'd caused him pain, I was a little happy that a reminder would be with him, wherever he went.

"Ah, found 'em," I muttered.

He started to ask me, "What?" when I playfully glided the very tip of my tongue over the vague white line. He cut off what he was saying, and a shudder rippled through him. Emboldened, I let my tongue make a trail between his shoulder blades and up the back of his neck. Kellan squirmed and dropped his forehead to the pillow; his breath quickened. Another old memory seizing me, I very gently bit the back of his neck, making him groan.

Before I could process it or stop it, he twisted beneath me, bringing his arms up to pull me down to the bed. All of the air whooshed from my lungs with the force he used to extract me from his back. I giggled when he crawled on top of me. His lips attacked mine, his tongue practically searching for my tonsils.

I pushed him away from me. With desire clear in his smoky bedroom eyes, he growled, "I said don't tease me."

I smirked and ran a finger across his parted lips. "Payback." I raised an eyebrow at him. "At least I didn't do that in a crowded club."

His face started. It was almost like he'd forgotten about that very intense moment when he licked me in the middle of a packed dance floor. Denny and Anna had been somewhere in that club at the time. His brow scrunched together as his eyes turned recalcitrant. "That wasn't very nice of me, was it?"

I slung my arms around his neck and shook my head. "No, it wasn't…but I liked it."

His guilty eyes turned playful again as he thought about that night. "I couldn't resist." His fingers trailed up my arms, raising them over my head and causing delightful shivers to course down my body. "You had your arms up here." He raised one over my head and brought the other one above it. Holding both wrists in one hand, he trailed his finger down my nose to my mouth. "You were biting your lip as you danced." I bit my lip again as I watched his hungry eyes recreate the imagery of me that had pushed him over the edge. His finger glided over my lip and down between my breasts. I closed my eyes but he kept going, dragging his finger over my still exposed belly button to my shorts. He played with the waistband before bringing a hand to my hip bone. "And these…these hips…" He leaned over me to lightly breathe on my face, our lips brushing together. "These hips drove me straight to madness."

He brought his lips down to mine and released my hands. I wrapped my arms over his head, firmly holding him to me. When we paused for air, I muttered, "You were watching me?"

He ran his nose along my jaw, flicking his tongue for an occasional taste. "Ceaselessly." His lips traveled back and forth along my jaw. "I have many things to atone for, and I hate what happened between us later, but I'll never be sorry for tasting your skin that night." I gasped and arched against him, lifting my head so his lips could revisit my neck.

He obliged and feather-light touches made their way down my skin. His mouth still on my neck, his fingers tore at the knotted section of my shirt. In one smooth move he lifted the dark material up and over my head. His eyes lingered over my body for a second before he harshly unhooked my bra and ripped it off. My body pulsed with need as his burning eyes visually caressed me.

With a sigh, he dropped his head to my stomach. "I need this flesh," he muttered as his tongue ran up my body.

Fire shot through me at the contact and I writhed under his touch. "I need you too, Kellan."

He dragged his tongue between my breasts. "I need to see your face when I do this." He flicked his tongue all the way up to my neck and I closed my eyes and groaned in response.

"I need to hear you when I do this." He brought his lips, and that miraculous tongue, to my breast, swirling it around the nipple.

I arched my back and dug my hands into his hair. "God, yes…"

His breath heavy, he brought his lips to my ear. "I need to be inside of you…as deep as I can go." My body ached with his words, my light shorts suddenly horribly uncomfortable as the pleasant tingling between my thighs shifted to a full-on throbbing ache. I moaned loudly and tried to kiss him but he pulled away.

He hovered above me and I opened my eyes to gaze at the Adonis before me. His expression burning with desire for me, he swallowed heavily. "And I need to hear you beg for it." His expression asking so much more than his words, he added, "Do you want me?"

The throbbing that I didn't think could get any worse intensified, and my mouth found his. "God, Kellan…please, yes, God…please. I want you…I want you so much." I also meant more than just the words. He was asking me if he was truly the one I wanted to be with. I was telling him, as plainly as I could, that he was.

I mumbled more pleas for him while our mouths enacted what we both wanted. With heavy breaths and frantic fingers we pulled off the rest of our clothes and he did exactly what he said he needed to do.

Smiling as I woke up the next morning, I yawned and stretched. My arms and legs didn't collide with another warm body in my chilly bed, but that wasn't too surprising. Kellan was almost always up before me. I wasn't sure why, but the boy was an early riser; he got up at the crack of dawn nearly every day. He was also a night owl, usually staying up just as late as I did, even on nights I closed at the bar. The man was sort of miraculous when it came to sleep. It did eventually catch up with him, hitting him like a brick wall and knocking him out for twelve hours straight, but it amazed me how he could go for days on very little of it.

Shaking my head at him, I inhaled deeply, my smile widening. My favorite smell in the world, besides Kellan's natural scent, was wafting through the house—coffee. Kellan was brewing a pot in the kitchen. That was definitely one of the perks of waking up with him.

Prying an eye open, I saw that he had left my bedroom door ajar. From the other room I could hear the pot percolating and the sound of Kellan getting cups ready. He was humming a song. Relaxing back on my pillow, I enjoyed the sound for a minute. I pictured him out there, singing away in just his boxers. It was a delightful image.

The sound of a key entering a lock broke the stillness of the morning. It was immediately followed by the front door cracking open. Sitting up on my elbows, I frowned. Was Anna just getting home now? I knew she'd worked the night shift yesterday, and she'd mentioned that she was going out afterwards with some of the girls from work, but this was late, even for her. Unless, of course, she slept…somewhere else.

Perhaps she met up with Griffin, to congratulate him on his big event. But it just as easily could have been some random guy that she hooked up with. Anna and Griffin had a bizarre relationship. When they were together, they were inseparable—all hands and tongues and, ugh, grinding. But when they were apart from each other…well, you'd never even suspect their involvement with each other. They were very open about being with other people. The situation was odd to me, but it seemed to work for them, so I didn't say much about it.

When Anna's bright voice sounded a greeting, I immediately hoped Kellan wasn't in his boxers. I inspected the ground to see if his clothes were still on my floor. Luckily, they weren't. Although he and Anna were only ever affable with each other, I didn't need my sister ogling him any more than she already did. My sister had physically kept her distance from Kellan once she realized we were in a relationship, but her eyes lingered on him, appreciating the masterpiece before her as she would appreciate any other fine piece of art. I understood. I appreciated him daily.

"Hey, Kellan, good morning."

"Mornin', Anna. You're out late…or early."

Anna sighed as a heavy bag clunked to the floor. "Yeah, went to Pete's. Ran into the guys."

Kellan chuckled lightly, probably surmising what I had guessed earlier, that she'd been entertained by Griffin until the wee hours of the morning. It hurt my stomach a little to think about what they'd probably been doing, and as I forcefully made my sluggish body stand up, I tried not to.

Anna laughed huskily while I grabbed some lounge pants out of my dresser, quickly throwing them on my naked body. "I heard you guys did great at your big show." Anna sighed forlornly. "I'm sorry I had to miss it."

Nonchalantly, Kellan replied, "It was just a show, nothing you haven't seen before. Don't worry about it."

I shook my head as I threw on a thin, comfortable shirt. Just another show? He was so indifferent about the whole thing. But I knew that it meant something to him. It excited him, invigorated him. He'd made that evident when he'd shoved me against the door last night. I bit my lip at that thought and quickly ran my fingers through my thick hair a few times, eager to see the passionate man again.

Stealthily walking out of my room, I immediately saw Anna and Kellan in the kitchen. He was leaning back against the counter, facing me, his arms crossed over his chest as he carried on a quiet conversation with my sister. Her back was to me, her long, luxuriously shiny hair ridiculously perfect for the early hour.

Watching them, I couldn't help but think that if my sister had had her way last year, the two of them would have ended up together and I'd be walking up on a couple, instead of a couple of friends. As Kellan's lips curved into a small smile while he spoke softly—his hair a distractingly charming mess—I could easily picture them as the gorgeous pair they would have been.

Raising my chin, I inhaled a big breath. That wasn't what had happened.

He'd never touched her. My sister had no idea what his lips felt like, what he tasted like, what his fingers felt like, what he sounded like when he was making love. She'd never heard him say *I love you*. But I had…repeatedly.

My confidence pushed aside my lingering insecurities as I meandered into the kitchen. They both twisted to look at me when I stepped into the small room. Kellan's small smile for Anna turned into a wide one for me, his deep eyes brightening.

I slung my arms around his waist. "Mornin', sleepy," he breathed, kissing my head.

Exhaling contently, I buried my head in his neck. "Good morning."

My sister sighed. "God, you two are adorable." Smacking my arm, she rolled her eyes. "It's annoying."

I smiled, laughing a little. "Good morning, Anna. Late night?"

Grinning devilishly, she bit her perfect, red lip and cocked an eyebrow just as expertly as Kellan. "Oh, yes." Her finger shifted between the two of us. "And I can guarantee you it wasn't as cutesy as your night."

I flushed and looked away from her, and she laughed, her voice throaty and seductive in a way that mine never would be. Kellan laughed with her, squeezing me tighter. "I wouldn't say our night was cute, Anna."

I flashed my eyes up to Kellan and smacked his chest, my face reddening even more. While our love life might be a bit tamer than he was used to, and tamer than my sister was used to for that matter, I didn't need him chatting about it. Grinning down at me, he said nothing further and I relaxed. Kellan wasn't exactly an open book, and he generally didn't talk about his life much. Thankfully, that included our sex life.

Anna snorted, and I looked back at her. Her face in a playful grin, she said, "I know." She poked my shoulder. "I know how hot you guys can get." My jaw dropped, and my face paled. She laughed and jerked her thumb towards the hallway. "My bedroom is only one room away from yours, Kiera." Raising her eyebrows, she leaned in and muttered, "Maybe the two of you could remember that in the future?"

I covered my face with my hand and twisted into Kellan's body. God, sometimes I did forget. Being with Kellan could be so…consuming. Chuckling as he held me close, rubbing my back, Kellan casually answered her. "We'll try and keep that in mind, Anna. Thanks."

Laughing, Anna rubbed my shoulder. "I'm just teasing you, Kiera. Go ahead and scream away, I don't mind." As I peeked at her from between my fingers, I watched her eyes rake over Kellan's body. "Lord knows I would," she murmured.

Kellan shook his head before kissing mine again. Winking at him, Anna patted my arm. "Well, I'm off to bed. I'm beat."

Twisting away from us, she started sashaying back to her room. The tight pants she wore emphasized the curve of her hips. Anna was definitely beautiful and provocative. Sometimes it was hard to live with her never-ending perfection, but she was family, and she'd swooped into my life when I needed her the most. She'd helped me get back on my feet when both men in my life had dumped me. She'd secured a place for us to live when I had nowhere to go. She'd helped me heal my shattered heart when I was sure I couldn't. She'd even aided in restoring my relationship with Kellan. No, whatever her eccentricities, I loved her.

I was smiling and shaking my head at her when she tossed back, "I'll be out like a light if you guys want to go at it again?"

I sighed as Kellan laughed. Pulling back to look at him, I smacked his chest again. "Would you stop encouraging her?" He smiled, still chuckling and I sighed again. "I wish the two of you had a better hobby than trying to embarrass me."

Turning me around to face him, he placed a tender kiss on my forehead. "Well, you wouldn't have to worry about it at my place." Rocking my hips back and forth, our bodies touching and retreating enticingly, he added, "Maybe I'll just embarrass you back to my home?"

Raising an eyebrow, he grinned crookedly at me. I wanted to smack him again, but that look was too damn sexy. I ended up kissing him instead, which of course, made him chuckle.

Kellan stayed with me all afternoon, helping me go over anything and everything that had to do with school. I was starting my last year soon. I had everything ready to go—all my classes lined up, and all my books purchased—but going over my schedule helped ease my anxiety.

I had no idea why I was still apprehensive about the first day of school. You would think that after sixteen grades, I'd be used to it all, but I wasn't. That first day of school phobia effectively caused me to defer college immediately after high school.

My parents were furious about that, but I was too distressed to do it. My mom was experiencing a small cancer scare then; the doctors detected a malignant tumor on her breast and removed it. Even though they'd protested, I'd taken the opportunity to stay home with her while she underwent treatments. She hated the idea of me deferring school, but it worked out for the best anyway. It gave me the chance to give her some much-needed palliative care and allowed me to delay doing something that terrified me.

My mother went into complete remission long before the school year ended. She begged me to quit wasting time and enter mid-semester. I'd already deferred for a year, though, so I took all the time I could. I might have delayed for another year, but eventually Anna became agitated at my indecision. She marched me down to the registry office after my year hiatus and forced me to enroll at Ohio University. And, of course, once I was there, I was fine. The hardest part for me was always getting through the door. I was working on that, too.

I suppose my deferment ended up being a good thing. I wouldn't have met Denny if I hadn't taken that year off to procrastinate. If I'd never met Denny, I definitely wouldn't have met Kellan. Even though I hated how we started, how much we had hurt Denny, I was still grateful that fate had led me to Seattle, to Kellan.

Kellan thought my nerves were cute. He didn't seem to get nervous about anything. He could probably walk into the first day of school, thirty minutes late, completely naked, and be absolutely fine. I smiled to myself as I reconsidered. No, people and places might not affect him, but feelings did. Telling me that he loved me for the first time had sure scared him, probably worse than all of my first day jitters combined.

Well, it was nice to know that he wasn't impervious to nerves.

English was my major this year, a fact that Kellan teased me about incessantly. He seemed to think I'd be better suited for Psychology. I'm sure he wanted me to take another class like the Human Sexuality course I had taken the year before. He was sort of incorrigible when it came to the baser instincts. Not that I had much room to talk, at least, not when it came to him. I just couldn't resist him when he was near.

After a full day of mapping out everything, right down to the most convenient route to my classes, it was finally time for me to go to work.

Smiling as we walked through the apartment's parking lot, I proceeded to grab the keys from his hand. "Can I drive?" I asked playfully, walking backwards in front of him as I tried to jiggle the keys out of the death-grip he had around them.

Scowling wonderfully, he shook his head and jerked his hand away. "No, you cannot."

Stopping and putting my hands on my hips as he walked past me, I stuck my lip out. "Why not?"

He took two steps and then stopped and walked back to me. His mouth was instantly sucking on my pouting lips. I instantly stopped pouting. With his lips against my skin, he murmured, "Because…that is my baby, and I don't share her," he growled.

"I thought I was your baby?" I managed to squeak out, my pulse quickening.

Smiling, he grabbed my hips and pulled me into his. "You are." His lips returned to mine, his kiss deep and territorial. I felt that familiar fire starting to ignite and I longed to yank off that bothersome t-shirt and glorify his body with my tongue. At that moment, he broke away from me and breathed, "And I don't share you, either."

A delightful, gooey, warm sensation permeated my body; I could have melted right there into the sidewalk. He laughed and pulled me to the car. I—quite happily—scooted into the passenger's side.

Still smiling over his possessive declaration of love, I hardly noticed arriving at Pete's—my second home here in Seattle. Well, third really, Kellan's place would always feel like home to me. Even with all of the bad memories that lingered there.

Parking in the stall that his Chevelle frequented so often that it was unofficially known as "Kellan's Spot," he shut off his mechanical baby. If only he could turn me off so easily; I was still a little worked up. Not the best way to start my shift, but that was probably his true intention all along. He might have called me a tease, but that boy enjoyed making me squirm.

S.C. Stephens

I stepped out of his car right as he walked around to open my door. He frowned that I hadn't waited and let him be chivalrous. He held out his hand for me. I took it, and we strolled together towards the large, rectangular building where Kellan found peace.

While Pete's was comforting and familiar to me, the place provided solace for Kellan. He came here to play, to socialize, and at one time, to pick up girls. But mainly I think he came here to escape life's harsh realities, to shut off his mind. While being conflicted over which man to give my heart to, I'd disrupted his sanctuary. The ordeal of dealing with our confusing relationship was a turbulent time for him, but his tranquility was back, and it clearly showed through the lazy smile that curled around his lips as we stepped through the door.

Holding one set of the double doors open for me, he gallantly led me in, kissing my hand as it extended away from him. He generally did something physical when we walked through the door. Sometimes it was a peck on the cheek, sometimes his hand snuck around my waist, but there was always something. Some sort of announcement to the room—I was his.

He'd wanted that when our relationship was secret, and now that it wasn't, he let everybody know it. Including Rita, the sulking bartender who was watching us.

Rita had been a fixture at Pete's since long before Kellan's band arrived. From the second she had set eyes on Kellan, she'd shamelessly pursued him, husband be damned. It made me nauseous to know that she succeeded in having her way with him. She was at least twice his age, with over-tanned leathery skin, over-bleached blonde hair, and a sense of fashion that left nothing to the imagination. I've never asked Kellan about their hookup. Honestly, I didn't want to know…ever.

Her lips twisted up when Kellan shifted his head to acknowledge her. All he gave her was a slight incline of a greeting, but by her reaction you'd think he'd just walked up and licked her. All sultry smiles and hooded eyes that were, I'm sure, mentally undressing him, she leaned over the aged bar that ran the length of the wall beside the front doors.

Practically purring, she murmured, "Hey there, Kellan…Kiera." My name was clearly an afterthought.

I smirked at her and twisted to face Kellan. "I have to go put my stuff away. Usual?"

I tilted my head and he ran a finger back through my hair, tucking a lock behind my ear as he bit his lip in that charming, attractive way. "Yeah, thanks, Kiera."

Smiling at him, I reached up to kiss his cheek. Dissatisfied with just a peck, he twisted and found my lips. My face heated, knowing Rita and Pete's customers were staring, but I allowed myself to indulge in a small moment of PDA. I abruptly stopped the moment when I felt his free hand move around to squeeze my backside. Kellan didn't always do subtle PDA.

Pushing his shoulder back, I pointed at him in warning. Laughing, he shrugged and gave me an *I'm innocent* smile. It was a complete and total lie, Kellan was nowhere near innocent, but the reaction was nevertheless adorable, and I rolled my eyes and laughed as I turned away from him.

As I made my way to the hallway, I passed about five sets of tables with women who all had their eyes glued on me. They alternated between watching Kellan and watching me as Kellan made his way to the far corner of the room near the stage, where the guys traditionally sat. I could feel myself being assessed with every step I took. Self conscious, I kept my head down and walked a little faster. It was one thing for Kellan to be admired by so many people, it was quite another to for me to be judged on whether or not I was worthy of his affection. And by the leers and twisted lips I saw, it was clear that I was falling short of their expectations. Again, I tried to not let it bother me, but the ego is a frail, tender thing.

Exhaling in relief when I was through Kellan's admirers, I made my way to the back room, where the employee lockers were kept. Jenny and Kate were leaving as I approached. Kate, a tall, graceful girl with the world's bounciest, most perfectly put together ponytail, beamed at me. I'd seen her work a double shift two nights in a row, and her hair always looked well-groomed, like she'd just done it five minutes ago. I don't know what she uses on it, but she should look into endorsing the product.

"Hey, Kiera. I hear the show rocked yesterday!" A long, auburn strand curled around her neck as she spoke. Her neck was so slim and elegant, it was practically begging to be draped in diamonds.

I nodded eagerly as I worked past them in the door frame. "It was. They were incredible!" I sighed, reminiscing about how perfect Kellan had looked on stage. They say some people are just born to be in the spotlight. Kellan was one of those people. Idly, I wondered what that meant for us...long term.

Jenny tilted her head and looked at me curiously, her red Pete's shirt emphasizing the curves that men swooned over. She was the sweetest person, though, and completely devoted to Evan. "You okay, Kiera?" she asked.

I shook my head. "Yeah, just nervous about school starting up." And Kellan becoming a bona fide, across-the-globe rock star. It was weird to both want a future for someone, and desperately not want it at the same time. I wished him all the success in the world, but only if I didn't have to share him. Man, one more thing I needed to work on. Good thing college was all about self-discovery.

Jenny smiled and patted my arm. "Don't worry. You're super smart. You'll do great."

I nodded, feeling ridiculous for worrying about school. Jenny was right. Kellan was right. I knew the grounds. I knew a lot of people there. I knew a lot of the professors. And I had a scholarship that nearly paid for all of the tuition. I had nothing to worry about. Nothing to fear but fear, right?

Kate nodded with Jenny, her light brown, almost topaz eyes wistful. "Yeah, you're so much smarter than me. I gave up after one semester." I frowned sympathetically, but then she swished her head to look down the hall. "Hey, is Kellan here? I want to ask him about the show."

Shifting to a smile as I pictured Kellan leaning back in his chair, people watching while he waited for me to bring him his "usual," I nodded. "Yeah, he's here."

I couldn't keep the dorky grin from my face and they both giggled at me before shuffling off together. What? My boyfriend was a super-hot musician with fabulous hair, a rock-hard body, and my name tattooed over his chest. Who wouldn't grin about that?

I shoved my stuff in a locker and hastily threw my hair up in a ponytail; it was nowhere near as perfect as Kate's. Sunday nights were generally slow since the band didn't play, but there was still a lot of activity and not having my hair flopping all over my face was a good thing.

When I returned to the main part of the bar, I saw that my D-bag boyfriend wasn't alone anymore. Leaning back in his chair, a foot casually propped on a knee, he was chatting amicably with Sam, the bouncer.

Sam was a big, burly, muscular guy. He sported a shaved head and an intimidating scowl on his face. It made him seem all the more menacing. He and Denny became friends when Denny had been here for high school as an exchange student. It was Sam who took Denny in after we broke up, when Denny just couldn't live with Kellan anymore. Understandable, given the circumstances. From what I heard, Sam and Denny still talked occasionally.

Kellan had also attended school with Sam and Denny. It was how they'd all known each other. Although Kellan was a few years younger, he'd formed tight bonds with Sam and my ex. And it never ceased to amaze me to know that Kellan still talked to Denny, too.

Kellan and Sam were now conversing on more pleasant topics than last year's drama. Kellan wore a huge smile on his face and occasionally flicked his hands in the air, gesturing. Sam listened with a small grin on his usually imposing features. I surmised by his expression that Kellan was telling him about the show.

Shaking my head, I went about getting Kellan's beer. I just couldn't get over the fact that my boyfriend had played a major venue. Even if his band didn't play anywhere else, that would be an awesome story to tell his grandkids. I smiled even wider as I approached Rita. Kellan with kids…even the thought gave me goose bumps.

A few hours later, the rest of the band strolled in. Kellan was at the front of the bar when they burst through the doors. Wanting information on yesterday's event, Kate had finally cornered him. I heard Kellan play it off like it was nothing, but Kate wouldn't let it go and asked him question after question, most of them along the lines of—"Weren't you nervous? Didn't you feel like peeing your pants?" Kellan always laughed at her and told her no, but I don't think she bought his answer.

After being hounded by her for a while, Kellan almost looked relived when he twisted around to see his band mates strolling in. Once the quartet united, the bar broke out in ear-splitting whistles and applause.

I joined in with the merriment; I was just as proud of them as the patrons. Evan smiled as he looked around, his warm eyes grateful and appreciative. Matt seemed horribly embarrassed. His face flushed with color as he quickly looked back at the door, like he wanted to bolt. Kellan chuckled and shook his head as he put his hand up in acknowledgment. They all looked thrown by the attention.

Except Griffin, of course. He was throwing kisses with his hands in-between deep, dramatic bows. If Kellan hadn't clapped him on the back to make him stop, I think he would have started in on an Oscar-worthy speech.

Still shaking his head, Kellan said a polite thank you to the crowd once it was quiet enough to hear him. Matt immediately darted to their table, thankful to disappear. Laughing at the guitarist, Evan walked over to Jenny, lifting her into a mammoth embrace. Kellan shoved Griffin forward, but not before the bassist loudly exclaimed, "My johnson is gladly accepting all forms of praise...if anyone wants to congratulate me privately."

I rolled my eyes and looked away as Kellan smacked him across the back of the head. Seriously, my sister must have a screw loose to date that man. If what they were doing could even be considered dating.

With the guys seated, Pete, the middle-aged, weary owner of the bar came out to congratulate them. With a thin smile on his lips, he shook hands with each band member. While Pete looked far from unhappy at the prospect of losing the band, he didn't seem thrilled either. Kellan had told me once that Pete was terrible at booking bands. It was the main reason the D-bags played here so much. Pete and his business partner, Sal, made a deal with the band, giving them exclusive rights to the stage every weekend. It gave the boys a home base to play from, and a safe place to store their instruments. As for Pete and Sal, it gave them a reprieve from searching for bands that would bring in the customers. It was a win-win; the D-bags brought in a lot of customers.

From the slight frown on Pete's brow as he shook Kellan's hand, it was obvious that he was starting to believe his act might outgrow him...and then he'd have to start looking for talent again.

Once Pete left the guys to their drinking, clapping Evan on the back as he left, the bar returned to normal. Most of the people started engaging in their own conversations, with only a few going over to congratulate the boys personally. Thankfully, none of those few were women congratulating Griffin in the way that he wanted.

A few female fans did eye Kellan, but nothing more than the I-want-you eyes I was used to him getting. None of them seemed brave enough, or drunk enough, to approach his table, though, and I was just fine with that.

Throughout the course of the evening, the D-bags eventually left their bar. Matt left by himself an hour or two after arriving, a shy smile on his face as he said that he had plans with Rachel. Griffin rolled his eyes as his cousin left, gesturing obscenely with his hand in the air over his naughty parts. Thankfully, he also left about an hour later, some blonde bimbo on his arm. She gave him sultry, seductive eyes as they left, and I was pretty sure she'd give him the praise he'd wanted earlier. I shook my head and ignored the sight of Griffin leaving with another woman. It happened all the time. I had asked Anna about it once, but she only shrugged and said she didn't care. He was free to do whatever he wanted. So was she.

Evan stayed until closing, escorting Jenny out when her shift was over. Kellan stayed, too. Feet kicked up on a chair, he watched me with a deliciously provocative smile while I wiped off some tables nearby. And Rita watched him just as provocatively.

Yep, everything was back to normal.

Refusing to sleep in my lumpy bed for another night, Kellan drove us to his place later. A small, peaceful smile was on his lips as he pulled into his street. I wasn't sure if it was because he was coming home after a few days away, or if he just enjoyed having me come home with him. I supposed it was a little of both.

His tiny, white, two-story house was dark as he turned off the ignition. When the three of us had lived here—Kellan, Denny and I—the house was warm and alive with activity. Now that it was just Kellan, the house seemed a little quiet. As Kellan cracked his door, I thought maybe that was the real reason for his smile. Kellan preferred a bustling house. I'd pried that out of him when I asked him if he'd rent out his room again.

With a slight frown, he'd told me, "I've thought about it. But I don't know…it feels like yours, and I don't want to give it to someone else." Those words had warmed me considerably, but when I asked him if he needed the rent money, he only shrugged and said, "No, renting out the room was never about money." Sighing, he added, "I just don't like being there alone."

God, sometimes he just broke my heart.

Stepping into the entryway, my eyes drifted around the familiar space. It was sort of a double-edged sword for me. I loved being here with Kellan. I loved the memories of cuddling with him on the couch and making love to him in his room, but…Denny was here, too.

His ghost seemed to linger in the spaces he'd been. Leaning against the kitchen counter, drinking a mug of tea. Lying back on the couch, watching sports on TV. Showering in the bathroom, sometimes with me. And our room, the first room we'd ever shared as a couple, was the room that Kellan refused to rent out again. The ghosts were heaviest in there. So heavy that I refused to go in there. I couldn't even look at the door. Noting the closed door when Kellan and I walked into his bedroom, I thought that Kellan probably didn't go in there, either. Like I said, double-edged sword.

Propping his guitar case in the corner of his room, Kellan watched me as I sat on his bed. With soft eyes, his vision flicked to the closed door across the very short hall upstairs. "You all right?"

Throwing on my brightest smile, I leaned back on my elbows. Kellan's face brightened considerably. "Of course, I'm fine." That was mainly true. I was fine. I'd let Denny go and I'd slowly begun to forgive myself for being unfaithful. But being here was sometimes difficult and Kellan knew it. I think that was the real reason why he didn't pressure me more to move in with him. I just wasn't ready to deal with the ghosts every day.

Sitting down beside me, he laid a palm on my thigh; it ignited me instantly. "I'm glad you're here," he whispered.

Sitting up, I laced my arms around his neck. "I had no choice. You wouldn't let me drive your car, remember?"

He chuckled and leaned in to kiss me. Lightly laughing myself, I threaded my fingers back through his shaggy hair and laid myself back on his pillows, bringing him with me.

He was instantly engaged, hands running over my body, his own body sneaking into position alongside mine. As I thought of all the women who had wanted him this weekend, women whom he'd flirted with only briefly, or politely acknowledged, or in some cases completely ignored, my heart swelled. He didn't want them. He wanted me. He loved me. And God, how I loved him, too.

Chapter 3 – Distractions

Kellan's room was still dark when I peeled my eyes open. Moonlight filtered in through his window, highlighting the objects that he'd collected over the years. There wasn't much—some paperbacks on his bookshelf, a few CDs scattered along the top of it, the Ramones poster I picked up for him last summer while out shopping with Jenny. Besides some pocket change and a couple of well-used notebooks, the only thing on his dresser was a bottle of some sort of hair product. Kellan said that a woman from high school had turned him on to the stuff and he'd been using it ever since to "manage the mess." I was fairly certain from the slight smile on his face when he said it, that he literally meant the words "woman" and "turned on." His high school years scared me a little bit.

Other than our clothes strewn about the floor, the only other things of note in his room were his guitars. His main guitar, the one still tucked away in its black carrying case, was leaning against the wall beside an older, clearly worn one. Since Kellan never played with the older guitar, I figured he kept it for sentimental reasons. Plain and seemingly inexpensive, he'd told me it was the first guitar he'd ever had, and the only possession he'd taken to L.A. with him when he'd run away. It was quite possibly the only thing from Kellan's childhood that was a happy memory for him. And, since his parents had literally thrown out all his possessions when they moved to this house that he inherited, it was also the only memento of his youth. His childhood scared me too, but for a completely different reason.

As I fingered the silver guitar pendant around my neck, a symbolic keepsake from Kellan that never left my body, I twisted my head to look at what had awakened me.

With sheets tangled and twisted around his body, his bare chest silver in the faded light pouring through his window, Kellan moved restlessly beside me. His brow furrowed, his face distraught, he was shaking his head and murmuring something I couldn't make out. I twisted around to touch his cheek, but he flinched away from me as if in pain.

"Kellan," I whispered, "you're dreaming…wake up."

His hand fisted the sheets near his hip. His breath picked up as he shook his head again and whimpered. Carefully adjusting my body to a comforting position beside him, I leaned over and soothingly hushed him. Draping my arm over his chest, I could feel how rapidly his heart was racing. Tears pricked my eyes as I wondered what he was dreaming about. With Kellan, it could be any number of horrible things.

Leaning my head against him, I kissed his shoulder. "Wake up, baby, it's just a dream."

He started saying, "No," then, "Please." His face cringed away from me. His legs drew up to reflexively curl into a ball. Kissing his shoulder again, I lightly shook him. "Kellan, wake up."

Taking quick, shallow inhales, his body trembled under my fingers. Just as I considered turning on his lamp to wake him up, he gasped and his eyes flew open. Immediately propping himself up on his elbows, he shied away from my embrace. Looking around with wide eyes, he seemed lost, like he didn't know where he was.

With his breath still quick and his body still quivering, he swallowed over and over.

I reached out and cupped his cheek, forcing his gaze to mine. His confused eyes narrowed. "Kiera?"

I nodded, scooting closer to him. "Yeah, it's me. You're okay. It was just a dream, Kellan."

His rigid posture slumped back and he closed his eyes and hung his head. "Just a dream," he muttered. My heart cracked a little watching his face. Kellan's nightmares weren't really just dreams. They were more like memories. I wasn't sure which ordeal Kellan had been reliving, but I knew it had terrified him.

Inhaling slowly, he took a couple of deep breaths. When he was calmer, he peeked back up at me. Running a trembling hand across his mouth, he shook his head. "I'm sorry if I woke you up."

Swallowing the emotion in my throat, I flung my arms around him and crushed my bare body to his. His arms loosely came around me and I could still feel his heart surging as adrenaline coursed through him. "It's okay." Kissing his cheek, I gave him a few moments to collect himself. When he settled back down to the pillows, his fingers rubbing the bridge of his nose like he had a headache, I propped myself up on his chest. "You want to talk about it?"

Bringing my hands up to his temples, I pressed my thumbs into the soft spots, taking over his headache reducing massage. He closed his eyes and relaxed into my touch. "I was back at home and my dad…" he stopped and swallowed, "it was nothing…just a dream."

I bit my lip to stop a sigh. His past was just something he didn't like to talk about. In fact, I was certain I was the only human on earth that he'd ever confided in. Evan knew about the physical abuses he had endured, since Kellan drunkenly spilled the beans to him, and Denny knew about the abuse, having witnessed it himself, but Kellan had never revealed to them that his father was not his biological father. No one knew that his mother had been unfaithful to her husband, and had become pregnant by the other man. Then that horrible woman claimed that she'd been raped. Because of the lie, or maybe because of the truth, the man who raised Kellan had brutalized him repeatedly…and his mother had done nothing to prevent it.

I hated them both.

"Are you sure you don't want to talk about it?" I whispered, kissing his jaw.

He stirred, inhaling deep. Opening his eyes, he gently pushed me off him and rolled me to my side. Pressing his body into mine, he cupped my cheek and tilted my head up. Attaching his warm lips to my neck, he murmured, "Yes, I'm done with talking."

My heart picked up its pace as his hand left my cheek to run down my side. I knew he was diverting his mind with my body. I knew it, yet I couldn't seem to stop him from doing it. He pushed me on to my back, leaning over me as his lips worked their way down my throat. My fingers automatically locked into that marvelous hair as every section of skin that he touched on me suddenly burned.

My breath was embarrassingly fast as his hand rubbed a circle into my hip.

He was purposely avoiding every spot that I most wanted him to touch and it was driving me crazy. I shoved his head down a smidge when he kissed along the top of my breast and he chuckled before conceding. All thought of his earlier grief was gone from the both of us as his mouth closed around a nipple, his tongue drawing a circle around the peak. Aching, I cried out and rocked my hips towards him.

With a deep sound of satisfaction rising up his throat, he seemed just as pleased being the one giving the pleasure as I was receiving it. As his teeth lightly dragged across my tender flesh, his finger, equally light, ran right between my legs. I was ready for him; I think I was in a constant state of semi-arousal just being near him. I arched my back and ran my hands over my face and through my hair.

"Oh God," I muttered as his finger down below matched the movement of his tongue up above. The two hot spots were making every coherent part of my body melt away—I couldn't even come up with my own name at that moment.

Chuckling again, he peeked up at me with a devilish smile. "No, just me," he whispered. The part of me that could still get embarrassed wanted to smack him, but then he switched to the other breast and my head dropped back, my eyes closing.

"Oh God…yes."

Groaning a bit himself, he left my breast and slid his tongue up my throat. His finger also changed position, sliding inside where I wanted him. Working his way up to my ear, he sucked in a quick, erotic breath. "I love it when you say that," he whispered huskily.

I groaned and found his mouth, not even caring anymore that I hadn't brushed my teeth. He didn't either, eagerly kissing me just as fiercely as I kissed him. His finger moving gently inside me was joined by another; I moaned, clutching his hair. His thumb joined the action, swirling around the most sensitive part of my core. I cried out again, my hands switching to his shoulders, forcibly trying to move him on top of me.

He resisted, chuckling and groaning almost simultaneously. "I love how much you want me," he muttered, his mouth moving to my jaw.

My body moving in perfect rhythm with his hand, I squirmed and whimpered. I hated how easily he could reduce me to a begging, quivering mass of hormones…and I loved it, too. "Yes, I want you…now…please."

I could feel him grinning as he placed kisses along my skin. He did love it when I asked for it. Pressing his body into mine, I could feel how much he wanted me, too. I whimpered as he pulled his hand away from me, but then he settled himself between my legs, the hard length of him resting tantalizingly close, and my complaint shifted to a moan. Then he did…nothing, nothing but continue to kiss me.

It was torture. Pure, blissful torture. Having him so close sent my body into overdrive. I was practically clawing at his back, squirming underneath him, doing anything I could to move him into position. I couldn't, though. He held himself against me, but perfectly out of reach. It drove me crazy.

And my reaction drove him crazy. His breath was fast, his lips frantic. He groaned as his fingers explored my body. He moaned my name as he dropped his head to rest in the crook of my neck. Barely able to stand it another second, my hand trailed down his chest, his abdomen, the deep V that led straight to what I wanted, what I needed. My hand wrapped around him, hard, ready, and pulsing under my fingers. A slight wetness coated my thumb as I swirled over the tip of him and he clutched the sheets again, but in a good way this time.

"God, I need you," he breathed in my ear. I started to feel like he meant more than just for a physical release, but he adjusted his hips and plunged right into me, and I thought nothing more of it.

My hand fell away as he sunk in deep. We both made equally passionate groans of relief. Then we started moving together. In-between fast breaths and soft moans of pleasure, our lips searched the other's. He quickly brought me right to the brink, my cries more frantic with each thrust. Then, right as I was about to go over, he stilled his hips, not moving at all. It was an aching torture that made me dig into his backside, trying to get him to keep going.

With a strained voice he whispered, "Just wait, Kiera." I didn't think I could. I felt like I was going to explode. I wanted to whimper, I wanted to cry. Then he moved again.

Holy hell, the fire that surged through my body…I never knew anything could feel that good.

He did it two more times, stopping, then starting; I even begged him to do it on the last time. Then he didn't stop anymore. I didn't think he could, even if I asked him to. With his head buried in my shoulder again, he groaned so erotically, I instantly clenched around him, finally having the release that he'd kept from me for so long. It was…glorious.

He cried out as I squeezed around him and I felt him releasing into me. After a few final thrusts, he stopped moving, breathing heavily as he lay on my chest. I was a little surprised to feel that we were both slightly damp from the exertion. You wouldn't think sex could actually be a workout, but if done right…

Feeling light-headed, I closed my eyes, wrapping my arms around his head. When our breaths stabilized and our bodies cooled to normal, I looked down at him still resting on top of me. He hadn't moved at all. He was still…a part of me.

Hoping he hadn't fallen back asleep like that, I poked his shoulder. "Are you going to…move?"

He grunted then stretched, still not pulling out. "No, I'm good."

I giggled as I threaded my fingers back through his hair. "You can't stay there, you know." I felt myself flushing horribly and was instantly glad the room was still dark.

He peeked up at me, the moonlight glinting off his mischievous eyes. "I'm just saving us time." He grinned crookedly as he moved his hips a little. He was still sort of semi-aroused and the movement sent a shiver though my body. My eyes fluttered before refocusing on his smug, attractive face. He raised an eyebrow. "You know, for when you're ready for round two."

Rolling my eyes, even though a part of me was considering it, I shoved his shoulders off me. He laughed genuinely, finally removing himself and slinking to my side. "I was just being practical," he murmured, nestling into my body and kissing my shoulder.

His eyes closed as peace washed over his face. Sighing, I kissed his forehead, making his smile widen. Curling into him, I thought of his face before that little romp. What he'd done to block out the memory had been pretty spectacular, but now that it was over, I was thinking about it again. I hoped he wasn't thinking about it anymore. I didn't really want to bring it up, but I did want to make sure that he was okay.

"Are you all right?" I asked, running my hands up his chest.

He made a deep, satisfied noise in his throat. "Completely," he murmured, his smile a charmingly crooked one. I smacked his shoulder and he opened an eye. Seeing that my face was serious, his smile faded. His finger came out to tuck a damp lock behind my ear. "I'm fine, Kiera," he said, his tone more subdued.

I nodded, burying my head into his shoulder as he put his arm around me.

I kept a close watch on him for the next few nights, but he slept soundly from what I could tell. Only the normal nighttime adjustments that we all make during sleep, not the restless thrashing that comes from nightmares. I didn't stay with him every night, but more often than not, I fell asleep by his side.

It was comforting, having our bodies touching as I drifted into dreamland, but I think it meant so much more for Kellan. He would pop into my apartment at the crack of dawn after gigs at other bars and clubs around the Seattle area. He said he didn't like slipping into a cold bed. Well, okay, the way he phrased it was: "If I'm going to slip into a bed in the early hours of the morning, I want it warmed up by your hot little naked body."

I didn't actually sleep naked. Not unless he was there to put me to bed that way. Wearing pajamas was a habit that he was constantly trying to get me to break, saying, "Why do you need clothes if I'm just going to rip them off?" But the gist of his comment was that he wanted to be warm with me, not cold and alone by himself.

But after a few weeks of watching him closely as he cuddled next to me, I stopped worrying about the dreams that sometimes plagued him. Instead, I became increasingly anxious about my upcoming reentry into higher learning. I had a demanding schedule this year which meant it would be necessary for me to study nearly every waking moment I had. While I was one of those weird people who thrived on the challenge of school, I wasn't looking forward to so much of my free time being absorbed with it. But Kellan was patient and a pretty good study buddy— when he wasn't trying to distract me with sex. And the fact that he was free during the day meant we would still spend a great deal of time together.

But I meant what I said when I'd told him that living with my sister brought balance to my life. I was aware that I needed to spend time with other friends besides Kellan. So when Jenny invited Kate and me to try out a new art class with her, I obliged. We met every Monday and Wednesday morning, usually stopping for espresso afterwards.

The Monday before school commenced was my last class. If a grade was given for this course, well…I would have received my first "F" ever.

"Well, Miss Allen, it's a very nice use of…color."

Our instructor was a kindly, retired high school art teacher who taught the class in her home. She patted me on the back, and with a tight-lipped smile, complimented me on the only positive thing that she could say about my elementary level bowl of tropical fruit. Although I had worked on the portrait for three weeks, it looked like something a six-year-old had drawn and colored in one afternoon. Artist, I was not.

As she walked over to commend Kate on her perfectly proportioned apples, I wondered if the retired school teacher had been around when Kellan was in school and if she had taught him. Maybe he'd taken her class? Maybe she'd been his teacher, complimenting him on his sketch of the female form. Instantly, I started to wonder if maybe she'd "taught" Kellan in more ways than one; a scowl formed on my lips.

A light laughter broke my train of thought, and I looked over at Jenny watching me. "It's not so bad, Kiera."

With the end of her pencil, she pointed to my pathetic attempt at realism. "It's sort of…Picasso-ish."

I frowned, but then laughed with her. Picasso wasn't really what I'd been going for, but then again, art was subjective. One man's garbage was another man's Monet. Maybe I had a future in it after all. Looking over at Jenny's drawing, I reconsidered. No, out of all of us, Jenny was the artist. She'd moved on from fruit bowls ages ago, and was now sketching people. What she'd created with just a pencil blew my mind.

Jenny had created a close-up portrait of the band on stage…our band— Griffin and Matt jamming on their guitars, Evan beaming with joy behind his drums, and Kellan, singing into his microphone. She even managed to capture the devilish curl of a smile that Kellan wore when he sang. It was breathtaking, and put my sad little bundle of grapes to shame.

Sighing, I pointed at her drawing. "That's amazing, Jenny. Really, you've got a knack for this."

Her face blossoming into a wide smile, she looked back at her picture. "Thanks." Erasing a minute pencil line on Matt's guitar, she looked back at me. "I was thinking of having Pete put it up at the bar when I'm done with it." She shrugged. "You know, as an homage to his boys."

She giggled and I nodded. "No, that's a good idea." Watching her perfect a shadow line across Kellan's jaw, making the masculine right angle stick out even more, I shook my head. "I think they'd really like that, Jenny." She nodded as she went back to work on it, and thinking of the bassist she was working on, I snorted a little. "You should probably draw a flasher in there somewhere for Griffin."

She laughed. "Yeah, definitely." Scrunching her pale brows, she shook her head. "What is up with him and your sister anyway? Are they together or not?"

Sighing as I turned back to my misshapen fruit, I shrugged. "No idea. They don't act like they're together, and they certainly aren't exclusive if they are." Looking back at her, I shook my head. "But they, um, see each other at least a few times a month."

Jenny nodded, her blonde locks dangling around her shoulders. "I know. He talks about it when they do." She shrugged one shoulder. "I asked him once what they were and he said…"

Biting her lip, she didn't finish that sentence. Not sure if I really wanted to hear anything Griffin said about my sister, I raised an eyebrow. "He said what?" I asked cautiously.

Avoiding my eyes, she sighed softly and looked around. I didn't take that as a good sign. While no one was close enough to hear her, she leaned in towards me anyway. "He called her his…fuck buddy." Her lips twisted into a grimace and she rolled her eyes.

My cheeks flamed red-hot and the only coherent sound I could make was one of disgust. Seeing my expression, Jenny shook her head again and went back to her pencil drawing of the revolting man. "Yeah, I know," she flicked the image of him on her paper with her pencil, "he's a tool."

Adjusting the eraser of the pencil to his waistband she grinned at me mischievously. "Maybe I should just neuter him?"

I busted up laughing, and the entire room of studious art novices twisted around to look at me. My cheeks heated even more, and I dropped my head into my hands and let the giggles take me over. If only taming Griffin could be that easy.

Kellan and I both had the evening off, so after art class I headed to his place. Driving over, I realized how rare it was for us to get a matching night off; unless we asked for it, it usually didn't happen. I had an inkling that perhaps Kellan had asked Matt to keep this evening free, knowing that I was a bundle of nerves before the first day of school. It wouldn't surprise me if he had.

Jenny and Kate dropped me off at his place and waved goodbye. I still had Denny's beat-up little Honda, but Anna had pretty much taken it over. She always asked before using it, but I was actually a little relieved that she did take it so much. It seemed more like her car now than my ex-boyfriend's. Besides, I was terrible with stick shifts.

Kellan was out when I arrived, his front door firmly locked as I jiggled it. His car was still parked in the driveway, so he must've taken advantage of the beautiful, sunny afternoon to go for a run. Pulling my keys out of my bag, I flicked through the ring until I found his house key. We'd exchanged keys recently. "The next step," Kellan had called it. Stepping into his home, the coolness of his empty entryway hit me. I set my heavy bag on the floor with relief. Knowing I'd probably end up staying the night, I had packed everything I needed for the next day—clothes, books, paper, pens and pencils.

Examining the book bag, I took a mental inventory for the hundredth time. Just as I was wondering if I'd packed the Lit book that I needed, Kellan's front door opened. I glanced over at him, looked back to my bag, then snapped my head back to him. He must've overheated while running; his shirt was draped over his shoulder. His lean, toned body was glistening as he stepped through the door, wiping his face off with the edge of his tee. He was still panting from the exertion, and his abs clenched and relaxed in such an appealing way that I could not stop staring.

"You're obsessed, you know?" he laughed out, scrubbing dry the edge of his hair with his shirt. I flushed instantly, thinking he meant the way I was so engrossed by his body all the time, but he raised an eyebrow and pointed to my bag. "You're going to be just fine."

I relaxed, feeling my embarrassment slide away. Rolling my eyes, I shook my head. "I know. I honestly don't know why it twists my stomach so much."

Grinning, he turned and shut his front door. My eyes darted down his bare back to the loose track pants he had on, but I managed to snap them back up to his face when he turned around again.

"I know just how to get your mind off of it."

Enjoying the playful look in his eye, I tilted my head as he came up to me, slinging his arms around my waist. "Oh?" I asked, lightly resting my fingers on his damp chest, his skin deliciously soft.

Grinning crookedly, he raised an eyebrow and looked down my body. "Yep." I bunched my brows at the amused look on his face. Laughing, he released my body and kissed my cheek. "Just let me clean up first."

Watching him move around me to go upstairs, I nodded, my lips still twisted as I wondered just what he'd come up with to occupy me. Still laughing at my expression, he smacked my bottom before hopping up the stairs two at a time.

Smiling at his mood, I walked into the living room to distract myself from thoughts of Kellan in the shower. It was hard to do once I heard the water running. I had to turn the television up and force myself to be suddenly fascinated with marine botany.

By the time I actually *was* interested in estuary ecosystems, even leaning over my knees as I focused on Kellan's big screen, he finally came down. Twirling a lock of hair around my finger, completely absorbed with the program, I didn't hear his approach. Not used to being ignored, he grunted and leaned over to kiss my neck. I started when his lips brushed my skin, then smiled and closed my eyes. I angled my head to give him better access.

"Is this how you're going to distract me?" I asked in a low voice, starting to feel like he could distract me that way all afternoon long.

Chuckling deep in his chest, he grabbed my waist and pulled me from the couch in one swift, playful move. "Nope." Smiling, he flicked the end of my nose with his finger. "I have a better idea."

Taking in the sight of him dressed in my favorite deep blue shirt, a color that made his eyes seem impossibly beautiful, I pursed my lips. "You're not interested in…playing with me?" I really had thought that would be his plan.

His lips curved up into a smile that screamed sex, but he shook his head. "Oh, I intend to play with you." Laughing, he grabbed my hand and led me into the kitchen. Over his shoulder, he added, "Just not in the way that you're thinking."

Sitting me down at his table, he leaned over the back of me and kissed my cheek again. "At least, not yet anyway."

As I shook my head and furrowed my brows, wondering what the heck we were doing, he started rummaging through his kitchen drawers. Humming to himself, a small smile on his face, his hair wonderfully messy and slightly damp around the edges, he opened and shut every junk drawer he had.

When I was just about to ask him what he was looking for, he finally made a happy noise and grabbed something shoved in the very back of a crammed drawer. A crooked smile on his face, he looked back at me sitting at the table and lifted his hand to show me what he'd found.

"Playing cards?" Smiling, I shook my head. "Are we playing pinochle all afternoon?"

Frowning at me, he raised an eyebrow. "Pinochle? Are we sixty?" His grin returning, he opened the pack of cards, tossing the jacket back to the counter. Shuffling the cards, he sat down opposite me at his table. "No, we're playing poker."

Shaking my head, I murmured, "I'm really not that good at poker."

His smile brightened gorgeously. "Well, that is actually perfect, because we're playing strip poker."

Flushing all over, I immediately stood up. Laughing harder, he grabbed my hand. "Come on, it will be fun." He lifted his eyebrows suggestively. "I promise."

Knowing my face was bright red, I slowly sat back down. "Kellan...I don't know..."

Leaning back in his chair, he eyed my body across from him very slowly. When he reached my face, he asked, "Have you ever played?"

I sighed and shrugged. "No."

Grinning, he nodded, still shuffling the cards. "Good. Then it will be a new experience for you." He curled his lip...perfectly. "And I like giving you new experiences."

The flush from my cheeks rushed down my body as he intently stared at me. I suddenly wanted to play more than I've ever wanted anything. I couldn't even remember what he was distracting me from, and I supposed that was the point.

Tucking my hair behind my ears, I pointed my thumb at his wide-open kitchen windows. "What about...your neighbors?"

He shrugged. "What about them?"

Looking away from the heat in his eyes, I swallowed. "I don't want them looking...at me."

Laughing huskily, he stood and pulled down some blinds rolled up near the top of the windows. Once closed, he sat back down and raised an eyebrow. "Better?"

I nodded, not believing that I was actually considering this. Smiling at me, he laughed again. "Would it make you feel any better if I told you that I'm not very good at this either?" Laughing more, he shook his head. "I'm generally the first one naked."

My eyes widened as I flashed down his body. "You've played?" I asked, quite stupidly. It was Kellan after all, the man who used to have threesomes like they were everyday occurrences. Of course he'd played strip poker. He'd probably played far more intense games, games that I did not want to think about.

He only smiled and nodded to my question, his face amused. Then he started dealing cards and explaining rules. I sighed listening to them, then mentally thanked myself for wearing a bunch of light layers today.

Over the course of the afternoon, I lost my shoes, socks, jeans and all but one of my short-sleeved t-shirts. Kellan was no better off, having lost his shirt on the very first hand and his jeans on a really bad bluff. Thank goodness girls generally wear more clothes than boys. More relaxed than when we'd started this little game, I laughed, watching him reach down to take off his last remaining sock, as I set down a pair of queens in triumph.

Shaking his head, he muttered, "Trumped by the queen....story of my life."

Giggling, I kissed the air and dealt another hand. Scooping them off the table, he fanned the five slick cards in his hand as he studied them. We were playing traditional poker, not the Texas Hold 'Em style that's all the rage on TV. Much like his car, Kellan liked the classics. His face was expressionless as he leaned back in his chair. Not that I really noticed his face. His bare chest was far too appealing. He looked very comfortable being nearly nude by the refrigerator.

I tried to match his casualness, since I was still far more dressed than he was, but it was odd to be sitting at the breakfast table in just my underwear. I played with the necklace at my throat while I studied the cards in my hand. Not bad, a low pair, but not great either; I'd have to take three on my turn and hope for the best. Glancing up, I found Kellan watching me with a small smile on his lips. He raised an eyebrow. "Nervous?"

His eyes flashed to my necklace and I instantly stopped playing with it. So much for tells, although the thought of taking off my last shirt was making me far more nervous than my lack of cards. Of course, if I won the hand, Kellan's next piece of clothing was those delightful black boxers he liked wearing. And I was pretty sure he wasn't wearing two pairs today.

Smiling effortlessly, I shook my head. "No?" I glanced down his body and raised my eyebrow. "You?"

Biting his lip, he shook his head. "Nope. In fact, I don't even need any more cards. How about you?"

I contained the frown I felt coming. I really didn't have the best hand, just a pair of threes. Kellan would know that if I dealt myself more cards. I really didn't want to give him that satisfaction, especially when his lips started curving into a smug, seductive smile. Lifting my chin, I reminded myself that Kellan was awful at this game and he probably had nothing. Smiling softly, I shook my head. "Nope, I'm good."

He ran his tongue over his bottom lip, then drug his teeth over it. It was freaking hot and my mouth dropped open a little. "Yeah, I know," he whispered, laying his cards down. Blindly, I laid mine down, too.

Still staring at his mouth, I didn't notice what he had. When he chuckled, I finally blushed and looked down. "Crap." Shaking my head, I stared at his low pair...of fours. He had made me believe that he was bluffing, and unfortunately, I'd fallen for it.

Sighing, I gave him sad eyes. "Really?"

Laughing, he leaned back and crossed his arms over his chest. "Deal's a deal, Kiera." His smile not leaving him, he blatantly stared at my chest.

Sighing again, I plucked at the fabric near my waist. It wasn't as if he hadn't seen me before, it wasn't as if I didn't still have a bra on, but there was something nerve-wracking about causally taking off my clothes in broad daylight with Kellan staring holes through me but not being anywhere near me. It quickened my breath.

"How did you ever talk me into this?" I muttered, lifting the fabric up and over me.

With my plain, white, practical cotton bra exposed, Kellan's eyes started to smolder. Running my hands along my arms, I resisted the urge to hide myself. It helped that Kellan looked like I was wearing the sexiest lingerie on the planet, like my slight curves were the most voluptuous he's ever seen. Finally peering up at my face, his grin turned devilish. "I love this game."

Laughing a little, I tossed my shirt at him. Just as he was inhaling it, a dopey grin on his face, the doorbell rang. I immediately tried to snatch it back, but he stood up with it and took a step away from me. His face lit up as he set it on the counter. "Oh, good, food's here."

Crossing my arms over my chest and my legs over each other, I was instantly conscious of how little I was wearing. As Kellan stood tall and straight, hands on his hips, he seemed oblivious to the fact that only one piece of dark, loose fabric was hiding him away from the world.

"What food? What are you talking about?" I squeaked out, feeling my cheeks heat.

Grinning, he shrugged. "I thought you might be getting hungry, so I ordered some pizza on your last bathroom break."

As I gaped at him, he turned to leave the kitchen. "Kellan!" He looked back at me and I flung a hand out at his glorious—but mostly bare—body.

His hands patted his chest, then his hips. "Oh...right." Smiling, he walked over to his pile of clothes near the table. I expected him to step into his jeans and pull them up, but he only rifled through them to get to a pocket. Seconds later, he pulled out his wallet. "I should probably pay them, huh?"

I sputtered something unintelligible, and he leaned up and gave me a brief kiss. As my hand was still gesturing to the expanse of smooth, muscled skin he was showing, he finished standing and hurried out to grab our food...in just his boxers.

Shaking my head, I grabbed his shirt by my feet and held it up over my chest. It wasn't as if I could be seen from the entryway, but if they saw Kellan like that, well, then they would probably assume that he wasn't half-dressed alone. It made my cheeks heat and I sunk my head into my hands. Well, that's what I got for being with a man who had no idea what being self-conscious felt like. He knew he looked good, and he didn't care who else knew it, too. Some days, I'd give anything for that sort of confidence. Yeah, that was also on my list of things to work on.

I heard him open the door and greet someone. Then I heard giggling...female giggling. I sighed. Of course the pizza person would be a girl tonight, on the night that Kellan decided to answer the door in his skivvies. I pictured him leaning against the door frame, every wondrous muscle distinct and defined as pizza-chick drooled over our pepperoni. At least my name on his chest would be distinct and defined for her, too.

Sorry, girlie, but the hot man handing you a twenty belongs to me. See, it says so right there on his pec. I smiled and rolled my eyes at myself.

The incessant giggling continued the entire time she was here, and it seemed like forever as I waited. When the door finally shut and Kellan sauntered back into the kitchen, pizza box in hand, his smile was magnificent. It faded a little as soon as he noticed that I'd covered up with his t-shirt in his absence. He pointed at me, a smaller box in his other hand. "Uh-uh, that's cheating. You have to stay as naked as you were when I left."

I rolled my eyes and dropped his shirt to the floor. "Even when you're flirting with the delivery girl?"

Setting the larger box on the counter, he twisted his lips at me. "I wasn't flirting."

Deciding to try on the self-confidence that oozed from him so fluidly, I stood up. His eyes traveled down and back up my body, his smile evening out. "You weren't?" Coming up to stand in front of him, I leaned back on a hip and mimicked a pose that every sexy underwear model used. Pointing at the smaller box in his hand, I asked, "Then what's that?"

Shrugging, he bit his lip. "She had some extra bread sticks. She said we could have them if we wanted."

I shook my head, and he chuckled. Quickly setting down the box, he wrapped his arms around my waist, pulling me tight to his body. I laced my arms around his neck while his lips traveled up my throat to my ear. "I can't help what women find appealing." His mouth danced over mine, soft and feather-light, while his hand ducked inside my underwear, cupping my bottom. "But I only find you appealing," he murmured.

Breathing heavily, I attached my mouth to his. He could have given her a lap dance for those bread sticks and I wouldn't have cared. Well, okay, I would have cared, but I would have let it go. He was the object of many people's affections, but I was the object of his.

Just as I considered removing the last piece of his clothing, he stepped away from me. Grabbing my hand, he twirled me out from him and then back to him. Laughing, my hand touched his chest for a moment before being whirled away again.

His laughter joined my own, and with only the merriment of our joy as music, we danced in his kitchen…in our underwear.

We didn't return to our game, we just snatched up greasy slices between dips and twirls. Eating and laughing, Kellan completely swept away any lingering nerves I had about school. He also successfully wiped away any remnants of self-consciousness. By the time we were a few slices into our pie and through a few of his hard-earned bread sticks, I was shaking my modestly covered booty for Kellan. I was in hysterics when he imitated my move and it felt good to finally have a small speck of his confidence.

And he was the reason I felt it. His gaze, his touch, his smile, his laugh, no one had ever made me feel…worshipped…quite like he did. I felt like I could have done anything as I danced in that kitchen with him and I knew, without a doubt, that I really would be fine tomorrow.

Chapter 4 – Gossip

I woke up the next morning far earlier than I'd intended. A small flutter of nerves in my stomach warned me that something potentially embarrassing could happen today. I suppressed the feeling as I sat up. Unlike the dream I had just awakened from, I wouldn't be tripping in front of the class today. No, the only sort of embarrassment I'd feel was walking the halls with a rock star. I was certain Kellan would feel obligated to walk with me to my first class, like I was a kindergartener going to school for the first time, but that was okay. Having him beside me drew all the focus to him, and he didn't mind being the center of attention.

Surveying his empty bedroom, I wondered where the rock star was. I slipped on my underwear and grabbed one of his t-shirts from his drawer. It smelled amazing as I slipped it over my head and I briefly considered wearing it to school. My first class today was British Literature with a focus on turn of the century feminism, but surely those long-deceased, forward-thinking writers would understand the allure of Kellan Kyle's clothing?

Knowing I was up way too early, hours before I needed to get ready, I headed downstairs to find Kellan. Expectedly, I found him in the kitchen, perfect and casual, dressed in worn jeans and a light shirt. He was leaning against the counter as the coffee brewed. With the aroma of coffee mingling with his own wondrous scent, I smiled and walked over to where he was watching me.

Before I could say anything, he spoke one of my favorite words. "Mornin'."

Wrapping my arms around his waist, I snuggled into his chest. "Good morning." It still being an indecent hour, I yawned after my greeting.

Chuckling, he rubbed my back. "You don't have to wake up with me. You can sleep in until school starts."

Resting my chin on his chest, I peeked up at him; his dark blue eyes seemed completely rested, intense and alive with a passion waiting to be stoked. "If you're up, I want to be up." Scrunching my brows, I added, "Why do you get up so early, when you've got nowhere to go?"

Sighing softly, he looked away from me. "Well, let's just say that my childhood trained me to wake up at the crack of dawn." Looking back to me, he shrugged. "Waking up on my own was preferable to being woken up." Shaking his head, he softly added, "I guess the habit stuck, now I can't seem to stop waking up early."

I hated the abuse his parents had inflicted on him at such an early age, and the effect it still had on him, even years later, despite the abusers being dead and gone. Seeing the melancholy in his eyes, I shook my head and forced myself to smile brightly. "Well, I'm glad you do. Quiet mornings with you are some of the best memories that I have."

His sad smile widened into a peaceful one as he ran his fingers back through my hair. "Me too," he whispered. "I always looked forward to you coming down to see me." He shrugged. "Even if it was just for a little while, it still made me feel like we were…together."

His smile started to fade and I reached up to cup his face. "We were, Kellan. We were together...even if it was just for a little while."

Memories of all of our stolen moments together flooded me as I touched his face—the laughter, our quiet conversations, holding him, being held by him, being angry with him, being insanely jealous over some harlot he'd been with the night before, even though I had no right to be. Falling in love with him... Most of it had started right here in this kitchen, waiting for the coffee pot to finish brewing.

Lost in the memories, lost in the dark blue depths of his eyes studying mine, I nearly jumped out of my skin when the phone rang. Kellan chuckled at me as my heart raced about a million miles per hour. I smacked him on the chest as he gently pushed me back and walked over to the obtrusive thing. The shrilling stopped as he picked up the corded handle.

"Hello?" Leaning back, Kellan smiled at me as I took some deep, calming breaths. Then his eyes shifted over to stare out the window as he listened to the voice on the other line. "Hey, Denny, long time, no hear."

My eyes widened as I listened to my boyfriend greet my ex-boyfriend. It was...odd. I knew they still talked, I still talked with Denny too, it just rarely happened when I was in the room. Shifting my weight, I considered leaving Kellan to have a private conversation with the man who I knew he still considered family, despite everything.

Just as my body turned away, Kellan's voice stopped me. "Yeah...she's right here...hold on."

I turned back to Kellan holding out the receiver of the clunky, green phone to me. Shrugging a little, he whispered, "He called here for you."

His face and voice were smooth as he said it, but I thought I saw a slight crease in his brow, and I wondered how he really felt about me still talking to Denny. He had nothing to worry about. Denny and I were completely over, not to mention separated by over seven thousand miles since Denny had returned home to Australia. I smiled comfortingly and grabbed the phone from him. Kellan remained where he was against the counter, making no attempt to leave me to my privacy. I understood.

The butterflies in my stomach flared up as I brought the receiver to my ear. It had been a while since I talked with Denny last, a couple of months actually. The time apart was making me nervous to talk to him again. Well, that and Kellan was standing a foot away from me. Remembering that Denny was still a good friend to both of us, I relaxed as I greeted him. "Good morning, Denny."

He laughed, the sound instantly taking me back to the countless lazy afternoons we'd spent together in Ohio. It tightened my heart a little. Over or not, I still missed him. "Actually, it's evening here. Did I wake you?"

His accent was thicker now that he was back at home. It was delicious to the ear and I laughed at his comment, remembering the massive time change between us. "No, Kellan and I are up."

I bit my lip, remembering that he'd called me here, and asked if I was awake, which meant he figured I'd spent the night, which meant he probably also assumed

I'd slept with Kellan, in the figurative sense. And he was right, if he thought that. I hated him thinking about it, much like I still hated to think about him with his current girlfriend, a sweet woman named Abby that he'd been with for a while, longer than Kellan and I had officially been together.

He didn't react to me lumping myself together with the man who'd stolen me away from him, though. Kellan, however, smiled devilishly. "Ah, good. Did I miss it?" Denny asked anxiously.

I furrowed my brow and shook my head. "Miss what?" Kellan repeated my gesture and I shrugged at him.

Denny quickly filled in the blanks for me. "Your first day back to school. Is it today, or did I miss it?"

My mouth dropped open as I understood why he was calling. "Did you call just to wish me good luck on my first day of school?" Tears stung my eyes that he would still be so sweet to me. He shouldn't, not after everything I've done to him. He should curse my name and vow eternal vengeance on me. But that…just wasn't Denny.

I heard him clear his throat and pictured him running a hand through his chunky, dark hair, a goofy smile on his beautiful face. "Well, yeah, I know how nervous you get about stuff like that." He paused and my throat dried up, amazed and stunned by his level of forgiveness. Kellan narrowed his eyes at my reaction, but didn't say anything. In the silence, Denny asked, "Should I not have called, Kiera? Is this…weird?"

Swallowing repeatedly, I shook my head. "No, no, I'm sorry. Yes, of course you should call me. And no, you didn't miss it, and yes, I'm a little nervous." Not liking the tension that had built up, I said all of that really fast.

Kellan crossed his arms over his chest, but Denny laughed. "Oh, okay, good. Well, I just wanted to wish you well, and let you know that I was…thinking about you today."

Denny cleared his throat again while I blinked back the tears again. God, he was just too good of a person. Sometimes I thought I was an idiot for ever hurting him. Okay, I perpetually thought I was an idiot for hurting him.

"Thank you, Denny…for remembering. That was incredibly sweet of you." I felt a flush creep over my face as I peeked up at Kellan. He sniffed and quickly looked away. I felt that age-old guilt wash over me. And just when I thought I'd never have to feel guilty again.

Softly, Denny responded with, "No problem, Kiera. I know that Kellan," he swallowed after saying his name, "is probably doing a lot to help you out today, so you probably don't need to hear it from me, but, good luck."

Not knowing how else to respond, I only whispered, "Thank you, Denny." Kellan, still not looking at me, took a step away. I immediately grabbed his arm. He paused, but still wouldn't look back at me.

Denny laughed a little into the receiver. "Uh, and tell your sister sorry for me. I called there first and I'm pretty sure I woke her up."

I laughed. Anna did not like being woken up early in the morning. "Yeah, I'll be certain to do that." Kellan's arm under my fingers turned rigid, but he stayed where he was, staring at the coffee pot like it was the most important thing in the universe. I hated that this was bothering him, but it shouldn't. Denny and I were nothing anymore, and he knew that.

I soothingly stroked his arm with my thumb as Denny laughed and said, "Well, Abby and I are at a party for work, so I should get going. She'll fillet me if I stay on the phone all night."

Laughing lightly, I told him, "All right. Tell Abby hi for me, and have fun." After he responded that he would, I turned from Kellan, angling my head away from him. "Hey, thank you so much for remembering, Denny...that means a lot to me." Before he could respond, I added, "I'm so sorry, Denny, about everything."

He sniffed and was quiet a moment, then, "Yeah, I know, Kiera. Have a great day at school. I'll talk to you later, goodbye."

Closing my eyes for a second, I exhaled, "Bye."

Hanging up the phone, I kept my eyes closed as I twisted back to Kellan. When I opened them, he was still staring at the dark coffee resting in the full pot. Although his face was blank, a myriad of emotions were shifting through his eyes. He took another long second, then finally looked back at me.

Smiling encouragingly, I brushed a strand of hair off his forehead. "Hey, you okay?"

He nodded, a smile seamlessly brightening his face, if not his eyes. "Of course, I'm fine. Denny called to wish you luck, that was nice of him." There wasn't a trace of jealousy or sarcasm in his voice, but I heard it anyway.

Sighing, I laced my arms around his neck. "You know that doesn't mean anything, right? You know that I love you, and Denny is nothing more than a friend now, don't you?" I searched his eyes as his smile faltered. "Don't you?"

He started to look towards the pot again and I caught his cheek, making him look at me. His smile returned, perfectly natural. "Yes, I know, Kiera." In a softer voice he added, "I know exactly what you and Denny are."

Not entirely sure what he meant by that, I decided to just take it at face value. Leaning up, I gave him a soft kiss. "Good, because, while he's important to me, you're more important, and I don't want my talking with him to hurt you."

His eyes widened as he stared down at me, like he was really surprised to hear me say that. It pained me that he still didn't understand. Kissing him again, I whispered, "I know what you're thinking, and you're wrong. You're not second best. I could have fled to him, but I went to you. I couldn't live without you. I chose you. I love you."

Swallowing, his moist eyes searching mine, he whispered, "It still feels...unreal...I guess. I'm not used to being...loved by someone. I keep waiting to wake up."

Biting my lip, I shook my head. "Well get used to it. I'm not going anywhere, Kellan."

After a leisurely breakfast, Kellan helped me get ready for school. Well, okay, Kellan lay on his bed and stared while I got dressed. I'd already had to tell him that he couldn't help me in the shower. Firmly pointing at him to stay put on his pillows, I proceeded to slip my bra on under my towel. Kellan shook his head at me, rolling his eyes. "I've seen you naked, you know?"

Flushing as I turned around, I muttered, "I know, but you just staring at me like that is…different."

He snorted and I peeked over my shoulder at him as I slipped on some clean underwear, also under my towel.

Grinning crookedly, he raised an eyebrow. "It's just skin, Kiera." Sitting up and scooting to the edge of the bed, where he could just reach me, he grabbed my knee. His hand started to slide up my leg. "And it's far too beautiful to keep covered up."

Loving the shivers he was sending up my body, but knowing that I couldn't lounge in a bed with him today, unfortunately, I stepped away and again pointed to his pillows. "I don't need to get you any more riled up than you constantly are, by giving you a peep show."

Expertly slipping on my jeans while the towel was still firmly wrapped around my chest, I watched him chuckle and relax back down on his mattress. "Fine," he muttered sullenly. "I'll just remember that the next time you're staring at my body."

I paused in the process of pulling my blouse out of my bag and met his eye. Knowing that I actually did stare at him quite a bit, I sighed, and let the towel drop to the floor. His smile was glorious as he took in my plain, cream-colored bra and I looked away, embarrassed and a little turned on by his attention.

Quickly counting to five, figuring that was long enough for him to get a decent mental picture for the day, I tossed on my fitted, button-up shirt. Pulling my long hair out of the back, the bulk of it still damp, I rolled my eyes at the heat in his expression while he continued to stare at my covered-up chest. Men.

My throat clearing finally brought his eyesight up. Locking gazes with me, he smiled devilishly. "Well, now I'm turned on, and you can't go. You're just going to have to stay here with me today."

Laughing, I leaned over the bed to kiss him. He seemed to think that was a green light and grabbed my body, pulling me on top of him. Giggling in his mouth while we softly moved against each other, I was grateful that his mood had improved from the conversation earlier this morning. I really didn't like him glum about Denny, especially since there was no reason for it. I understood though. I'd hurt him so many times while I'd been with Denny. I had hurt them both. I didn't want to ever hurt another man again.

As our kiss became intense, Kellan's body started telling me that he really wasn't kidding about being in the mood. I reluctantly pulled away from his mouth. "I wish I could stay with you." Frowning, I sulked, "I'm not really looking forward to today."

Sighing, he cupped my cheeks and searched my eyes. "Someday I'll get you to feel like the confident woman who was prancing around in her underwear last night all the time." Running his hand back through my hair, he added, "You are a beautiful, intelligent woman with a boyfriend who adores you. You have nothing to fear...ever."

Smiling, I blushed and looked away. "Easy for you to say, rock star."

Pulling back, I stood and found my comb. Running it through my locks, I watched him laugh and sit up. "I get nervous."

I gave him a wry smile as I stopped mid-stroke. Yeah, right. Kellan Kyle was never nervous. Not around people. Not about his body or his looks. He oozed confidence in nearly everything he did.

Tilting his head, he shrugged. "No, it's true. In the beginning, I used to get nervous on stage."

Scrunching my brow, I finished de-tangling my hair. "Let me guess, you picture the crowd naked now?"

Chuckling, he stood up. "Nah, I had to stop doing that...turned me on."

Pushing his chest back as he came up to me, I laughed unintentionally. "You're impossible."

Shaking my head, I rolled my eyes; he only grinned wider. "We all have our weaknesses," he muttered playfully, sneaking around behind me and holding me tight. "You will be great and I'll drive you every day if you want." Chuckling, he added, "Maybe I'll sit in on a class or two."

I laughed at the image of him beside me, bored to tears, during lectures. "I doubt the professor would like you snoring during class." Chuckling more, he kissed my neck.

Sighing, I rested my wet head on his shoulder and closed my eyes, letting his peace-inducing smell wash over me. I'd decided to forgo wearing his t-shirt to school, but maybe I could get his scent to leech into my clothes. Keep him with me olfactorily. God, what was I saying about not being consumed by him? I couldn't help it. He was just...consuming.

Much sooner than I would have liked, it was time for class. As promised, Kellan drove me to school. His smile was peaceful as he leaned back in his seat, one hand draped across my thigh, the other casually holding the wheel straight. He looked like someone returning to a favorite activity after a long absence. It made me smile that chauffeuring me around was such a pleasant experience for him. I think most people would have tired of it after a few weeks. Not Kellan, though. He never complained about all the places that I needed to go. It was one of the many ways he expressed his affection. For a guy who had never been a boyfriend before, he was surprisingly good at it. Then again, Kellan was good at most things he tried...except pool...and, as I had found out last night, poker.

Smiling at the image of him in his black silky boxers, pizza in hand as he twirled me around the kitchen, I didn't even notice when we finally stopped. I blinked and looked around when he shut off the car.

The University of Washington. Located on the other side of Lake Union from the heart of downtown Seattle, it was a massive campus, more like a small city. Several of the local businesses surrounding it survived solely on the influx of college students arriving every year.

I knew this area pretty well after my time here. I wasn't really that nervous about knowing where my classes were. It was more walking into a room full of strangers that tangled my nerves. I was not a big fan of being the focus of people's attention. Which made walking beside Kellan both a blessing and a curse.

It was a blessing because I loved having him around, and also because when he was with me, people tended to stare at *him*. Kellan just possessed a certain aura. He drew people to him. The face, the hair, the body, the swagger—everything about him made you notice him. And for girls, the intense inspection of him was usually long and thorough.

It was a curse because, now that we were a couple, he was a fountain of affection. Our previously friendly handholding was now loving embraces. And as he laughed along to some absurd comment my parents had made last week about him needing to earn a real living, since being in a band was not a viable career choice for the man their daughter was dating, I noticed that a lot of eyes shifted from him to settle on me. Much like what frequently happened at the bar, I was being judged on whether or not I was worthy of belonging to the rock-god. And because Kellan was right about my general lack of confidence, I couldn't help but think that I came up short in their eyes.

Head held high, I forced it from my mind. It was irrelevant what these strangers thought of my relationship with him. And it didn't matter if a bunch of random people thought I was unworthy of Kellan. Kellan thought I was, and really, that was the only opinion I needed, right?

Laughing along with him, I nearly ran right into a small cluster stopped in the hallway.

Kellan pulled me back right before I collided with a man who seemed about seven feet tall. He hovered over Kellan, who was at least a couple of inches over six feet himself. The dark-haired boy had a huge smile on his face as he pointed at Kellan.

"Hey, aren't you that guy? The singer of that band? The D-Bags?"

Kellan's face shifted from a cautious expression into a relaxed smile, and I couldn't help but wonder if he'd been expecting the guy to engage him in a fight. There was a time when Kellan didn't care too much about other people's relationships. "Kellan, yeah….I'm a D-Bag." He laughed a little after his comment, amused by his own band's name.

The man and his group of equally tall friends circled Kellan, eager to talk to the celebrity they'd stumbled upon. Reaching out, the imposing fan grabbed Kellan's hand and shook it. "You were great at Bumbershoot, man!" Then the group started in on the compliments and questions.

They were relentless. The flattery went on and on, and I started getting nervous that I would be late if we stayed any longer. Kellan answered all of their questions and politely thanked them for their praises, then expertly released himself from the conversation, waving goodbye as he turned us to walk around the group. By the time he successfully disengaged himself, Kellan had received invitations to at least three different parties.

Shaking my head as we approached my classroom, I laughed. Looking over at me, he bumped my shoulder with his. "What?"

I gave him a crooked grin. "Look at you, finally getting some male fans."

Laughing as he opened the door for me, he shook his head. "We've always had male fans, Kiera." Raising an eyebrow, he added, "You just choose to fixate on the female ones."

Brushing past his body as I walked by him, I paused and leaned into his face. "Well, that's because they fixate on you," I whispered, letting my mouth almost touch his.

He bit his lip, and I heard him groan a little. "Look at you…becoming a seductress," he whispered.

I blushed and immediately stepped away from him.

I heard his laughter behind me, but didn't turn to look. Soft lips greeted my cheek as his hands rested on my hips. "Have fun," he whispered in my ear.

I wanted to sigh and lean into him again, but female giggling reminded me that I was no longer alone with him in his bedroom. No, I was in front of a classroom, sort of being inappropriate with my boyfriend. Oh well, at least he'd managed to not make me nervous about my entrance.

With my cheeks flaming red, embarrassed by our private moment being watched, I gave him a soft peck and told him that I would have fun. Then I made a beeline to a seat in the middle of the room, away from the chuckling women watching my man's backside as he waved and left the room.

After a rousing debate on how sexism influenced early feminist literature, I was feeling right as rain with school again. I knew that would happen. Once I settled in, things always worked out. It was just the process of getting there that frazzled my nerves. After lit was my ethics class. Now that I was comfortable, I was looking forward to this course, although, I had a feeling I would be doing a lot of soul-searching in it. Ethics and I had crossed paths recently, and I was not sure that I'd fallen on the right side of the morality line. No, no, I was pretty sure I'd failed miserably. Kellan and I both. It would probably be cathartic for me to write a paper about it.

Walking into an aesthetically beautiful and functional structure, my eyes came across a face I haven't seen in a while, someone I didn't really care to see again. Hovering by the front doors, I watched a familiar redhead with tight, bouncy curls chatting to a couple of her friends. I recognized all three—Candy and her cohorts. They'd each interrogated me about Kellan last year. Mostly Candy, since she found sleeping with him to be such an enjoyable pastime.

Well, that diversion was no longer available to her now; she'd just have to get her kicks somewhere else. With a small smile playing on my face, I watched as they cackled and strolled down the hall a few paces in front of me. I sighed when they all walked into my designated classroom. I'd had a class with Candy before, last spring actually, when Kellan and I finally reunited. I guessed I had another class with her. And, of course, this would be the class I'd have every day. And an ethics class to boot. Joy. I bet the universe was laughing its ass off at the irony.

Shaking my head and rolling my eyes, I walked into the room amidst a small flurry of butterflies in my belly. They settled quickly once the people already seated looked up, then looked back down. Well, all but three. Candy and her minions continued to stare as I made my way to the section farthest from them. I felt their eyes on my back as I sat down, grabbed a notebook, and started doodling like a mad woman.

I nearly expected Candy to move to take the seat beside me. I cringed and peeked up when I finally felt somebody approaching. Thankfully it was only some strait-laced guy. He gave me a look that clearly said, *Good, she doesn't seem like a talker, maybe I'll be able to hear the lecture if I sit next to her*, then proceeded to sit down beside me. I resumed my drawing, glad that at least Kellan's ex-fling wasn't going to disrupt my learning.

No, she left me completely alone...until after class.

I was still absorbed by the professor's explanation about the difference between ethics and morals, and Candy's approach caught me off guard. Before I could take action, she and her friends had me surrounded. Looking between them as we walked from the classroom, I sighed softly and prayed that Kellan was waiting for me by his car, and not right outside the front doors.

Sidling up close to my side, Candy tilted her head at me. "So, rumor has it that you and Kellan Kyle are a thing now. Like, a real thing."

Peeking over at her, I considered stopping and extending my hand in a formal introduction, since we've never had one, but I didn't. I merely shrugged and muttered, "Yep."

She scoffed, the clone-like friends around her giggling. "So it doesn't bother you that he's a whore."

Stopping in my tracks, I glared over at her and wondered if I could slap a girl in the middle of school and not get in trouble. This was college, right? Wasn't it all about the freedom of expression? "He is not a whore. Don't ever call him that again." I felt the heat in my tone and was a little proud of myself that my voice didn't tremble at all.

She put her hands on her hips, her sycophants rotating to stand behind her, like backup singers or something. "Huh, I guess you're right." She leaned in, an eyebrow raised. "Whores get paid. He does it for the fun of it."

I literally had to grab my jeans to not deck her. Seriously? Deciding that getting arrested for assault wasn't a good way to start the school year, I stormed off down the hall. She, of course, followed me.

S.C. Stephens

"What? Can't handle the truth? I just wanted you to be aware that he still gets it on with every girl he can." She laughed, dryly. "It's not like being with you has miraculously turned him into a good boy now. Men are what they are, and Kellan is a sex addict."

Tears of anger stinging my eyes, I twisted to face her. "You don't know anything about him. You don't know anything he's been through." Leaning into her, I raised my eyebrow. "I know you've slept with him, but don't confuse sex for intimacy." Irritated that I let her get to me, knowing full well that she was just trying to rile me up, I jerked open the front doors. Luckily, Kellan was not there.

Right on my heels, she snapped back, "Hey, I'm doing you a favor. You think he's changed, you think he's suddenly a faithful, one-woman man now? A tiger doesn't change his spots!"

Groaning as I dashed down the steps, I tossed over my shoulder, "A tiger doesn't even have spots. Get your metaphors straight."

Prissily, she marched beside me. "Whatever. My point is that Tina here," she jerked her thumb at the blonde striding next to her, "saw him after a show in the Square just last week." Smirking, she yanked on my elbow to hold me in place. "He was shirtless and about to get it on with some skank."

Tina nodded her agreement, adding, "And in a storage closet, too...how romantic."

Glaring between the two of them, I felt my body ice over. Kellan did play several shows during the week at different venues. He got home really late after those shows because he had to help pack up their equipment. He could have... I shook my head. No, not after everything...he wouldn't do that to me. A nagging voice in my head added, *Right, just like you wouldn't do that to Denny?*

Ignoring that voice, I narrowed my eyes at the gossipers. "You didn't see what you think you saw. I trust him." With that, I jerked my arm away and sauntered off.

Light snickers followed me, along with, "You know, him having your name across his heart doesn't mean he's not loaning out other parts of his body!"

My jaw dropped open as I looked back at her. Few people knew about Kellan's tattoo. He was much more reluctant to strip at shows now, like he didn't want the world to see his romantic proclamation of devotion. It meant a lot to me that he felt that way. It was private, between the two of us. How did this group of girls know about it? Had Tina really seen him half-naked? I didn't want to believe it, but my mind vividly pictured him undressed, panting with desire, with some harlot fan attached to his mouth. Then I pictured him closing the storage room door and doing all sorts of unseemly things to her.

I felt my stomach rising as I gaped at them. They only chuckled at me, Tina giving me a fake, apologetic smile while Candy shrugged. "Dogs are dogs, Kiera," she said sweetly.

I bit my lip and forced myself to walk away from them...and not run. They were lying...they had to be.

At the parking lot, I spotted Kellan's shiny black Chevelle right away. Sighting him, I instantly understood why he hadn't met me outside of class on my first day of school. A group of about five girls surrounded him. He was casually leaning against his car as he talked to them. They giggled, tittering like thirteen-year-olds as he spoke. Even from the distance between us, I could see the small, amused smile on his face. After my meeting with Candy, it boiled my blood.

My hands in permanent fists, I strutted over to him. I tried to calm myself down, but instead I seemed to get angrier with each step. Where had they seen that damn tattoo? Where was he exposing himself? Was I being naïve in thinking that what we had was so monumental that he would never stray from it? Was he still being a whore?

Laughing at something one of the hussies said, Kellan turned his head and spotted me. His small smile brightened at seeing me approach, then dimmed when he noticed the scowl on my face. The tittering girls didn't back off at all, and I had to elbow my way through them to get to him.

"Let's go," I bit out, not really in the mood to be around his fans for another second longer.

He nodded, his brow furrowed as he opened the passenger's door. After shutting it behind me, I heard him say to his adoring entourage, "I'm sorry, but I have to go. It was nice meeting you all." There were whines and groans of disappointment as he walked over to his side of the car. I rolled my eyes.

Kellan watched me curiously as he started the car, the roar of the engine matching my foul mood. Cocking an eyebrow, he put the car in reverse. One eye on me, the other carefully tracking the girls, so he didn't run them over as they watched us pull away, he asked, "You want to tell me what happened that's got you all ticked off?"

Gritting my jaw, I glared at the floosies staring after him. Most turned away from my eye line, while a couple glared back. "Not really," I muttered under my breath.

Sighing, he put his hand on my thigh. I instantly wondered where else that hand had been recently. "Will you anyway?" I looked back at him, trying to keep my expression and my mood even. He frowned before turning on to the road. "You're the one that said we should talk things out…and you look like you need to talk something out."

Grunting, and wishing I'd never said that to him, I crossed my arms over my chest. "I have another class with Candy this year. She made sure to say hello afterwards."

I watched him carefully as he studied the road he was driving along. He narrowed his eyes and tilted his head; it was an adorable expression of confusion. "Candy…?"

I rolled my eyes that her name didn't immediately register with him. Well, when your little black book was about as thick as the local yellow pages, I suppose it took a while to mentally filter through it.

A second later, as I was sighing, recognition flared in his eyes and he peeked over at me. "Oh, right...Candy." Twisting his lips, he shrugged. "What...did she say?"

Glaring at him, I tightened my hands across my chest. If I didn't, I was sure I'd smack him. "She just mentioned a show that you had last week. You played in Pioneer Square, right?"

He looked up. I wasn't sure whether he was accessing his memory for that particular event, or whether he was accessing the creative part of the brain that made up rapid-fire lies. Looking up and to the left meant one, looking up and to the right meant the other. I just could never remember which one was which. "Yeah, yeah we did." He looked over at me. "Was she there? She didn't say hello." He added that last part quickly, as if he was reassuring me that he hadn't seen her.

I narrowed my eyes even more as I studied him. Had I just had sex last night with a man who was having sex with a bunch of other people too? God, it made me sick just to think about it. "No, a friend of hers saw you there...in the back."

I said that suspiciously and he looked at me strangely before shifting his attention back to driving. Shrugging, he said, "Huh, well, okay." Peeking over at me, he raised an eyebrow. "Why is one of her friends seeing me making you look like you sucked on a lemon?"

Exhaling in a tightly controlled way, I resisted the urge to smack the crap out of him. "Because she said she saw you doing things...with someone who was not me."

His eyes widened as he stared at me, then he jerked the car over to the side of the road. I had to hold on to the door he moved over so fast. With the car slightly on the curb, he slammed it into park and shifted to face me.

His expression deadly serious, he held my eye; I could feel mine stinging as my fears bubbled up to the surface. "I am not doing anything with anyone who is not you. Whatever she said was a lie, Kiera."

I lifted my chin, but I could feel the tear building, swelling until it rolled down my cheek. "She knew about the tattoo, Kellan."

He cupped my cheek, brushing the moisture off my skin. "Then she saw it somewhere else or someone told her about it, because I'm not fooling around with anyone." Unbuckling his seatbelt and scooting closer to me, he rested his head against mine. "I'm only fooling around with you. I'm only getting naked with you. I'm only having sex with you, Kiera." Pulling back, he met my eye. "I chose you. I love you. I'm not interested in anyone else, okay?"

I nodded, feeling more tears slide down my cheeks. I felt the truth in his words, words that were similar to the words of comfort and reassurance that I often gave to him. I hated that one conniving, jealous bitch had made me doubt him. If she hadn't had such a good point I wouldn't have, but Kellan had a long, sordid history of poor decisions when it came to women. I didn't always feel special enough to stop that cycle of behavior.

He leaned in to tenderly kiss me and I felt myself relaxing as he poured his heart into his soft touch. Tasting the salt of my tears between us, I tried to let the doubt go. We'd gone through so much. I'd seen a side of him, a vulnerability, that I was positive no other girl had seen before. I was certain that I had his heart, and surely he wouldn't risk losing his heart over some stupid desire his body might be feeling. Not when he could satisfy that ache with me. Not when I would take him into my bed every night, and the brand new bed that he just purchased for me the other day, too.

As our kiss ignited, and our bodies inched closer as our breaths quickened, I wanted to remind him what I could be to him, and I wanted him to remind me exactly what we had together—a bond that no eager fan could break. Knowing that I had a couple of hours before work, and an empty apartment, I dragged my lips up to his ear. "Show me that you want me, Kellan. Take me home."

He had the car back in drive and flying down the road a microsecond later.

Chapter 5 – A Dream

It never ceased to surprise me how quickly Kellan Kyle could turn my mood around. One minute I felt certain that I'd made a mistake and we would never work out, and the next I'd be languidly getting out of bed with him, a dopey, satisfied smile on my face and the notion that all was right and good in the world. Elated, I gave him one last peck before heading to the bathroom to get ready for work. Pulling out my curling iron, I made room for it on the small counter already littered with Anna's beauty products. I listened to Kellan humming in my bedroom. It was a comforting sound and my dopey smile widened in the mirror.

Sighing at the frazzled state of my I-just-had-sex hair, I yanked a brush through my waves. Kellan just had a way about him. He could ruin everything, or he could make everything perfect. Candy was just trying to interfere with our relationship because she was the jealousy harpy that I was trying not to be. I'd heard her brag to students about being with a rock star before. While I sometimes wished Kellan wasn't a celebrity, she adored that he was sort of famous around here. She wanted more of that fame. I'm pretty sure she'd date him just to attach her name to his. It sickened me that some people were so obsessed with their fifteen minutes. For me, his status only complicated our lives. It'd be so much simpler if no one knew who he was.

When I finished freshening up my makeup and taming my locks into a functional-but-cute ponytail, I headed back to my room. Kellan had made himself comfortable on the queen-sized mattress that dominated my tiny bedroom. Propped up on my pillows, he was happily rubbing his sock-covered feet together. Once again fully dressed, he was reading one of my romance novels with a small, amused grin on his face.

Glancing at the cover, which featured some bronze, buff man holding a scantily clad woman to his bare chest, I shook my head at Kellan. "What are you doing?"

Not looking up at me, his smile widened. "I'm reading your porn."

Smacking his foot as I walked by, I scoffed, "That's not porn...it's romance."

Snorting, Kellan looked up at me. "Really?" Glancing down at the book, he started reading a passage from it. "She gasped in his mouth when his erection slid against her. He groaned when her desire coated him. They were both so ready to be together, guilt and remorse free...finally. Her legs wrapped around him as her hips rocked him into place. As he felt the tip of himself press against her entrance, he heard her groan, 'I want you buried in me, I want to be consumed by you.'"

I flushed red all over, remembering the part that he was reading. It was a pretty hot scene, and usually did turn me on a bit. And the way he read it was so sensual... Embarrassed that he was sort of right, I snatched the book away from him, tucking it into a dresser drawer. I was pretty certain that the next time I read it I would hear Kellan's sultry voice in my head. It made me ache just thinking about it.

Kellan gave me a sly smile. "See...porn." He leaned forward. "And hot porn too." He pointed to where I'd tucked the book away. "I wouldn't mind trying that thing on page--"

I cut him off, my cheeks hot to the touch as I yanked on his arm, pulling him to his feet. "Get your shoes on, it's time to go."

He laughed at me as he steadied himself. "Yeah, all right...maybe next time then."

Walking into Pete's with Kellan a while later, I was greeted by a bubbly Kate. Since Jenny had the night off, she was my partner in crime for the evening. "Hi guys!"

"Hi, Kate." I smiled at the bouncy woman and attempted to disengage myself from my boyfriend so I could go put my purse away. Just as our fingertips separated, Kellan grabbed my waist, pulling me back into his hips.

"I'll have my usual," he growled in my ear.

I bit my lip as his voice sent shivers down my spine. Twisting to give him a dirty look, I shook my head. "I know what you like, Kellan."

He grinned impishly, his hand slipping around to slink inside the back pocket of my jeans. "Yes...you certainly do."

Realizing how suggestive what I'd said was, I pushed him away from me. He had such a dirty mind sometimes. Well, most of the time actually. He laughed as I blushed, then kissed my cheek. "You're so adorable." Leaning in he whispered, "Have I mentioned how much that turns me on?"

Laughing as I untangled myself from him, I murmured, "What doesn't, Kellan?"

Smiling, he shrugged one shoulder and walked back to his table. I sighed, watching his back pockets walk away from me. Kate, beside me, sighed too. I turned to look at her as she dreamily said, "God he's got great hair. He always looks like he just got out of bed." Meeting my eye, she frowned. "How does he do that?"

Biting my lip, hoping my face wasn't beet red, I shrugged. I couldn't exactly tell her that he was currently rocking an amazing head of sex-hair because he'd just had sex. That was a little too much information to give my co-worker. Shrugging, she shook her head and handed me a fistful of lollipops from the pocket of her apron. "Here, Pete had these made to give out to the customers."

Unwrapping a red label with "Pete's Bar" clearly written across it, she popped one in her mouth. "I keep forgetting to give them out though." She smiled around the stick in her mouth. "They're apple flavored."

I smiled, thanked her, then went to put my stuff away. Once I was back on the floor, I unwrapped one too and stuck it in my mouth. God, I loved apple flavor. It tasted so much better than real apples.

Rita had Kellan's beer ready before I got to the bar to pick it up. Staring across the room at Kellan, she sullenly handed it to me. "Here...this is for sweet cheeks."

Snatching it from her, I murmured, "Thanks," and rolled my eyes as I walked away. It was so irritating to have my guy mentally undressed over and over again. And people think men are the hornier bunch. I was beginning to doubt that.

Pulling the sucker out as I approached Kellan's table, I handed him his drink. "Here you go…your usual."

He smiled at me as he took the beer from my hand. His other hand reached up and grabbed the hand holding my sucker. Closing his fingers over mine, he brought the treat to his lips and closed his mouth around it. Not breaking eye contact, he sucked on my lollipop for a moment, then let it go. It was horribly erotic and I heard a few groans from a nearby table of girls watching him. Wanting to lean down and taste the apple on his tongue, I instead decided to stick up for my rights.

Shoving his shoulder back, I frowned. "Eww, Kellan. That's mine."

Nothing about his mouth on or near anything of mine actually grossed me out, but it was the principle of the thing. You don't suck another person's sucker uninvited. Smiling, like he knew I'd let his lips go anywhere, he asked, "What? I can put my mouth on your--"

I covered up that mouth, taking a quick peek at the girls at the table next to him, subtly leaning over in their seats to hear him speak. "Kellan!" I hissed under my breath.

Removing my hand from his lips, he continued undaunted. "…but I can't enjoy your sucker?"

Shaking my head at him, I felt a smile creep into my mouth. He was giving me a slight frown and puppy dog eyes. And damn if it wasn't hopelessly attractive. Giving up, I shoved the sucker in his mouth. Those eyes had earned it. He smiled around the stick and I sighed in annoyance. "You could at least ask first."

Removing it, his lips curving over the edge of the ball seductively, he raised an eyebrow. "I didn't think I had to ask to suck on your…candy."

I frowned genuinely. "Don't say candy." After the afternoon I'd had, I really didn't want to ever hear that word again.

The smirk fell off his face as he understood my expression. "Sorry," he whispered.

Shaking my head, I leaned down and pressed my lips to his; the apple was as marvelous as I thought it would be. "It's all right." Ignoring the disgruntled noises from the table of women to my left, I softly kissed him again. "Just ask next time, sucker thief."

He was grinning and thoroughly enjoying his sweet treat as I walked away.

Not too much later, as I was relaying my day at school to Kate, minus the Candy-fiasco of course, the doors burst open. Startled, I looked over to see Matt stepping through them. His face was beaming as he immediately looked back to the guys' table. Seeing Kellan, his smile expanded as he practically bounded to the table.

Not used to seeing the shy man so exuberant, I looked back at Kate. She shrugged. We both twisted back to the front doors when we heard it open again. Griffin stepped through this time, with Evan right behind him. Both men were glowing as brightly as Matt had been.

They both darted towards Matt, who was approaching Kellan, fervidly telling him about something. Kellan frowned and looked over at the rest of the guys coming towards him. Furrowing my brows, I tried to figure out what was going on.

"What's up, Kiera?" Kate asked me, pointing to where Matt, Griffin and Evan were all seated around Kellan, leaning into him as they all talked at once. Kellan's expression was one of shock as he looked between all of them. He occasionally asked questions when one of them paused long enough for him to do so.

"I have no idea," I murmured, stepping away from her to find out.

Kellan's eyes snapped up to me when I was almost within ear shot. I paused when he leaned back and ran a hand over his mouth. His eyes looked worried, really worried. Suddenly my feet felt like lead, and I was afraid to move any closer to him. I thought it was good news by the look on the guys' faces, but Kellan didn't look like he'd just received good news. He looked like they'd just told him life as he knew it was coming to an end.

Excited, they all patted his shoulder. They were trying to get him to smile, but Kellan shook his head and murmured something to them, his gaze still locked on me. Eventually they all turned to look at me. I actually took a step back as each of their eyes met mine. Evan's was sympathetic; that scared me. Matt's was appraising; that concerned me. Griffin's was irritated; that...was really nothing new.

Kellan leaning forward brought all of their attentions back to him. He started talking, low and intensely, and I couldn't make it out. The guys were instantly shaking their heads and throwing their hands about, irritated. I'd never seen the group fight before and I had the horrid feeling they were somehow fighting about me.

Someone nearby called out to me, asking for something, but I couldn't move to respond to them. Something big was happening. Something that Kellan wasn't thrilled about, but the rest of the group was. Something that seemed to involve me. Ice poured through my body as I tried in vain to snap the puzzle pieces together.

Griffin suddenly shouting, "Oh, come on, Kellan! Fuck!" made me flinch. Kellan raised a calming hand to Griffin and quietly said something, shaking his head. Griffin shook his, crossing his arms over his chest. Griffin scowled back at Kellan while Matt hung his head, disappointed. Evan clapped Kellan on the shoulder and leaned in to tell him something. Evan's hand swung back to me and Kellan's eyes followed the movement.

My heart raced as I watched Kellan sigh and scrub his face with his hands. Slumping back in his chair, he finally shook his head and looked at his friends. Nodding, he said something, then slowly stood up.

His eyes met mine, and he sighed again. I felt like my heart was going to explode as I watched him excuse himself and walk towards me. I nearly wanted to run away as I felt that tension from his table follow him up the aisle. Maybe it was all in my head, but the bar seemed deathly quiet. Kellan and I had a history of making scenes in this bar. I wasn't sure if that was going to happen, but the rest of the patrons seemed to think so as they eagerly waited for us to meet.

His head down, Kellan stepped in front of me. I held my breath. "Can

I...talk to you," he looked up, his expression tight, "outside?"

I gave him a wooden nod, wanting to do anything else but go outside with him. I couldn't move my feet, but he grabbed my hand and started dragging me away. The action prompted the muscles in my body to involuntarily respond, and I followed him out of the double doors.

A flurry of whispers started right before the doors shut. Then all of the sound from the bar ceased. Kellan dropped my hand and ran it through his hair. Looking around the lot, he seemed to be focusing on anything except me. I felt tears in my eyes as fear roiled in my stomach.

"Kellan?" I whispered, my voice shaky.

He finally looked at me when he heard my tone. Sighing, he cupped my cheek. "I need to tell you something, and I don't know where to start." He bit his lip as my heart thudded against my chest.

"Just tell me, because you're really starting to scare me."

He swallowed and looked down, his hand dropping to my arm. "Matt has been doing a lot over the summer for the band." He looked up at me and shrugged. "Lining up more gigs, scoring that equipment so we can work on soundproofing Evan's place, getting us that spot at Bumbershoot..."

I nodded. None of this was news to me. My heart on hold, I waited for the part that was. Stepping up close, Kellan began stroking my arm. "A band that he's been trying to get in with saw us at Bumbershoot. They were...impressed and..." He sighed, his other hand coming up to wrap around my fingers. "They want us to join them on their tour," he whispered.

I blinked and pulled away from him, his face torn in the moonlight. "You got invited to join a tour? An actual band tour?"

Nodding, he shrugged. "It's a pretty decently sized one, about six other bands are already on it, from what Matt says. We'll be a...last minute addition, bottom of the lineup, but on it, at least."

Amazed and overwhelmed with pride, I threw my arms around him. "Oh, my God, Kellan! That's amazing!"

He sighed as I hugged him tight and I pulled back to look at him. He wouldn't look at me and the brief joy I felt faded. Cupping his cheek, I stroked his skin with my thumb. "You're not excited about this..." Feeling my heart turn to lead, I began to understand. "Because of me, right?"

Meeting my gaze, he shrugged. "It's a six month tour, Kiera...coast to coast." I bit my lip. My eyes started stinging as I considered just what that meant for us. He'd be leaving, for quite a while.

Forcing a smile, even though I wanted to feel as melancholy as he did, I shook my head. "It's okay. Six months isn't so long. And you'll have breaks, right? I'll still get to see you?"

He nodded and looked down. "I don't have to go, Kiera." Looking back up at me, he shook his head. "I can tell the guys no."

My mouth dropped open as I realized what the band had fought about. He'd told them no in the bar, because he didn't want to leave me. I searched his face in disbelief. "This is your dream, Kellan, and this could be it for you. This could be your moment, your chance. Isn't this what you want?"

He shrugged, looking over my shoulder to the bar. "I'm fine with my life the way it is. Playing at Pete's," he looked back at me, "being with you."

Running my hand back through his hair, I pressed our bodies together. "But you know you're too talented to keep doing that forever, Kellan. Even though I'd like to keep you to myself, I know that I can't hide you away from the world." He looked at the ground and I sunk down to meet his eyes. "And it's not just your dream, Kellan." I glanced back at the bar and he followed my gaze. "You know how much this means to them." Looking back at him, I shrugged. "You can't say no because of me."

"I know." He sighed. "They're the only reason I'm even talking to you about this right now." Shaking his head, he added, "But, Kiera...you have another year of school, you can't come with me. I don't want to leave you..."

I shook my head, cutting him off. "Not because of me, Kellan." Feeling tears sting my eyes again, I swallowed hard. I was going to miss him so much, but I couldn't keep him from this. I couldn't be that person...again. "I won't keep another man from his dream," I whispered.

He pulled me in tight, clasping me to him like I was going to vanish. I felt like sobbing but I knew that I couldn't, not when I could feel him shaking in my arms. Concerned, I whispered in his ear, "You're scared, Kellan...why? You never get scared."

He shook his head. "That's not true. I'm scared all the time." I pulled back to look at him with furrowed brows and he swallowed. "I remember, Kiera." I furrowed my brows even more and he shook his head. "I remember when Denny left you...what it did to you." His eyes searching mine, he whispered, "I remember how we got together."

Heat pricked me as what he was saying sunk in. He thought if he left, I'd cheat. I'd be so lonely and pathetic without him that I'd reach out to the next available man and do...exactly what I'd done to Denny. Knowing I couldn't hate him for his fear, but feeling the anger anyway, I pushed him back from me. "You won't leave me because when Denny left..."

"I know you don't like being alone," he murmured.

Anger stirring my belly, I spat out, "I'm not going to freak out because you're gone and cheat on you. I'm not... I wouldn't..." I stammered with something that didn't sound childish. "Why would you think I would do that to you?"

"Because I was there...when Denny thought the exact same thing, when he thought you'd never cheat on him either." He sighed and tried to wrap me in his embrace again but I kept him at arm's length.

I tried to raise my chin, but I felt it quivering as my emotions ran rampant. "That's not fair. I've grown, Kellan. And you and I were a completely different situation. You can't throw that in my face."

Looking apologetic, he shook his head. "I know, I do know that. And I know you've grown, Kiera, but still…" Closing his eyes, he looked away.

Open-mouthed, I could only shake my head at him. "Are you always going to wonder about me?" I whispered.

I wished we had the sort of relationship where we could smile and congratulate the other, wishing them well, knowing that nothing bad would happen. We didn't have that though. We had a relationship filled with doubt and fear, even though I sometimes tried to naively pretend that we didn't.

Peeking up at me, he raised his eyebrows. "Just like you wonder about me? Just earlier today you thought I was cheating on you. You won't worry when I'm gone? I mean, if I go on the road for months…with Griffin…it won't cross your mind?"

My eyes narrowed as I considered just what kind of trouble he could get into with *that* D-bag. "Well, now it will." I crossed my arms over my chest and glared at him until he turned away. He sighed, looking out over the parking lot. I sighed as well, my posture relaxing as my residual anger faded. I couldn't be angry with him for wondering about something that I often wondered about too. "I guess we'll just have to try and…trust each other."

When he solemnly nodded, his gaze dropping to our feet, I looked around at where we were—outside, alone. A second wave of understanding hit me. Cupping his cheek, I brought his gaze back up to mine. "Did you tell me this out here because you thought I would break down?"

Nodding, he whispered, "I remember that night that Denny told you he was leaving. I remember holding you while you cried…for him. I saw you when his plane left. You were devastated, like a part of you had left with him. I don't want to hurt you like that, Kiera."

His eyes saddened as he looked over mine…over my completely dry ones. Kissing him softly, I rested my forehead against his. "Are you upset that I'm…not more upset. Was this a test?"

Sighing, he shook his head. "I wouldn't test you, Kiera, but I did think you'd…at least cry, maybe beg a little."

He tried to turn away again, but I held him in front of me. "I will. Trust me, when you actually leave, I will be a blubbering wreck. But I meant what I said, Kellan. I've grown. A lot has happened since Denny left me that first time. I've done some maturing." Remembering how I was back then, I shook my head. "I was so scared to be alone." I shrugged my shoulder as he watched me. "I still don't like it, but I'm more secure now, I think. Mistakes in the past have aged me some."

He cracked a small smile. "Ah, the wizened twenty-two year old."

My smile was a small one as well, but some of the earlier tension evaporated in it. "Kellan, you may have a lot more experience, but don't act like you're not the same age I am. I've seen your driver's license."

Grinning crookedly, he raised an eyebrow. "The real one?"

Shaking my head at him, I held his face. "Do you think I loved Denny more, because it bothered me so much when he first told me he was leaving?"

Shrugging, his smile turned sad. "Can you blame me for thinking that?"

Enveloping my arms around him, I laid my head on his shoulder. "No, I guess not." We were silent a moment, rocking slightly as we held each other. I waited a moment longer, peace and a bit of sadness creeping into me. "I didn't love him more than I love you, Kellan." Pulling back, I met his eye. "I love *you* more. I love you enough to let you go and live your dream." I shrugged. "Don't you see…? I love you more."

He smiled softly and I brushed some hair off of his forehead. Running the backs of my fingers down his cheek, I whispered, "And, yes, I will miss you, more than you can possibly imagine, but I know that you have to do this, Kellan. And you know it, too."

Stubbornly, he shook his head. "No, I know that I have to be with you. Everything else is just…details."

I smiled and kissed him. Against his lips I murmured, "This isn't just your dream though, remember." Sighing, I pointed back to the bar, to the other people his decision involved. "There's Evan and Griffin, and Matt…he's worked so hard for this."

He watched my fingers then sighed, "I know…"

I laced my arms around his neck. "And that's why you'll do this. It's their dream too, and you can't take it away from them…for me, for us."

Leaning his head against mine, he closed his eyes. "I know." We rested against each other for an achingly long time, then Kellan pulled back. "I guess I should go tell Matt the good news," he said, a little sullenly.

I nodded, biting my lip and fighting the tears starting to sting. I'd always suspected this would happen one day, just not necessarily today. "When does the tour start?"

Looking down, he quietly said, "First part of November."

Now I looked down, too. "Oh."

November. It was the end of September…November wasn't all that far away, just around a month really. We were silent a moment longer, processing our impending separation, then Kellan grabbed my hand. Squeezing it as he placed a light kiss on my lips, he nodded over at the bar doors. I took a deep inhale and nodded back. A part of me didn't want to go back through those doors. It felt like everything I knew would change once I stepped over the threshold. That was a ridiculous feeling of course—everything had already changed.

Pulling on my hand, Kellan led me through the doors. Curious bar patrons eyed us as we entered, maybe to see if I was red and splotchy…or if Kellan had a black eye. Since we both looked the same, although much more melancholy than before, they soon shifted back to their own conversations.

Sighing, Kellan led us back to his table. The guys were still there, waiting for Kellan's answer. Since he was the front man for the band, they couldn't do much without him. They could certainly replace him, head out on their own with another singer, but it wouldn't be the same without Kellan's talent. I couldn't even picture the D-bags without their head D-bag. And I knew that most of the guys felt that way as well. Evan especially, would rather hang it up than quit on Kellan. So they sat, and waited for him to tell them if their dream was a go or not.

Arms crossed over his chest, Griffin glared at me. I felt like Yoko walking up to their table, clutching my man's hand. Matt watched me respectfully, but his face was full of disappointment; he wanted this so bad. Evan was the only one that looked torn. I knew he wanted the success—what rock band member didn't want to hit it big—but Evan's heart was anchored in Seattle with Jenny. He'd be separated from her just as Kellan would be separated from me. He smiled sympathetically at me as I stepped to the edge of the threesome.

As Kellan cleared his throat and ran a hand through his hair, all of their eyes shifted back to him. After a long and controlled exhale, he took a moment to gather himself, then locked eyes with Matt. "I'm in," was all he told him.

Matt, ecstatic, jumped up from beside the table as a chorus of excitement erupted from the guys. Throwing an arm around Kellan's shoulder, the blond's slim face was ear-to-ear smiles. "This is gonna be great, Kell. You'll see." He nodded enthusiastically as Evan and Griffin stood and swarmed around Kellan.

After that there was playful shoving and elbow ribbing. Evan grabbed Kellan's head and rumpled his hair as he laughed. Griffin stepped between Kellan and I, jarring us loose as he slugged him in the shoulder. As they all animatedly talked about their upcoming adventure, I found myself forced back a few steps, watching them from a distance.

Kellan looked back at me for a split-second, but his attention was quickly diverted back to the guys. Sighing, I twisted around and left them to their moment of glory. I had to go back to work anyway.

As I meandered over to assist a couple that had just arrived, I listened to the band in the back corner. Their laughter was loud, their voices gleeful. Several regulars asked me what was going on and I morosely told them.

"They're going on tour. They're going to spread their talent over the nation and some record label is going to notice and sign them up. After that, they'll be played on the radio every five minutes, headline a solo tour in every major city in the world, and be swarmed by people nonstop. They'll be booked on every talk show, play at every award show, and Kellan will end up on every magazine's "Hottest Guys" list. After that, he'll receive invitations from groupies and celebrities alike. Eventually he'll give into an A-list starlet and they'll be the talk of every tabloid in creation. And I'll be here...pouring you your drink and reminiscing about the rock star that I used to date."

Well, okay, I may have only told the customers that very first sentence, but the rest of the speech echoed in my head on a never-ending loop. Kellan and I could try to trust each other, sure, but that only meant he wouldn't sneak around behind my back. There were no guarantees that he'd stay with me once he was exposed to…well, literally, everyone.

The customers were all elated with the news. Several fans walked over to the guys' table to slap them on the back in congratulations, while the girls gave them appreciative hugs. Surprisingly, the only person who seemed as disheartened as I was by this latest development was Rita. She sulked as much as I did as I approached the bar to get yet another round of congratulatory drinks for the foursome.

Her collagen-injected lips puckered into as much of a scowl as she could make as she arranged their shots. "I can't believe he's leaving," she murmured over the noise in the bar. Glancing up at me, she narrowed her eyes. "Aren't you going to stop this? Put your foot down?"

Looking back at Kellan smiling and shaking Sam's hand, finally looking happy about the idea of touring the country, I sighed and shook my head. "No, he deserves this. I'm not going to try and keep him from fulfilling a dream."

Rita reached across the bar and smacked me on the shoulder. I glared back at her as she adjusted the deeply plunging neckline of her altered Pete's shirt. "Then you're an idiot." She pointed over to Kellan and the guys and crassly verbalized every fear I had. "He's going to get famous after this little stint. Then he's going to realize that he's famous, and gorgeous, and can screw just about any woman in the world. You think he's going to stay with an ordinary nobody after that?"

Harshly grabbing my tray of shots, a good quarter of the drinks splashing over the edge, I raised my chin to her. With a confidence that I wasn't sure I really felt, I shook my head. "You don't know Kellan, not like I do. He's not like that. He's not interested in the fame, in the power, or in the women." Lowering my chin, I shrugged. "He's interested in me."

Rita folded her arms across her chest and smirked at me. "Right. And he wouldn't dare cheat on you, because he's such a…moral guy."

She eyed me up and down and I flushed all over. By the tone in her voice I knew what she was referring to when she questioned his morality. The affair Kellan and I'd had was never openly admitted by anyone who knew, but our public fights, followed by Kellan's beating—that we still claimed was a mugging—and Denny leaving the country, had clued most people in on the situation.

Since Kellan had once been immoral with her too, I no longer wanted to discuss my life with Rita. I muttered, "You don't know him," and stormed off to their table.

After another couple of free rounds, the guys finally had to leave for a show at another bar. Kellan lingered after the other guys exited to a spattering of cheers and whistles. Before he left, Griffin paused at the door, exclaiming, "Thank you all, my loyal subjects. And don't worry, I won't ever forget you when I'm famous, I'll only refuse to acknowledge your existence!"

Most of the bar laughed at that, maybe thinking he was joking. Knowing Griffin probably meant it wholeheartedly, I rolled my eyes and shook my head. Jackass. Someday I was going to have to stage an intervention for Anna. She could do so much better. Well, she certainly couldn't do any worse.

S.C. Stephens

Also rolling his eyes and shaking his head, Kellan strolled up to where I was standing beside a recently emptied table. Giving me a crooked grin, he nodded at where Griffin had disappeared to. "What do you think will do him in first? Drugs, money, or women?"

Smiling, I slung my arms around his waist and raised an eyebrow. "I'm pretty sure it will be a combination of all three."

Kellan chuckled and looped his arms around my waist. As he leaned down to kiss me, I found myself inadvertently spouting, "And what about you? What will be your downfall?"

He paused before our lips touched. He started to frown, then smiled. "You think I'll have one?"

Embarrassed that I had asked, I shook my head, then shrugged. "It has occurred to me that you're on the path to fame and fame brings certain…hazards with it." Sighing, knowing now wasn't really the time to have this conversation, I stared up at him. "You'll be surrounded by so much…temptation." I bit my lip. "And I've seen 'Behind the Music.' I know what gets offered to rock stars."

He narrowed his eyes but then laughed. "Wait, 'Behind the Music?' You've already mapped out my career, haven't you?" Smiling devilishly, he ducked down and looked me in the eye. "So what is it? Booze? Gambling? Buying too many yachts?"

I twisted my lip at his comment and smacked his chest. "No, for you, it's women." Sighing, I shook my head. "Always women."

The smile on his face faded as he looked over mine. "You have to trust me, Kiera." His smile returned a little, but it was tinged with sadness. "Just like I have to trust you." The sudden seriousness in his face instantly shifted to an impish grin and the air of heartache around us lifted. "I know I'll never find anything out there that will top you, but really, it is quite possible that you may lose interest in me once I've sold out and hit the bottle. Maybe you'll decide you can do better…start dating one of the Jonas Brothers or something."

Laughing, even though my stomach hurt a little at our conversation, I smacked his chest again. Leaning up to kiss him, I muttered, "Never. You're mine, washed up or not."

Chuckling against my lips, he murmured, "Good, because none of that is going to happen." Pulling back, he raised an eyebrow. "It's just a six month tour with a bunch of other bands, most of which are small and unsigned…just like us. And when we're all crammed together on a smelly bus, I'll be wishing that I was back at home with you." Leaning in, he rested his head against mine. "And when the six months are up, that's exactly where you'll find me…in bed with you."

I nodded against him as tears stung my eyes. "I hope so," I whispered.

"I know so," he whispered back, his voice just as wistful as mine. Then his lips crashed down to me and my hands came up to possessively tangle into his hair, holding him against me. Kissing much more aggressively than we usually did in public, I let the feeling of being watched evaporate from me and only concentrated on his touch. He was mine, I was his. This didn't have to be a life altering event if we didn't let it. It could just be a brief separation while he did something amazing that most people would never get the chance to do. We would both stay faithful to the other and then we'd be back together and all the happier for it.

After that…well, I'd tackle that hurdle once it was upon me.

Chapter 6 – Time Flies

You are told from the moment you enter school that time is constant. It never changes. It is one of those set things in life that you can always rely on…much like death and taxes. There will always be sixty seconds in a minute. There will always be sixty minutes in an hour. And there will always be twenty-four hours in a day. Time does not fluctuate. It moves on at the same, constant pace at every moment in your life.

And that was the biggest load of crap that I've ever been taught in school.

Truth was, time did fluctuate. It was easy to lose hours or even days in a blink of an eye. Other times, it was a struggle to get through a mere hour. It ebbed and flowed as relentlessly as the tides, and just as powerfully too. The moments that you wanted to last forever were the ones that washed away all too soon. The moments that you wanted to speed up, slowed down to a snail's pace.

That was the truth of the matter. And my life…was fast forwarding, and there was nothing I could do about it.

It seemed only yesterday that Kellan had reluctantly agreed to go off and tour the country, but, all of a sudden, his departure was only a few days away. It was Monday morning…he was leaving Saturday morning. And as much as the last few weeks had rushed by, I knew that the universe would cruelly make the next six months drag on and on. I knew that I would feel every second of our separation and it was going to suck…but I had to let it happen. I would not selfishly guilt another man to give it all up for me. I would never do that to anyone again…..no matter how much it hurt.

Hearing a knock on my apartment door, I snapped myself out of my thoughts and slapped on a smile. Kellan was also having a hard time with our upcoming separation. I didn't want to make it even more difficult by being forlorn in his presence. Over the last few weeks I'd perfected the art of feigned excitement. Not that I wasn't excited for him, and endlessly proud of him, I just didn't want him to go. If he could somehow have it all but stay close to my side, well, then my forced smile would be a natural one.

Walking past a folding card table, a wobbly contraption that my sister and I were calling a fancy dining table, I smiled at the present sitting on top of it. When I opened the front door, Kellan was leaning against the frame. He smiled crookedly at me. I bit my lip as I absorbed his features, then stepped back so he could enter.

Stepping through, he murmured, "Mornin'."

Attaching his lips to my neck, he swung me around and pulled my hips into his. Closing the door behind him, I giggled quietly; my sister was still asleep. "Good morning, yourself."

Sighing, he slinked his arms around my waist. "I'm going to miss taking you to school every day," he sighed. Shaking his head, he added, "You'll nearly be graduating by the time I'm back."

Stepping up my smile, even though my heart was breaking, I tilted my head at him and stroked his cheek. "At least you'll be back in time for the ceremony. You can watch me walk down the aisle."

Smiling softly, he cinched me a little tighter. "I'd love to watch you walk down the aisle."

My heart starting to race a little, I suddenly wondered just what aisle he was referring to. I opened my mouth, not sure what to say, but Kellan looked over his shoulder and noticed the bright red gift bag. His expression genuinely gleeful, he looked back to me. "What's that?"

Releasing him, I giggled again. "It's for you. Sort of a going away present."

Frowning, he shook his head at me. "I know money is tight for you. You didn't have to get me anything."

Pressing myself against his back, I shoved his shoulders towards the table. "I got a good deal, it didn't cost me much and it's sort of a present for the both of us."

Slowly walking towards the gift, he turned his head back to me and grinned devilishly. "Is it handcuffs? Did you get the furry kind? Because those feel really nice against your--"

I smacked his back and turned his head away from me, so that he couldn't see the blush spreading over my cheeks. "No!" I felt him chuckling as he picked up his gift, but my head was busy imagining him locked to my bed...naked. I guessed that would be one way to keep him near me. Rolling my eyes, I contained a sigh. And of course he'd had enough experience with handcuffs that he had a style preference.

Still laughing a little, he pulled the tissues out of the bag. When he got to the real present, he pulled it out and looked back at me, confused. "What's this?"

Now I laughed as I moved around to stand beside him. "Well, I know you're a little behind on the times, but they call that a cell phone. It works just like your corded one...but you can walk around with it." Leaning in, I whispered, "You can even use it outside."

Giving me a dry look, he shook his head. "I know what it is...what's it for?"

Smiling, I pulled a matching one out of my jacket pocket slung over a nearby chair. "It's so we can keep in touch while you're gone. So you can always get ahold of me, and I can get ahold of you." I shrugged, feeling my throat starting to close up. "So we can try to stay close...even though we'll be really far apart."

I watched his eyes search mine as he swallowed a few times, like his throat was closing up a little, too. Nodding, he leaned in and kissed me. "I love it, thank you."

I closed my eyes as we kissed a few times, savoring every second that his skin was on mine. Pulling back from me, his breath a little heavier, his eyes slightly hooded, his gaze focused on my mouth. I got the distinct impression that if he hadn't had to take me to school in a few minutes, he would have swept me up and taken me to my bedroom. And even though I knew school was important, and I needed to focus on my last year, I wanted him to.

His eyes flashing up to mine, he gave me a breathtaking grin. "Can I sext you on it?"

I blinked at his question then felt my cheeks flame red hot again. Not giving him an answer, I grabbed my jacket. Just as he was chuckling, tucking his new phone away in his leather jacket pocket, I heard a bedroom door open. Kellan turned towards the sound, ready to greet Anna, but the person who stepped out of the door was not my sister. He was also not dressed.

Scratching his freely swinging man parts, Griffin yawned and squinted at us. "Dude, what are you doing here so early?"

I immediately looked away from the naked man. Kellan smirked and shook his head. "It's ten thirty, Griffin."

I heard Griffin snort, but didn't look back at him. "I know, man, it's fucking earlier than shit." Kellan looked down at me and rolled his eyes. Anything before eleven was practically the crack of dawn for Griffin. I wanted to roll my eyes as well, but I heard Griffin coming closer to us. I froze. I seriously wanted to scream at him to get some clothes on.

Yawning again, Griffin lazily said, "Hey, Matt wanted me to tell you that if you miss another rehearsal, he's tossing you from the band."

Kellan looked back up at Griffin and raised an eyebrow. "Really?" Laughing lightly, he shook his head. "Tell him I'll be there." Looking down at me again, Kellan shrugged. "I guess my head has been other places lately."

I saw Griffin's hand come out to push back Kellan's shoulder, but I refused to look at the nudist. "Well zip your head back in your pants and get back in the game. We need you on board."

Sighing, Kellan looked up at him. "I'm on board, Griff. I'll be there, okay?"

"You better."

Just as it sounded like Griffin was turning to leave, I watched Kellan shake his head, his lips twisting. "Hey, Griff? You mind not walking around my girlfriend's place buck naked? I'd really prefer her only staring at my junk, if you don't mind."

My eyes widening, I inadvertently looked back at Griffin. Smirking at me, he took himself in hand. "Dude, if she's peeking at another man's schlong, then that's between the two of you." Raising his eyebrows at Kellan, he shook his blond head. "The Hulk needs to breathe."

Kellan bit his lip, struggling to not laugh. I had no such luck with my control and had to slap a hand over my mouth. Griffin glared at both of us, then sauntered back to Anna's room. Once the door closed again, Kellan burst out laughing. I joined him, the tears springing into my eyes gladly obscuring the after image of Griffin's pierced manhood.

Between giggles, I managed to laugh out, "The Hulk? Does it turn green when it grows?"

Holding in his stomach, Kellan shook his head. "Oh God, I hope not. Come on, let's get out of here before we find out."

Grabbing my book bag, we hastily escaped from where we could hear Griffin start to wake up Anna. Once in the hall, our laughter slowly subsided. When I could talk without giggling, I smiled over at Kellan. "Thank you for trying. Seeing Griffin in all his glory...will be one of the things that I definitely won't miss."

Slinging his arm over my shoulders, Kellan shook his head. Still laughing over his ass of a band mate, he said, "I wish I could say the same, but the green mutant's coming with me."

Laughing a little myself, I raised an eyebrow at him. "You have any...nicknames?"

Kellan gave me a charmingly crooked smile. "None that I've given myself, but from what I've heard said in the bedroom, it would probably be something like, 'The Oh-God-yes-harder-faster-don't-you-dare-stop-yes-fuck-me-now-you're-freaking-amazing Machine'." He shrugged. "But that's kind of a mouthful."

Frowning, I elbowed him in the stomach and shrugged his arm from me. Sometimes he could be just as much of a jackass as Griffin...almost, anyway. Laughing, he came up behind me and spun me around. As I squealed in protest, he lifted me up over his shoulder and smacked my bottom. "I'm just joking. Come on, let's get you to class." As I squirmed against him, he added, "Maybe while you're learning, I'll go get some of those handcuffs...then you can give me a better nickname."

I stiffened in his arms, wondering if he was serious about that; his only response was to laugh.

After depositing me at my place of higher learning, Kellan went off to go do...whatever he did while I was in school. Maybe think of new ways to mortify me. Hopefully he really was joking about the handcuffs.

Over the past weeks I'd gotten to know some of the other graduating English majors and I met up with a few of them before my Critical Practice class. It was an intense course and we'd all agreed to meet early and study for an hour before we went in. Sitting in a group of six or seven like-minded individuals, contemplating the importance of interpretive practices when studying literature and culture, I felt more like my own person, with my own hopes and dreams, and less like one of Kellan's entourage. It made me feel whole, complete, and made the process of him leaving slightly less nerve-wracking. Slightly...I still wasn't ready for that day to come.

The near two hour course was a brain burner, and by the time it was over, I was grateful for my slightly easier ethics class. Even if ethics brought Candy...and not the apple-flavored kind. Gritting my teeth, I did what I did nearly every day when I walked into the classroom—I ignored her and her friends. It was fairly easy to do since she'd started ignoring me too. After her failed attempt to make me break up with Kellan, she'd seemed to give up on it. Either that or she was busy plotting and scheming a more masterful plan than merely spreading gossip. I liked to believe the woman had more important things to do with her time, though.

Quickly absorbed in the lecture, I forgot all about Candy sitting a few rows in front of me with her friends. Once the class was over, I grabbed my belongings and started going over the paper I planned to write tonight during my shift. The paper was on the ethical responsibility of various websites. I was thinking of doing mine on a popular medical advice site, to illustrate how important it is to give potential patients the correct information.

Already outlining my debate in my head, I bumped into Kellan in the hallway. Grabbing my shoulders, he held me in place in front of him. Lost in thought, I blinked at him stupidly for a second before smiling and engulfing him in a hug. "Hey, you're picking me up inside."

Laughing at my obvious comment, he scuffed up his hair with his hand. "Yeah, it's pouring out there. I thought I'd go for a swim instead of waiting in my car." I cringed away from the water droplets flicking me and he laughed a little more.

Looping my arm through his, I smiled and leaned into his side. "Well, I'm glad you did. I can run my idea for a paper by you…even though you'll probably have no idea what I'm talking about." I smiled, knowing that Kellan rarely went near a computer, let alone searched the Internet.

He grinned as we started walking away. "Hit me."

Just as I began my speech, someone jostled me so harshly that I was knocked a step away from Kellan. Frowning, I glanced over at the rude person who thought they ruled the hallway. Flaming red curls met my eye as a snide Candy glared back at me. Sighing, I rolled my eyes and reattached myself to Kellan. He didn't let me, though. His eyes narrowing at her, he mumbled, "Stay here a second," then strode over to where she was eyeing him with pleasantly curled lips.

Irritated, but curious too, I stopped where he asked and watched him approach her and her friends. Tina and Genevieve looked about ready to faint as he stepped up to them. I figured it was the closest they'd ever actually been to him. Kellan, however, looked about ready to rip somebody's head off. Glaring at the trio, he finally rested his eyes on Candy. She backed up a step as his dark expression settled on her.

Grabbing her arm, he leaned into her face, whispering something heatedly. I didn't know what he was saying, but Candy's eyes widened. Shaking her head, she started muttering something and pointed at Tina. Tina put her hands in the air and started sputtering something, too, when Kellan's glare swung around to her. Releasing Candy's arm, Kellan said something to the three of them that had them quickly nodding and scurrying off.

Straightening as they left, Kellan turned and faced me with a perfectly normal smile, like nothing odd had just happened. He walked back to me and grabbed my hand. He started pulling me towards the doors, whistling as he did. Raising an eyebrow at him, I waited for an explanation. When he didn't give one, I cleared my throat. Looking down on me, he shrugged. "What?"

Pointing to the doors we were approaching, the window wet from the downpour he had mentioned, I indicated where Candy had fled. "What was that all about?"

Smiling charmingly, he shrugged. "I just let them know that it wouldn't be prudent for them to spread anymore lies about me, and I suggested that they leave you alone."

Grinning, he opened the door for me and moved aside so I could step through. Narrowing my eyes at him, I prepared myself to step past him into the downpour. They'd seemed pretty startled by whatever he'd said, so my mind was running over a list of threats that he could have used. I've seen Kellan's anger several times before, and he could be intimidating when he wanted to be. I figured they really would leave me alone for the rest of the school year.

Smiling, I leaned in and kissed him. "Did they happen to mention how they saw your tattoo?"

Rolling his eyes as he held the door open, he shook his head. "Tina saw me working out in the park near here. I got hot, I was shirtless."

Biting my lip, I glanced down his body. Yes, he was certainly hot. I supposed that explained the story. I watched his face for a minute, gauging the truth I saw in his eyes as he steadfastly held my gaze. I saw no deception there and smiled wider. Raising a corner of his lip, he indicated outside. "Are you gonna head out there? Cuz this door's getting heavy."

Laughing, I kissed him lightly and then sucked in a quick breath, preparing to make a run for it. Halfway down the steps, I felt like a waterlogged rat. Groaning, I dashed for the parking lot and wished I'd brought an umbrella.

Coming up behind me, Kellan smacked my bottom. "Hurry up, pokey, you're getting soaked." Laughing, he ran his fingers back through his hair. The mess slicked back in a way that reminded me of a less pleasant moment in the rain with Kellan. I pushed aside the memory and focused on his body twisting away from me and running hard.

Adjusting my bag, I yelled out, "No fair! You're not carrying anything."

He only looked back at me and chuckled. By the time I got to the lot, he was already in his car, feet propped up on my side of the seat and leaning his back against the driver's side door with his eyes closed, like he'd fallen asleep waiting for me. I batted his shoes as I stood in the rain, but he ignored it, and continued to take up my spot. Cursing that I was still getting soaked, I crawled over his legs to lie on top of him. That got his attention.

His eyes opened with a wide smile. Twisting my body to shut the door, I unhooked my book bag and tossed it into the back seat. His arms came out for me, pulling my soaked body into his soaked body. Scooting down the seat, he laid his back against the cushion. He adjusted my legs so my hips straddled his.

"There, that's better," he muttered, lifting his head to kiss me.

Assaulted by more wet memories of him, I pulled back. His eyes were lustful as he stared at me, his breath heavier, and not just from the exertion of running all the way out here. My wet hair hung down around my face, the long strands dripping on his clothes. His scent beneath me mixed with the smell of clean water, both of them stirring something within me.

Cupping his cheek, I stroked his rain-softened skin with my thumb. Looking over his midnight blue eyes, the specks of water glistening in his hair, the full, partly opened lips, the strong jaw, I sighed. "You're so attractive," I whispered, my words oddly in tune to the pounding rain in the background. "You're the sexiest man I've ever seen."

Feeling completely alone with him in here, even though it was the middle of the afternoon, I leaned down to kiss him. His soft lips melded with mine, tasting, searching. After a brief moment, he frowned and shook his head. "I may not always be." Shrugging, one hand clenching and unclenching my hip while the other indicated his face, he added, "This could vanish overnight, you know. I could be mauled by a bear while walking down the street tomorrow." He lifted an eyebrow. "Would you still want me then?"

I smiled at his comment. "Of course. Your face isn't the only thing that makes you attractive, Kellan. Your looks aren't why I love you." He smiled, his hands running up my back, urging me down to him. Before our lips met again, I gave him a pointed glance. "A bear? Really?"

Chuckling, he pulled me all the way down to him. As our hips met, rocking lightly against the other's, the windshield quickly fogged up. I felt bodies hurriedly walking past the car, but with the noise of the rain and the windows tinted with moisture, I felt like we were the only two people around. As our breaths and kiss heated, Kellan murmured, "God, now I'm going to have to do something I never thought I would."

Moving up to kiss his cheek, I dug my hips into his. "What?" I breathed, the tip of my tongue lining the edge of his ear.

He sucked in a quick breath, his hips under me rising off the seat. "I'm going to have to take you in this car," he murmured back, his voice low and husky.

He was suddenly moving underneath me, trying to twist us around so he was on top. I quickly sat up before he was successful. While I felt alone out here, I knew we weren't, and I wasn't about to advertise what we were doing by rocking the car. He sat up on his elbows, breathless. Spreading out his hands, he frowned. "Why did you stop?"

Biting my lip and carefully moving away from his hips, I pushed his feet off the seat so I could sit comfortably. Pointing at him as menacingly as I could, I sternly said, "Because you have a rehearsal to get to, and if you blow it off again, Matt is going to kick you out of the band."

Sitting up, he wrapped his arms around me. "It's *my* band, they can't kick me out."

He started kissing my neck and I tried not to lean into it, tried not to start panting with desire and clawing at his clothes. Pushing him back, I dug my finger into his chest. "I'm not having sex with you in the parking lot of my school."

He glanced around, his eyes playful. "No one will notice." Looking back at me, he raised an eyebrow. "Have you ever had sex in a car?"

Blushing horribly, I tucked my hair behind my ears. "Yes, Denny and I…"

I didn't finish that and Kellan's playful grin faded. Releasing me, he scooted over to his side of the seat and nodded. "Oh, yeah…your road trip." Sighing, he dug his hand in his pocket and took out his keys.

I tilted my head to see his face better, to see if he was upset or not, but I couldn't tell from the angle. "Hey, you all right?"

Smiling, he looked back at me as the car roared to life. "Yeah." He shrugged, then he smirked. "I was just hoping to give you another first experience." I watched his smile falter as he turned away from me. "I guess I missed my shot, though."

Placing my hand on his thigh, I whispered, "There will be other firsts that you can give me, Kellan."

Looking back at me as he put the car in reverse, he shook his head. "I know, Kiera."

Wishing I could rewind time and avoid bringing up an intimate moment with my ex to my current, I looked out the passenger's side window as we drove to Kellan's rehearsal. The guys generally met once a day to create new material or work out kinks in the older stuff. Since it was how they made their living, they were all surprisingly dedicated to it. Well, except recently. Lately, Kellan had been blowing off rehearsals to spend some quality time with me. Matt was in a snit over it. Even though the band was technically Kellan's, since he'd created it, Matt was the one that directed it. He lined up the shows, worked on marketing, arranged rehearsals, and he demanded professionalism from the quartet of easily distracted twenty-somethings. The band was Matt's baby.

Heading over the bridge connecting the U-District to the heart of Seattle, I watched the towering Space Needle fill my window. It was beautiful, iconic, and held a soft spot for me, as it was where Kellan had poured his heart out to me. He'd opened up and divulged secrets about himself that he hadn't revealed to anyone, ever. It saddened me incredibly that Kellan's life could have been so different if he'd just told someone about the abuse. Perhaps then Child Services would have intervened and placed him in a loving foster home. Anything would have been preferable to his nightmare.

Looking back at him, I put my hand over his knee. He smiled at the contact, quickly glancing at me before shifting his eyes back to the road. A small, dark part of me wondered if Kellan had only been attracted to me, stayed with me, fallen in love with me, because his messed up psyche craved the pain I had given him. Maybe he had a masochistic streak. If so, I certainly stoked it…repeatedly. It truly was a miracle that he took me back.

Sighing, I leaned over and placed my head on his shoulder. He relaxed his head against mine, his hand coming out to rest on my thigh. As the Needle left my vision—tall skyscrapers holding thousands of businessmen and women trailing along after it—we approached the industrial district. That was where Evan had his loft. It was a perfect spot to rehearse, since he didn't live in a residential area like Kellan and the others. The few neighbors that he did have didn't seem to mind the noise so long as the guys didn't play too late into the evening.

Driving past the two sports stadiums, Kellan arrived at Evan's place. He switched off the ignition, opened his door, and grabbed his guitar out of the back seat. I got out and waited for him near the front of the vehicle. Thankfully, the earlier squall had passed, and only light droplets fell on our damp bodies. When Kellan stepped beside me, his hair still attractively slicked back from the rain, he smiled and nodded towards the stairs leading to the loft.

Evan lived above an auto body shop. The mechanics loved it when the boys practiced during their shift. They even sometimes requested that the guys leave the door open so the music would resonate downstairs. One of the mechanics once informed me that listening to the band play made going to work feel like going to a rock concert. I understood the sentiment; they constantly made my job feel that way.

One of the garage doors opened as we walked by. A man was guiding a car that was backing out of the door, so the driver didn't accidentally back over the mechanic's pit. Once the car was free, the man smiled and waved at Kellan.

"Where you been, man? Matt's gonna evict you."

Kellan rolled his eyes and shook his head. "Yeah, that's what I hear."

The man laughed while a grease-smeared woman got out of the car she'd just parked along the curb. She walked up to Kellan and bumped his shoulder with her fist. "Knock 'em dead on tour, Kell." She sighed dramatically while I glanced up at the rain falling on us. Maybe the woman could flirt with my man inside...where it was dryer. Shaking her shaggy crop of dark hair, she frowned. "We're gonna miss you around here. It just won't be the same with Evan's place empty."

Kellan smiled back at her and I mentally frowned at the warmth I saw on his face. I knew Kellan had female friends, Jenny was one of them, but I instantly wondered how friendly this mechanic-girl had been with my boyfriend. I squeezed his hand tighter, subconsciously leaning into his side as he said, "I doubt that, Rox. You probably won't even know we're gone." Raising an eyebrow, Kellan leaned over to her. "Besides, it will finally be quiet enough around here for you to work on that book."

She laughed, her face brightening, and I hated even more that not only were they friendly, but they knew things about each other. They even abbreviated each other's names. The familiarity bothered me and a rush of jealousy threatened to sweep me away. I struggled to restrain myself from pushing her back, stepping in front of Kellan, and growling possessively. I wouldn't ever actually do that...but I was thinking it.

A whistle from within the garage forced the two reluctant mechanics chatting with us to return to work. Kellan waved goodbye. Rox, Roxie or Roxanne, whatever her full name was, looked back at Kellan before disappearing. She wore that same interested expression that I'd seen all too often. Not once in that interaction did she acknowledge me, as if I was inconsequential. I wanted to sneer at her retreating form, maybe stick my tongue out and say, "neiner-neiner," but I wouldn't stoop to five-year-old behavior. Yet.

Pushing aside yet another woman's desire for him, I followed him up the stairs to Evan's place. Kellan barged through without knocking; treating the place like his own. Matt's eyes were on us the second we stepped through the door.

"'Bout freaking time!" he glared at Kellan, and Rachel leaned over and whispered something in his ear. His features calmed, and he relaxed a little, smiling over at where she stood by his side.

I waved at Rachel, the shy, exotic beauty, then waved behind her at Jenny sitting on Evan's lap behind his drum set. The two of them were banging out some rhythm, Jenny giggling as Evan nuzzled her neck.

Closing the door behind us, Kellan grimaced when he met Matt's eye. "Sorry...things have been coming up."

Kellan walked us into the room. Being at Evan's loft was like being at a smaller version of Pete's. There was a tiny kitchen, a living room with one couch facing a TV, and a rumpled bed in the far corner, a dresser and nightstand beside it. The rest of the place was a stage. The guys stored their equipment here between shows, except for the gear they kept at Pete's on a daily basis. It was well known in the bar that touching their stuff on stage resulted in immediate eviction from the premises.

Here at Evan's, they had the sound equipment, Evan's spare drum set, Griffin's bass guitar, and Matt's guitar; Kellan preferred to keep his guitar close and lugged it around from place to place. With all of their instruments waiting for them beside plugged-in microphones, they just needed some spot lights and a couple of bouncers, and they could do a professional show from here. They were even working on erecting a studio with sound proof walls, so they could make their own recordings. They had the walls constructed, but not assembled; the materials were leaning uselessly against the wall behind Evan's drums. I knew Matt really wanted to finish the project, but Bumbershoot, and now the tour, had put it on hold. I was certain that when they returned, it would become a top priority.

Kellan set his guitar case on a kitchen counter and propped it open. I smiled at a picture of the two of us tucked away inside the lining. As he pulled out his most prized possession, aside from his car, Griffin walked up and smacked him on the back. "Yeah, I know what's been...up."

Twisting to face me, Griffin's eyes locked straight on my hips. It was horrid, having him stare at me like that, knowing that in his mind...right now...we were having sex. With my hands, I hid as much of my body as I could; his smile widened.

Finally noticing that Griffin was mentally assaulting me, Kellan frowned and smacked him across the back of the head. "Don't eye-fuck my girlfriend, Griffin."

Sniffing indignantly, Griffin shrugged. "What? A fella can't daydream anymore?" Kellan rolled his eyes and walked away. Griffin turned backed to me, sneering devilishly as he pointed to his head and whispered, "Later."

I felt like taking a shower.

Quickly turning my back on Griffin, I walked over to where Rachel and Jenny had gathered. Forming a sort of band-wives club, we knelt on the couch and leaned over the back to cheer for our men from the front row of our very private concert. Watching Kellan converse with Matt and Evan, while Griffin picked up Matt's guitar and started rocking out like he was Slash, I sighed softly. I'd miss this when they were gone.

Rachel and Jenny both sighed right after me. I observed them watching their men, their loves. Jenny had been tearful when the band announced that they were going on tour. She was excited for Evan to go, but she didn't want to be separated from him. She didn't want it any more than I wanted to be apart from Kellan. She wasn't concerned that Evan might stray, though. Her unwavering confidence in his faithfulness was inspiring. I wished I shared that certainty. That was something I'd had with Denny—a nearly unbreakable faith that he would never cheat on me. It was a comfort that had somehow slipped away from me once I cheated on him. Now, I sort of felt like anybody could do anything to anyone. It was a horrible feeling to have.

Rachel looked over at me, her deeply tanned skin looking a little pale "I can't believe they're leaving Saturday." She shook her head and shrugged. "Where did the time go?"

I sighed again, having had the exact same sentiments earlier. "I know…" I looked back to the guys. Kellan had slung his guitar across his chest and was nodding at Matt, while Matt mimed guitar chords in the air. Evan watched the interaction between the two, occasionally nodding. Griffin was tuning them all out, bowing to his imaginary crowd. Shaking my head, I muttered, "It seems like just yesterday that we watched them play Bumbershoot."

Jenny sighed, sitting back on her heels. "Matt's having a going away party at his place after their performance Friday night." She sighed again, forlornly. "Their last performance."

I swallowed as I looked over at her. Her eyes were just as glassy as mine. It was so difficult to let people follow their dreams, especially when those dreams took them thousands of miles away. Nodding, I leaned over and hugged Jenny who was sniffling a little. Rachel's arms circled around the both of us and we started our left-behind-girlfriend pity party. We were interrupted by the sound of soft chuckling in front of us.

As we broke apart, we all looked up at Kellan, smirking as he looked down at us. "Group cuddling…and I wasn't invited?" he asked, raising an eyebrow suggestively.

Jenny and Rachel giggled and I smacked him in the stomach. Chuckling a little harder, he grabbed my hand and pulled me across the couch into his body. I squealed, but his lips came down to mine and I instantly stopped. Forgetting that everyone was around, I closed my eyes and tangled my fingers in his drying hair.

Losing myself in the moment, I moaned a little when his tongue brushed against mine. Nervous giggles met my ear, but I didn't care. I only snapped out of it when I heard someone shout, "Hey? We playin'…or screwing the girls?"

Kellan and I separated as we both looked over at Griffin grinning mischievously. Grabbing his pants, Griffin shook his head. "I'm cool either way, I just need to know which instrument to pull out."

Kellan frowned and stood up straight. I flushed bright red and laid my head down on the couch. Jenny and Rachel laughed, Jenny's hand sympathetically patting my back. From above, I heard Griffin being hit hard. Smiling, I peeked up in time to see Griffin flip Kellan off with one hand while massaging his arm with the other.

Kellan stifled a smile as he took his spot behind his microphone. Locking gazes with me, he waited while Evan tapped out an intro.

Matt and Evan started the song perfectly, their instruments filling the space around us. The room vibrated with power and energy, and I giggled, loving it. Kellan smiled, watching me appreciate his craft. Griffin joined in a few beats later, Kellan joining the fray last. With all of their sounds mixing and surging perfectly, Kellan started to sing.

He was perfect. He elongated words and phrases effortlessly. He sucked in quick breaths suggestively. His voice was clear, strong, pitch-perfect…amazing. I could listen to him sing all day long. If I had an iPod loaded with his music, it would be on endless repeat. The song was a new one that they were preparing; Matt wanted to include it on the tour. Their first performance of it would be Friday night, as sort of a thank you to the diehard fans that had stuck by the band from the very beginning.

Matt worked the rehearsals around everyone's schedules, so they sometimes played later in the evenings, when I was at work. I did, however, make an effort to get to the practice sessions before my shift. I just loved watching the creative process. I'd watched Kellan write the lyrics in his kitchen over coffee, and I'd watched him, Evan and Matt shuffle through the melody at the bar. It was amazing, to watch an idea in someone's head blossom into a powerful song about coming to a personal crossroads and emerging out the other side a stronger person. It was a beautiful piece. I liked to think that the song was somehow about us.

When they came to the chorus, Kellan frowned and abruptly stopped singing mid-sentence. He looked over at Matt and eventually the other instruments died out, Griffin stopping last. Matt frowned and shook his head and Kellan pointed to his guitar. "What are you doing? That's the bridge, not the chorus."

Matt sighed and raised his hand into the air. "Dude, that's what I've been saying. You're so spacey lately." He pointed back to Evan. "Since you've been missing rehearsals and leaving us without a singer, Evan and I have been tweaking the music. We flopped the two sections and it sounds about a million times better." Frowning, he stuck his hand on his hip and shook his spiky head. "And you'd know that if you were around more."

Raising his hands submissively, Kellan backed off. "Fine, dang, just asking." Looking between Evan and Matt, Kellan sighed. He quickly glanced at me before returning his eyes to Matt. "I'm sorry, okay, but I'm here now, and I'm committed to this, so just…fill me in, all right?"

Matt pursed his lips but nodded.

"Any other changes I should know about?" Kellan asked.

Matt started to shake his head, then tilted it to the side. "Oh, well, we added a solo for me before the last chorus." He smiled, just slightly, and raised a pale eyebrow at Kellan.

Kellan looked away, a small smile on his lips. Chuckling a little, he shook his head. "I guess that's what I get for being a flake." Settling his eyes on me, he smiled a little wider. "Worth it though," he muttered to me, then louder to the guys, "Okay, back to where we left off."

They finished the song with no more interruptions from Kellan, and Matt reveled in his new mini-solo while Kellan shook his head, amused. At the end of the song I had to agree with Matt, the changes were small, but overall the song did sound better. They were going to rock Friday.

When the guys were finished rehearsing for the day, it was time for Jenny and me to start our shifts. The guys followed us over to Pete's, eager to relax with a beer after their "hard" day at work. I had to roll my eyes as I handed it to them. Sometimes I was envious of how easy their lifestyle was—drinking, partying and playing music all night, being swarmed by fawning females—but I saw how seriously they took it, and I knew how hard they worked behind the scenes to keep their success going.

Truly, their job was probably just as taxing as mine. At least my work hours were finite, theirs was twenty-four-seven. This was reaffirmed for me when a couple of college girls worked up the nerve to approach their table later in the evening. They chatted with the fans amicably. Kellan politely brushed off the blonde's affections and shook his head when she nodded to the front doors and raised her eyebrows in a clearly sexual way.

I frowned disapprovingly as I watched the display, wanting badly to "accidentally" dump my tray on her. No, aspects of their job were never-ending...unfortunately.

Chapter 7 – History Lessons

After getting chastised by Matt for missing practices, Kellan was diligent about not missing any more. Unfortunately, things worked out so that I couldn't go to another rehearsal, so I saw less of Kellan in that last week than in all the weeks before. We'd been hovering around each other lately, blowing off friends and easy-to-miss obligations to roll around in Kellan's bed for a few hours. It was inexcusable of us really, since his practice was important and the few classes I skipped had also been important. But we'd needed the time together as each looming day brought our separation to the forefront.

So having that cycle of irresponsibility broken by Kellan, who was suddenly focused again, was a struggle for me. I adapted though, throwing myself into work, school and friends. And Kellan made our time apart interesting by trying out his new cell phone. He interrupted me a few times during class by texting highly inappropriate comments. Most of them made my cheeks flush bright red. Honestly, he was too seductive, even through technology.

But eventually Friday was upon us.

When I awoke in my new spacious bed, there was a feeling of goodbye in the air. I woke up with Kellan's arms around me, my cheek resting on his chest. He was stroking my hair in a soft, repetitive fashion, his fingers gently tucking strands behind my ear, so I knew he was awake.

Stretching, I lifted my head and looked up at him. Midnight blue eyes, deeper and more beautiful than the darkest oceans, stared back at me. Smiling, he ran the back of his finger down my cheek. "Mornin'," he whispered.

Smiling, I leaned up to gently touch my lips to his. "Good morning."

We didn't say anything more and I laid my head back down on his skin and held him for at least another hour. He held me as tightly as I held him, occasionally kissing my hair. It was one of the most comforting experiences I'd ever had, and I knew a part of me would remember this morning forever, tucking the memory away to pull out at a later date, when I was missing him so much I physically ached.

After what felt like a fast eternity of bliss, it was time for me to get ready for school. I grudgingly pulled away from Kellan, but he came with me, a playful smile on his face. That impish grin followed me into the bathroom, all the way into the shower. Watching the stream of water flowing down the lean muscles of his frame, I let him pamper and caress me. He lathered me with soap and affection, touching me everywhere but refraining from turning the moment into a sexual one. He only washed me, and I in turn washed him. It was comforting, too.

When the water turned chilly on us, he wrapped himself in a towel and headed out to make us some coffee. I smiled at the low-slung cotton riding just over his backside, and hastily got myself dressed so I could rejoin that half-naked body.

I threw on a pair of jeans and a few layered t-shirts and opened my door just as my sister opened hers. Blinking sleepily, even though it was well past eleven, she scratched her wildly attractive bed head. "Hey, sis, you headed out to school?"

Nodding, hoping my sister didn't decide to go to the kitchen for any reason, since Kellan was only rocking a towel-skirt, I stepped in front of her line of vision. "Yeah, pretty soon. Kellan's taking me, so you can have the car today."

Anna nodded and yawned. She had the car most days so that really wasn't news to her. Stretching so that the tight t-shirt she'd slept in rode up her bikini-clad hips, she nodded towards the kitchen. "He in there? I should wish him a good show tonight."

Hearing Kellan humming, I tried to block my sister's vision even more. She might not care if I saw her boyfriend in all his glory, but I didn't need her ogling Kellan in his. That was my job. "Yeah, he's making coffee." When she smiled and took a step towards me, I grabbed her shoulder. Looking down at her scantily dressed body, I raised an eyebrow. "Would you mind putting on some clothes before you go waltzing out there?"

Covering a yawn, she shook her head. "He doesn't care, Kiera. I'm like a sister to him."

Sighing at the impossible beauty of the sexpot before me, I shook my head. "Please?"

Maybe seeing my expression as I wistfully glanced over her curves, she finally nodded. "All right."

After she slinked back to her room, I darted into mine and grabbed Kellan's clothes. Holding the bundle tight to my chest, I hurried down the short hall into the kitchen. Kellan was leaning against the counter with his hands behind him, his glorious chest on full display. I paused a moment to just blatantly stare at him.

His hair was a damp, disheveled mess, and water drops occasionally dripped onto his shoulder. One drop followed the curve of his collarbone before trailing over the elegant script of my name above his heart. From there, the frisky ball of water rolled over his pec, across his ribs, and straight down to the deep V-cut of his lower abdomen. It traveled that line quite a distance before finally hitting the absorbent towel slung around his hips. It was the luckiest damn drop of water on earth.

"Kiera?"

Kellan's entertained voice brought my eyes back up to his highly amused ones. Grinning crookedly, he raised an eyebrow. "See something you like?"

Flushing, I tossed his clothes at him. He flinched at the sudden move but managed to catch them. "Anna's awake and getting ready to come out here. Can you get dressed please?"

I said that last part forlornly as I glossed over his body again. Lightly chuckling, he set his clothes on the counter and watched me watch him. I bit my lip as another drop traveled down his broad back. "You sure?" he asked, still amused.

Sighing, I took a quick glance back at Anna's room. Luckily, the door was still closed. "Yes."

When I looked back at him, he shrugged and unwrapped the towel from his waist. In the middle of my tiny kitchen, he let the material fall right to the ground. My eyes widened at the sight of him completely bare. Kellan didn't need to...um, glorify his manhood with accessories like Griffin did. He was absolutely perfect in his natural state. Flushing red-hot, I watched him shake his head at me and very slowly grab his underwear from the pile. I wanted to snap at him to hurry, and at the same time I wanted him to slow down even more. Smiling, I knew this mental snapshot would also come back to me when I was missing him.

When the last piece of clothing was on his body, I sighed sadly and walked over to lace my arms around his neck. "I'm gonna miss you," I murmured, shaking my head at him.

He smiled, lacing his arms around my waist. "I'm gonna miss you, too."

We were softly kissing when my sister entered the room. "Damn it, was he in a towel?"

I looked over at my sister frowning playfully, pointing at the evidence piled on the floor. Grinning, I laid my head on his chest. "Yes, sorry, you missed the peep show."

Sighing dramatically, she reached into the cupboard next to us and grabbed a few coffee mugs. "I always do," she muttered, handing one to me and one to Kellan.

Laughing and shaking his head, Kellan disengaged himself from me so he could pour everyone coffee from the pot that had just finished brewing. When he handed a full one to Anna, she politely thanked him. Taking a small sip, she raised her eyebrows at him. "Hey, good luck at your show, Kellan. I'm gonna get off work a little early so I can catch the tail end of it."

Kellan nodded and smiled, handing me a cup with room to add creamer; I couldn't stand black coffee like he and my sister could.

"Thanks, Anna. I'm glad you'll be able to make it to this one." Smiling at me, he poured a final cup for himself. "It should be good." He shrugged casually, like it was just another show and not his farewell show.

I bit my lip to stop the stinging sensation building in my eyes as I poured a good helping of flavored creamer into my mug. I didn't want to get emotional already. There would be time for tears later, I was sure. Anna sighed, the sound matching my mood. "I wouldn't miss it for anything, Kellan."

She gave him a supportive pat on the shoulder then left us so we could have one last peaceful morning together with our cups of coffee. And it was the most comforting of all.

After driving me to school, Kellan threw his arm over my shoulder and walked me to class. The students were finally used to seeing him walking down the hall, since he escorted me to class nearly every day, but the girls still stared appreciatively. I had considered skipping today, so we would have all the time in the world together, but Kellan had firmly said, "No." School was important, he said, and I'd missed too much already. Knowing he was right, I'd reluctantly agreed.

Surprising me, Kellan walked me all the way into my classroom. When he walked me over to a row with a couple of open seats, I rolled my eyes at him. "I can handle this part. You can go...nap or something."

Chuckling adorably, he shook his head and, holding my hand, walked backwards down the aisle with me. "I'm not walking you to your seat." Edging past a couple of girls staring at him wide-eyed, he sat down and motioned for me to sit beside him. "I'm joining you," he said, smiling brilliantly as he crossed his arms over his chest.

I stared at him open-mouthed. He'd teased about sitting through a class before, but I didn't think he'd ever actually do it. Kellan wasn't dumb or anything, but he wasn't exactly the academic type, either. He'd be bored out of his mind sitting here with me while the teacher droned on and on about morality clauses in contract agreements. Shaking my head, I sat down beside him. "All right."

Chuckling, he wrapped his arm around my shoulder. Looking over at him, I raised an eyebrow. "No falling asleep." He laughed a little and stroked my arm with his thumb. Smiling, I added, "And no funny business. I actually need to learn this stuff."

Kellan rolled his eyes and made a pledge over his heart. "I'll be the perfect student." Facing forward, he whispered, "And if I'm not, you can punish me later." His grin was so devilishly attractive, I had to look away. Unfortunately, I looked right across the room at Candy.

She was sitting with her sidekicks, her head turned all the way around as she stared at the rock star sitting in on her class. Her surprised expression nearly matched what mine had been. As I leaned into his side, resting my head on his shoulder, her expression relaxed into a neutral one. Rolling her eyes and muttering a word that I could clearly tell was, "Whatever," she jerked back around to the front of the room.

I grinned and waited for my boyfriend to receive his first college lecture. I hope he liked it.

In a way that surprised me, Kellan *was* the perfect student. He leaned in and listened, enraptured. During discussion period, he even piped up with a couple of well thought out questions. I smiled as he got into a debate with a guy a few rows down from us. Kellan's argument was much more persuasive, and the legitimate student conceded in the end. The professor commended Kellan on his perspectives, then cocked his head like he was trying to place who Kellan was...and if he was actually a student. Eventually he gave up trying to figure it out and dismissed the class for the day.

I was very proud of my boyfriend as we left the room. In another life, he probably would have excelled at college.

Kellan was ear-to-ear smiles as I clenched his hand, loving that he'd enjoyed it so much. Everything was going great, until he walked past a group of giggling girls. Feeling bold, they stepped right in front of us and blocked our exit. Still on cloud nine, Kellan smiled at the group. "Ladies?" he asked politely.

They giggled even more at being addressed. I wanted to sigh in exasperation. There was something about him that turned mature, educated, enlightened women into fifteen-year-old school girls. I've seen it happen way too often.

The boldest of the group stepped forward. "You're Kellan, right? We just love your band."

Nodding politely, an odd expression passed Kellan's face as he studied the group of women assembled before him. It was something that the girls probably wouldn't have noticed, but I did. It was almost like he was trying to place a name with a face. Throwing on an effortless grin, he smoothly said, "I'm glad to hear you enjoy us. Our last show is tonight at Pete's." Leaning in, he husked, "I hope you guys can make it." His tone was so suggestive that I actually raised my eyebrow. I was used to Kellan flirting with female fans a little, but this was excessive.

They, of course, ate it up. Kellan smiled as he flicked his eyes over the group. He kept looking at the girl in the back, and I curiously started examining her too. She was biting her lip and eyeing him in an intimate way, a way that clearly said she was a step above the other fawning fans. It was a look I'd seen before on women who approached him, or sometimes even showed up at his place. It was the look of a woman who'd shared a bed with him and probably wouldn't mind sharing a bed with him again.

As his eyes kept flashing over hers, I finally registered the look I was seeing on his face. It was an expression of, *I know you...how do I know you?*

Irritated by the whole situation, I started to subtly pull away from him. Maybe taking the hint, he excused himself from the gawkers. "It was nice to meet you all...I'll see you at the show." I groaned a little that he tossed that in at the end. Now they all probably assumed that he literally meant he'd spend some time with them at the performance tonight. And I've-slept-with-you girl was probably expecting a great amount of personal attention.

I was scowling by the time we were outside. He noticed. "Hey, what's wrong?"

Glaring over at him, I rolled my eyes. "I hope you all can make it. See you there, ladies," I mocked, not really meaning to.

He stopped and stared at me. "I was just being friendly with some fans, Kiera. It doesn't mean what you think it means."

I stopped, setting my hands on my hips. I was fine with the fans, truly, I was, but that girl in the back had gotten under my skin. It was so weird to have so many people know what being with him was like...in that way. And they kept popping up everywhere. This girl, Candy, Rita, and I was pretty sure about that mechanic chick too...and that was just in the small circle that I saw often. I knew the list was much, much longer than that.

Pointing back to the building, I snapped out, "You've had sex with that girl!"

He blinked at my tone and my words, then his face heated. "And?"

I blinked that he didn't even try to deny it. "And...and..." Not having a real argument, I sighed and hung my head. "And I'm tired of running into girls who know what making love to you feels like."

He sighed and stepped into me, cupping my face. His voice and face softer, he shook his head. "No one but you knows what making love to me feels like." Raising his eyebrows, he rested his head against mine. "*I* didn't even know what making love was like until you."

Pulling back, he indicated the building. "What happened with that girl…was just sex. A mindless, physical act that had no meaning or feeling behind it. It was just pleasure…and I don't even really remember it."

Squatting down, he met my eye. "I remember every single time with you. Even before we were together, being with you haunted my dreams. I couldn't forget, even when I wanted to…" His thumbs brushed over my cheeks as I felt tears falling down them. "You…seared me. That's making love. That is something that none of them have over you. You are…unforgettable…and I love you."

Sniffling, I swallowed a couple of times before I could finally say, "I love you, too."

He kissed me then, and I felt the passion and the truth in his words. They'd had him, but not like I had him. For some reason, I was different to him, and I was eternally grateful for that. I was still thinking about all of his conquests on the drive to his place, though. Feeling a little melancholy, I sat on his couch after we walked in his door. He sat beside me, a little cautiously.

"Kiera? You're not still mad, are you?"

I shook my head as I looked over at him. "No, I'm not mad, I'm just…"

Sighing, I bit my lip. Looking nervous, he shrugged. "You're what?"

Knowing we had to have this conversation sooner or later, I gritted my teeth and inhaled. On the exhale, I calmly said, "I'm curious…about the women."

Looking away, Kellan sighed, like he'd known this was coming. "Kiera…you know why I used to…"

He trailed off, staring at the floor. Grabbing his cheek, I made him look back at me. "I know, Kellan. I know why, I just don't know…how many."

He pulled back from my fingertips, his brows pulling together. "How many? Why do you…? Why does that…?" Shaking his head, he shrugged again. "What difference does that make, Kiera?"

Sighing as I stared at the floor now, I shrugged. "I don't know why, Kellan. I guess I just want to know how many….others…I could potentially run into." I peeked back up to look at him; his brow was still furrowed. "Do you know how many there are?"

He swallowed, his eyes avoiding mine. "Kiera, I'm not really comfortable with…" He sighed and finally looked at me. "Can we not do this, please? Not today, not when I'm leaving tomorrow."

I paused, wishing I could just let it go again. But I'd let it go too many times already and really, this was the perfect time to discuss it. "We should have this conversation, Kellan. We should have already had it, but you and I had…different problems getting together, so this just kept getting put on the back burner. But it's important…we need to talk about it."

Exhaling, he shook his head. "Why? It's ancient history. I'm not that guy anymore, Kiera. I'm not gonna be that guy again. Can't we just ignore it?"

Stroking his cheek, I shook my head. "We can't ignore things and have a solid relationship. And...it's not ancient, Kellan. That girl today proves that it's still relevant. We're going to run into these girls over and over and I need..." I exhaled in a rush, "I just need to know what I'm up against, Kellan."

Dropping his head he muttered, "You're not up against anything." I didn't speak and he peeked up at me, hope in his eyes that I'd drop this. When I didn't, when I just kept silently sitting and waiting for him to answer, my heart in my throat, he resignedly sighed. "I don't know how many, Kiera...I'm sorry."

Looking around the room, he leaned over and rested his elbows on his knees. "I suppose if you did the math..." He looked down at his hands. "I've been having sex for about a decade, with two or three different girls a week," he peeked up at me, guilt all over his face, "on average," he looked back down at his hands, "so that's...."

I held my breath, already having calculated the answer. He looked up at me and blinked after he did the math. "Crap...that's over fifteen hundred girls." He looked back down to his hands and muttered, "That can't be right..."

I sighed, knowing it was. Even if he only had sex twice a week with a different girl each time, that was over one hundred girls a year. Since he started so young, and he had almost ten years of that sort of behavior under his belt...well, that was almost a thousand girls. And that was assuming a low average. I had a feeling some years had been much higher than two or three a week. Sometimes he'd had two or three a day.

He looked a little ill as he sat on his couch, considering that. He clearly never had before. "Jesus," he muttered. "I really am a whore."

Actually feeling bad for him, I put a hand on his knee. "Well, I can see why you don't remember them all," I whispered.

He looked up at me, horrified. "I'm so sorry, Kiera. I didn't realize..."

He shook his head and I shook mine too. "I wasn't trying to make you feel guilty, Kellan, I just...we should talk about this openly, honestly."

Sighing, he leaned back against the couch. Nodding, he splayed his fingers out to me. "What do you want to know?"

"I know you don't remember all of their names, but do you remember their faces? Would you recognize them all if we ran into them again?" I cringed, thinking of this afternoon.

He bit his lip, thinking. "Maybe girls from the last few years, but before that...no, I'm sorry, the faces blur together and, you know, I didn't always ask..." he looked down, "...their names."

I squeezed my hand on his knee, and asked the one question that I really needed answered, the one that seemed the most relevant...and the one that terrified me a little. "Were you safe...with all of them?"

My heart thudded in my chest. True, STDs and other communicable diseases were high up on my list of concerns, but the one thing that scared me the most was the idea of some woman out there having had his child after a one-night fling with him. It happened all the time. It was so plausible. It terrified me to no end that some woman knocking on his door would also come with a toddler...with midnight blue eyes.

His eyes immediately flashed up to mine. "Yes," he whispered, his voice sounding completely sure.

Sighing, I slumped against the couch. "Kellan, you don't have to lie to make me feel better...just be honest."

His hand came out to cup my cheek. "I am. Even from the first, the very first, we used condoms. I always carried some with me after that day. I didn't want..." he sighed and shook his head, "I didn't want another...me...to happen to some girl."

I stared at him blankly, amazed that the circumstances of his own conception had scared him straight, so to speak, even at the tender age of twelve. Without thinking about it, I murmured, "How can you be sure...if you don't remember them all?"

He shook his head. "Because it was my rule, and I never broke it. It was the one thing I...was good about."

Frowning, I pushed his hand away from my face. "You weren't with me. You never even thought about it with me."

There was a little heat in my tone as I thought about all of our skin-on-skin moments. He looked down, his eyes flicking back and forth. "That's because..." he peeked up at me, "it was you." I furrowed my brow, not understanding. He sighed, bringing his fingers back to my cheek. "I wanted you...so much...and in a way I'd never wanted any girl." He rested his forehead against mine, exhaling lightly. "I loved you...even that first time. I didn't want anything between us. I wanted..."

Pulling back, he looked away. Grabbing his cheek, I made him look at me. "You wanted what?"

Looking guilty again, he shrugged. "I wanted...to own you. I wanted a part of me in you." He cringed. "I wanted to mark you, make you mine." Sighing, he shook his head. "Because I knew you really weren't...but it made me feel...closer to you, to think that way."

He lowered his eyes as mine watered. "I'm sorry...I shouldn't have done that."

Swallowing, I brought his mouth to mine. "I love you, too," I muttered between our lips.

Grabbing his head, I pulled him back as I laid myself down on the couch. He went freely, settling himself over the top of me as our mouths moved in perfect synch. Breaths heavier, our kiss intensified and my body melted under his, ready for him to stake his claim on me again. But when I tangled my fingers in his messy hair, lightly scratching his scalp, he pulled away from me.

Staring down on me, he shook his head. "Don't take this the wrong way, but can we not have sex right now? Can we just…cuddle…until you have to go in to work? I just want to be close to you for a while."

Shifting my fingers to brush some stray hair from his forehead, I searched his eyes. "Yeah, of course."

He smiled lightly and kissed me one last time before shifting to lie beside me. His head on my shoulder, he wrapped his leg over mine and laced our fingers together. Kissing my knuckles, he sighed softly. "I love you, Kiera," he whispered.

Kissing his forehead, I rested my cheek on his head and absorbed the feeling of his body sprawled across mine. I had been wrong before. *This* was the most comforting thing ever.

We stayed that way, cuddling and silently comforting each other, right up until it was time for me to go to work. Immediately upon entering the bar, Sam handed Kellan a shot of something. A big grin on his imposing face, the huge bouncer clapped Kellan's shoulder. "Here, man, it's your night, drink up!"

Kellan swished it back without hesitation. "Thanks, Sam." He laughed a little as he handed the empty glass back to him. "I never thought you, of all people, would hand me alcohol."

Kellan laughed a little more, and Sam rolled his eyes, his smile dropping. "Well, since you're not going to end up on my doorstep tonight, I'll allow it."

I frowned at Kellan, remembering his confession about getting himself obliterated at Sam's doorstep because of me. I'd had to deal with the inebriated idiot that night, when I had no idea why he'd gotten tossed. It was a little surprising that he could joke about that evening now, but that was Kellan—resilient. I suppose, with his life, he'd had to develop the ability to bounce back.

Sam shook his head then laughed and clapped Kellan's shoulder again. "We're gonna miss you, Kell." Walking away from Kellan, I thought I heard Sam mutter, "Drunken idiot."

Ignoring that last part, Kellan shouted back, "Thanks!"

I tried to walk with Kellan to his table, but with every step we took, someone halted him, offered him a drink, and toasted their congratulations. He happily took them all, slinging them back and thanking the person offering it. After the fourth such stoppage, I gave up walking with him, kissed him on the cheek, and told him that I had to get to work. He nodded as he took another shot. Shaking my head, I hoped he slowed down enough so that he could actually give his final performance tonight. It would be quite a disappointment to his fans if I had to drive the drunken idiot home in an hour.

By the time I officially started my shift, Kellan was surrounded by a boisterous crowd. Everyone seemed to want some time with him before he left tomorrow. I was grateful that we'd already had our tender moment back at the house, although I was somewhat saddened by the fact that our private time was over. I'd have to share him from here on out.

About an hour into my shift, the rest of the band showed up. The place erupted into fanfare with the whole group assembled; it was easily ten times louder than the applause they received after Bumbershoot. Everyone was proud of their boys and wanted to wish them well. The bar was bursting at the seams, and it was still a few hours before the show officially started.

Hearing the ruckus, Pete popped out of his office. He sighed despondently at the sight of his entertainment moving on from him, then shook his head and raised his hands into the air. The place quieted as everyone twisted to look at him. Kellan worked his way through the crowd to stand near his band mates and locked eyes with Pete.

Smiling at the singer, Pete said, "Kellan…boys…you've done wonders for my little pub and I'll never forget that. If and when you return, you will always have a place here." Kellan smiled, his eyes drifting to the floor. The other D-bags beamed, smiling at each other. Sniffing in a clearly emotional way, Pete shook his head. "Anyway…a round for everybody, on the house!"

The bar erupted in cheers and my eyes widened. There were a lot of people here. As Pete went over to chat with his band, Jenny, Kate and I got busy distributing free beers to the exuberant masses. It felt like an eternity before we satiated the crowd, but eventually, with Rita and the day bartender, Troy, helping out, we did. As a content murmur filtered throughout the place, I leaned against the bar and sighed, already exhausted.

Kate and Jenny leaned against the bar with me; one on either side. Kate blew a stray piece of hair out of her eyes, the first stray piece of hair I'd ever seen on her. "I'm gonna miss those guys, but, whew, this is gonna be a long night."

Rita popped over behind us, pouring us each shots. "A round for the ladies!" Troy walked up to her side, and Rita gave him a suggestive smile before pouring him one. "And you too, I suppose." I hid my smile from her, not bothering to tell her that I was pretty sure Troy would never be interested in her the way her smile insinuated. I was pretty sure Troy's interests lay elsewhere…like in my boyfriend.

Clinking glasses, we all took a quick shot. It burned going down, but afterwards it was warm and calming, just enough to help me get through tonight's chaos. As Rita and Troy moved off to help start the next round for people, Jenny sighed and laid her head on my arm. "I'm going to miss Evan…and the guys. Pete's just won't be the same."

I nodded, resting my head against her. "I know…nothing will be the same really."

Kate sighed and we both looked over to her. "Yeah, I have some really good memories of those boys." Giggling, she twirled a lock of hair around her finger. "A couple summers ago they kidnapped me for my birthday." She grinned at Jenny. "Evan made me wear that stupid birthday hat, remember?"

Jenny grinned back at Kate and shook her head. "Yeah, that was fun." Wistfully, she looked over at the guys. "I remember when they did a show in Eastern Washington. A group of us decided to road trip it over the pass with them. We all got stuck halfway through when Griffin's Van broke down. We had to camp at a rest stop." Jenny started laughing, Kate and I joining her. "Matt never booked another show over the mountains after that."

Jenny wiped her eyes as the memories of that trip washed over her. I sighed, wishing I had been here for those happy times. Kate reached over and tapped Jenny's shoulder. "Remember the water slides fiasco?"

Jenny nodded. "Yeah, Griffin still isn't allowed to go back there."

They both started belly laughing, and I frowned, wondering what the cretin had done. Tears streaming down her cheeks, Jenny said, "And remember the rooftop party? The heights freaked Matt out and he spent the whole night in the exact center of the roof." Wiping her eyes, Jenny laughed out, "Kellan had to sling him over his shoulder to get him to leave."

I laughed with them, imagining that, then I sighed. I'd missed so many memories. Giggling nonstop, Kate added, "Remember when you walked in on me and Kellan that one New Year's Eve?"

I instantly stopped laughing and swung my head around to Kate. She instantly stopped laughing too, remembering who I was. "You and Kellan?" I looked her up and down with narrowed eyes, like it had just happened. "What?"

My tone was bitter and Jenny put a hand on my shoulder. Kate blanched and shook her head. "We didn't have sex...it didn't get that far." She pointed over to Jenny. "She..." Biting her lip, Kate shrugged, looking very apologetic.

My eyes narrowing even more, I put my hands on my hips. "Why didn't you ever mention this before?"

Kate cringed a bit. "What was I supposed to say? Hey, I nearly had sex with the guy you're seeing? That's not cool." She shrugged again. "Besides, it was a while ago, and we were really, really drunk. I don't think he even..." Looking around self-consciously, she shrugged again. "I should get back to work."

Feeling my cheeks heat, I didn't respond, and she quickly turned and fled. God! He'd done Rita, he'd asked Jenny out, and now I'd found out that he'd seriously made out with Kate. Did Kellan not have a history with anyone at Pete's!

Seeing me fuming, Jenny stepped in front of me, putting both hands on my shoulders. "He's different now, Kiera." Looking over to where Kate had disappeared, Jenny shook her head. "And don't hate her for caving into him." Looking back at me, she raised an eyebrow pointedly. "You know how persuasive Kellan is."

I flushed for another reason and slumped a little against the bar. "I know...I just wish everyone in the entire world didn't have some sort of sexual history with the man I'm in love with."

Laughing softly, Jenny ducked down to meet my eye. "It's a lot, Kiera, I know, but I'm sure it's not everybody." Shaking her head, she smiled cheerily. "I don't have a history with him. I've never even kissed him." She instantly frowned and pulled away, her eyes suddenly deep in thought. "Hmmm..."

My mouth dropped as she shook her head, her frown lines getting deeper. I smacked her shoulder. "You have kissed him, haven't you?"

Looking back at me with a small grimace, she shrugged. "There was this one time after he drove me home from a shift." My mouth dropped wider and I made a very unladylike noise. She twisted her lips and shook her head. "Sorry, I forgot. It wasn't too long after I started working here. He was looking sad and lonely and he offered to drive me, so I caved and said yes. Then we were talking in my driveway and he leaned over and kissed me." She shook out her beautiful, blonde head of hair. "I pushed him back and told him I didn't want to." Rolling her eyes, she added, "I think that's what started him hounding me for a date, until I finally put my foot down."

She shrugged as she stared at me, like it was no big deal. Closing my eyes, I stormed off to the back room. I needed to go some place where another woman that Kellan had been intimately involved with was not. And right now, that meant I needed to be alone.

Chapter 8 – The First Farewell

Shutting out the noise and the chaos of the bar calmed me down some. It really wasn't my friends' fault. I shouldn't be angry or upset with them. Kellan either. He'd been looking for something. Unknowingly, he'd been looking for a genuine, loving connection with someone. He'd just gone about it all wrong—jumping into the physical aspect of a relationship without building up the emotional part of it. No wonder the feeling had never lasted long after the sex for him. No wonder he'd flitted from person to person, desperate and unhappy.

And besides, his past was his past, and it was all behind him. He found what he'd been missing. The only person he was being overtly sexual with was me...and that was the way it should be.

Lightly laughing as I organized stock shelves that didn't need organizing, I tried to imagine the funnier stories the girls had told about the group. I could just picture them all drinking stale coffee at some middle-of-nowhere rest stop, complaining about Griffin's crappy car.

Smiling at the image of Kellan in wet board shorts at a water park, I re-folded the stack of Pete's shirts for the third time. Eventually I would need to go back out there. Maybe after I filled all the extra salt shakers. Vaguely, I heard the sound of the door opening and closing, the noise of the bar increasing and decreasing. Sighing that an employee was messing with my chi, probably about to bite my head off for hiding out during the busiest night we'd ever had, I kept my back turned, trying to appear horribly busy in my quest for...something.

But then, I felt a body come up right behind me, way too far into my personal space. Alarm washing through me, I started to twist around. Strong hands rested against the shelves on either side of me while a firm, hard body pressed into my back.

A mouth hovered near my ear. "Don't turn around."

My heart surged, racing through my veins and thudding in my ears. A list of harrowing, life-changing images rushed through my mind. Was I being attacked? Was I about to be raped? Would anyone hear me scream back here? Would anyone rush to my rescue? Where was Kellan?

Panic stricken and scared out of my wits, I instantly turned around. Or I tried to anyway. The strong hands jerked my head straight. The body behind me pressed me up against the shelves, the arousal of the man clear against my low back. Oh God, so this *was* going to be rape then? I started shivering as the voice growled in my ear, "I said, don't turn around."

Just as I was debating which part of my body to hit him with first, my attacker started laughing. The ice and fear leeched from me as I instantly recognized the amused chuckle. Rolling my eyes, heat taking over fear, I twisted to face him.

"Kellan! You scared the shit out of me!" I smacked him in the chest, then did it again for good measure.

He backed away a step, then pulled my body flush to his. Still chuckling, he shook his head. "You're disobeying me..." Grinning fiendishly, he leaned his face against mine and backed me up into the shelves. I could smell the wave of alcohol on his breath. "I may just have to punish you tonight," he whispered.

It was so erotic, I instantly wanted him, then hated my treacherous body for submitting so fast. It was hard to think, though, with his evident pleasure pressed right where I needed it. Grabbing my leg, he hitched it up to his hip, and pressed that marvelous hardness against me even more. I groaned softly, closing my eyes and wrapping my arms around him.

"Don't...I'm mad at you," I muttered.

A low rumble came up his throat as his mouth attached to my neck. "It makes me hot when you're angry," he murmured, dragging the tip of his tongue from my neck to my ear. I sucked in a breath, my head dropping back to the shelf behind me while his ready body rubbed against me.

Oh, damn.

His fingers deftly untucked my Pete's shirt, one hand dipping underneath to cup my breast. His teeth lightly tugged on an earlobe before his hot lips closed around it. He groaned low and seductive as he pressed against me, and before I knew it, I was nearly panting, silently begging him to take me.

Hissing through his teeth, he murmured, "God, I want you...do you want me?"

The hand not engaged in fondling me, slinked inside my jeans and darted inside my underwear. I exhaled in a rush, my eyes flying open. "No, Kellan, don't." I grabbed his hand right before his fingers could reach me. God, if he actually touched me...we'd be undressed and all over each other a second later. And I knew from experience that this room wasn't exactly secure.

Frowning, he pulled back to look at me. Or he tried to look at me. His eyes focused and unfocused. "Why'd you stop me?" he said, slurring a little and blinking slowly.

Sighing, I tried to get his hand out of my pants; somehow he managed to inch it down a little more. "Are you drunk?" I whispered, bringing my other hand down to try to yank his up.

He laughed lightly, his stronger hand not budging, even with all my efforts. God, I hoped no one walked in on us like this. "Probably," he giggled a little, "and I want that sex now."

Shaking my head, I set my mouth in a firm line. "No, I'm not having sex with you in the back room."

Frowning, he brought his lips to mine. I resisted, but he teased me with light flicks of his tongue against my skin and I had no choice but to let him in. My grip on his hand relaxed just a fraction, too. "Why not?" he murmured. "I had Pete fix the door...it's locked, if that's what you're worried about." His hand slid down a half-inch lower, and I let it. "Besides, it *is* my big night."

Summoning all of my will power, I pulled back from his mouth. "Why would you have Pete fix the door?"

He shrugged, heading back towards my lips. "I like it back here. This room holds...happy memories for me."

Avoiding him, I raised an eyebrow. "Happy? Us screaming at each other is a happy memory for you?" I cringed at the reference to the night when we'd finally blown up at each other. It was the worst verbal fight I'd ever been in, and hoped to ever be in, again.

He grinned lazily, the alcohol flowing through his veins clear in his features. "Remember what I said about you being angry making me hot?" The tip of his finger brushed over a curl below and I hissed in a breath, yanking his hand up a smidge. He grinned wider, then exhaled softly. "I told you I loved you in this room." His voice wistful, he shook his head. "I should have said it earlier."

Seeing the love in his drunken gaze, I smiled and released one of my hands from his arm to stroke his cheek. "Yes, you should have." Sighing, I shook my head. "And I should have said it back."

His expression turned serious for a second and he lowered his head against mine, closing his perfectly deep eyes. "Yes, yes you should have." Giggling, he added, "You always were stubborn as shit, though. It took you forever to admit you even had feelings for me."

Pulling back from him, I frowned as deeply as I could with his hand still down my pants. He giggled more and leaned over to kiss me. "What? You know I'm right." His tongue brushed against mine and I moaned. I considered letting him do whatever he wanted with me. He did get the door fixed after all...

Maybe sensing where my head was, or maybe too drunk to care, his hand slid down to cup my body. I groaned, aching with the need for him to lift a finger and touch me. He didn't, though, just held his hand there and passionately kissed me. His breath was harder, and as my fingers reached down to tentatively touch his arousal, I could feel that it was harder too.

Wanting to scream, "Okay, okay, just take me!" I suddenly remembered the chaos we'd left in the bar. Releasing my hand from him, I pushed his shoulder back. "You have to go play, Kellan." Narrowing my eyes, ignoring the throbbing in my body, I looked over his slightly glazed face. "Can you even do that?"

Laughing, he nodded. "There's a lot I can do when I'm drunk." He laughed again, and I frowned, also remembering the earlier revelations from my coworkers.

"Yeah, I hear you make out with Pete's waitresses on New Year's Eve when you're wasted."

He looked at me blankly, a dopey, satisfied smile on his face, then he frowned. "What?"

Rolling my eyes, I yanked on his hand still happy and content on my privates. "Kate, you ass. You never told me you almost had sex with her...Jenny too."

He rolled his eyes and slurred, "I never got anywhere near sex with Jenny. She said no. And Kate....doesn't count."

I narrowed my eyes, leaning into his face. He blinked as he readjusted his vision to look at me. "What do you mean she doesn't count?"

He shrugged slowly. "Almost doesn't count."

Grunting, I successfully yanked his hand free from my jeans. He openly pouted at me as I handed his hand back to him; he even gave me puppy dog eyes. Smiling, in spite of my objections to his comment, I shook my head. "What am I going to do with you?"

His smile turned lascivious as his eyes locked on my pants. "I could think of a few things."

Chuckling, I physically turned him around. Hopefully his…situation…wouldn't be too apparent to the patrons when I stormed him back out to the bar. That could be a little embarrassing for him. Then again, maybe not. Kellan didn't get embarrassed by things that would mortify most people. He'd probably just shrug and drink another beer.

He sighed morosely while I pushed him forward. I chuckled again, realizing something. He looked back at me once we got to the door. Frowning, he muttered, "What's so funny?"

Smiling at the look of insolence on his face, I grinned and laughed a little more. "Well…Casanova…since you are obviously living it up on your night, guess what I get to do later?"

He grinned again, bringing his still ready body around so he could press it into mine. Unfortunately, I was still ready too, and it felt, really, really amazing when we pressed together. I started to close my eyes but opened them when he mumbled, "Me?"

Pushing him back, I raised a finger in warning. "No…" Smiling innocently, I reached behind him to open the door. "I finally get to drive the Chevelle again."

He frowned and instantly started protesting, but I shoved his drunken ass through the door. There was no way I was letting him drive to the after party.

Just as he backed out into the hallway, adorably sputtering that he was fine to drive, he started ringing. Well, the cell phone in his front pocket started ringing, but since Kellan wasn't used to wearing one on him, he looked around himself like he had no idea why he was making noise. He started patting his body, looking for the source of the sound. Laughing, I stopped his hands and put one of them on the slight bulge that was his cell phone.

Giggling to himself as the people walking past us looked at him oddly, he muttered, "Oh thank God, it's the phone. For a minute, I thought my cock was ringing."

As my cheeks flamed bright red and my hand slapped over my mouth, Kellan dug his phone out of his pocket and answered it. Upon hearing his greeting, I instantly wondered if Kellan should be speaking on the phone in his condition. I also wondered who could be calling him…most of us were already here, or on our way here.

"Yo, talk to me," he spouted merrily, sitting back on a hip. Shaking my head at him, I rolled my eyes. Lord help whoever he was talking to. I figured out who that was a moment later. His face dropping in complete surprise, Kellan loudly exclaimed, "Dude! Denny, man! You have, like, fuck-tastic timing. Tonight's my last show and Kiera and I were just--"

My eyes widened and I immediately tried to take the phone from him. Of all the people for Kellan to talk to drunk, Denny was the worst one. There were way too many delicate topics he could accidentally start talking about.

Glaring at me, Kellan twisted out of my reach, stumbling back a step. "Relax, Kiera, I wasn't going to tell him that you just blew me off." My mouth dropped open; he'd just said that directly into the phone and it had sounded really, really bad. His hazy mind registering what he'd done, Kellan blinked and quickly covered with, "Oh, Denny, not that she actually blew me or anything, she didn't, she doesn't really hang out down there, if you know what I mean," he paused to giggle, "and I guess you do, huh?"

Attempting to snatch the phone away before the idiot told Denny everything that he didn't need to hear, I watched Kellan frown as he batted me away. "Sorry, man, you probably don't want to hear shit like that." There was a pause from Kellan as Denny spoke, then Kellan laughed. "Yeah, well, at least I didn't say you caught us in the middle of doing it...that would have been awkward."

I closed my eyes and shook my head. Idiot. Joking or not, Denny really didn't need to picture Kellan and I together. I heard silence and peeked an eye open at Kellan; he was frowning. "Denny? You still there?" After another second his frown lifted to a medicated smile. "No, the tour starts tomorrow, we're livin' it up for our last night in Seattle."

Sighing, I grimaced. I hadn't realized that Kellan had told Denny that he was leaving for a few months. I could just imagine what Denny thought about that. Denny probably wouldn't say anything directly, but I was sure, in his head, he was making some comparisons to when he'd left me.

Wondering how to get Kellan out of saying something stupid to his friend, potentially ruining the already-tenuous relationship that they had, I tried for the phone again. Kellan held me back at arm's length as he blabbered on. "Yeah, I know. Six months, Denny. On a bus, man! An actual tour bus, can you believe that shit?" Kellan paused, then tilted his head. "Yeah, I'm seriously buzzin'...why?"

Taking advantage of Kellan's brief moment of confusion, I snatched the phone out of his hand. Denny was laughing when I put the cell up to my ear. "Hey, Denny, it's me. Sorry about that, he's been...celebrating."

Still chuckling, Denny murmured, "I can tell. Hey, how are you?"

I knew he was asking about Kellan's upcoming departure, but I answered like I didn't know he was asking that. "Oh, I'm doing great. Work's busy and school's crazy, but I'm getting by."

There was a pause and I studied Kellan. He'd crossed his arms over his chest and was tapping his foot like a petulant teenage girl. I bit my lip to not laugh. After the silence, Denny seriously said, "No, Kiera, I meant with Kellan leaving."

Sighing, I closed my eyes and concentrated on the phone. "Yeah, I know that's what you meant. I'm fine...really." Opening my eyes, I smiled at Kellan; he smiled back, wobbling a bit on his feet. "This is a big moment for him. I'm not going to ruin it by..." I bit my lip, not wanting to say it to Denny.

Sighing, I heard him fill in the blanks. "By breaking up with him so he gives up everything to rush back to you...even though it's too late."

Swallowing, I turned away from Kellan. "Denny..."

Clearing his throat, Denny sniffed into the phone. "Hey, sorry. I didn't mean to go there. I really didn't, Kiera." Sounding uncomfortable, he cleared his throat again. "Look, I'll call back later when he's sober. I just wanted to wish him good luck on his tour." He laughed softly. "Not that he'll need it."

I smiled a little, looking back at Kellan who was leaning against the far wall, staring at the exit sign at the end of the hallway. "Yeah...I'll tell him later. Thanks for calling, Denny. I know it means a lot to Kellan."

A brief silence, then, "Yeah...goodnight, Kiera."

"Goodnight, Denny."

Ending the call, I held the phone in my hand a moment before turning back to Kellan. He was staring at me again, blinking slowly. When I walked over and held the phone out to him, he numbly took it, still expressionless. Shoving it in his pocket, he finally grimaced. "I'm hungry...do you want to split some fries with me?"

Exhaling in a long, relieved breath, glad that he wasn't going to start a drunken fight with me for chatting with my ex, I nodded. "Sounds great. I'll get some cooked up for you."

He nodded, smiled brilliantly, then gave me a swift kiss on the cheek. Then he tipsily swaggered down the hall, getting distracted by every person that spoke to him along the way. Slowly shaking my head, I prayed he didn't get sick before the night was through.

About an hour later, he paraded up onto the stage. The sound was deafening as the boys took their places for their last official performance here. Kellan had an adorable expression on his face. It was a mixture of joy, contentment, and excitement, with a touch of wistfulness and a good dollop of alcohol. He'd sobered up some after I'd made him down a plate of food, but I was pretty sure he was still feeling no pain.

Slinging his guitar over his body and grabbing his mic, he held his hand up to the massive crowd that had turned out; there were people still outside, the bar too packed to let them in. As the other boys adjusted their instruments, Kellan's eyes swept over his well-wishers. I swear the blue depths were a little misty as he shook his head, his face in disbelief.

"Wow...there's a lot of you here." He smiled gorgeously after speaking and a shrill scream of approval rang through the crowd. I flinched at the sound; Kellan grinned wider.

Popping the microphone off the stand, Kellan stepped to the edge of the stage; I prayed he wouldn't fall off of it. "I want to thank you all for coming, for supporting us for so long." He paused, waiting for the sudden noise to die down. The wistfulness in his expression took over as he locked gazes with some of the fans directly in front of him. Sighing, he shook his head. "I'm gonna miss this…"

He lifted his eyes and found mine. It took him a second to focus on me, but when he did, his entire face lit back up. Giggling, he muttered, "I'm so wasted right now."

The crowd cheered, screaming again, and I rolled my eyes. God, I hoped he could still play, I'd hate for his last show to suck. The melancholy of it being his last performance tried to sneak up on me but I pushed it back. There'd be time to dwell on it later. For now, while it was happening, I wanted to enjoy it. Smiling at him, I shook my head and went back to my duties. I heard him laugh again, then Evan started his intro.

They played their new song first, and I listened intently for any sign that Kellan was off. He wasn't. He was pitch-perfect, even his playing was right on. You wouldn't know by listening to him perform that he couldn't walk in a straight line anymore. Muscle memory…truly one of the marvels of the universe.

After their new song, the band rocked the bar with all of their greatest hits. I watched them whenever I could. Kellan smiled and flirted, looking right at home up on that small stage. There was nothing more natural to me than seeing Kellan singing with his friends, the black wall behind him, decorated with various styles of guitars, as his backdrop. While I was thrilled about Kellan's potentially exciting future, I was going to miss this.

Halfway through the set, Kellan played my song. I stopped working, taking my break so I could listen. It was the song he'd been singing the night we'd gotten back together. It was the song he'd written about us, after I'd broken his heart. I hated it…I loved it.

Edging my way through the fans, I squeezed into the front row. Someone threw their arms around me and I blinked at seeing my sister there. She'd stopped in after her shift at Hooters and melded into the crowd. I smiled at her, then focused all of my attention up at my boyfriend. He'd watched my progression through the pack of people and his eyes were burning holes through me as he sang his melancholy ode to heartache. It still brought tears to my eyes.

He stepped up to the edge of the stage. The fans went nuts at how close he was, their hands shooting out to touch him. Ignoring them for a moment, he dropped down to a knee right in front of me. Shutting out the world, shutting out the fans stroking the edge of his jeans, he locked his eyes on me and sang his heart out. The tears were streaming down my cheeks by the time he finished with his song.

Smiling, still dropped down on his knee, he crooked his finger at me and leaned forward. Forgetting that he was in the middle of a show, I swiped the tears away and leaned up to kiss him. The shrieks and hollers as our lips brushed together reminded me that we weren't alone in the back room anymore. I instantly wanted to pull away, embarrassed, but his hand reached out to grab my head. Chuckling in my mouth, he held me against him, deepening our kiss.

I flushed red-hot everywhere, feeling every eye in the bar on me. When he finally broke away, his grin was devilish. He knew how much stuff like that bothered me. I'd rather slink in the back unnoticed than have every woman gaping at me. Smacking him on the arm, I gave him my best, *We'll talk about this later*, look. Laughing, he stood back up.

As fans jostled against me, some asking questions, the rest trying to take my place and lean up to attach their lips to him somehow, I wiggled past my sister and past the mob of people now studying my every move. Even mortified, though, my lips burned in the absolute best possible way from where he'd touched me.

When the band's long set finally ended, the crowd erupted into applause and cat calls. Kellan grinned as he took it all in, looking a little more sober after his couple of hours onstage. Evan beamed as he clicked his sticks together. Matt looked down at the floor as he unstrung his guitar from around his neck, and Griffin raised his chin and surveyed his kingdom with the air of someone who felt entitled to it.

Grabbing the neck of his guitar, Kellan raised his hand for quiet. The bar hushed almost instantly, the opening and shutting front doors the only sound for a moment. Smiling warmly, Kellan said, "The band and I would like to thank you all again. You're the best fans that we ever could have asked for and we're going to miss playing for you every weekend…"

He paused, absorbing the sight of everyone enraptured by him, then, grinning wickedly, he pointed over to Matt. "Now, let's all go over to Matt's place and get royally fucked up!"

There was an ear-splitting noise of agreement by the crowd as Matt frowned at Kellan. Griffin patted him on the back as the group hopped off the stage. Kellan put his guitar back in its case and slung it over his shoulder; he was the only one that didn't just leave his instrument at the bar. I thought that maybe Matt and Griffin might grab their instruments this time, too, since they weren't coming back, at least, not for a really long time. But then I remembered that the girls and I were planning on packing up their stuff—Evan's drums, the guitars, and all of their sound equipment. We were closing up shop for them, so the guys didn't have to do it after the bar closed tonight, so they could relax and enjoy their last night in Seattle.

As I dwelled on that, Kellan pushed his way through the people to get to me. It was a process; at every step the crowd stopped and fondled him. He even brushed past I've-slept-with-you-girl that we ran into at school earlier. She and her friends had accepted his invitation to see the show. Glancing up at me, he quickly disengaged himself from her. I couldn't stop the small grin on my face at the disappointment in hers.

When he finally made it to me, he threw his arm around my shoulders. Sighing in my ear as he hugged me, he muttered, "I can't believe that was our last show here." Pulling back, he shrugged. "This place is home to me."

Shaking my head, I ran my knuckle over his cheek. "You'll be back," I said matter-of-factly and Kellan raised an edge of his lip. We really didn't know if the band would be back. Touring could lead to all kinds of possibilities, and all of them were bigger than playing at the same small bar every weekend.

Not wanting to think about it, I pointed to his guitar. "Why don't you go put that in the car and go with Matt to his place?" Sighing, I shook my head. "I'm sure you're eager to get to your after party." Noticing my sister behind him, I briefly waved at her as she darted out of the doors with Griffin.

Smiling, Kellan moved his arm around my shoulder down to my waist. "No, I thought I'd help you clean up here before we headed out…together."

Inwardly touched, I frowned. "It's your party…don't you want to go?" I looked around at the mass of people leaving the bar and the mess they'd left behind. "I might be stuck here another hour."

Chuckling, Kellan darted back into my vision. "Not if I stay to help." Smiling, he shook his head. "Besides, I want to spend my evening with you…not a bunch of drunk people I barely know."

Grinning, I leaned up to kiss him. "Okay, good. Then come back here after you put that away." He nodded against my lips and laughing a little, I added, "And don't forget to give me your keys."

Pulling back, he raised an eyebrow at me. "I sobered up on stage. I'm completely fine to drive."

Furrowing my brow, I narrowed my eyes. "You remember telling Denny earlier tonight that I don't hang out 'down there'?"

Kellan's eyes widened as he remembered that horribly embarrassing conversation that he'd drunkenly had earlier. Biting his lip as he backed away from me, looking for all the world like he was worried that I'd slap him again, he mumbled, "Oh, right…yeah, I'll get those keys to you."

I smiled knowingly and nodded. Yes, letting me drive his buzzed butt was the least he could do for me after that little comment.

Kellan ended up chatting with some of the longtime regulars instead of actually helping me, but that was all right. At least he was still with me, throwing me smiles whenever he looked my way. That was preferable to him at a party with a bunch of women who'd love a chance to give him a very intimate farewell present. And they'd probably have no qualms about hanging out "down there."

When the last customer had finally left and the place was clean enough that the day crew wouldn't cuss us out too bad, Kellan and I finally headed out to his car. Kate, Jenny and even Rita all followed us as I led the way to Matt and Griffin's place. Sulking the entire time I drove, Kellan told me to head to the outskirts of the city. Oddly enough, Matt and Griffin shared a townhouse in suburbia. It was an odd thought to have in conjunction with Griffin. Honestly, I'd always pictured him living above a brothel or something. I supposed he would, if they were legal here.

Parking about a half mile away from the house, our group walked up to the bustling home. As Kate and Jenny relayed funnier memories to Rita, making her laugh, I looked around the cramped neighborhood and wondered when the homeowners would called the cops on the noisy rockers in their midst.

Kellan opened the front door and walked through—another home-away-from-home for him. The noise of the stereo hit me first, the bass deep and thumping, then the rustle and hiss of dozens and dozens of bodies filled my ears. The sound only amplified when Rita shut the door behind her. Kellan smiled back at me and nodded his head in the direction he wanted us to go. Taking a second to put my bag and jacket in the already crammed full coat closet, I grabbed his hand.

He started leading us directly through the mass of people in the living room. Matt and Griffin's place was spacious compared to Kellan's. The open floor plan created ample space for dancing in the center of it. A group of clearly intoxicated partiers were already doing just that. A rotund guy was doing some sort of seductive shimmy, shaking his beer-belly to a group of giggling girls. Kellan chuckled at him as we passed, patting his shoulder to give us space. The girls instantly locked onto Kellan, ignoring the dancing joker in their midst.

I clutched Kellan's hand tightly, and we finally made our way through the gyrating swarm to the dining room, where another group of people were sitting at a six-foot-long dining table. The table had seen better days, the hard wood scraped and dented, but the dipsomaniacs in the room were too preoccupied with their drinking games to care. Kellan paused at the table, watching the chaos for a few seconds with an amused grin on his face.

As some perky blonde pouted that she had to finish her nearly full beer, Matt came up to our side and clapped Kellan's shoulder. "Hey, you made it. People have been asking for you."

I smiled over at Matt's cutely flushed face. His eyes were slightly unfocused. I figured he'd been indulging at his going away party. Rachel, behind him, placed her chin on his shoulder and smiled over at me. Her eyes were clear and bright. If Matt was caving in, she was not. I smiled and waved at her, instantly grateful that at least one person at this party was being sober and responsible.

Smiling over at me, Matt raised his eyebrows. "Hey, Kiera. We got everything…what's your poison?"

Glancing behind him into the kitchen, I noticed every beer and liquor on the planet covering the long counters. They seemed better stocked than Pete's. Laughing at Rita, who'd slipped into the room the other way and was now serving drinks, like she did back at the bar, I shook my head at Matt. "I'm good, really, thanks."

Matt nodded and let it go. Kellan twisted around and frowned at me. "Uh-uh, you need a drink."

Twisting my lip at him, I raised an eyebrow. "You're going to peer pressure me to drink?"

He smiled and rolled his eyes. Leaning into me, he placed his lips on my ear. I had to stop breathing for a second as his breath washed over my neck, igniting my body. "I don't want you spending the entire evening thinking about me leaving."

His words washed my brief desire away and I pulled back to look at him. Frowning, he added, "I don't want you spending our last night thinking about it…and you will, right?" Sighing, I reluctantly nodded. Yeah, his approaching departure was about all I could think about. Even the many distractions here couldn't really keep my mind from that path for long.

Sighing himself, he slung his arms around my waist and kissed my forehead. "I want you to loosen up and have a little fun with me." Sinking down to my eye level, he raised a brow. "Can you do that?"

Exhaling, I took a moment to memorize his features. Twisting back to Matt, who'd spent our brief discussion sucking on Rachel's neck while she tried to get him to stop, I tapped his shoulder. When he blinkingly looked at me, I pointed to the alcohol flowing freely around the room. "I'll take something…sweet."

Matt brightened and leaned in to hug me. I wasn't used to receiving this much affection from him, and I giggled as I patted his back. "I'll hook you up, Kiera!" he exclaimed, leaping to his assignment like I was a royal debutante that he had to please.

Kellan laughed at his friend as he kissed my neck. "Thank you," he murmured in my ear.

I was about to tell him that he'd be thanking me later if I got tipsy and threw up in his car, but just at that moment a scream sounded over the music in the living room. Kellan and I stepped back so we could peek into the large room. I started laughing instantly. Evan had found Jenny and had picked the tiny woman up and slung her over his shoulder. Jostling her a little bit, he was playfully smacking her bottom while she squealed.

While Kate tried to help her down, Jenny laughed and clung to her teddy bear of a boyfriend. Spotting me, she lifted her hand up. "Kiera, help me!"

Evan twisted around to look at us, also rotating Jenny around in the process. She kicked her feet but Evan had her tight. Smiling at Kellan and me, he waved a quick greeting. Kellan waved back and chuckled. Smiling down at me, a playful glint began to glow in Kellan's eyes.

My eyes widened as I stepped back. "Don't even think about it, Kyle." Putting my finger in his chest as his playful grin turned impish, I backed up into a dining room chair. The girl sitting there drunkenly stood up and grabbed my shoulders.

"Here, I'm done…you play." She forcefully plopped me down and I sat in a whoosh.

As soon as my bottom hit the seat, Matt was beside me, handing me a large glass filled with something orangey-pink in color. "Here you are, Kiera. Something sweet," he laughed as he straightened, "like you."

I smiled at Matt and thanked him just as someone placed a pair of dice in front of me. Frowning at the brunette who'd handed them to me, I started shaking my head. I really hadn't intended to play. Rolling her eyes, she put the dice in my palm and made my palm drop them.

The entire table mockingly groaned as I looked at a pair of ones. They all seemed to know what that meant…I had no clue. Kellan started laughing, and I glanced up at him, irritated. As Matt consolingly patted my shoulder, muttering something that sounded like, "I'll make you another one, Kiera," Kellan pointed to my glass.

"Snake eyes means you have to pound your drink." My mouth dropped open as I stared at him. Rita handed him a beer, her hand resting a little too casually on his shoulder. Kellan raised his beer to me. "Bottom's up, babe."

I smirked and shook my head. "I wasn't really playing…"

The entire table started booing and groaning; someone even threw a bottle cap at me. Kellan laughed and shrugged as I took a hold of my drink. Knowing that he wanted me to loosen up and have a little fun, and figuring this was as good a way as any, I tipped the drink down and forced myself to swallow it as fast as I could.

It freaking burned.

Whatever the hell Matt had made me was strong. By the end of the glass I was coughing and my eyes were stinging. A pleasant warmth filled my belly, and my head swam a little. I grinned up at Kellan as the table burst into cheers. God, by the approval level, you'd have thought that drinking was a sport, and I'd just scored the winning point.

As Matt handed me another beautifully peachy drink, someone commented to Kellan, "Dude, your girlfriend can really suck 'em down…lucky bastard."

Kellan started laughing but immediately stopped when he met my icy glare. Grabbing the commenter's jacket, Kellan hauled him from his seat. "My turn," he told him, sitting in his spot. I smiled as the dice made their way around to him. Jerk. I hope he got snake eyes, too.

As the evening progressed, my luck with the game didn't improve. I swear to God, every time anyone did anything, I was the one that had to drink. My glass never strayed from my lips long, and my head got fuzzier and fuzzier the longer I sat at the table. The drink, however, got smoother and smoother. It was practically candy at one point.

The brunette bitch to the right of me, the one who had made me start this little fiasco in the first place, giggled and gave me five drinks…just because. As I cursed and then started taking them, she adorably peeked her head at Kellan. "Sorry, Kellan, I'm really not trying to get your girlfriend drunk."

I wanted to leer at her and mutter, "Yeah, you are," but I wasn't finished with my assigned drinks yet.

Kellan smiled at the cute girl next to me, but before my jealousy could really start to flare up, his gorgeous blue eyes turned to mine. Even my slow head could appreciate the beauty in those dark depths. Keeping his gaze on me, he told her, "No, go ahead, get her drunk." Grinning devilishly, he added, "The odds of me getting lucky tonight will only increase if you do."

I wanted to blush and be embarrassed, but really, I'd had far too much alcohol by that point. In-between sips, I laughed and tossed out, "Since when have you ever needed help with your odds?" Surprisingly, I only slurred that a little bit.

Kellan charmingly cocked an eyebrow at me while the table rolled with laughter. He'd sobered up a bit on the stage, but with how long he'd been playing this game with me, he had to be as buzzed as I was. Smiling crookedly, he leaned forward on the table. "True…" he murmured drunkenly.

He was sitting kitty-corner to me at the massive table, but our feet were touching underneath it. Even with the table packed with people, the room crammed with watchers, with Kellan keeping his simmering eyes locked on mine, my body flaring with heat in response...we might as well have been alone.

He ran his teeth along his bottom lip, the move so sexy I bit my own, then he dropped his voice to a seductive level that I usually only heard when we were alone, wrapped in each other's bare arms. "But, maybe I could get you to do that one thing with your--"

Suddenly remembering that we were not alone and wrapped in each other's bare arms, I partially stood from the table, cutting him off. "Kellan Kyle! You shut the hell up!"

He laughed and sat back in his chair. Quite a few people in the room laughed with him and I finally felt that blush creeping into my cheeks. He shrugged and shook his head. "Just saying..." As I narrowed my eyes at him, making the room crack up even more, he stared at me in an unmistakably loving way. "You're such an adorable drunk, Kiera."

Grinning, my mood shifting again, I stood up. He watched me curiously as I leaned over the table, completely pausing the drinking game as everyone stared at us. For once I didn't care if they did. Kellan was my focus and I wanted him to kiss me...even if I had to crawl over the table to get to him.

Smiling at the image in my head, I crooked a finger at him. One edge of a lip curling up in a way that was dangerously attractive, he stood slightly and leaned over the table as well. Our lips met in the middle, my mouth parting as his tongue lightly brushed against me. My sloppy mind heard a few giggles and whistles, but Kellan's soft skin took up all of my concentration. I nearly wanted him to lay me down on this damaged, beer-stained surface.

As I was considering yanking him over the table so his entire body could be on mine, a particular voice broke through the chaos. "All right! We playing spin the bottle?"

Kellan and I broke apart at the same time and glared over at the annoyance who had just distracted us. As Griffin strode up to the table, I suppressed a sigh. Well, I'd known he was here...it had really been only a matter of time before Griffin made an appearance. Glancing behind him, I noticed my sister leaning against a wall, a familiar, satisfied expression on her face. I instantly did not want to know where they'd been hiding.

As Griffin stood beside Kellan, clapping a hand on his back, Kellan fully stood and shook his head. "No, we're not, Griffin."

Ignoring him, Griffin reached down to the table. Finding an empty beer bottle, he laid it on its side and spun it in a circle. The table instantly started laughing at the new aspect being introduced to our game.

With everyone chuckling around us, I sat back down, blushing. I hadn't played spin the bottle since the eighth grade, and I was pretty sure I didn't want to ever play it with Griffin. Even my frazzled brain knew that much. The brunette beside me bit her lip as she stared at Kellan; I knew exactly where she was hoping her turn would land her. I had no intention of letting her wish be fulfilled. Breech of party etiquette or not, no one was kissing Kellan tonight but me.

Griffin had an eager look on his face as he watched the brown bottle start to spin slower. As the room quieted in anticipation, I glanced over at Kellan; he was still standing in front of his seat, arms crossed over his chest as he watched Griffin with a smirk on his face. I wondered if Kellan was just as against anyone kissing me as I was against anyone kissing him. I wondered what he'd do if the bottle stopped on me? Oh God, what would I do if the bottle stopped on me? Griffin wouldn't let it go with a simple refusal. Even if he had to hunt me down, he'd stop at nothing to get his kiss.

Just when I was about to gather all of my slow senses together so I could make a bolt for the back door, the bottle stopped spinning and the room started laughing...hysterically. I couldn't figure out why until I looked down at the bottle, then I started laughing hysterically too. It had finally stopped moving with the neck pointed perfectly...at Kellan.

Kellan was twisting his lips unhappily as he stared down at it, then he suddenly looked back up at Griffin who was still staring at the bottle, maybe thinking it was going to move again. Griffin looked up at Kellan who adamantly shook his head and said, "Nuh-uh." The table laughed even harder and so did I, my eyes starting to water as I clutched my stomach.

Matt and Evan sauntered up to see what all the fuss was about while Griffin scowled, then shrugged. "Sorry, man. House rules, you play the bottle where it lies."

Kellan shook his head again while Evan and Matt joined in the laughter bouncing off the walls in the room. "Griff, we're not playing--"

Kellan couldn't finish his sentence. Griffin reached out and grabbed his head, pulling him in for a kiss...and not a peck. Kellan struggled for a second, then managed to break free. He took a step back with his hand raised at Griffin in warning. Several people around the table had to wipe tears of laughter out of their eyes, me included. I guessed I had been wrong about no one else kissing Kellan tonight.

"Dude! What the fuck!"

As Kellan glared at Griffin, Griffin took a step back and regarded Kellan with a puzzled expression. "Huh." Cocking his head as he looked Kellan over, he shrugged. "Yeah, I don't get what all the fuss is about...I've had better." He gestured with his hand while Kellan scowled, re-crossing his arms over his chest. "Maybe if you did this thing with your tongue..."

Evan and Matt bent over they were laughing so hard. Jenny and Kate joined them as they peeked their heads into the room. My sister was in hysterics against the wall, and even shy Rachel was quietly laughing. The few people who had dared to take a sip of their drink, were desperately trying not to sputter their drink everywhere. I really didn't want to laugh at a man kissing my boyfriend... and then calling him bad at it, but it was too funny, and I was too drunk. I laughed as hard as the rest of them, maybe harder, since I couldn't imagine anything worse than being Frenched by Griffin.

Kellan backhanded Griffin across the chest for his comment, then let out a small chuckle and shoved his shoulder away from him. "Get the fuck out of here, Griffin."

With an offended look, Griffin backed away from the table. "Whatever, man, it's just a suggestion. Take it or leave it." Clutching my sister's waist, he drew her in for a deep kiss. I cringed until they pulled away. Smiling at her breathless face, Griffin smirked. "I'll just save my skills for people who appreciate them." Anna laughed and brought his lips back to hers while Kellan rolled his eyes.

Matt clapped Griffin on the back and they left the room with Anna and Rachel. Matt was holding his stomach he was laughing so hard. Kellan closed his eyes and slowly shook his head. Opening them, he turned to look at where I was still giggling. He smiled at my enjoyment of his situation and then shook his head at me.

Kellan glanced around the room of people all still laughing at his misfortune. Chuckling himself, he picked up his beer from the table and motioned with it to the now-forgotten game. "Well, needless to say…I'm done."

Chapter 9 – A Night to Remember

The dice game resumed as the residual laughter died down with Griffin's departure. I blinked and watched Kellan's empty seat quickly become occupied by a fresh-faced boy who looked entirely too young to drink. Walking around to where I was sitting, merrily sipping away on my fruity drink, Kellan extended his hand out to me.

"Dance with me, beautiful girl?" Kellan cocked an eyebrow after he asked, and I swear I heard someone sigh…or maybe I did. My hazed brain couldn't really tell anymore.

Nodding, I grabbed his hand and let him pull me up. The alcohol already in my system rushed to my head as I changed positions. I'd been feeling pretty buzzed sitting at the table. Suddenly standing, I felt blitzed.

I giggled and stumbled a little as Kellan wrapped his arms around me. Unsteady himself, he asked, "You all right?"

I laughed and nodded again as he helped me take a few steps away from the loudly cheering table. The poor, fresh-faced boy had rolled the dreaded pair of ones, and he cringed as he stared at the amount of alcohol left in his plastic cup. I instantly felt sympathy for him, since that was the roll that did me in. Oddly enough, I wanted to give him a big hug and tell him that everything would be fine. I even made a drunken step towards him before Kellan pulled my arm in the other direction.

"This way, sweetheart."

Leaving the youth to his chosen fate, I twisted back to Kellan. Giggling, I tangled my arms around his waist. With stumbling, erratic steps, we both made it to the center of the packed living room. People wished Kellan luck whenever they came upon him, but Kellan's eyes never left mine as he acknowledged them. It was like we were alone in this house swarming with strangers.

As a heavy beat thumped out a seductive rhythm, Kellan's hands slid up my back, then down to my hips. My extra-sensitive body felt every section that he touched. It was as if he was dragging a mild electric current over me; a tingling sensation lingered long after his fingers passed. When he put one of his legs between mine, forcing our bodies to straddle the other's, I gasped. The tingle shifted to a full-on fire.

Our hips moved in time to the beat in such an intimate way that I should have been embarrassed. One of the wonders of mind-altering substances…pesky little things like inhibitions flew out when alcohol flew in. As Kellan's hands continued to caress my body, his palm running up the front of my red Pete's shirt, he rested his forehead against mine. More grinding than dancing, we lightly breathed on each other. It was maddening, and the rest of the world fell away.

When his hand blatantly stopped on my breast, his thumb running back and forth over the dangerously sensitive spot, I whimpered. He smiled at hearing it, even over the music. Feeling numb and incredibly turned on, I reached up and buried my fingers in his thick hair, closing the distance between us and pulling his head down to mine.

Whatever Griffin had been complaining about was beyond me—Kellan was fabulous with his tongue. As his lips melded with mine, our light breaths became nearly frantic pants. He squeezed my nipple between his thumb and finger and I groaned...loudly. He hissed in a breath, his other hand sliding inside my pants to rest over my cotton-covered backside.

I wanted his hand on the other side. I wanted all of his body on the other side. Jerking his head down so I could moan in his ear, I whispered, "I want you...now." Well, I think I whispered it.

Kellan pulled his head away and stared at me. The heat in his eyes was glorious. Those I-want-to-have-sex-with-you eyes had a way of turning my insides into molasses, warm and gooey...delicious. His eyes darted down my body as he adjusted the way our hips lined up. He didn't have to say a word; I could feel the hardening mass in his jeans that was telling me that he wanted me, too...right now.

Licking his lips, he looked up at where we were—surrounded by a bunch of dancing, drunk people in the middle of Matt's living room. Bringing his eyes back down to mine, he reached up to disentangle my fingers from his hair. Lacing our hands together, he nodded his head towards the hallway.

Leaning into my body, he growled into my ear, "Come with me."

God, I nearly did.

Clutching his hand with both of mine, I bit my lip and eagerly nodded. I had no idea where he intended to take me or even what exactly we were going to do once we got there, but I really didn't care either. I just wanted to be alone with him.

Giggling, I pressed into his back as he worked us through the throngs of people. Most clapped him on the shoulder as he walked by, the girls that were brave enough dragged their fingers down his arm suggestively. I glared at those girls but Kellan ignored them, focused on his task of getting us alone. As one trio of women blatantly stared at his ass, I nearly yelled, "Stare all you want, I'm the one he's about to screw!"

Thank God Kellan jerked me forward just as I was about to say it. Stumbling a little, I forgot to. Smiling back at me as I regained my balance, he laughed as he managed to finally get us into the hallway. Twisting to face me, he brought his free hand around to cup my cheek. Pulling my head into his, he found my lips again. I groaned as the sweetness of his breath hit me. I normally didn't care for the smell of beer, but Kellan could make anything sexy.

Kellan walked us down the hallway backwards while we made out, occasionally running us into a few partiers that didn't move aside fast enough. He stopped beside a closed door. I didn't know whose door it was or where it led, and as his tongue flicked along mine, I didn't care, just so long as he opened it soon.

Missing the handle on his first attempt, Kellan tried again. He finally opened the door on his third try, and we hurried inside. He closed it blindly, flicking the light switch on afterwards. As Kellan locked the door, I briefly looked at what room we were in. My light-as-air head hoped it wasn't Griffin's. Luckily it wasn't...it was the bathroom.

Frowning, I looked up at Kellan. "This is a bathroom."

He nodded, his mouth parted as his eyes locked on my lips. "Yeah, I know."

I wanted to object or something, but his mouth came back to mine and the only sound I made was a moan of delight. Wanting him so bad I ached everywhere, I threw my hands back into his hair and pressed my body against his. Our lips were frantic as the passion within us boiled over.

Overcome with desire, I growled, "You always make me feel so good...I'm going to make you feel good, too, Kellan. I want you so much."

He nearly panted as my lips shifted to his neck. Kellan closed his eyes and let his head drop back. "Oh God...I love it when you're like this."

Breathing heavy myself, I peeked up at him. "Like what...drunk?" I started to laugh, but his skin was calling me and instead, I drug the tip of my tongue along his throat.

He hissed in a quick inhale, then swallowed. "No," he breathed. "Confident...like you finally get it."

I pulled away to look at him and he brought his head back down to stare at me. "Get what?" I whispered, licking the edge of his lip as I pressed my aching body into his clearly strained one.

His eyes fluttered for a second before he refocused on me. "That I'm yours...that you can take me...anywhere, anytime, anyway. That you own every piece of me."

Heat and desire pooled in me. "If I own you, then I want to take you...now...here. I want to make you come," I murmured, surprisingly myself.

As he smiled crookedly, I pushed him against the counter, grinding my hips into his and yanking his head back down to mine. I wanted him so bad that it didn't even bother me anymore that we were in a tiny bathroom, making out in the middle of a raucous party. I moaned in his mouth, panting with need as his tongue brushed mine. His breath was equally fast as he cupped my bottom, pulling me tighter into his fully ready body.

"God...yes. I need you, Kiera," he breathed into my mouth. "Can you feel how much I need you?" I could only whimper in response, my fingers brushing down his chest to pull feebly at the denim looped around the one button holding his jeans closed.

People knocked and banged on the door, but we ignored them and they eventually walked away, grumbling something my buzzed mind couldn't make out under the loud music streaming in from the living room. Breaths and hearts racing, our mouths attacked each other's. While my numb fingers tried unsuccessfully to unfasten his jeans, his slid up my ribs, sweeping my t-shirt with it. Giving up on the button, since my drunken fingers never could unfasten them, I helped him pull my shirt over my head.

My hands came down to his shirt as the beat boomed on through the door. Within seconds his bare chest was before me and I pressed our stomachs together, relishing the similar heat. Tangling my hand back through his hair, I forced his lips back to mine. His fingers slid across my necklace, feeling the symbolic representation of him on my skin. Then they slipped into a bra cup, pinching a nipple. I cried out, the sound echoing in the tiny room.

"Uh, Kellan? You in there?"

A voice behind the door broke through our growing moans of passion, but I was far too drunk to care. I ignored the irritated person just as much as Kellan did. His mouth broke away from mine, sweeping the cup of my bra aside to lock around a nipple, his tongue swirling around the rigid peak. Groaning, I held his head to me and ground my hips into his, needing to feel that wonderful hardness, that connection full of erotic promises.

"Dude, Kellan, I know you and Kiera are in there…people saw you two head that way. Open the door."

Cursing, Kellan separated from me. I instantly went for his mouth, but he pushed me back a little and unlocked the bathroom door right next to us. Cracking it open, he scowled at the person on the other side of it. "What, Matt?"

I laid my head on Kellan's chest and stared blankly at Matt looking at us through the slit in the door. He didn't look happy. "Are you about to have sex in my bathroom?"

Without missing a beat, Kellan responded with, "Yes," and started closing the door. My hazed mind found it funny, and I started laughing.

Matt stopped the door with his hand. "Kell, we only have one bathroom. I don't want people peeing in my kitchen sink."

Sighing in irritation, Kellan opened the door wider and glared at Matt. Matt looked down at Kellan's bare chest, then my half-naked chest, then snapped his eyes up to Kellan's eyes. Kellan shook his head and shrugged. "Bedroom or bathroom," was all he said.

Matt scrunched his brow and Kellan repeated himself, raising his eyebrows. "Bedroom or bathroom? You pick, Matt."

Sighing, Matt rolled his eyes. "Fine, but make it quick."

Grinning, Kellan slammed the door shut and locked it again. I giggled as my mind swam. On the other side I heard Matt slurringly yell, "And clean up when you're done, damn it!"

Already ignoring him, Kellan and I resumed attacking each other. My amped-up body responded instantly to everywhere he touched me. I was on fire as his fingers traveled around to unsnap my bra. I moaned, "Yes," quite loudly, as his mouth took me in. Pushing against him, I tried undoing his pants again. He laughed when I still couldn't.

"You never could do drunk undressing," he murmured, loosening the button and shoving his jeans down.

Not answering him, my hand slipped right into his boxers. Grasping the thickness I wanted more than anything, I squeezed the base. He whimpered and pushed me against the wall. My head thudded as I lightly bumped into it. I heard myself murmur, "Yes," again, but it nearly felt like someone else was saying it.

Panting in my ear, his fingers worked on removing the rest of my clothes. As I slid my hand up and down the hard length of him, he ripped down my jeans, shoving them harshly off my hips.

Backing away from me, he disengaged my hand from himself so he could slip off my shoes and rip my pants and underwear off my legs. Completely bare before him, and way too drunk and horny to care, I ran my fingers up my body. Cursing under his breath, he slipped off his shoes, then the rest of his clothes. Licking my lips at the sight of him, I moaned that I wanted him in me. It echoed around the room, and I smiled.

Grinning devilishly at me, his own eyes unfocused, he shook his head. "Not yet."

I frowned as I leaned against the wall, watching him standing before me, but way too far away for what I needed. Then he dropped to his knees in front of me. My slow head couldn't figure out what he was doing, especially when he grabbed my leg and pulled it up over his shoulder. I realized right where his head lined up when he brought his mouth to my aching core.

Crying out, I smacked my head against the wall again. It felt incredible, and as he sucked, swirled and stroked the most sensitive part of me, I made noises that would have had me burying my head in embarrassment on a confident day.

Just as I was moaning his name, rocking my hips against him, he separated from me. Stumbling back a step, he brought his mouth back up to mine and shoved his tongue inside. I tangled my fingers in his hair, pulling him flush to my body.

It seemed deathly quiet in the house. I couldn't even make out the thump of the music anymore, but I could not have cared less—I needed him so bad. Groaning, I grabbed his throbbing mass and tried leading him to where I needed him. He stubbornly removed my hand...tease. "I want you inside me...now," I begged out, panting.

Pulling me away from the wall, he stumbled back a step. His finger came down to swipe across my wet flesh and I cried out. "Oh God, please...take me, Kellan."

Muttering, "Yes," to himself, he kissed down my neck, down my collarbone, and down to my breasts again. I swiveled against his hips, desperate for more. I was nearly ready to climax from the anticipation alone.

Walking backwards, he stumbled into something and sat down. He looked around, surprised, then laughed when he realized he was sitting on the closed toilet. He smiled, looking up at me, but I couldn't smile anymore. I had an ache that I needed him to finish satisfying.

Straddling his hips, I lowered myself onto him. He stopped smiling when he penetrated me. Closing his eyes, he sucked in a quick breath through his teeth and dropped his head back to a stack of towels behind him. "Oh God, Kiera...yes."

Watching him closely, I rocked my hips. The feel of him in me was the most fulfilling thing my drunken body had ever experienced. He cringed in ecstasy, biting his lip. I smiled, loving how I affected him, and loving how he affected me. Rocking against him again, I arched my back and cried out his name. He opened his eyes and looked up at me. "You're beautiful," he murmured, caressing my chest, my hips.

I bit my lip at his words, rocking against him again. The sensation heated up my numb core and I quickly felt the desire rising to a nearly painful level. Dropping my head back, I cried out repeatedly in an ever escalating rhythm. I couldn't stop myself...it felt so good. I was so close.

"Fuck," he muttered, sitting up to suck on my breast again.

I moaned at how delicious that word was, but frowned on principle. "Don't swear," I muttered, pressing into him harder so he slid even deeper inside of me. Standing slightly, I used my body weight to slam myself against him. It was hard, deep and intense.

He cringed and panted, grabbing my hips encouragingly. "I'm sorry...fuck, I'm sorry...just please, don't stop." He pulled my hips into his body in a faster rhythm than I was going and I matched him.

Feeling wild and uncharacteristically unrestrained, I bucked against him, thrashing my body into his. He was moaning just as hard as I was as I felt the buildup approaching. By the look on his face, I knew he was there, too, and I begged him heatedly to come with me.

He opened his mouth, his breath halting as I felt him starting to explode. He groaned low and intense right after, but the sound was lost in the cry I made. I clutched his head to me as I hit my peak. I swear my vision phased in and out, and not because of my intoxicated state. Every fiber of my body tingled with pleasure, starting from my belly and expanding out. My toes even curled as I rode out the sensation coursing through my body with a chorus of, "Yes, yes...Kellan...God...yes."

As we panted against each other, holding the other tight, I thought I heard a strange sort of clapping and laughing from the hallway, but I was way too far gone to care. "I love you," I murmured, burying my head in his shoulder.

Sighing contently under me, he rested his head in the crook of my neck. "I love you, too."

We stayed like that for a minute more, until I started to shiver and people started knocking on the door again. Stumbling and fumbling around, we managed to get dressed with everything we'd come into the room wearing. At least, I hoped so. I'd have hated for Griffin to find anything of mine that I might have missed.

When Kellan opened the bathroom door and we stepped through it, every eye turned our way. I blinked, my head swimming as I wondered why everyone was staring at me. Then the whistles started and people nearby clapped Kellan on the back. Thinking they were still congratulating him on his upcoming trip, I shrugged and smiled. People laughed even more at my reaction.

Biting back a smile, Kellan led me into the living room. Once we were in the center, Griffin approached us. I naturally took a step away from him, but grinning broadly, he stepped right up to me, handing me a bottled beer.

"Kiera, I think I love you," he gushed. Cringing, I took the beer and drank it, just so he'd back up a step.

Laughing, Griffin smacked Kellan on the chest. "You are the luckiest fucking son of a bitch." Handing Kellan a beer from his other hand, Griffin playfully scowled. "I mean, I hated you before, but now, I really can't stand you."

Kellan started nodding and pushing Griffin's shoulder away, repeatedly glancing at me with a look of concern, like he thought that I might start to flip out. My fuzzy mind was too hazed to know why. Shaking my head at Griffin's odd comments, I tipped back my beer again. The alcohol had just hit my lips when Griffin said, "That was so hot…like, off the scales hot. You guys should make a porno…I'd totally buy it!"

The people around us laughed at his comment and I started choking on the beer I'd just swallowed. Wait? What was Griffin talking about? What was hot? Wait…did he say porno? My drunken cheeks flushed at just the thought.

Just as comments and the crowd's stares and laughter slowly began clicking into place for me, Kellan shoved Griffin away from us and made his way to the stereo. Turning it up loud again, he hopped onto a nearby coffee table. With Kellan dancing up there like he was at a club downtown, I stopped trying to piece together the mystery that was Griffin. I really didn't want to think about him and his rude comments anyway.

Kellan extended a hand out to me as a group of girls immediately started circling on the floor around him. Giggling, I joined him on Matt and Griffin's sturdy furniture. Laughing, Kellan and I finished our beers as we danced. Kellan sang all of the fun, anthem songs to the crowd, riling them up to party more, but he sang the sweeter songs directly to me, moving our bodies together in a rhythm that was both beautiful and erotic. I finally felt equal to every gorgeous girl in the room with the way he stared at me, moved with me, sang to me. For several wonderful, hazy-brained hours, we were all able to put aside the painful moments that were quickly approaching with the dawn, when the boys would be leaving, and we danced the rest of the night away. Well, the rest of the early morning.

My head felt like someone was banging on a gong when I groggily woke up the next day. My mouth was dry, too. So dry it hurt. I wanted water, but I was too afraid to move. I didn't want my banging head to turn into a spinning stomach.

Peeking an eye open, I risked a glance at my environment. I really didn't see anything, other than the body crushed against mine. A t-shirt filled most of my vision and I froze, trying to remember how and when I'd fallen asleep. Everything from last night was so blurry that I wasn't even sure where I'd fallen asleep.

Hoping against hope that the body lying underneath me was Kellan, I attempted to lift my head. The gong increased in volume; my vision flexed in and out. Finally, I was able to focus on a pair of perfectly plump lips. Exhaling in relief as I took in Kellan's familiar face, I focused on the rest of my body.

Sore and a little achy, I was lying on top of Kellan, nearly head to foot. The two of us were cuddled up on a long, narrow couch, Kellan just inches away from the edge of it. It wasn't my garish couch or Kellan's lumpy one either. My arms were heavy as they rested on his chest. My legs tangled up with his felt leaden. Even my girly parts felt overworked…although, I wasn't sure why.

I was sure I would be paying for last night's overindulgence for the next three days. Groaning softly, I felt the warm arms laced around my waist tighten. "Mornin'."

Flinching a little at his soft words, I shut my eyes. Peeking just one open, I looked up at him. "I'm right here, you don't have to be so noisy," I whispered.

Chuckling as he stretched his body beneath mine, he opened his eyes to gaze at me. Bringing a hand up to run a finger back through my hair, he quietly whispered, "How do you feel?"

Cringing, I leaned into his hand and he obligingly held my head. I was immediately grateful, since I didn't have the strength to keep it up anymore. "Like a marching band took up residence in my skull."

He grinned, looking tired but in much better shape than I. His eyes glanced down my body. "How's your stomach?"

Not wanting to give my stomach the opportunity to revolt by giving it any attention, I shrugged. "It's fine…for now." Grimacing and trying to swallow with my completely parched throat, I added, "I'm mainly thirsty."

Kellan nodded, like he'd expected as much. "Matt's not up yet, but I'm sure he wouldn't mind you getting some water out of his fridge." He grinned a little wickedly, then added, "Unless you'd prefer the water from the bathroom."

My eyes widened at hearing that we were still at Matt's. I supposed that was a good thing, since neither of us had been in driving condition last night. We must have literally danced until we crashed. I vaguely remembered being tired and sitting down with Kellan. Sitting must have turned into lying, and that must have turned into sleep.

Lifting my head off his hand, I took in his playful expression as he watched me. Shaking my head, very carefully, as it was still throbbing, I furrowed my brows. "Why do you look like…?" My thoughts drifted off as his comment stung my ears. The bathroom… Even vaguer memories of a tiny, enclosed place echoing with heated sounds of sex filled my brain.

Forgetting my head and my hangover, I sat up straight on his lap. He grunted a bit as my weight shifted to his sensitive parts. My eyes wide, I said at full volume, "Did we have sex in the bathroom?"

We both cringed at my statement and I rethought my assessment that Kellan was fine. Peeking an eye at me, he chuckled. My cheeks heated as I desperately hoped no one else had heard me say that. Slow and seductive, Kellan murmured, "Oh…yeah."

My eyes widened and I hoped that nobody at the party knew about that moment. As Kellan smiled at me, a satisfied expression sliding over his momentary pain, memories fought their way to the surface. Memories of people clapping…whistling…cheering…Griffin…

My hands flew to my mouth as I started shaking my head. "Oh, my God."

Slowly lowering my fingers, my head suddenly felt fine in comparison to the dread in my veins. I whispered, "Did they all hear us?"

Looking anywhere that wasn't me, Kellan bit his lip. "Well...we really weren't being quiet and it is a pretty small bathroom...so..."

Groaning again, I dropped my head to his chest. "Oh, my God," I muttered, mortified.

Chuckling under me, Kellan rubbed my back. "Don't worry about it, Kiera. Everyone told me they thought it was hot."

I jerked my head up, regretting the quick movement, but needing to glare at him. "Everyone?"

Twisting his lip, he shrugged. "Just the few I talked to after you passed out."

Dropping my head back to his chest, I whimpered. Good God, everyone at the party had listened to me having sex. And I was remembering it more and more now that we were talking about it. It was good sex. It was great sex. It was loud sex! I could never show my face in public again, let alone ever go back to Pete's. "Oh, my God..."

Still chuckling lightly underneath me, Kellan kissed my head. "You were letting go, Kiera...I liked it." As I collected my embarrassment, mixing that pain with my aching body, Kellan whispered, "Was that your first time in a bathroom in the middle of a party?"

I lifted an eyebrow and pursed my lips. "Yeah, that was a definite first."

Fully smiling, he laced his arms over my back, pulling the rest of my body down to his. "Good," he replied spunkily. When I furrowed my brows, he shrugged and added, "I like giving you firsts, remember?"

Not able to help myself, I shook my head and smiled at him. Then, remembering something else, I frowned. "Did Griffin seriously say we needed to make porn?" Kellan twisted his lips and nodded. I groaned, sagging my head back down to his chest. "Oh, because he heard us...heard me. Goddamn it."

Kellan laughed at my seldom use of swear words and rubbed my back soothingly. "You'll live, Kiera. And on the bright side, it will be a night you'll probably never forget." I took a second to peek up and smirk at him before lowering my head back to his chest. He was definitely right about that...I would never forget Griffin telling me that he'd gladly buy my sex tape. "And don't be embarrassed...I'm not."

I lifted my head to look at him again and he happily shook his. "You were hot, and every guy in that place wished they were me in that bathroom. I don't feel the least bit bad that every man was jealous," he grabbed my hips, pulling me into him, "as long as you're only mine."

Smiling, I answered, "I am."

Lifting his head to lightly kiss me, he grinned. "Good."

Snuggling back down with him, I tried to let the drunken evening go, so I could concentrate on this moment. I only had a few hours left with the man who had my heart, who stole my breath. There would be time later to beat myself up over the mortifying situation I had put myself in at a huge going away party.

Sighing, I snuggled my head into his chest and tried not to think about his departure. I couldn't yet, it was too hard. Instead, I focused on what my body was telling me—I needed water...and aspirin. While he rubbed my back and kissed my head, I murmured, "Do you want some water? I could bring you some?"

Stretching underneath me again, he inhaled a big breath. "No, but I could use some coffee...I'll come with you."

I nodded and prepared my body to move. Kellan was so comfortable to lie on, my body rebelled, staying exactly where it was. Kellan chuckled a few moments later when I still hadn't moved. "Need help?" he whispered.

I smiled, my head still resting against his chest, almost above the tattoo of my name. His arms holding me close to his body, he sat up. I could feel his muscles flexing under his clothes and I couldn't stop myself from picturing that hard body in its natural state—completely bare.

I giggled as he adjusted us to a standing position, then groaned as my head painfully complained about the new angle. Biting my lip, I swayed a little on my feet. Kellan's hands came up to massage my temples and I smiled at him gratefully; it felt wonderful against my throbbing skull. His face was weary, but still perfect. He did not look like a man who'd been slinging back alcohol all night. With his hair all crazy from sleeping on the couch, and slight stubble along his jaw, he looked...yummy.

I turned away from his perfection, positive that I did not look quite so...appealing. His warm lips rested on my forehead for a second, then he pulled me into the kitchen. We stepped around people lying on the floor. Apparently, we were not the only ones that slept over. In the kitchen, a pair of partiers was at the table playing poker from what I could make out. Thankfully, not strip poker, since the guy and girl were still dressed.

Kellan nodded at them as they blinked and looked around, like they'd just now noticed it was light outside and the party was over. You'd think that the person snoring at the end of the table would have clued them in to that fact.

While I rested my tired head on his back, Kellan went about making a pot of coffee. He knew exactly where everything was in Matt's house. When the pot started percolating, Kellan grabbed me a glass from the cupboard and filled it with water. I inhaled it I was so thirsty.

He smiled at me, kissing my head as I sputtered on some of the liquid going down the wrong pipe. As I was trying to cough quietly, Matt shuffled into the room. Yawning as he scratched his chest, he nodded at us. Remembering that he'd seen me half-naked last night, I averted my beet red face from him.

"Hey, guys...good morning," he mumbled. Cautiously, I peeked back at him. Matt had been pretty far gone last night, maybe he didn't remember?

Leaning against the counter with his arms wrapped around me, Kellan nodded. "Mornin', how do you feel?"

Matt ran a hand through his disheveled hair, then massaged his temples; I figured his head was throbbing too. "Peachy," he muttered sullenly, opening a cupboard to get a glass.

Kellan chuckled as he held me tight, looping his thumbs through my belt buckle straps. Matt looked over at his friend as he ran some cold water into his glass; the sound of the running faucet pierced my aching head. I laid my head back against Kellan's shoulder, wishing I could fast-forward through this excruciatingly painful part of my recovery.

"God, it's annoying how chipper you are in the morning," Matt muttered, taking a long gulp of water. Kellan only smiled wider, rocking me a bit in his arms. When Matt paused, he added, "I hope you're not like that on the road…it would really get on my nerves."

Kellan laughed, and I frowned, not wanting to think about that part yet. Matt made it worse by adding, "Bus leaves in a few hours, so we should start getting people up…especially Griffin."

Kellan sighed and nodded. I bit my lip; I *really* didn't want to think about this yet. Finishing his glass, Matt frowned at me. "You okay, Kiera?" Adjusting my face, I gave him a small nod. He smiled back warmly, then his lips twisted. "You, uh…have fun last night?"

He asked it innocently, but his face flushed a little when he said it, and I knew that he did indeed remember. Wanting to bury my head in the sand and stay there, I gave him a small smile and squeaked out, "Yeah…thanks for…letting us come…"

My voice trailed off as I realized what I said. Matt's light flush turned as red as mine. In recovery mode I quickly added, "Over, thanks for letting us come over," but it was too late…I'd already said it in a horribly embarrassing way. Matt mumbled something about needing to get ready and quickly fled the room.

Kellan struggled to not laugh, but as soon as the poker players started busting up, he too gave up trying to hold back. Twisting around, I smacked him repeatedly in the chest. It only made him laugh harder. Wiping his eyes, he shook his head at me. "Oh God, Kiera, you're so damn cute."

I crossed my arms over my chest and tried to walk away from him, but he held me tight, pulling my body back into his. Turning me around, he wrapped his arms around my waist, holding me in place. Sighing at the look of total embarrassment on my face, he shook his head. "I'm gonna miss your adorable awkwardness." He sighed again, sadder this time. "So much," he whispered.

I bit my lip as I searched his face, feeling the impending farewell in the air. I wasn't ready for it. I didn't want to say goodbye to him. Slinging my arms around his neck, I held him as tight as I could. I'd have held him to me forever if there was a way, but I knew there wasn't. I had to let him go. I had to let him live his dream, no matter how much it hurt.

Eventually the rest of the partiers woke up and shuffled off, wishing Kellan and Matt a great time on their adventure. As the poker players were blinking at the sun in the doorway, Evan and Jenny stepped through it. Feeling grimy and tired, I waved at a fresh-faced Jenny. She and Evan clearly hadn't celebrated as hard as I had.

Seeing my worn features, she walked over to the couch to give me a hug while Evan excitedly clapped Kellan on the back. "You all right, Kiera?" she laughed out.

Groaning, I laid my head back on the cushions. "Yep." Looking over at her, I frowned. "I don't remember you and Evan leaving last night?"

Her cheeks flushed a little as she glanced at the boys standing a few feet away from us. "Yeah, well, you were a little preoccupied at the time." Kellan glanced her way mid-conversation and she chuckled at him.

I covered my face with my hands. God, this humiliation was going to last all friggin' day. Laughing a little harder, Jenny pulled my hands down and gave me a warm smile. "I'm glad you had a good time, Kiera." Shaking her head, she added, "Evan and I were afraid you'd spend the night moping."

I smiled and looked over at Evan, the tatted, buzzed-cut rocker with a heart as big as Jenny's. Meeting my eye, he nodded at me warmly and I let the lingering discomfiture fade. These people loved me, they wouldn't deliberately make me regret a carefree moment with my boyfriend. Especially since the release was a much needed one, in light of our imminent, emotional goodbye.

Rachel quietly joined us on the couch while Matt took a shower. I longingly listened to the flowing water, wishing I could take one next. A shower might help ease the incessant throbbing in my head. Then, of course, hearing Matt in the bathroom reminded me of being in that bathroom myself. Just as my face was flushing, Kellan turned from his conversation with Evan to grin at me, like he knew exactly what I was thinking. Biting my lip, I looked away.

"Kiera, when Matt's done, what's say you and me go suds up?"

Frowning, I glanced over at the last band member to enter the living room. Griffin was smiling at me in a way that I didn't care for, his eyes clearly imagining me in a sexual scenario. Giving me a kiss in the air, he added, "I want to hear you moan my name like you did Kell's."

I was just about to walk over and pummel the man when he was hit by about four different people. My sister, sleepily shuffling up behind him, smacked him over the head. Jenny, beside me, chucked a couch pillow at him, hitting him in the face. Rachel even got into the mix by tossing the TV remote into his gut. But Kellan was the one that fazed him the most.

Striding the few steps over to him, Kellan grabbed a thick section of his chin-length hair and jerked Griffin's face into his. "Knock it off, Griffin, or I'll knock it off for you." His indigo eyes dark and cold, Kellan searched Griffin's face. By the chill in his voice, I knew that Kellan wasn't joking. He was finally fed up with Griffin teasing me, sexually assaulting me with his comments.

As tension built up in the room, Evan placed a hand on Kellan's shoulder, trying to calm him down. Anna tried to push Kellan back, but Kellan didn't budge and kept his stony face an inch away from Griffin's. Griffin's light blue eyes looked scared for a moment...then he started laughing.

"Did you want another kiss, bro? All you had to do was ask."

Exasperated, Kellan finally released the idiot. The tension in the room immediately dissolved as Griffin doubled over. "Dude, you should have seen your face! That was awesome! I really thought you were gonna hit me." Kellan grunted and walked away as Griffin stood straight and draped his arm over Anna. Pointing at Kellan's retreating back as he walked into the kitchen, Griffin laughed out, "Say it again, Kell!" Mocking his voice, Griffin growled, "Knock it off, or I'll knock it off for you."

Anna smacked him in the chest, but laughed a little too. Sighing, Griffin shook his head. "Ah, that was classic."

Chapter 10 – This Isn't Goodbye

Once the boys had cleaned up and gotten their stuff ready, it was time to head out. Kellan had already packed a bag and shoved it in his trunk, probably figuring that the party would be an all nighter. I hadn't, and was still wearing my Pete's uniform under my jacket as I slid into Kellan's Chevelle beside him.

I hated the drive there. I felt like how an army wife must feel, driving her man off to war. All right, I take that back, the situations were nothing alike. Those women lived with the knowledge that they may never see their husbands again. Kellan touring wasn't nearly so treacherous. But…it still felt the same. And in all honesty, the possibility that I could never see him again was there. Not because of him being killed in battle, but because he could be swept away by fame.

He could be discovered by some record big-wig, offered the world, then sent off to parts unknown to become a cog in the entertainment industry wheel. He wouldn't have time for me then. And, if he was constantly surrounded by dying-to-please star-effers…he might not want me then either.

Rolling my eyes as I watched the tail lights of Griffin's van and Evan's car, I reminded myself that Kellan wasn't interested in a woman who was only interested in his fame, and not in him as a person. He'd had that…for years…and he wanted more. He wanted me. Even if this was his moment, he wouldn't give up on us. I just had to keep believing that.

Setting his hand on my thigh, Kellan looked over at me. "It won't happen."

I blinked as I looked over at him, wondering how he knew my thoughts. Smiling, he shook his head and pointed at me. "Whatever bad scenario you've created in your head, where I become a rich and famous douche and leave you high and dry…it won't happen that way."

Frowning, I tilted my head at him. "I thought you said you couldn't read minds."

Laughing, he twisted back to the road. "I can't…I just know how you think is all." Glancing back at me, he added, "You think you're not enough for me. You think I'll see all the hot tail in front of me and I'll dive into it without a moment's hesitation. You think I'll cheat…because I won't be able to help myself."

He scowled and I sighed. Shaking my head, I said, "And now you're thinking that I'll be so lonely and depressed, imagining you with every starlet wannabe out there, that I'll find comfort in another man's arms. You think I'll cheat…because I'll assume that you already are."

Exhaling, he muttered, "Well, aren't we a pair."

Resting my head on his shoulder, I whispered, "I won't, Kellan. Even if I do think that about you, and I'm not saying that I will think that, but…either way, I won't…I'm yours."

He laid his head over mine. "And I won't…because I've only ever been yours."

I closed my eyes, desperately wanting to believe him. Moments later, we arrived at our destination. Kellan pulled into a parking space next to Evan and shut the car off. We sat for a moment in silence while Evan opened his door beside us. He rapped on our window, a wide smile on his face. Jenny opened her side and joined him, waving in our direction. As the pair met up with Matt, Griffin, Rachel and Anna, Kellan and I still sat in his car, enjoying the last moment of quiet before he had to go.

There was a flurry of activity a few rows behind us. Several guys, who I assumed were members of the other bands, were bustling around three long motor home-like busses. Uniformed bus drivers talked with a few of them. There were a lot of guys around, girls fawning over them as they said their goodbyes. With a lot more passengers than busses, I figured Kellan was right about being cramped. He might not know the other band members now, but he certainly would by the end of the tour. At least, with that many people already on board, there wouldn't be a lot of room for girls. Although...I supposed nothing would prevent them from caravanning after the busses, stopping at the various places along the way. That was a disheartening thought, and I immediately forced it to the back of my head.

As I looked back at the mass of people at the very edge of the super mall parking lot, Kellan twisted the keys out of the ignition and handed them to me. I blinked as I took them. "Take care of her for me, okay?" His deep eyes seemed reluctant to let the keys go as my fingers curled over them.

My eyes widened. "You're giving me your car?"

Slightly frowning, he shook his head. "I'm just letting you borrow her." He lifted an eyebrow. "I'll want her back." I smiled a little at the thought of cruising around in his muscle car and his frown deepened. "Make sure you get the oil changed and fill her up with premium...and don't drive on the hills if it snows and no joy riding..." Pondering for a moment, he quickly added, "And don't let Anna drive her." Rolling his eyes, he muttered, "I've seen what she did to Denny's car."

I smiled, my fingers tightening on the keys. No, I wouldn't let Anna turn another one of my boyfriend's cars into her personal, portable closet. "I won't," I whispered. "I'll keep your baby in mint condition, Kellan."

He smiled that I'd personified his car, then sighed. "It just seems a shame for her to sit in a driveway while you argue with Anna over who gets that P.O.S. Honda." Running his fingers through my hair, he shook his head. "I want you to be able to get to...wherever you need to go while I'm gone."

Swallowing, I nodded. Somehow, Kellan handing over the rights to his baby seemed more final than staring across the lot at his future home for the next six months. My eyes stinging, I shoved the keys in my pocket. Kellan's eyes followed them for a second before he finally cracked open his door. Reluctantly, I followed suit.

There was an excited buzz in the air as men loaded the bands' heavy equipment, securing them into a couple of trucks that would follow the busses. Twenty-something boys everywhere were tucking bags and instruments under the bus, jabbing and mocking each other, or kissing the few women in the crowd.

Matt and Evan walked up to a couple of guys that I recognized. They were in a bigger band with a couple of hits on the radio. I loved their stuff, and sang along jovially whenever one of their songs came on the radio. Kellan said they were headlining the tour, but it was totally surreal seeing them, and seeing my friends talking to them.

Grabbing his guitar case from the back seat, Kellan slung it over his shoulder. Retrieving his bag from the trunk, he grabbed my hand and started pulling me towards the celebrities in our midst. I froze up, not wanting to go anywhere near them.

He looked back at me, his brow furrowed. I shook my head and whispered, "Don't you know who they are?"

Kellan smiled and nodded. "Yeah, they're sort of the reason we're on this tour. I was going to go say hello and thank them." Seeing my horror at the idea of talking to them, he said, "I've heard you sing their stuff. Don't you want to meet them?"

I shook my head even harder. No, I tended to look like an idiot meeting people. Meeting people I actually admired would be…unimaginably mortifying. Laughing at my reluctance, Kellan pulled my arm a little harder. "They're just people, Kiera. They started out as nobodies," he laughed a little harder, "just like me." Raising an eyebrow in a suggestive way, he yanked my body into his side. "And you don't seem to have a problem talking to me."

I giggled despite myself and reluctantly allowed him to lead me their way. I was embarrassingly shaky when we stepped up to the pair of bona fide rock stars. Before Kellan addressed them, he whispered in my ear, "You're trembling just like some of my fans do…I'm a little jealous. I'll try not to be offended that I don't make you…quiver."

I busted out laughing, right as the men turned to look at us. My cheeks flamed red-hot as they both bunched their brows like I was a mental patient. God, I sucked at introductions.

Lightly laughing himself, Kellan dropped his bag and stuck his hand out; I clung to his other one like a lifeline. "Kellan Kyle, D-Bag, I wanted to thank you for inviting us to this."

Justin, the blond, phenomenal lead singer of the band, clasped Kellan's hand and shook it. "Yeah, man, we're honored to have you. You guys rocked the festival."

Kellan beamed. "Thanks." Looking over at where I was hiding behind his shoulder, blatantly staring at the tattoo across Justin's collar bones, Kellan bumped my shoulder. "This is my girlfriend, Kiera." I glanced up at Kellan, wishing I could tell him to shut up. He chuckled as he added, "She's a huge fan of yours…more so than she is of me, I think."

Justin looked straight at me and I wanted to crawl into a hole. He had pale eyes and they held the same amused look Kellan gave when he ran into shivering, shaking female fans. Throwing on a professional smile, Justin extended a hand out to me. I was positive mine was clammy as all get out, and I really didn't want to gross him out by taking his, but I didn't have a choice if I didn't want to offend him either, so, reluctantly, I did.

Tilting his fabulous head of layered hair, Justin casually said, "It's always nice to meet a fan. What's your favorite song?"

As his skin touched mine, all coherent thought left my brain. I couldn't think of a title of any of their songs. Not a damn one. I stammered and stuttered, my cheeks heating to a nearly uncomfortable level until I finally spat out, "I like them all..."

Kellan quietly laughed at me while I realized that I'd been shaking the rock star's hand for an inordinately long amount of time. Dropping it, I cuddled into Kellan's side, again wishing I could disappear. Justin and his friend looked over at Kellan and Justin clapped him on the shoulder. "Well, we're just about ready to roll. We'll see you later."

Kellan nodded and the two walked off to enter the first bus in line. That had been just as embarrassing as I'd thought it would be...I wanted to die. After they were gone, Kellan peered down at me, an eyebrow raised. "You couldn't think of one song, could you?" I sighed and shrugged, and Kellan rolled his eyes. "I'm not sure how I feel about another man making you so nervous." Slinging his arms around my waist, he smiled. "I want to be the one that makes you sweat."

Rubbing my hands on my pants, my eyes widened. "Oh, my God, was I sweaty?"

Kellan squatted down to meet my eye, his lips pursed. Laughing at the expression on his face, I exhaled a calming breath and looped my arms around his neck. "I am your biggest fan, Kellan Kyle." Leaning in, I kissed him. "And don't you forget it."

Languidly kissing me back, he murmured, "Well, I do aim to please the fans." He slid his tongue into my mouth, but I smacked his shoulder on principle. He chuckled, pulling my body into his and I melted, letting his passion seep into me. My hands tangling into his wonderfully shaggy hair, I lost myself in the moment, in his body. Just as our kiss was intensifying, and I started hoping that he'd press me into the bus and claim me again, someone tapped Kellan on the shoulder.

"Uh, man, it's time to go."

We broke apart and glanced over at Evan with Jenny attached to his side, slight tears in her eyes as she clung to him. Behind him, Matt was quietly saying goodbye to Rachel, both of them lightly kissing in-between words that I couldn't hear. Griffin had Anna pressed against the bus.

Kellan nodded as Evan reached down and picked up Kellan's bag for him, giving us a few extra moments. Straightening, Evan gave me a swift goodbye hug and then he and Jenny walked to the doors of bus number three. Not able to watch their painful goodbye, since my own painful goodbye was upon me, I jerked my head back to Kellan. He swallowed and brought his eyes back to mine. Cupping my cheeks, he looked over my face, memorizing me.

"This isn't goodbye, okay. There are no goodbyes...not between us." Whispering intensely, he lowered his forehead to rest it against mine. His scent overwhelmed me and I inhaled it, savoring it. Tears were already stinging my eyes when he continued. "This tour is just me being gone for another show...a really long one. But when it's over, I'm coming home to you, to slip into your warm, inviting bed, like I always do…"

I nodded, not having any words.

He swallowed again and closed his eyes. "I'll still be with you every night, Kiera. Every night, no matter where I am, I'm crawling into bed with you. Our bed will be a lot bigger, miles wide, but it will still just be you and me inside it…okay?"

I nodded again and he whispered, "This doesn't have to change anything…if we don't let it." Swallowing, he choked out, "So let's not let it, all right?"

Tears sliding down my cheeks, I sputtered, "All right…"

Pulling apart from me, his own eyes moist, he searched my face again. "Are you okay?"

Feeling the weight of his absence crushing down on me, I choked on a sob. Hating myself, but not able to stop the words from forming, I shook my head in his hands. "No, no, I'm not okay. I've changed my mind. I don't want you to go. I don't want this. I don't want you to leave. I want you to stay here with me. I want you to give it all up and stay here with me…please."

Tears coursed down my cheeks as I started to sob. I hated that my feelings were coming out this way. I didn't really want him to give up his dreams…I just didn't want to see him go. I loved him too much.

Surprisingly, he exhaled in relief. Smiling softly, he brushed the tears off my cheeks. "Good, I'm glad to hear you say that. I really thought this wasn't affecting you." He kissed me twice, then pulled back and held my gaze. My sobs eased at the look in his eyes. "I love you too, Kiera…so much." Shaking his head, his eyes moistening again, he added, "I'm gonna miss you…every second."

I nodded and swallowed, trying to reign in my explosive feelings. I felt like I was going to break down into hysterics any second, and I didn't want our last moment to be that way. Even if seeing my grief reaffirmed things for him, I didn't want to drown him in tears. This was a good thing for him, an exciting thing. I wanted him to go off happy, knowing that I'd be here when he got back. And like Jenny was always telling me, I had to have faith that he *would* come back.

Closing my eyes, I tried to imagine the reverse of this moment, six months from now, when he came home. We'd embrace. We'd shower each other with affection. Then I'd drop my reluctance to move in with him, and we'd go home together. Then we'd make love for hours. Just the two of us, twisted in his sheets, moaning in passion. It ignited me a little already, just thinking of it. We just had to get through this winter and then we'd be reunited in the spring…like last year.

My eyes flew open at the thought of winter. "You'll be gone," I whispered.

He bunched his forehead, not following my vague statement. Shaking my head, I clarified. "This will be our first Christmas…together…and you'll be gone."

The sadness threatened to drive me over the edge again, but he smiled. "I won't be working over the holidays. I do get some time off."

I sighed. "But who knows where you'll be. You couldn't possibly fly across the country just to spend a couple of days with me."

Frowning, he shrugged. "Why not? People do it all the time."

I shrugged, feeling like it was too much of a hassle to ask him to jump on a plane, not once, but twice, during the busiest traveling time of the year. Tilting his head at me, he twisted his lip. "Where will you be for Christmas?"

Shaking my head, I shrugged again. "With my family in Ohio, I guess. I'll probably spend my winter break there."

He nodded, his smile widening. "Then I'll meet you there...in Ohio."

I raised an eyebrow at him, shaking my head. "Kellan..."

He interrupted me with a swift kiss. "No, I've always wanted to meet your parents, see your home town." Pulling back, his face excited, he smiled wide. "When I get the time off, I'll come to you." He shook his head, his eyes glowing. "We'll do Christmas with your family. It'll be great, Kiera."

Sighing, imagining him sitting on my parents' couch, sipping eggnog, I nodded and bit my lip. "All right...it's a date."

Both of us feeling better, we kissed again for a few long seconds. Band members brushed past us as we nonverbally said goodbye, but we ignored them. I even managed to ignore Griffin grabbing my butt and murmuring in my ear, "Yes, Kellan...God, yes." Then, we were alone and the bus driver was snapping at Kellan to get on or he'd leave him here.

Sighing, we broke apart...for the last time. I didn't want to think of it that way, but there it was, the last kiss we'd have for what I knew was going to feel like an eternity. Swallowing as he nodded at me, he took a step back. Our hands trailed across the other's arms and it took every amount of will power I had to not grab his fingertips as our hands broke apart.

I didn't want to, but a sob came out of me when his skin left mine. Even though we'd made plans to see each other again, it felt like things were irrevocably shifting. We'd never be Kiera and Kellan again...not like we were anyway. I hoped that the new Kiera and Kellan would be stronger and more trusting of each other...but I didn't know for sure where we'd end up. And the unknown is a terrifying thing.

Kellan adjusted his guitar strapped on his back, then stepped onto his bus and out of my sight. Jenny, Rachel and Anna came up to clump around me. Windows opened along the sides of the bus, and strange guys leaned out of them to wave to strange girls. Then our D-Bags appeared near the back. Kellan leaned on his elbows over the glass, lifting his hand in a small wave. Tears in my eyes, I waved back.

With all of us girls sniffling, we watched, disheartened, as the bus rumbled to life. Stringing my arms over Anna and Jenny, Rachel leaning on Jenny, we all softly cried while our men departed for their war with fame. Even through my sorrow, I wished them luck.

As the bus pulled away, the boys popped back inside it, closing windows after them. All but Kellan. He stayed propped out his window, watching me fade into oblivion as he sped away from me faster and faster. It was so metaphoric, a physical example of everything I feared our relationship would become, that I couldn't keep watching. When he was far enough away that he wouldn't be able to notice, I closed my eyes. Sadly, that felt metaphoric too.

When I reopened them, the busses had vanished from sight, off to destinations unknown. The random girls wandering around the parking lot chatted briefly with one another in clumps before heading off to their separate vehicles. Most of them looked fine, like their boyfriends disappearing down the path to fame and fortune was no big deal. Shaking my head at the more chipper girls in the crowd, I wanted to run over and tell them, "What are you so thrilled about? Don't you know the odds are that you'll be replaced as soon as they become household names?" But I was trying to keep my head in a positive place, so I didn't.

Sniffing back the tears, I suddenly wanted to go home and cry my way through a box of Kleenex. My friends had other plans, though. Jenny stepped in front of me, cupping my cheeks. Her face hazed in my watery vision as I stared at her. Shaking her golden waves, she said, "Kellan gave me instructions that I wasn't allowed to let you mope after he left...so stop picturing all of the bad things you're picturing and smile, so I can tell him that I did my job."

She grinned after she said it and I blinked. "He...gave you instructions on how to handle me?"

Jenny shrugged, dropping her palms from my face to grab my hands. Anna laughed and put her chin on my shoulder. "Yeah, he talked to me, too...said I should take you out a lot, make sure you had fun and didn't wallow too much." I looked back at my sister and she giggled, rolling her eyes. "It's like he knows you or something."

Quiet Rachel put her hand on my arm and I looked over at the mixed beauty. "He cares a lot about you, Kiera. He wants you to be happy while he's gone."

Blinking at her, I shook my head. "He talked to all of you?" They all shrugged and smiled, and I shook my head. "I can't believe my boyfriend assigned my friends to be my keepers...like I'd be popping Prozac and walking along bridge rails once he left." Smiling, I laughed a little. "That jackass."

They all laughed with me, and I took a moment to look over each woman's face. Even smiling, I could see a sadness in each of them and I swallowed, remembering that I wasn't the only one suffering here. Putting my arm around Rachel, I asked, "I know I'm not the only one going through this...how are you guys?"

Rachel shrugged, her deeply tanned skin flushing. "All right, I guess. Matt says he loves me and he's not interested in anybody else. It's all about the music with him...so, I think we'll be fine."

I hugged her briefly, agreeing with her. Matt wasn't the type to go after a girl when he had one waiting at home. Even before he'd started dating Rachel...that just wasn't him. Jenny in front of me sighed morosely. "I miss him already, but I know Evan will come back for me." She shook her head. "We've been friends for so long...I just can't see him doing anything..." she bit her lip and glanced at Anna,

"…stupid."

Anna snorted and we all turned to look at her. "Well, Griffin and I aren't the lovey-dovey couple that the three of you are, so I'm completely fine." Smiling, she shrugged. "He gives me what I need when he's around, and when he's not…" her smile widened, "there are plenty of others who can."

She winked at us, and I laughed and shook my head. At least Anna wasn't head-over-heels for Griffin and wouldn't get hurt over his…antics. I was fairly certain that he wouldn't even try to be faithful and committed to her while he was gone. Hell, he wasn't faithful and committed to her while he was here! But she wasn't faithful to him either, and they both seemed fine with the situation.

Jenny smirked and shook her head while Rachel frowned. Being Matt's girlfriend meant she saw Griffin the most, since the twin-like cousins were inseparable, and if she was anything like me, she probably found him repugnant. Anna sighed and laid her head on my shoulder. "I will miss the multiple orgasms, though." She sighed, forlornly. "No one can stroke me like that boy."

Jenny giggled while Rachel's flush deepened. I reached over and smacked my sister's shoulder, pushing her away from me. "Ewww, Anna, too much information…seriously."

She laughed while I shook my head in disgust. I might have to go home and take a shower now. I felt a little dirty just hearing her comment, let alone the visual I now had. Anna chuckled, her finger looping around a perfect, silky lock of hair as she raised her eyebrows suggestively. I was still shaking my head at her when my pocket vibrated.

A bit startled, I reached into my jacket and pulled out my phone. The most glorious words imaginable flashed across the screen—Incoming call from Kellan Kyle. Giggling at the marvels of technology, I pressed the connect button and put the phone to my ear. "Hello?"

A husky voice greeted me, along with a lot of background noise, boisterous boys laughing and talking. "Hey, is it too early to miss you?"

Laughing a little as Jenny and the girls watched me, I shook my head. "No, it's never too early for that. I miss you too, Kellan."

Anna rolled her eyes while Jenny and Rachel grinned. Kellan laughed in my ear, the sound instantly taking me to my happy place. "Good…is it too early for phone sex?"

Straightening, I felt my cheeks heat. "Kellan!" He laughed even harder in my ear, and Anna stopped smirking, raising an eyebrow instead. I could only shake my head at her, my mind too busy wondering what phone sex was exactly, since I'd never done it. I couldn't imagine anything more horrifying, although…the thought of Kellan panting in my ear, touching himself, moaning my name, thinking of me…it did send a rush through me.

But there was no way I'd even consider it in the company I was in now.

I stammered for something to say and he chuckled, amused. "I'm just teasing, Kiera. I'm glad you're okay. I thought you might be a blubbering mess by now."

Relaxing a bit as Anna, Jenny and Rachel moved on to their own conversation, giving Kellan and me some privacy, I twisted my lip. "Yeah, well, your recruits have done their job well." My voice came out a little dry and he laughed again.

"Good, then part one of my plan has been successful."

I blinked. "Part one? Wait...what plan?"

Vaguely, I heard the girls start to make plans of their own, mainly to head over to Pete's, to tear down the guys' equipment and move it over to Evan's place, since Jenny had the keys to his loft. My main focus was on Kellan, though...and this mysterious plan that he had.

Chuckling a little, he murmured, "Just a little something to keep you occupied while I'm gone."

I smiled, wondering just what he had in mind. "Hmmm, I see." As Jenny tapped my shoulder, mouthing that they were going to head over there, I nodded.

While I walked over to our cars, well, the cars the boys were letting us drive in their absence, Kellan sighed in my ear. "I'm liking this phone idea you had. This is nice, being able to talk to you whenever I want to."

I waved at Jenny as she opened Evan's car door, ducking inside it with Rachel. Anna blew me a kiss as she opened Griffin's van door and ducked inside. Smiling at Kellan's comment, I cracked the Chevelle's door open and sat inside. It was strange sitting here without him. But with his voice in my ear and the residual smell of him in the car, it was almost like he was here, sitting beside me. I smiled as I answered him. "Yeah, see, I knew you'd like it better than handcuffs."

"Oh, hey now...I didn't say that." He chuckled as I bit my lip. Pulling the keys out of my pocket, I twisted the ignition and the solid engine roared to life.

Kellan sighed. "Did you just start my baby?"

I laughed, waiting while Jenny and Anna pulled their vehicles out of their respective parking spots. "Well, I do have to drive her home, so...yeah."

"Well, you shouldn't drive and talk on the phone, so I'll let you go."

I frowned, wishing for a moment that we could spend the entire time apart connected on the phone. I knew that was horribly impractical, though. "Okay...I love you."

He sighed, the sound a happy and content one. "I love you, too. I'll call you later tonight."

I nodded, then remembered he couldn't see me. "Okay...bye."

"Bye." He disconnected and the rambunctious laughter in the background faded. I sighed, then smiled. At least I'd get to talk to him a lot while he was gone. And perhaps, if I felt brave enough someday, we'd try that phone sex thing. I was insanely curious to hear what he'd sound like, making love from a distance...and I could always fake my end of it anyway.

Sighing, I popped the phone back in my jacket. Feeling warmer with a connection to Kellan inside my pocket, I smiled and wrapped my fingers around the steering wheel. The power of the car reminded me of the power of the man who owned it. Sleek and sexy, strong and hard, it fit Kellan perfectly, and I knew I'd think of him whenever I drove it.

In a much better mood than I'd have ever thought possible, I headed over to Pete's Bar, to remove all traces of my boyfriend from it. That thought managed to diminish my good mood a little.

Parking in Kellan's traditional spot, I turned off the ignition. I pictured his sexy half-smile as I sat there in contemplative silence. I was jerked back into reality by a rap on my window. Anna smiled at me, signaling for me to get out of the car. Inhaling Kellan's lingering scent within the car, I knew I needed to get a handle on my revolving emotions as I pushed open his heavy door.

Anna slung her arm over my shoulder as Jenny and Rachel got out of Evan's car, laughing about some story they'd been telling on the ride over. Smiling at my friends and family, I perked back up. Almost our own quartet, the D-Bag-ettes, we strolled through the double doors. Nearly expecting the reaction Kellan and the guys got when they busted through the doors, I was a little disappointed when not one person in the lunch crowd looked our way.

Troy, back to his normal daytime hours at the bar, waved at us. His face was forlorn, like he missed Kellan, too. I almost wanted to go over and hug him, talk to him about the man we both mutually crushed on, but considering that I had Kellan's heart and poor Troy never would…I thought that might be mean. Best to leave the man alone to his grief.

As we headed towards the stage, Jenny waved at the elderly waitresses who'd been working at the bar since its inception, or so it seemed. The black wall covered in guitars behind the equipment we were tearing down seemed a bit morose today, or maybe that was just my lingering mood. Stepping up onto the worn-with-use oak, I walked up to Kellan's microphone, alone in the center. Running my hand up the shaft, I imagined Kellan's fingers doing the same.

Twisting to face the crowd who was largely ignoring us, I imagined what he felt standing up here. Looking out over the now empty dance floor, I envisioned it packed with people, as it normally was when the boys played. Just the thought made my stomach twist. How did he do it? And now he'd be playing even bigger venues…it boggled my mind.

Gripping the mic at the top of the stand, the sound equipment set way too tall for me, I mentally pictured my rock star boyfriend.

"You wanna sing something, before we tear it down?" I looked over at Jenny. She was watching me as she twisted some of Evan's drum sticks in her hands. Smiling as she walked over to sit behind Evan's drums, she pointed to Kellan's microphone. "We could play one of theirs." She laughed a little. "We could be their cover band."

I paled at the idea, but Anna thought it was a great plan, and immediately strung Griffin's bass guitar over her shoulder. Chuckling softly, Rachel took Matt's guitar off its stand and looped it over her shoulder. Then, they all looked expectantly at me, like I was actually the leader of this fake band.

I shook my head, but Jenny started clicking off a beat with her sticks. Then they all started playing. I was so busy laughing, I couldn't be embarrassed. There was one prerequisite that even a cover band needed to be successful—they needed to know how to play, and none of us did. As Jenny made random hits on various drums, Anna plucked whatever chord struck her fancy on her unplugged instrument; Rachel strummed hers like she held a ukulele. I heartily laughed.

A few patrons glanced up at us, but since the equipment wasn't powered up, and Jenny was smacking the set as softly as she could, we really weren't making that much noise. They all went back to their meals and conversations. Still curious about being a rock star, about what that would feel like, I closed my eyes and started singing one of Kellan's songs. Well, singing was a stretch. I was murmuring, my voice nearly lost in the chaos around me.

At hearing my band mates giggle, I opened my eyes. They were all smiling at me, rocking out hard on their borrowed instruments. Grinning, my courage building the longer I was up here, I unfastened the mic from the stand and raised my voice...a little.

Mimicking the moves I'd seen Kellan do a thousand times, I started to pretend that I was him. My eyes swung over the empty patch where the crowds would have been, and I pictured them there, cheering for me. I even pictured Kellan among them, grinning crookedly and shaking his head at me. I focused my attention on the mental image I had of him, trying to be sexy for him, since he so often was for me.

My imagined version of Kellan smiled wider and bit his lip. I heard whistled encouragement from behind me and the picture of him in my head vanished. I giggled over at Anna, nodding at me as she faked her way through playing a D-Bag classic. My cheeks heating, I switched my view to Rachel, merrily strumming away like we were doing a skit at summer camp. Jenny behind me started playing her version of a disorganized solo and I giggled mid-sentence at the musical mess we were making.

When the song was over, I made a small bow, the girls joining me. From across the bar I heard a small splattering of applause. Looking up, Troy was clapping, beaming at us. I laughed, embarrassment flooding me but held back from completely absorbing me by a flash of pride. I did it. I sang on stage. Granted, I wasn't plugged in and no one but Troy had really been listening, but still, I felt like I could cross it off my bucket list now.

Kellan would be so proud. I couldn't wait to tell him.

S.C. Stephens

Chapter 11 – Gone But Not Forgotten

After our jam session, the girls and I finally got everything squished into Griffin's van. I sighed when we all looked at the empty stage before us. It was dark and lonely as its owners traveled farther and farther away. I wasn't even sure where they were right now. Matt had given us all a tour schedule and their first show was tonight in Spokane, on the very east side of Eastern Washington. They were probably close to heading up the mountain passes by now. The same passes that Denny and I had traveled on our way here. The same mountains that had brought me to the place where one love had eventually superseded another were now taking that love away.

Interesting, how life had a way of coming full circle.

Jenny, beside me, sighed, her melancholy matching my own. Suddenly straightening, she turned and dashed out of the front doors. We all watched her leave, curious at her sudden departure. She returned a few minutes later, beaming as she carried a large poster frame under her arm.

I smiled as she walked up to me. "I nearly forgot I brought this." Twisting the poster around so we could all see it, she displayed the finished artwork that she'd been doing in class—the drawing of the band. I had tears in my eyes as I gazed at her perfect re-creation of Kellan. Nodding at the stage, she smiled. "It's wrong to leave that stage without a piece of them up there, right?"

I eagerly nodded and helped her rearrange some of the decorative guitars hanging on the wall so we could hang it. After centering it, we took a step back and admired her handiwork. She'd turned her pencil drawing into a stunning black and white sketch. It was incredible. She really did have a knack for it.

Nearly wanting to place a kiss on the lifelike vision of my boyfriend, I slung my arm around Jenny's shoulders. "It's perfect, Jenny." Laughing a little, I added, "I think the boys won't be the only famous people to come out of this bar."

She flushed and laughed, looking down. "It's all right, I guess." Staring at it in awe, Anna and Rachel both assured her that it was better than all right.

Before leaving, we said goodbye to the staff we didn't spend too much time with—Sal, the part owner of the bar, Hun and Sweetie, the longtime waitresses, and lastly, Troy. He seemed brighter with the addition of Jenny's portrait on the back wall; at least we'd made him feel a little better.

Getting back into our cars, we headed out to Evan's. Mechanic girl was walking across the lot when I pulled up in Kellan's car. Her eyes instantly swung to the Chevelle. She looked highly disappointed when I stepped out of the vehicle, and not her former…whatever. She waved at me, then stepped into the shop. Maybe she was going to go write her book: Groupie Lovin' 101.

Exhaling, I rolled my eyes. Grabbing instruments from Griffin's van, I followed Jenny and Rachel up to the loft, Anna trailing behind us. I knew I was being too hard on mechanic girl, especially since I wasn't even really sure if she had been with Kellan or not. And even if she had, it was in his past and it shouldn't really matter anymore. I was being jealous without justification…and that needed to stop if Kellan and I were going to work as a couple.

Evan's place was oddly bare when we stepped into it; the guys having taken their travelling instruments on the road, only Evan's drum set remained. As the various groups on the tour had decided to share a drum set, Evan had left his in Seattle. Used to playing other people's equipment, Evan was fine with the arrangement. I smiled, thinking of Kellan lugging his guitar onto the bus. He'd never settle for playing somebody else's instrument.

As I set down Griffin's bass, I noticed a small note taped on the back. Now, normally, I wouldn't touch anything of Griffin's, even handling his instrument was questionable, but the note had my name on it. Curiosity getting the better of me, I tore off the securely held piece of paper. Unfolding it, I cringed, waiting for some horrific comment from the crude bassist. I was pleasantly surprised at what I discovered, though.

> I know you hate touching anything of Griffin's, so I thought I'd make it a little more bearable for you. Thank you for doing this. I love you, Kellan.

Grinning like an idiot, I tucked the note into my pocket. Warmth flooded through me, both from the fact that he knew me so well, in regards to Griffin, and also from the fact that he'd been thinking about me far enough in advance to plan leaving that message behind. He must have put it there before the show. Biting my lip, I wondered if this was also a part of his plan. I wondered what else I might find, tucked here and there, just waiting for me to discover them.

We eventually brought in all the instruments and equipment. After Jenny arranged Evan's second drum set next to his first one, she sighed and came over to rest her head on my shoulder. Placing my hand over the normally perky blonde's head, I offered her what comfort I could. As much as Kellan and the boys missed us, being left behind was so much harder than leaving. I knew we'd all be sifting through our emotional baggage for a while, finding a new mood every ten minutes. Jenny confirmed that for me by brightly popping her head up.

"Oh, we have to remember to pay the neighbors."

I stared at her blankly, not having a clue what she meant. Rent or something? Noticing my puzzled expression, she shook her head. "You know, Matt and Griffin's neighbors." Still confused, I shook mine. Jenny tilted her head. "Kellan didn't tell you what he did?"

Narrowing my eyes, I wondered just what he'd done. "No…"

Laughing a little at my sullen tone, she pointed out the window in the direction of Matt and Griffin's suburban utopia. "He paid all the neighbors to not call the cops if the party got a little…noisy."

My mouth lowered. "He paid all the…what?"

Jenny shrugged. "Well, since he knew the party would get started late, I guess he figured it would go until the early morning. Most suburbanites aren't okay with that, so he gave them money to encourage them to let it go for one night." She shrugged again. "He said if they did, he'd double the amount. We're supposed to deliver that payment."

I shook my head at how much that must have cost him. And all so he could give everyone a good time on the band's last night in town. Shaking my head, I glanced out the window. "That must have cost him a fortune." I looked back at Jenny. "Is that even legal?"

Jenny shrugged. "I don't know, but I told him I'd take care of it. He left some money here…somewhere."

As Jenny began to search for the envelope padded with hush money, I frowned and put my hands on my hips. "Why didn't he ask me?" I muttered.

Anna, resting on the couch with her feet up, heard me. "Probably because he knew you'd get that look on your face, and object to him throwing his money away."

She smirked after she said it, and I scowled at her. Damn right, I objected. But still…I was his girlfriend, not Jenny. Slipping money under people's doors should have been my job. Laughter swung my attention around. Jenny and Rachel were in the corner of the room reserved as the kitchen, and were staring into a can of coffee grounds, chuckling.

Curious, I walked over to them. Jenny shook her head, pulling a thick envelope out of the can. "Kellan and his coffee," she murmured.

I flushed, my own memories of Kellan, coffee, and an espresso stand that I would never forget mixing erotically in my head. Not noticing my face, Jenny opened the envelope and did a quick count of the cash. When she got to the end of the wad, she pulled out a piece of paper. Seeing my name on the outside, she looked up and handed it to me.

"Here, it's for you."

I smiled as I grabbed it. I smiled even more reading it.

> Don't be angry. I asked Jenny to do this because I knew you'd be upset with me for spending so much money. I had to, though. I had to give you a memorable evening, and preferably one that didn't end with us all being arrested…although, seeing you in handcuffs…
>
> Anyway, please don't be mad. I did it for you. You deserved a good night last night. You deserve everything.
>
> I love you, I miss you.
>
> Kellan.

Gazing stupidly at his handwriting across the paper, I didn't notice the person reading over my shoulder. I noticed when she shoved me. "Goddamn, he's sweet. I really wouldn't have expected that from him."

Folding the note, I looked back at Anna. She giggled and hugged me. Kissing my head, she added, "You're one freaking lucky girl, sis. I hope you know that."

Smiling, I raised my chin a bit. "I do."

Squeezing my shoulders, Anna laughed a little harder. "And I'm lucky, too.

I'm going to have the hottest brother-in-law on the planet!"

I playfully pushed her away from me. "We're not...he's not..."

Slinging her arm around Jenny, Anna continued undaunted. "Can't you just picture what my nieces and nephews are going to look like?" Jenny laughed as Anna sighed. "Those deep blue eyes, that jaw, those lips..."

"That hair," Rachel quietly added.

I flushed and smacked my sister on the arm for starting this whole embarrassing conversation. And as family, I had the right, no...duty...to whale on her; I'm pretty sure they had covered that topic in my ethics class.

Stepping away from me, Anna leaned over to Rachel. "And you know I'm going to have loads and loads of them, because their parents can't keep their hands off each other." As I covered my face with my hands and shook my head, Anna sighed again. "I'll have to get a bigger place, just so all the beautiful little babies can visit me."

Removing my hands, I rolled my eyes. Anna shrugged. "Just saying." Finished with moving the equipment and instruments, I turned to leave the loft. I heard my sister murmur to the girls, "I cannot wait to see our dad's expression when he finds out that a rock star impregnated his daughter...it'll be epic."

They were all laughing as I left the room, my body heating at just the thought of one day carrying Kellan's child. It was a very nice thought. I wondered how Kellan felt about having kids... Hmmm, maybe I should consider how he felt about getting married. First things first and all.

I smiled as I opened the door to his Chevelle. I'd never truly considered marriage with Denny. Maybe because we'd been so young, maybe because I always knew he'd never agree to it until he was established in his career. With him, it had just seemed a distant goal that we'd eventually reach someday, and I hadn't felt the urge to make that day come any faster than was necessary. But with Kellan...well, my pulse raced at just the thought of wearing his ring on my finger. And besides the honor of being his wife, a ring on *his* finger might ward off every other girl out there.

I paused as I inserted the key into the ignition. I didn't like that thought. I didn't want to marry him just so he'd be "off the market." I wanted to marry him because he was my world. And he was...but there was an ulterior motive in being his wife that didn't sit well with me. Maybe I wasn't ready yet. I had to stop being so possessive with him first. I had to be so comfortable in our relationship that no one outside of it mattered.

I had to learn to trust him.

We both had to learn to trust each other...and this tour was just what we needed, really. It provided an opportunity to test our fidelity. I knew I wouldn't stray, and I prayed that Kellan wouldn't, but either way, we'd know for sure after this.

Anna had to go to work so she headed home, while Jenny, Rachel and I completed Kellan's task for him. Giggling, we stuffed envelopes with thank you notes into the cracks of people's doors. None of us wanted to knock on the doors to deliver the money personally, since we weren't really sure if any of this was legal. We felt a little spy-like dropping off the payment money, and I started to think that this was another thing I could cross off my bucket list. At this rate, I'd complete the entire thing while Kellan was gone. Well, except for the growing old with someone I loved part...I'd need him for that one.

Fortunately, there was a green belt behind Matt and Griffin's place, so we only had to worry about the neighbors on either side and across the street. We finished our task in no time. The last door we went to belonged to a sweet elderly lady. As Jenny was attempting to shimmy the envelope into the door jamb, it suddenly swung open.

A wrinkled woman smiled warmly at us and held her hand out for the envelope. "Ah, good, my bingo money, as promised."

Jenny and I glanced at each other and then Jenny handed over the wad of sealed cash. Taking it, the stooped woman tried to lift herself up to her full height and look over the top of us. Rachel quickly ducked behind me, trying to hide from the woman who I was pretty sure couldn't see farther than a few feet anyway.

"Is that good-looking boy with you?"

Shaking my head, I murmured, "No, ma'am." A little sadly, I added, "He had to leave town for a while."

The grandmother patted my arm consolingly. "Well, that's too bad." She leaned in to whisper, "He was very easy on the eye." I giggled as the woman leaned back. Yes, Kellan was very easy on the eye...effortless to look at. Shrugging her sagging shoulders, she added, "His bottom was very nice, too."

Jenny snorted, then girlishly slapped her hand over her mouth. Rachel popped her head up over my shoulder and giggled at the spunky old woman.

The neighbor's gnarled hand pointed across to where the party had been raging until the early hours of this morning. "That was some celebration you all had." Her eyes glossed over, reminiscing. "I used to tip back a few in my youth." Shaking her head, she grinned. "It was illegal back then, so we all met underground, in secret places." She lifted the envelope. "We had to pay people to keep the coppers away, too."

Shaking my head at her, I smiled wider. Man, she was way older than I anticipated. I hoped I looked this good when I was in my nineties. Glancing at all of our tired faces, she squinted her graying eyes. "You all look like you're suffering from the excess. Why don't you come in...I have the perfect cure."

Jenny and I looked at each other and shrugged. My headache had dialed back a great deal since this morning, but it still ached and throbbed, especially when I moved my head too fast. I also hadn't eaten anything yet so my stomach was feeling mildly queasy. I didn't want to push it over the edge but maybe the former flapper knew a sure-fire fix. We're told to listen to our elders, right? Surely that includes hang-over advice.

So, the three of us spent a good chunk of the afternoon consuming a really horrid cup of tea with a surprisingly interesting old lady. I'd have to tell Kellan all about her when he returned. He'd get a kick out of her. I probably wouldn't mention that she'd enjoyed his backside, though.

Afterwards, I went home to get ready for work. Anna was long gone and my home was empty. Running my hand along the back of Kellan's favorite chair, the chair he gave me when I involuntarily moved out of his place, I wondered where he was now. Probably in the middle of nowhere, and out of cellular range.

Sighing, I pushed it from my mind and went to take a hot, soothing shower. After partying all night, I felt absolutely grimy. The old lady's miracle cure kicked in once I was cleaned and refreshed, and amazingly, I felt one hundred percent better when I stepped out of the shower. Better…and starving.

Dressed in my work clothes, my wavy locks haphazardly tied in a pony tail, I made myself a meal fit for a queen. Okay, it was a bowl of spaghetti, but I was so hungry it felt like the best meal on earth going down.

Feeling full and content, more like myself, I pulled my cell phone out of my jacket and stared at it for a moment. Running my thumb over the screen, I considered calling Kellan. Maybe he was close enough to a large town that he could pick up a signal. On second thought, cell towers lined practically every freeway in the world nowadays. Maybe I was wrong about him being in the middle of nowhere. The middle of nowhere didn't really exist in our world anymore. With modern technology, you could be found almost anywhere you went.

But, we had just spoken this morning, and he'd promised to call tonight. I didn't want to be "that girl." The obsessive girlfriend that checked in every hour on the hour. I wanted to fully live my life—whether that was with him, or without him. That was the mistake I'd made with Denny. Letting my happiness revolve around him for so long.

When Denny had left for Tucson, it left a hole in my heart, a void that Kellan had easily filled. I didn't want to repeat that pattern. I had no desire for anyone to take Kellan's place, now that he was the one leaving. So I had to fill his aching absence with something healthy, something all my own. I wasn't sure what yet, but I was positive that I could. Losing Denny the way I did, doing what I'd done to him…had forced me to grow up some.

Guilt and regret flooding me, I dialed a number that I hadn't in a while, a number that I should really call more often. Bringing the ringing phone to my ear, I chewed on my lip while I waited for the other line to pick up. It did on the third ring.

"Hello?" A familiar voice said happily, clearly mid-laugh.

"Uh, hi…it's me." I rolled my eyes at my awkward greeting. Really, after everything, things between us shouldn't be awkward anymore.

"Oh, hey, Kiera."

Denny's accent wrapped around my name and I smiled, memories coming back to me. In the background, I heard a female voice asking him a question. I instantly did the time zone math in my head and cringed. It was late Saturday afternoon here, so it was Sunday morning in Australia. He was probably having a leisurely brunch with his girlfriend, Abby.

Being the honorable man I knew he was, Denny answered her question truthfully. "It's Kiera. I'll just be a minute, Abb, then I'll show you how to make pancakes without burning them." In the background I clearly heard, "That was not my fault! You completely distracted me."

Denny chuckled at her, and I instantly felt stupid for calling. He had his own life; he really didn't need me interfering in it. As I was thinking I should tell him that I'd call back later, his voice shifted back into the phone. "What's up? Everything all right?"

I sighed, forcing the image of him with another woman out of my head. He was happy and that's all I'd ever wished for him. "Yeah, no, everything's fine, Denny. I just, we haven't…" I sighed again, not knowing exactly how to put my feelings into words. I really needed to work on that, since English is my major. "It's just…we don't get to talk as much as we used to, and the last time we talked things were…awkward. I wanted to make sure you were…okay."

I bit my lip, hating that I'd brought up that conversation. Kellan, in his drunken state, had talked about our sex life with him. That was something Kellan was usually really careful not to do, not since the night that we'd provoked Denny into fracturing Kellan's arm and nearly cracking my skull.

Denny sighed. "Yeah…I already got a call from Kellan this morning, Kiera. The two of you really don't have to worry about me. You don't need to walk on eggshells. You don't need to treat me with kid gloves. I get it. You're together. I know what…that entails. I'm fine with it, Kiera. I left you. I broke up with you…but I never wanted you to end up alone, bab…"

He stopped himself short and my eyes widened. He nearly called me baby, right in front of his girlfriend. I closed my eyes as I heard him sigh again. "I know," I whispered. "But still…we don't want to hurt you. You're…a friend…to both of us. A close friend?" I added, my tone coming out as a question instead of a statement.

Denny chuckled. "You guys are close friends to me too, all right. So, let's just skip over this weird part…"

"But…?"

"Kiera, do you want to know if I hurt?" he whispered, his accent thick with the emotion building in it. "Yeah, sometimes I do. I mean, yes, it sucks that my girl cheated…" I hung my head as he broke off his sentence with a long exhale. "No, it's not that you cheated, Kiera. It's that you fell in love. If you'd just strayed a couple of times…I could have…I probably could have looked past that. But you didn't…you fell in love. So yeah, that hurts, okay?"

I sniffled, thinking I never should have called him. "I'm sorry…"

A long moment of silence was all I got, then, quietly, "I know, Kiera. You don't have to keep saying it. You can't…you can't help falling in love. It's not a reaction you can control. I get that, I really do. So please…quit apologizing, I don't want to hear it anymore."

I swallowed and whispered, "Okay." In my head I added another apology. I probably always would with him.

I pictured his dark brown eyes staring at me, a hand coming up to run through his chunky, dark hair. After another moment of silence, he finally spoke again. "What are you going to do with Kellan gone for so long?" Almost like he didn't want me to take that the wrong way, he added, "I mean, what are you going to do to keep yourself busy?"

I chuckled a little, in a humorless way. "No, you mean am I going to cheat on him?" He didn't say anything and I sighed. "No, I would never hurt someone like that again. It's not the person I want to be." Exhaling softly, I said, "I had a boyfriend once who was the best person I've ever known. Honorable, loving, sweet...sappy. He's who I aspire to be someday."

He chuckled now. "Well, sounds like you were an idiot for letting him go."

I grinned, shaking my head. "Yes, I don't think that's ever been in question."

Denny laughed genuinely and I reveled in the sound, my mind picturing the goofy grin he always wore, the warmth in his deep eyes. Once the moment of levity receded, he asked, "What about Kellan? Do you think he'll be...honorable?"

I blinked that he'd basically asked me if Kellan would cheat on me. As if, he too, questioned the solidity of our relationship. "Um, yeah, I think so..." I bit my lip, hating that I couldn't give Denny a definite and resounding, "Yes, of course, don't be ridiculous." That sort of bravado was pointless with Denny, though. We both knew Kellan's past, and we both knew how Kellan and I had first come together. Kellan was capable of being with someone in immoral situations. Our relationship was proof of that.

Denny sighed. It was a sympathetic sound. "I'm sure he'll be good, Kiera." He paused a minute while we both reflected on his statement. Softly he added, "He'd be an idiot not to be."

I smiled and sighed, feeling oddly reassured and a little sad. It wasn't as if I had left a bad relationship for a better one. I had left a good relationship for a different one. Things would be easier if I could paint Denny as an abusive, emotionally cutoff asshole. But he wasn't. He was as close to the perfect boyfriend as they come. Truly, his habit of getting wrapped up in his work was his only real flaw. And that was pretty minor, compared to the horror stories that I'd heard out there.

Shaking my head, I murmured, "Abby is very lucky, Denny. You're...a really great guy."

He laughed once. "Yeah, I tried to tell you that..."

I laughed once, too. "I know...I miss you." He didn't respond and I quickly added, "I should let you get back to your brunch. It sounds like you have some cooking to do." I did miss him, his friendship, his sweetness, his loyalty...but it was pointless and misleading to tell him things like that. Kellan had my whole heart.

Denny started chuckling, and I could hear the joy come back into his voice. "Yeah, Abby is many things, but cook isn't one of them. I don't even know how a person messes up pancakes...they're sort of...unscrew-up-able." I smiled, knowing that I couldn't make decent pancakes either. I guessed Abby and I had at least one thing in common. Well, two really. We both deeply cared for Denny, just in different ways now.

"Goodbye, Denny."

"Goodbye, Kiera. Everything will be fine, I promise."

I started to respond to that but he clicked off the line. "I hope so," I said anyway, the dust bunnies the only things around to hear me.

Walking into Pete's a while later, I couldn't help but look up at the empty stage. Jenny's beautiful drawing stood prominently on the black wall, and seeing our boys immortalized helped to ease the ache. But I'd have preferred to walk in on the foursome slinging back cold ones. That was one of my favorite things about working at Pete's—waiting on the band. Even Griffin, in a weird, unexplainable way.

It was a quiet night. With the band gone, only a handful of regulars came in. Pete let Jenny go home early, but Kate and I stayed to finish the late shift. At midnight, Kate handed me a note with a gleeful grin on her face. I bunched my brows together, wondering what she was up to.

As her bouncy pony tail swished over her shoulders, she giggled and pointed at the folded piece of paper in my hands. "Kellan made me promise to give this to you at exactly midnight tonight." Her topaz eyes lit up as she sighed. "He was so sweet when he asked. Sigh...I need another boyfriend." She twisted her lips and glided off, leaving me to puzzle over when Kellan had talked to her. When Kellan had talked to everybody. He sure had been busy before he left.

My heart started beating a little harder as I held his note. I leaned back against the bar. Rita, sullen as she stared at the empty stage and the half-empty bar, ignored me. Biting my lip, I unfolded the note. It wasn't sealed in any way, so I was pretty sure that Kate had already read it, but upon glancing at his handwriting on the paper, I didn't care. I was too happy that he'd left me another surprise.

Hey, just in case I'm a schlump and haven't called you yet, I wanted to say that it's not because I don't miss you...I do. Most likely my delay has something to do with Griffin...I'm sure the jackass will be a constant irritant on the road. Well, at least he won't be mentally undressing you for a while...that's my job. And if I've never told you...I do it constantly. When you walk past me, I picture those slim hips bare under my fingertips. When you lean over to hand me my beer, I picture those firm breasts, your rigid nipples just begging for my mouth.

My face flushing bright red, I stopped reading and glanced up at Kate across the room from me. Oh, my God, had she read this? Noticing me staring at her, note in hand, she started laughing. I figured she had. Well, at least Kellan had given this to her and not Rita...I probably never would have gotten it if that was the case. My face heating even more, I considered reading the rest of the note somewhere else, somewhere private. But curiosity got the better of me, and hiding the paper as much as I could, I continued on with Kellan's erotic love letter.

You wonder why I'm constantly aroused, and I guess I'm telling you. Your body fires me. Your fingertips brushing over my skin, ignites me. Your breath washing over me, enflames me. Everything about you is sensual, and you have no idea...none. When you stare at me with those smoky eyes, undressing me like I undress you, all the blood rushes down, and I want you...so bad. I'm pretty sure that wherever I am right now, I have an ache, a hard, nearly painful ache...because I'm thinking of you.

I had to stop reading again as a painful ache started building in me. Good God, if just reading his words did this to me, hearing him actually say these things would probably undo me. Adjusting my posture, I glanced around the room and then returned to my scandalous note.

My day isn't complete until I'm deep inside you. Your body wrapped around mine is the only way I feel whole. But don't think it's just sex and a physical response to you that I'm feeling. It's not...it's so much more. You've opened me in a way that leaves me bleeding, vulnerable. Being with you, making love to you, it only solidifies what I feel for you. I know that I've become one of those spouting, love-sick idiots, but what it all boils down to is three words that don't mean nearly enough...I love you.

I closed my eyes, silently sending my own repeated proclamation of love out into the ether, hoping he somehow heard it. Reopening them, I read his last line.

Anyway, I just wanted to let you know that I'm sorry for not having a chance to call you yet...and if I have called you tonight...well, then, disregard this whole letter. Kellan.

I laughed at his last line and shook my head. Glancing up, I noticed Kate still watching me, a wistful smile on her lips. Kate read a lot of romance novels in her spare time. I was sure she loved hearing Kellan's version of being romantic. Hot and sexy, but romantic, too...just like him.

Letting out a long, stuttered breath, I shoved the note in my apron and pulled out an apple lollipop. The suckers were meant for the customers but I suddenly needed something in my mouth to suck on.

Three hours later, when I was tiredly crawling into my bed, my phone rang, and the man who'd been cropping up throughout my day finally spoke to me again. Sounding energetically awake, he murmured in my ear, "Hey, gorgeous. Did I wake you or are you just lying down?"

Grinning ear to ear, I stretched out under the covers. "Just crawled into my large, cold bed."

Kellan sighed, the sound husky and sensual. "Ah...God that sounds nice. I wish I was there with you."

Sighing, I laid my hand over where his body would have been. "You are, remember? Our bed is just too big for me to feel you, is all."

He laughed, amused. "Yeah, that's right. Well, I'd wrap my leg around yours and bury my head in your neck if I were closer..." He sighed. "I miss the smell of you..."

I bit my lip, imagining his perfect bone structure in front of me. "I was going to say the exact same thing."

He laughed again, softly. "Hey, did you get any of my notes?"

Grinning like an idiot again, I rolled onto my back. "Yeah, I did." I laughed. "When did you find time to do all that?"

"What do you think I do while you're at school?" He laughed out.

Shaking my head, I shrugged, even though he couldn't see it. "Sleep would be my guess."

Kellan sighed, the sound full of love. "Not this week...I had much more important things to do."

My corresponding sigh matched his. "Well, I loved them all...it nearly felt like you were still here."

"Good, that was the point. Did Kate give you hers?" The way he said it was odd, like he wasn't sure how I'd respond to his seductive letter.

I flushed in the darkness, remembering the steamy things he'd written. Man, he was good at expressing himself on paper. "Um, yes, she did," I whispered, embarrassed, even alone.

"And...did you like it?" he whispered, his voice husky again.

"Yes," was all I could get out.

"Good...because I meant every word. What you do to me, the way you affect me... I know you don't think you're anything special, and I think you sometimes feel like you're not attractive enough for me, but you are. My body burns for you...I can't deny that...I never could."

"It's the same for me, Kellan...all of it. How you affect me, how much I love you...all of it."

He sighed, sounding completely satisfied. "Good...I like that we feel the same. It makes me think...everything is going to be fine."

Once again, I heard the words that I'd nearly said to Denny rattling around in my head—*I hope so*. I didn't dare say them to Kellan, though. Instead, I shifted the conversation to where his current location was and what he did today. He described all of the radio interviews he had to call in for immediately upon arrival. I began to understand a little more the time constraints he was under and why he wasn't able to call. Not that I'd really expected him to call. I knew he was busy. I knew I'd get to talk to him when he was ready.

When he finished recounting his day, I gave him a recap of mine. He was just as proud and amazed as I hoped he would be when I mentioned the girl jam session we had. And Matt's neighbor fascinated him enough for him to suggest visiting her when he came home.

I glossed over the phone call to Denny. It wasn't that I was hiding it or anything, but why bring up issues that might dredge up any insecurities in Kellan? I wanted him to feel good about our relationship, to know that Denny was no longer a concern for him. That romance was history, and while reminiscing about it sometimes brought up a smidge of the residual feelings from being in the relationship, it was just that—residual—more akin to enjoying a fond memory than anything relevant to my current emotional state. I wasn't certain if I could express that satisfactorily to Kellan, though, so I left it alone. Besides, he made no mention about his conversation with Denny today either. Some things, Kellan and I just didn't need to talk about anymore.

Chapter 12 – Love from a Distance

I reluctantly opened my eyes in the morning. I'd been sleep deprived since Kellan and the D-Bags had left town. There was an endless list of things that kept me up late each night: closing shifts at work, studying for school, Anna wanting to talk about the texts she was getting from Griffin, Kellan calling me at bedtime, tucking me in with his voice...

With sleep stinging my watery eyes, I wondered if Kellan was feeling the effects of his own late nights on stage and on the road. Was he sticking to his normal pattern of early rising? His tour mates would not appreciate it if he was staying true to form. At least, not as much as I appreciated it. I'd had to make my own coffee for way too many mornings in a row now...too many to recall.

Sighing, I reached back with my toes to feel the vacant half of the bed beside me. Oddly, it wasn't vacant. I jerked my head around immediately. Kellan was lying right there, resting on his stomach with his head facing me. A huge grin spread across my face as I propped up on an elbow to stare down at him.

Of course, how could I forget, his tour was over ...he was home. I couldn't remember the time passing. That was kind of strange considering how much of it had blurred past, but I somehow knew that it had. Six months had flown by and Kellan was home...in his bed. Looking around, my thoughts were confirmed. We were in his room. His Ramones poster was still perfectly pinned in place, his Bumbershoot poster right beside it.

Odd, I'd really thought the time would drag.

Not really caring how the time leap occurred, I leaned down and ran the back of my knuckle over his cheek. He moved his head a little, but his eyes remained closed in slumber. Sighing contently, I let my finger trail down his neck and over his shoulder-blade. Sometime in the night, I had become a bit of a bedcover hog and left Kellan with only the sheet. In his restless sleep he'd twisted the fabric so that only a corner of it was resting over his bare backside.

My knuckle traveled over his ribs, the long scar on his side the only mar on his otherwise smooth, pristine skin. I bit my lip as I traced it, enjoying a personal detail about Kellan that only a handful of people knew about.

He exhaled in a way that sounded like a sigh, but peeking up at him, he still seemed out of it. The tour must have exhausted him. It was unusual for me to wake before him. It was nearly unheard of that a touch from me wouldn't wake him. Unless he was deep in a nightmare, the slightest caress usually made his eyes crack open. He was just a very light sleeper.

Curious, I flipped my hand around so my palm rested on his low back. Still, no response. My own body fully alert now, I started sliding my hand down. As my hand slipped under the scant sheet separating his skin from the spring air, I angled my fingers down to feel his hip bone.

Biting my lip so hard I thought I might puncture myself, I pushed the heel of my hand all the way down the side of his hip. There was something insanely erotic about the movement, and I was breathing a little heavier when I reached his thigh.

Loving what just that small move had done to me, I brought my hand back up his hip. This time, I moved the sheet aside so I could see the skin there; it turned me on even more.

I glanced back up at him, but he was still obliviously asleep. I frowned, irritated that we weren't on the same page. I was getting all riled up and he had his head on his arm, contently unconscious.

His knee was slightly at an angle up his body, so there was a small, seductive gap under his hip. Containing a groan, I pushed my fingers into the gap. Maybe I could wake him up another way? He might be sleeping through me caressing his body, but touching *that* body part would surely get…some response.

Just as my fingers were wrapping around his hip bone, I heard a low and husky voice say, "Careful…you're about to make me very happy."

Smiling, I peeked up at him again. Insanely dark blue eyes stared down at me. One lip curling up into a devilish smile, he murmured, "Was there something you needed?"

Pressing my body into his, I nodded. "Yeah, I think so."

His smile widening, he inhaled deep and flipped onto his back. The scant covering that had been on him didn't survive the twisting process and fell off mid-turn. Putting his other arm behind his head, he tilted his chin up and closed his eyes. "Well then, go ahead."

That was when my eyes sprang open for real.

I knew I was really awake that time because my bed was completely empty. My bed was achingly empty, and I could remember every long second that had ticked by since Kellan's departure a month and a half ago. There was no glossing over time periods in reality. Every moment was catalogued in the brain, so every moment was known. You don't suddenly not remember six months passing. Unfortunately.

Sitting up in my bed, I cursed the erotic dream I'd been having. How unfair to wake up right as Kellan was exposing himself to me. I didn't even get to sneak a peek.

Sighing, I tossed the covers off. My dream had left me in a mood that required Kellan's attentions. Irritated, I decided to get ready for school. At least some education would help douse the fire in my body.

I turned the water all the way down to ice-cold when I got in the shower. It didn't entirely take the heat of the dream away, but the shivering and shaking did help. When I got out, I had to hop up and down to get my circulation moving again.

Teeth chattering, I smiled at a post-it note on the mirror as I ran a comb through my hair. I'd found it the morning after Kellan had left. Sleepy and a little forlorn, I'd found it hidden inside my mirrored medicine cabinet, waiting for me behind my stick of deodorant. In Kellan's neat scrawl, it read, 'Remember you're beautiful, and I'm thinking of you.' After I taped it to the mirror, my sister had added a sticky note beside it. Hers read, 'I'm jealous and I hate you…but you are beautiful.'

I shook my head at their written gestures. It still amazed me how much consideration Kellan had put into his departure. I'd discovered other notes tucked throughout my home. One in the coffee pot told me how many scoops to use to make the perfect batch. One in his car reminded me to drive slowly. One tucked in the back of my locker at work asked if I missed him yet. One at his house told me I could make use of his bed if I wanted to; it highly implied that I should enjoy myself, and if I felt like it, I could send him pictures.

After finding most of the notes in the first couple of weeks, I assumed that would be it. But gradually, like a never-ending Easter egg hunt, I discovered others that had been carefully hidden. In my down time, I searched for them. That was how I found my most prized possession.

Kellan had hidden it so discretely that it was by complete luck that I came across it. When my relationship with Kellan intensified, and he started frequently staying overnight at my place, I'd given him a drawer of my dresser, to store his stuff. And just because I loved him, I'd given him the top drawer. Wondering where the clever man would stash a note in my home, I rifled through his shirts and jeans. After checking all of his pants pockets, I started in on my drawer below it. Expecting him to leave something naughty in my underwear drawer, I was surprised to find it undisturbed. But upon closing the drawer, I heard a weird noise, like paper sliding against wood.

Removing the drawer, I flipped it over and found my prize attached to the bottom. Barely breathing, I stared at it for a solid five minutes. It wasn't a note that Kellan had left there…it was a photograph. Artistically beautiful, the black and white photograph was of his body… fresh from the shower.

I wasn't sure how he captured the image, but it started around his jaw line and cut off just centimeters before his…intimate parts. Everything in-between was covered in beaded drops of moisture, rivers of it running across the curves and lines of his well-defined physique. It was the single most erotic thing I'd ever seen, and I flushed whenever I looked at it. I flushed a lot throughout my day.

I kept it in my purse with me, carrying it everywhere I went. I pulled it out periodically, reading the inscription on the back whenever I did. In red ink he'd written, *'I know you enjoy looking at me and I wouldn't want to deprive you of anything that brings you joy.'* I usually fanned myself with it next.

When Kellan and I talked on the phone, I always mentioned what I'd found that day. He'd chuckle at me, enjoying that he could entertain me, even while away. I suspected that was only one of the reasons he did it. First as a game, and second as a way to keep me thinking of him. Like I'd ever stop thinking about him. The night I told him I found his naked picture, he'd made a deep noise in his throat, then asked, "Which one?"

I couldn't even answer him and he spent a good minute laughing. I had no idea if there were more naked pictures around, but I was determined to find out.

Sighing again, I cleared Kellan from my thoughts. I needed to focus on other things today besides missing him. I needed to stop wondering how he was doing and what he was doing. I needed to stop concerning myself with why, almost every time he called, there was a giggling girl in the background. No, those things could wait until later. Today I needed to focus on my last exam before winter break.

Afterwards, I could think about Kellan, about finally seeing him again in a week, when we met up at my parents' place for Christmas. I was trying to not get too excited about it, but it was too late, I already was. My parents…were not so thrilled. Convincing them that Kellan could join in our festivities had taken some work. They didn't hate him or anything, they just didn't know him yet. All they knew was what he did for a living, and for my dad, that was enough. While he didn't say it directly, I think my dad was expecting an STD-carrying, crack-smoking, foul-mouthed hooligan to show up. Dad always had been a little overprotective.

Throwing on a pair of comfortable jeans and the warmest sweater I owned, I bundled up in a thick jacket, grabbed my bag, and headed out to Kellan's second baby. I called her Babe-ette. Kellan asked about her well-being almost as much as my own. Starting the muscle car, I let the sound take me back to his smile. I couldn't wait to see him again.

Once at school, I found a seat and pulled out my notes. I had time to spare, so I quickly reviewed my scribbles before my ethics final. I waved at some of the schoolmates that I'd befriended during class. After seeing Kellan make it look so seamless and natural, I'd started participating in group discussions. Surprisingly, people listened and agreed with me. It was an exhilarating feeling, and I found myself piping up more often. As a result, the girls that used to ogle my boyfriend every morning while speculating about me now greeted me with warm smiles. Some even asked about Kellan. Like the girl sitting on my right, Cheyenne.

Perky and blonde, she was the sort of girl men noticed. Despite her attractiveness, she had a way of talking that made you like her. Nearly every girl in the class was her friend, but she always tried to sit by me. She said just being around me boosted her test scores.

"Hey, Kiera. Think you're going to ace this?" Cheyenne had a slight southern twang to her voice that made it even more adorable.

Smiling in the self-assured way that I'd often seen Kellan smile, I shrugged. "Sure, no problem." Then I grimaced. "I hope."

She smiled as she pulled out her own notes. "I'm sure you'll kick my butt." Glancing over at the chicken scratches on my papers, she asked, "You heard from Kellan recently? How's he doing?"

I sighed, trying not to think too much about those deep blue eyes that I missed, the impossibly sexy mess of hair. "Yeah, he called last night. They're doing good, working their way to the east coast. He's somewhere in Pennsylvania, I think."

Her eyes widened as she shook her head. "Pennsylvania? I've always wanted to head over there, see the history." Leaning back in her seat, her eyes got a little dreamy. "Lucky guy, he's getting to see the world."

Tapping my pen against my notebook, I nodded. "Yeah…yeah he is." Chuckling softly, I added, "Well, this country at least."

Students around us filtered in as Cheyenne and I went over possible test questions. Candy and her friends came in, sitting as far as possible from me. I had no idea what Kellan said to them, but she'd certainly backed off after his suggestion. I knew Kellan had a temper sometimes; I'd been the recipient of it on occasion. Perhaps Candy had never been reprimanded before.

As I debated it, Candy turned in her seat. Spotting me, she glared, then scoffed. Twisting back to Tina, she said something that made them all laugh, then Tina turned to watch me. I flushed deep, considering a list of insults that she might have said. I guessed she hadn't backed off as much as I'd thought. Maybe she'd regained her confidence with Kellan's long absence. Oh well, it didn't matter. Whether Candy liked or disliked me made little difference to my relationship with Kellan.

Noticing the look, Cheyenne commented. "Candy sure has evil eyes for you. What did you ever do to her anyway?" Leaning in, she smiled. "You're far too sweet for anyone not to like."

I smiled at Cheyenne warmly, thinking that she should have seen me last year. I'd been anything but sweet then, constantly betraying Denny, and repeatedly breaking Kellan's heart. Casting off the lugubrious memories, I responded with, "She wanted to be the one dating the rock star." Looking over at Candy, I smiled even wider. "But the rock star wanted to date me." Wishing the dream I'd had this morning had been real, I sighed.

Cheyenne laughed and muttered something about Candy needing to get over herself. A burly guy walked down the aisle in front of us. He sat in the seat directly in front of me, making the entire thing squeak a little. As he shifted his position, I noticed a scrap of paper oddly stuffed into the edge of the seat, nearly invisible.

Smirking, I wondered if Kellan had shoved it there, one last impossible note for me to discover. On a whim, I reached down and pulled the paper free. It took a second to jiggle it out and Cheyenne watched me curiously. When I finally had it, she pointed at it. "What's that?"

"Probably nothing." Probably just my overactive imagination.

Unfolding the wadded-up paper, I busted out laughing. I had to slap my hand over my mouth to not cause a scene in the starting-to-get quiet room. It *was* from Kellan. On the tiny piece of paper he'd written, *'Quit thinking of me naked and study, it's the ethical thing to do.'*

Still chuckling, I shook my head. How did he know I was having erotic dreams about him? Releasing my hand from my mouth, I trailed a finger over the words he'd created. Sighing, I wondered if he was having erotic dreams about me, too. I hoped so.

Cheyenne beside me giggled. "That from Kellan? He's pretty funny." She shook her head. "Gorgeous and funny, no wonder Candy hates you."

Laughing at her comment, my eyes swept over some of the other chairs. How did he know I'd pick this particular seat? I'd been extremely lucky to find this note at all. When I started spotting tiny corners of papers sticking out of some of the other seats, I reconsidered. I wasn't lucky…Kellan had tucked notes everywhere. My God, that must have taken him forever. When in the hell did he do this? And what did they all say? As the professor had just started class, I couldn't start collecting them yet. I'd have to wait until after class to find out. I could not stop smiling throughout the exam…I was quite possibly the happiest person taking it.

Cheyenne waved goodbye after class and wished me luck on my scores. Smiling at her, I deliberately took my time gathering my stuff together. When the room was mostly empty, I began my note-seeking quest. It took me a while, but I eventually recovered every scrap that Kellan had tucked away. When all the chairs were clean, I ended up with about a hundred little messages. I immediately went home, to read them all in the privacy of my room. Some were hot, some were sweet, but all of them were a joyful surprise. He'd done so much to make sure that I wouldn't forget him, almost like he was still scared that I would. Clutching the necklace around my throat, I shook my head. My eyes stung with tears. Like I ever could.

Tucking a note that merely said, '*I love you,*' in my pocket, I started to get ready for work. Since today was the last day of school we were expecting it to be a pretty busy night at Pete's. Especially since our new band had started to gather a fan base.

I wasn't too thrilled about seeing someone else performing on Kellan's stage, but even I had to admit that the group was good. Evan and Kellan signed them up for Pete before heading out of town. The Seattle music scene was a small social circle, and all the players were well acquainted with one another. Kellan thought that this particular group of guys would be the best fit for the bar.

When I say guys, I should clarify…I mean girls. Yeah, Kellan had signed up a girl band. Don't get me wrong, they rocked like any other male band on the planet, but, I smirked when I saw them for the first time. I had the distinct feeling that Kellan chose a group of girls on purpose. Wouldn't want me fawning over another male, moody artist.

As I was putting my stuff away in the back room, I found myself assaulted by my peppy best friend. Wrapping her arms around me, Jenny kissed my cheek. "Hey, Kiera. How was your last class?"

I grinned like a dopey idiot, thinking about the dozens of love notes now sprawled across my bed. "Wonderful…" I exhaled, a little dreamily. Jenny looked at me like I was mental. And I supposed my love-filled sigh was sort of a strong reaction to taking a final. Laughing a little, I shrugged. "What can I say, I love school."

Smiling crookedly, she shook out her golden locks. "You're so weird."

Playfully batting her on the arm, the two of us headed out to start our shifts. In the hallway, someone exiting the bathroom stopped us. "Oh, hey, Kiera, Jenny."

Looking over to the doors, I contained a sigh. A member of the girl band playing tonight smiled at me. They called themselves Poetic Bliss, and the girl heading my way was the lead singer. Her name was Rain, but I was pretty sure that wasn't the name on her birth certificate. Pretty sure, since the other band member's names were Blessing, Meadow, Sunshine, and…Tuesday.

I had a really hard time saying that last one with a straight face. I wasn't sure if they all changed their names upon joining the band, or if a group of uniquely named girls just happened to come across each other. I was leaning more towards the name change. The only thing I was certain of was that Rain knew my boyfriend in ways that most women around here seemed to know my boyfriend—intimate ways. That was the reason why I sighed every time she conversed with me. There was a definite downside to dating a former man whore.

As she jauntily walked up to me, I tried to not picture her entangled with Kellan. It was difficult not to, though. She was spunky and energetic, one of those people that was constantly moving. I kept imagining her being sort of...wild...behind closed doors. Knowing that I really wasn't outrageously great in bed or anything, I immediately felt like I fell short. But love and lust were different things, and all of her playful antics hadn't made Kellan fall for her, so I must have been doing something right. Besides...Kellan never complained about our sex life.

Rain came up and gave me a swift hug. "Hey, thank Kellan again for lining up this gig for me. It's awesome here, I love it!" The petite woman was three or four inches shorter than me but she made up for her stature by wearing six-inch heels on her chunky boots. With her jet-black hair cropped into a short, shaggy mess and her dark eyes highlighted in dramatic shades of gray and pink, she looked the part of a tough rocker chick. The clingy, low-cut shirt and barely-there pleated miniskirt completed the look. Well, that and the spiked collar around her neck.

"Yeah, I'll tell him," I mumbled, wishing I could go back in time and tell a much younger Kellan that saying 'no' was a perfectly acceptable response to come-ons, and that sex wasn't the same as love. But I'm pretty sure young Kellan wouldn't have listened. He'd had to figure that one out on his own.

Reaching my hand in my pocket to feel his note, I added, "Have a great night up there. You guys are sounding really good."

She bounced on her toes a little. "Thanks! I was so excited to play tonight. I couldn't wait to get here." She looked around the mostly empty hallway. "When do the cute guys come in, anyway?"

I bit back a smile. Well, they usually strolled in hours before they played, too. Shrugging, I only told her, "Business picks up in an hour or so."

She nodded, giggling. "I'm gonna shoot some pool then. Catch you later!" With that, she turned and skipped down the hall, the pleats of her skirt showing way more of her bare leg than I'd ever dare to show in public.

Jenny looped her arm through mine. "Stop it right now."

I looked back at her, frowning. "Stop what?"

"Comparing yourself." She nodded up the hall to where the sprightly girl had disappeared. "I know you heard her and Rita talking about having sex with Kellan. I saw your face when they were describing their moments." She frowned. "Well, before you hightailed it and ran...and I don't blame you for that one."

I cringed, remembering walking into a conversation that I'd never wanted to hear...ever. Apparently Rita and Kellan's hookup had happened right here at the bar, after closing one night. And when I say "bar" I mean that literally...he took her right next to the soda dispenser. I dashed out of the conversation just as Rain explained how they made his car shake so much she worried it would tip over. I was not thrilled to have that in my head every time I drove his...baby...somewhere.

I sighed as I started walking down the hall. "It doesn't matter. That's his history," I smiled weakly, "and I'm his future." Hopefully.

Jenny clapped me on the back, smiling brightly. "That's the spirit. Now the next time you say it, say it without looking like your puppy just died."

I laughed at her comment, genuinely feeling better. I still clutched Kellan's love note all throughout my shift, though, especially when Poetic Bliss took the stage.

When I got home that night and stared at all the evidence of Kellan's affection around my room—notes, lyrics, pictures—I grabbed a suitcase from my closet and started packing. I was leaving Monday with my sister to head back home for the holidays. By this time next week, Kellan and I would be reunited. Just the thought spurred me to action. I couldn't sleep, I needed to do something, and packing seemed as good a distraction as any.

Humming one of Poetic Bliss's songs to myself, I pulled out my warmest sweaters. I made sure I included the ugly green one that made me look like a frumpy housewife. My parents had given it to me last year and I knew my mom would ask about it if I didn't wear it. Since I'd invited Kellan to crash the party, I wanted them in the best mood possible.

Stuffing some socks around the edge of my bag, I started when my phone trilled at me. Seeing who was calling, I brightened immediately. "Hey, you," I sighed, "I've missed you all day."

Kellan laughed in my ear, the sound sending a shiver down my spine. "I missed you, too. Anything *note*worthy today?"

He emphasized the word note and I giggled, sitting down on my pile of them. "Ah, yeah, actually. The cleaning staff at school has been slacking off lately. I found at least a hundred slips of paper that the janitors missed."

"Hmmm...just a hundred? Guess some got nabbed by your classmates." He laughed again. "I hope they got the kinky ones."

I flushed, wondering what he meant by kinky. I smiled and ran a hand back through my hair. "I'm packing right now...I can't wait to see you next week." I looked out the window, east, to where he was miles and miles away from me. "Is there anything you need from your place? I could grab it?"

"I can't wait to see you either. In fact, I bought this lingerie for you before I left. I tucked it away for when I got back...you could bring that?"

I sat up straight, flushing even more. I had no idea if he was joking or not. "Uh, I don't...um..."

He chuckled in my ear as I stammered for a response. Just the thought of wearing something sultry and having those bedroom eyes wash over me...made me tingle. "I'm kidding, Kiera. You don't have to dress sexy for me...you already are."

Smiling, I looked down at the plain tank top and lounge pants I'd put on. Yep, that was me...sexy as all get out. I sighed and he heard it. "You okay?"

Not meaning to say anything, I blurted out, "Rain says thank you...again."

"Oh." His voice sounded surprised. He'd probably expected something much different to come out of my mouth. "Well, tell her it was no big deal. Her band is great, they deserved the opportunity."

"Yeah," I muttered, "And she's not one to pass up an opportunity." I cringed, hating that I actually said that out loud. I hated sounding jealous and petty.

Kellan, of course, heard my tone and deciphered it correctly. His voice a little tight, he quietly said, "She told you, didn't she?"

I exhaled in a rush, not really wanting to talk about this, but knowing I'd opened the can and Kellan wouldn't let it go until all of the worms were back inside it. "No, I overheard her and Rita comparing notes." I said Rita's name a bit harshly and clamped my mouth shut. God, the harpy was coming out of me today.

Kellan sighed. "Oh...did you know about Rita already?" he whispered that, his voice really tentative.

"Yes." The word came out short, clipped, and I forced myself to relax. History...future. I needed to remember that mantra.

Kellan was silent for a second and I nearly wanted to apologize for bringing it up. He spoke before I could. "I'm sorry, Kiera. I never wanted you to have to hear about...them. If I could stop the gossiping, you know I would."

Wearily, I laid myself back on the bed and propped my feet up. "You don't have to apologize, Kellan. It's...water under the bridge, really." Shaking my head, I tried to change the subject. "What about you, what have you been up to?"

He was quiet a moment, then murmured, "Just shows and traveling. I'm so sorry I haven't had a chance to come home yet. With us on the road between shows, there just hasn't been enough time to fly back to you."

I exhaled, the sound wistful to my ears. "I know. I miss you...so much." I closed my eyes.

He chuckled, his voice husky. "I miss you, too. I have the wildest dreams about you. You would not believe the hard-ons I wake up with."

My eyes sprang open as I listened to him chuckle in my ear. My body heated at his words. I imagined his response to his dreams and my reaction to mine. It warmed me that we were both waking up...unsatisfied. "Me too," I whispered, my face heating worse than my body. He laughed a little more and I slapped my hand over my eyes. "I mean, I'm not hard, but..." I groaned, hating the words that sometimes left my mouth.

In a low, seductive growl, he murmured, "Yeah, I know what you mean. I wish I was there, to touch you when you woke up that way. I wish I could feel how much you miss me."

I bit my lip, my fingers running over my mouth. Barely above a whisper, I said, "I wish you were too..."

He exhaled in a groan. "God, your voice…I'm hard right now, Kiera. I wish you could touch me."

My breath picking up, I heard myself murmur, "I want to." I had no idea if I meant that I wanted to touch him, or that I wanted to continue with where I thought this conversation might be going.

He paused for a second. When he spoke again, there was a heat in his voice that made me warm and luscious; it made me writhe. "Oh, Kiera…I want you so bad…what do you want me to do?"

Covering my eyes, I bit my lip. Oh, my God, I could not do this. Feeling moronic, I whispered, "Touch it, pretend it's me." Oh God, I wanted to crawl into a hole and never come out again.

I was expecting Kellan to chuckle, but he didn't, instead I heard some rustling around and I swear—a zipper un-zipping. Oh, damn…

He hissed in a breath, releasing it with a gasp. "Oh, I'm so hard…it feels so good. What now?"

Not believing this was happening, I swallowed. "Stroke it." I didn't just actually say that…did I?

He moaned in my ear, his breath faster. "Kiera…God…feels so good…I wish I was wet, though, like I am when I'm inside you."

I groaned, biting my knuckle. Jesus, was he really…? Insanely glad my sister was asleep, I whispered, "Do you have anything that would…?"

In a strained voice, his breath hitching, he gasped out, "Yeah…hold on." I heard a distinctly squishy noise and wondered just what sort of lubricant Kellan had on hand…and why. When he spoke again, though, I couldn't have cared less. "Oh…God…yes, it's warm…like you. You feel so good, wrapped around me…"

Aching myself now, I moaned a little. He was pretending, maybe I should too? "Do you want to touch me, Kellan?"

"Oh God, yes, please. I need to feel that warm, wet skin…I need to be inside you…"

Holy…hell. I ran my hand down my stomach, but I couldn't quite make myself go any further. I was far too embarrassed, even alone. Kellan didn't know that, though. "Does it feel good?" he groaned.

"Yes," I whispered. All of me felt tingly and nice, so that wasn't really a lie.

His breath increased. "Oh God, I need it harder…faster…"

"Yes, I whispered again. "Do it, do it faster…" I had to ceaselessly move my legs I was aching so bad, but I still hesitated to go through with my end of this.

Kellan, however, was not hesitating at all. "Oh God, yes…don't stop…that feels so good, please don't stop…" I moaned again, re-biting my knuckle so hard I thought I might break the skin. He groaned deep, his breath in a pant. "I want to come…Kiera…come with me…"

I ran my hand back through my hair. Oh, my God…he really was…

"Okay," I whispered, my voice husky. "Harder, Kellan, I need more of you in me," I murmured, my hand drifting back down to my stomach.

That got him going. "Yes…God, Kiera, you're so sexy, you feel so good. I'm in you…right now…can you feel me? Can you feel how deep I am?"

I groaned, louder than before and my hand strayed to the edge of my underwear. "God, Kellan, you're perfect…so perfect." My voice gained in strength as some of my inhibitions started leaving me. I wanted him. I wanted to do this. I wanted to finish this…together. "Yes, yes, take me…"

"Oh, my God, Kiera, I'm almost there…come with me…"

"Yes, Kellan, do it…come for me…" Not believing I said that, I finally tucked a finger on the inside of my underwear.

That was when I heard something that doused some cold water on my hot little moment. Kellan stopped breathing heavy and the phone muffled. Quieter than he'd been, but still loud enough to hear, I heard him say, "I'll have a Denver omelet…thank you."

I sat up in my bed, covering myself with my hands like we'd just gotten walked in on. Before he spoke to me again, I snapped out, "Kellan Kyle! Are you in a restaurant?"

"Well, I wouldn't exactly call this a restaurant…greasy spoon, maybe." His breath was still a little fast, but way more calm than it had been.

I closed my eyes, running my hand down my face. "Please tell me you are not about to be arrested for indecent exposure."

He laughed a little. "No, I'm not."

I dropped my hand to my knee, floored. "You faked all that? Why would you do that to me?" I brought my knees to my chest, feeling sort of weird. He'd told me before when he faked a sexual act that it wasn't his first time, but, damn…

Kellan sighed. "I never expected you to go along with it and when you did, well, I wasn't about to stop you from having your moment." In a whisper, he added, "Even if I can't come right now…I want you to."

I bit my lip, feeling a little bad. I had faked it, too. "I may have exaggerated my part in it…but I was thinking about it."

Kellan laughed. "Well, we'll call that a practice round then. Next time…I'll be somewhere private and you will actually touch yourself. Deal?"

I flushed, feeling that embarrassment creep back up. "Yeah," I mumbled.

I heard a voice in the background that sounded vaguely familiar. Sitting ramrod straight, I whispered, "Oh, my God, please tell me that you're sitting alone."

Kellan paused. I could almost hear him debating on whether or not to answer me. "Um, well, no…the guys are here…and Justin. He says hey, by the way."

"Oh, my God!" I exclaimed, disconnecting the phone in my mortification. Not only had he faked that little moment, but he'd faked it in front of his friends and the celebrity that I knew I'd never be able to look in the eye again. God…men…

Chapter 13 – Home for the Holidays

A week later, I was at my parents' place, staring at their Christmas tree, ticking down the minutes in my head. Ever since arriving in my hometown earlier in the week, I'd been hoping that Kellan's tour would end prematurely and he could join me. Sure, I would have to do some fanciful fast talking to get my dad to concede to letting him sleep in the house, but even if he had to stay at a nearby motel, at least he would be with me, and not…who knows where.

But the guys' busy schedule kept them working right until Christmas Eve. Just last night, he had played a show in New York. It was their largest show to date, and Kellan was exuberant when he finally called…at four in the morning. Now that our time zones were closer together, he was calling me well after I was asleep. I didn't mind though, groggily murmuring some sort of response to his stories.

My sister came out and joined me on our mom's plastic-coated couch. It squeaked a bit when she sat down. Looping her arm over my shoulders, she handed me a cup of spiced coffee. I took it, smiling as I watched the blinking Christmas lights reflecting in the white ceramic. The smell of cinnamon wafted up, reminding me of multiple things—baking with my mom, the candles my grandma had burned non-stop, and of course, Kellan. Anything with coffee always reminded me of Kellan.

Clinking our cups, Anna smiled brightly. "Merry Christmas, Kiera."

I tilted my head at her as I took a sip. "Merry Christmas, Anna."

Looking outside, to the light snow that was starting to fall, Anna shivered. "You excited to finally see Kellan again? It's been what…almost two months?"

I sighed and leaned back into the couch. "Yeah." It had actually gone by quicker than I'd anticipated. Kellan's phone calls, periodic texts, and his little scavenger hunt had eased the passage of time. If anything, Kellan was very good at keeping in touch. It was reassuring, and it confirmed how much he missed me, too.

Anna sighed and leaned back with me. "Yeah, I miss those guys." She frowned after she said it, and I leaned into her side. Other than a few phone calls and quite a few snapshots of Griffin's junk, Anna hadn't gotten much out of her pseudo-boyfriend. He wasn't even coming out to see her for Christmas, which I was sort of glad about. He and Matt were visiting their families in California, while Evan was going home to see Jenny. Rachel was flying out to visit Matt in L.A., but Anna hadn't shown any interest in flying out to meet up with Griffin. I was pretty sure Griffin hadn't invited her, either.

"I'm sure Griffin misses you, Anna. He wouldn't still text you if he didn't." I hoped that sounded encouraging, but really, their relationship mystified me.

Anna rolled her eyes and scoffed, bringing her feet up on the couch that our mom was anal about keeping clean. "Whatever…I'll see him when I see him." Her voice was a little strained and I thought she almost looked misty-eyed…but I couldn't really tell.

Shaking her head, she looked over at me. "When's Kellan coming up?"

I looked out the living room archway to the kitchen to see if either of our parents was listening. Mom was carving up a turkey, the sound of her electric knife filling the air. Occasionally I could hear her snapping at Dad to stay out of the olives. Smiling, I figured they were too engrossed in their own activities to hear me. I didn't want to bring up Kellan's arrival any more than I had to.

"Don't know." I lifted the phone I had in my other hand. "He's going to call when he knows for sure." As if on cue, the cell buzzed in my palm. I blinked at the contraption as Anna started laughing.

Impressed by Kellan's timing, I read the text message on my screen. 'I can't wait to see you tonight. I'll be in around nine. Should I meet you at your parents' place?'

Giggling that this was actually going to happen, I texted back a reply that was horribly impractical. 'No, have the cab take you here…'

I texted him the address of my favorite park. I knew it was romantic and sappy, meeting at a secluded spot instead of having him come to the house, but he'd been gone for an eternity, and I wanted to shower him in affection before introducing him to my parents. Besides, he did say that he wanted to see all of the places I loved.

'Okay, it's a date. I love you.'

I texted that I loved him, too, then held the phone to my chest as I sighed contently. God, I'd missed him. Anna just stared at me, an eyebrow raised. "Huh," she muttered.

Adjusting my posture so I didn't look so school girlish, I shook my head. "Huh, what?"

She smiled, then kissed my head. "Nothing…you've just got it bad, Kiera." She frowned, just slightly. "I hope…I hope you get what you want."

I started to ask her what she meant but she stood up and left the room. Maybe she was just conflicted about her own feelings towards Griffin, and she was transferring that doubt onto my relationship with Kellan. If she knew something…I was sure she'd tell me right away. Sister's code and all.

The rest of the day went by so slowly that I felt like another couple of months had passed. Kellan and I reunited, even for just one night, would be the best Christmas gift I could have asked for. Better than any material possession in this world.

Everyone dressed in their finest for our Christmas Eve meal. It was just the four of us, but we'd always made an elaborate gourmet feast fit to serve the queen; Mom even brought out the fine china. Dad dressed in his favorite sweater vest, looking very academic and proper, like he should be in a leather-bound chair, smoking a pipe while discussing Thoreau. Mom put on her pearls, her dress neatly steamed and pressed. I scrounged through my old closet and found a simple black dress. Anna outdid us all in a sleek, fitted red dress that she nearly spilled out of.

Glancing at the clock on the wall after arranging the table, the food so elegantly set that even Martha Stewart, herself, would have approved, Mom said, "Should we wait for Kellan, dear?"

My dad pursed his lips, not at all thrilled that a lazy, drug-induced rocker was about to throw off his Christmas traditions. I didn't bother telling him, again, that Kellan wasn't like that. "No, he's still a couple of hours away. I'll save him some for when he gets here."

Mom nodded and began serving the slices of poultry. Dad raised an eyebrow at me. "You know, we never fully went over where he'll be staying, Kiera...it won't be with you."

Sighing, I looked down. "I know, Dad...no boys in the house." Geez, you'd think I was still fifteen.

Anna crossed her arms over her chest. "Don't be ridiculous, Dad. Where exactly is he supposed to stay?" She pointed her finger out the window, to the city of Athens in the distance. "There were no rooms at the inn on Christmas Eve, remember?"

"Anna," Mom warned, her visage showing her disapproval of my sister's analogy.

Anna sighed and shrugged. "Just saying, things are going to be full. You can't just kick him out if he's got nowhere to be...that's not very merry." I smiled, loving that Anna was sticking up for him. Remaining quiet, since Anna could sometimes sway our parents more easily than I could, I watched my dad frown, then consider.

Rubbing his lip, he thought for a moment. Finally, he raised his eyes to me. "He can stay in the tent out back. I'll set it up after dinner."

"A tent? Dad!" I finally exclaimed. "It's snowing outside...he'll freeze to death." Crossing my arms now, I added, "You were going to let Denny stay with me last year...in my room."

Dad sighed heavily, like he was conceding a great defeat. He couldn't really argue with me on that point. My parents had acted hastily last year, in their attempt to lure me to their place when they thought I'd decided to go to Australia with Denny. Things hadn't worked out that way, but still, the offer had been made. They should honor it, no matter whom I was with.

Shaking his head, Dad muttered, "That was different. We knew Denny...and he was a good man. Made some bad decisions, left you alone when he shouldn't have, but...a good man, I think."

I sighed as Mom silently filled my plate. "Yes, Denny's a good man...and so is Kellan." Looking at the both of them, I shrugged. "You just have to give him a chance." Dad sighed again and I added, "Please...I really love him."

Mom paused, placing a hand on my shoulder and peering at my dad. He looked up at her, sighed again, then muttered, "Fine, he can stay in the house..." he pointed at me, "but he doesn't go up to your room...ever, and he sleeps on the couch!"

I rolled my eyes but didn't press my luck. Just Dad conceding to Kellan staying in the building was a huge victory. Anna smiled at me as she popped a forkful of stuffing in her mouth. She raised her eyebrows suggestively and I knew exactly what she was thinking—*Don't worry, I'll cover for you.*

After a leisurely dinner and a good helping of pecan pie, it was finally time to meet Kellan at my favorite park. I was giddy, envisioning our romantic moment. After I quickly threw on some warm clothes for my date, Dad sullenly gave me his car keys, complaining that if Kellan was truly a gentleman than he would've met me here. In Kellan's defense, I explained that it was my idea to meet in the park, as I wanted to show him a small bit of Ohio University.

Being a proud Alma Mater, that perked Dad up a bit. He watched me carefully as I took the keys though, and it was clear that he'd be listening for my return tonight. The private part of our reunion was going to be brief. Getting into my dad's Volvo, I started my drive.

The roads were kept pretty clear, so I had little difficulty traversing through the falling snow. Within minutes I arrived at our meeting place. Looking around, it was no surprise that the parking area was empty. It was late on Christmas Eve and most people were already snug in their beds, waiting for Christmas morning, not having a romantic rendezvous in a public place. Feeling excitement starting to course through me, I made my way through the park.

The freshly falling snow was adding a soft layer to the few inches already covering the ground. I wanted to run to the spot where I knew Kellan would be, but I resisted. Looking around the park, I hoped the directions I texted him earlier, were specific enough for him to be able to find this exact spot. Walking across the snowy lawn, my boots crunching a path through the pure white, I came up to a bench in front of a small duck pond. Even though I'd spent countless hours at this park while I attended college here, this place oddly reminded me of the park back home that Kellan and I regarded as ours. Strange, how I already considered Seattle my "home" and my birthplace was now the spot I visited.

Brushing snow off the wrought iron bench, I looked out over the pale moonlit night as I sat down. There were no fresh tracks in the snow. The ground was beautiful, perfectly pristine. Grabbing my cell phone out of the purse slung over my side, I glanced at the time. Nine-thirty. The local airport was nearby. Assuming his flight was on schedule, there had been ample time for him to get from the airport to here. But glancing around the sloping white hills, I only saw where my tracks led down to where I sat. Kellan wasn't here yet.

I tried waiting patiently, but I hadn't seen him in so long that I was edgy. Nervous energy shot through me as my feet bounced up and down on the insulated-with-snow concrete path. Light flakes were still falling, collecting in my hair and eyelashes, melting together then beading and rolling off my thick jacket. The longer I sat, the more I felt the cold. Sniffling a little, I suddenly cursed my romantic spot. I should have just had him drive to my parents' place. Less chance he'd get lost that way. Plus, parks weren't exactly the best place to wait around in the middle of the night…even on Christmas Eve.

That thought made me wonder what or who could be in this park besides me. I started when my phone vibrated in my hands. The tiny chime accompanying it seemed horribly loud in the still night and I cursed under my breath. Looking down, a puff of warm air from my mouth hazed the screen. Frowning, I wiped the condensation off…then I smiled.

New text message from Kellan Kyle.

Those words from my phone were some of my favorite. Right after, Incoming call from Kellan Kyle, actually. Pressing the view now icon, I waited to see what my man had to say for himself; he was nearly forty-five minutes late now. My heart dropped immediately.

'I'm sorry…I can't make it.'

I willed the disappointment to stop. It was hard. It came crashing through me like the storms hitting the east coast. Was that why he couldn't make it? Maybe he's snowed in?

With heavy fingers, I typed back, 'Really? But it's Christmas…'

I hoped he didn't think I was whining. I knew his schedule was grueling. I knew he was making an extraordinary effort to see me. Wiping a stubborn tear from my eye, I sniffed again for a different reason. I had wanted so much to introduce him to my family, to spend the holiday with him, to just…see him.

His reply came while I was wiping my nose with the back of my jacket sleeve. 'Yeah, I know. I tried…I'm really sorry.' While I tried to think of something that was encouraging and sympathetic, not snippy and childish, my phone buzzed and chirped again. 'Are you okay? You're not crying, are you?'

Sniffling and wiping my nose again, I frowned that he thought I'd turn into a blubbering mess so rapidly. True, my stomach was in knots and tears were freely rolling down my cheeks, but I didn't necessarily want him to know that. 'No…I'm fine. I know you tried. I'm okay…really.'

Thinking that I had no idea when I'd actually see him again, a stubborn sob escaped me. My phone sounded at me right after. I had to swipe my fingers under my eyes to read his message.

'You're lying.'

Sniffling as more tears embarrassingly ran down my face, I shook my head at the screen. "Am not…" My voice was a little petulant as I replied to a tiny piece of machinery that couldn't hear or understand me.

Just as my thumbs came down to type him a message reiterating just how completely fine I was, even though I wasn't, my phone chirped at me. Blinking, I opened his message.

'Are too.'

I stared at my phone like it had just grown lips and talked to me. I did say that smart ass comment out loud, didn't I? Did I subconsciously text it too? I was a little worn out from travel, and the holidays…and my parents. Flipping through my outbox, I double-checked all of my messages.

"How did you know that, Kellan?" I muttered as I looked for a message I didn't remember sending.

My phone buzzed while I was browsing yesterday's texts. Shaking my head,

I shifted back to the inbox. 'I know that because I know everything.' My eyes widened even more. Another message had come in while I was reading that one and I immediately opened it next. 'I also lied…turn around.'

My heart in my throat, I did as my phone commanded me. It was like emerging from a dream, or maybe, falling into one. Stepping away from the shadow of an oak tree at the base of the hill, just a few feet away from me, Kellan walked into the moonlight, tucking his phone into his leather jacket as he did. I stood from the bench as he came into view.

My God, he was beautiful.

My mouth dropped open as fresh tears sprang into my eyes, happy tears this time. Snow lightly gathering in his thick, messy hair, his lips curled into a devilish smile as he stared at me.

"Kellan," I breathed.

Then I was off, rushing towards him before my head even registered the movement. Chuckling, his face breaking into a playful grin, he started walking towards me. Walking wasn't good enough for me. I flew to him. I hadn't had his arms around me in weeks. I hadn't had more than his voice in my ear for weeks. I needed so much more now.

I leapt into his arms when I finally slipped and slid my way over to him. Kellan laughed as my arms cinched around his neck. The warmth of the reunion melted all the iciness from my body. I'd never felt such complete peace. He lifted me a good foot, swinging me around in a circle. I was laughing when he set me down, my earlier despair gone.

Just as his lips started coming towards mine, I shoved his shoulder back. My despair might have evaporated, but that was not a nice joke. "You were kidding? You're such a jerk."

Chuckling, his eyes even more blue in the blue light filtering through the trees, he raised an eyebrow. "I thought I was a prick?"

Shaking my head, I grabbed his cheeks, pulling his face towards mine. We could argue the semantics of his assholeness later. I needed more than just words right now. Kellan's arms wrapped around my waist as our lips melded together. Cold and hot at the same time, our mouths softly felt the other's. Our breath's vapor between us, he muttered, "I'm sorry I'm late."

My hands drifted up to tighten in his hair, the long strands on the top damp with melted snow. "I'm just glad you're here."

Our soft but intense kiss broke apart, and Kellan rested his head against mine. His eyes flicked over my face, studying me, maybe seeing how I'd changed in the past few weeks. "I've missed you…so much."

Grinning, I pressed my lips back to his. "I've missed you, too."

We kissed in the lightly falling snow, a few feet away from the frozen duck pond that students sometimes skated on when it iced over. We kissed until my fingers were so numb I could no longer feel the thick strands of his hair wrapped around them. That still didn't stop me though. I needed his lips on mine. I needed his body pressed into mine. I really didn't care if I froze solid, and became a living work of art here...as long as he was with me.

He pushed me back, though, when I went for his mouth again. "We should go, you're frozen."

His eyes traveled down my body and I felt the chill melt away. "I'm fine," I stuttered, my body actually colder than my mind believed it was.

He smirked, a cloud of moisture escaping his mouth. "Your teeth are chattering."

I leaned up, trying to will my frostbitten fingertips to pull his head back to me. "I don't care..."

Chuckling more, his hands grabbed my waist and twisted me around. Pulling my hips into his body and wrapping his arms over my chest, warming me, he murmured in my ear, "Well, I care." I closed my eyes and leaned back into his embrace; I'd missed this so much. His breath warm down the side of my neck he added, "Besides, I can't make love to you out here..."

My eyes sprang open and I took a step forward. Grabbing his hand, I started leading him away from my favorite pond. "You're right...it is getting pretty cold."

He looked down and shook his head. Small drops of melted snow in his hair fell to the ground as his amused smile widened. When he peeked back up at me, a drop landed on his cheek, sliding its way down to his neck...lucky drop.

His grin breaking into a mischievous one as I pulled him along, he told me, "I know my trick was a little mean, but it did prove one very important thing."

Turning to walk beside him, I looped my arm through his and peered up at him. "Besides the fact that you haven't changed...that you're still a prick?"

He chuckled and nodded. "Yes, aside from that." As I stared at him with a small smile on my face, his eyes searched mine and he shook his head. "You really did miss me," he whispered, his eyes looking almost...surprised by the information.

I stopped us in our tracks and stared up at him. He held my gaze, then swallowed. Shaking my head, I cupped his cheek. "Of course I missed you. I missed you every day, every hour...practically every second."

He smiled really quick and then looked away, as if embarrassed for bringing it up. "Yeah, I saw that." He shook his head, still not looking at me. "I just...no one's ever missed me before..."

I barely heard his voice, but I clearly heard the emotion behind it. Moving my hand to his chin, I forced his gaze back to mine. "I miss you when you're gone. I feel like I can't breathe when you're away. I think about you so often, it borders on obsession." I ran my frozen fingers over his jaw. "I love you...so much."

He swallowed and smiled, his jaw trembling. Not able to answer me, he only nodded.

After retrieving his bag from where he left it by the oak tree, we made our way to my dad's car. With the heater on high, we slowly drove back to my parents' house. Laying his head back on the seat, Kellan had a peaceful smile on his lips as he held my hand. Knowing that I'd given him a reason to smile warmed me more than the car's heater. He finally understood how it felt to be loved, cherished, and missed. The simple things we all took for granted…and he was relishing each and every moment, because he'd never had them.

It was later than I anticipated when we parked in the driveway. Examining the modest two-story house I'd grown up in, I looked up at the windows where my parents slept. The lights were all off—a good sign. Dad probably wanted to stay up all night, waiting for my return with my bad influence of a boyfriend, but Mom must have put a stop to that. Or Anna. She wasn't intimidated by them and would tell Dad exactly what an ass he was being if the situation required it. I wouldn't put it past her to march him to his room and make him stay there, like he was the child and she was the adult.

Anna…gotta love her.

Turning the car off, I giggled as I twisted to Kellan. He lifted his head, looking over the house, then over at me. "Want to see my room?" I flushed, feeling sixteen again…although I'd never, ever snuck a boy into my bedroom before.

Kellan tilted his head and smiled. "I'd love to."

He grabbed his bag from the trunk, then we quietly stepped into the deceptively empty-looking home. I cautioned Kellan to keep quiet. He smiled, containing a laugh as he shook his head. He might think it funny that his first visit to my family home involved sneaking around like we were robbing the place, but he'd understand why if we accidentally woke my dad up. If we did that, Kellan would be interrogated until morning.

Luckily though, my parents were the early-to-bed, early-to-rise type people. As I paused, listening for sounds, I clearly heard Dad's lumberjack snores echoing from upstairs. I pictured him asleep in his reading chair, book in hand as he drifted off waiting for me. Poor guy. He'd probably kick himself for falling asleep on duty. I smiled, wondering if Anna had snuck in and turned off his light when he finally passed out as a signal to me, to let me know that he was asleep and it was safe to…reunite…with my boyfriend.

Pointing at the couch, I whispered to Kellan that he could leave his bag there since he'd be sleeping there. He raised an eyebrow at me as he frowned, clearly unhappy with anything that involved him sleeping so far away from me. Smiling, I gave him a quick kiss before adjusting the pillow and afghan Mom had laid out for him. Kellan shook his head at the plastic-wrapped contraption and popped his shoes off. Slipping his jacket off, he looked about ready to crawl into the bed my parents expected him to sleep in.

Just as he started to sit, I pulled him back to his feet. "You're not actually sleeping there, silly," I whispered in his ear.

He grinned at me devilishly as he glanced upstairs. "Are you sure? I don't want to get you in trouble?"

I nodded, backing away from his pretend bed. "Yes…you're with me." He grinned more, rushing towards me to cup my cheeks, pulling me in for an intense kiss.

I stumbled as my heel hit the stairs. I nearly fell, but Kellan grabbed me and kept me upright. He chuckled while I clung to him. "Quiet," he whispered.

I nodded, giggling a little, then I found his lips again. We somehow managed to get up the stairs without waking anybody...or everybody. Our breaths were fast between our rarely parting lips. I felt every curve of his mouth, the warmth of his tongue. I'd imagined kissing him for weeks, but it was nothing—nothing—like the real thing. If there was one positive side to Kellan being so promiscuous in his youth...he was good at what he did. No, he was amazing at it. There wasn't one inch of my body that wasn't on fire by the time I opened the door to my bedroom.

Having removed my jacket on the way up the stairs, Kellan blindly tossed it into the room. I silently closed the door, taking a moment to press him into it. He sucked in a quick breath as my body compressed against his. "I missed you," he whispered.

I moaned some sort of answer, my fingers tangling into his thick hair. His hands traveled down my back, over my bottom. Squatting slightly, he grabbed my thighs and lifted me up as he took a step from the door.

Our mouths never parting, he walked me to my bed. Nervous, excited energy flooded into me. I'd never so directly defied my dad. He would be fuming if he knew Kellan was in here with me, about to...well, make me a woman, since in my dad's eyes I was probably still a virgin.

When Kellan bumped his legs into my bed, he leaned over and deposited me on to it. Holding his head to me, I scooted up the mattress so he could join me. Crawling on his hands and knees, he followed me until we were in the center. Then, with a quietly content groan, he lay on top of me. Instantly we both stopped breathing and broke apart.

Furrowing his brows, Kellan looked down at my bed. Propping himself up so that most of his weight was in his hands, he pushed down against the mattress. It squeaked...loudly. I bit my lip. I'd never noticed my bed did that before. Of course, I'd never had a boy in it while my dad was asleep in the next room. With a scowl, Kellan repeated the motion. The noise cut through the night...it was an unmistakable sound. It practically screamed—*Hey, listen to us, we're having sex!*

Looking down at me, Kellan raised an eyebrow. "Did your dad buy you the squeakiest bed in the world on purpose?"

Cringing, I sighed. "Yeah, probably." Damn overprotective father. When he couldn't stop us with a watchful eye, he managed to stop us with outdated technology.

I squirmed under Kellan's hips, wishing I could do more, but even that slight movement made a sharp sound. Now that my mind was clearer, even our crawling into the bed was noisy. I immediately stopped moving, afraid that we might have already woken my dad up.

Kellan shook his head, his lip curving into a delicious smile; it made me ache. "Well, your dad obviously doesn't know me very well, if he thinks that's going to be a big enough deterrent."

Slipping off me, the bed squealing in protest, he stood at the back of it. With a finger, he motioned for me to get up. I did, curious. Once standing, he grabbed all the blankets and laid them out on the floor on the other side of the bed. Next, he laid down some pillows, so we'd be sort of comfortable. Standing back, he smiled and spread his arms out. "Your love nest awaits."

Amused, I crossed my arms over my chest. Kellan walked over to me, grabbed my hand, and led me to our love nest. My heart accelerated with every step we took towards the spot he had laid out for us.

Pulling me into his body once we were standing before the blankets, he murmured, "Kiera?" He leaned down to place a light kiss upon my neck, just under my ear. I couldn't answer him, I started trembling. He didn't wait for my response. Placing a feather-light kiss below the first, he asked, "Will you...?" He paused to kiss farther down my neck. I tilted my head and closed my eyes, feeling dazed, like my head was spinning. He placed a kiss in the electric spot right by my collar-bone, then ran his nose up my neck to my ear. Once there, he finished his question. "...make love to me?"

I think I may have melted.

I kissed him hard, my breath back to pant-mode. Quickly, but quietly, we stripped off the multiple layers of clothing between us. When we were both bare, his fingers on my skin searing me, we lay down on my daisy covered quilt. Bringing the heavy, down comforter over the top of us, we melded together.

His skin, hot against mine, made my body feel like satin as we naturally entwined. His lips left warm, wet trails over my silky skin and I felt sensuous, seductive, and worshipped. He let out a soft groan in my ear as my fingers traveled down the most sensitive, private area of him. Desire shot through me, mixing with love and the residual loneliness of our forced separation.

Careful to keep as quiet as possible, I pulled on his hips, urging him to take me. He locked gazes with me, his breath fast through his parted lips. I reached up and sucked on one and his eyes fluttered closed. As we broke apart, I nodded, squirming my hips under his. I wanted this.

His eyes, dark in my dark room, skimmed over my features as his hand trailed down my body, to my knee. Slightly pulling my leg up and around his hip, he settled himself over me. My heart raced with anticipation. Resting his forehead against mine, he lightly breathed on me for a moment, pressing against me but not moving inside yet. Being this close, his smell overwhelmed me, and made me even more ready for him, for us, for this.

His breath hot but sweet, he let out an erotic exhale. "Nothing...compares to this..."

My fingers swept over his cheek. I wondered what he meant, but he closed his eyes and pressed into me and any attempt at speaking failed me. I clutched his shoulder, closing my own eyes as I swallowed repeatedly, anything to stop myself from crying out with the glorious intenseness of it. I heard him biting back his own groan as he dropped his head to my shoulder.

Effortless

Writhing with restraint, sucking in quick breaths, we began moving together. It was so intense—the weeks of waiting, the moments of telephone teasing, the anticipation I'd felt all day—my body hit the wall faster than I ever would have believed possible. I fought against the rising pressure, wanting to feel it with him. He grabbed my cheek, his pace staying slow and steady. Making me look at him as I fought against myself, he shook his head. "Don't...let go..."

I shook mine and he leaned down to my ear. "Don't worry about me...let me give this to you..."

He pushed a little harder and I lost whatever hold on my control that I had. The euphoria burst through me and I arched my back, panting as I struggled to control the vocal part of releasing. My body was shaking from the contained explosion and I dug my fingers into Kellan's shoulder. As my eyes rolled back, I thought I'd never felt anything so perfectly wondrous.

I ran a hand down my face as I drifted back from my high. Watching me intently, still smoothly sliding against my body, Kellan's face was a picture of love and lust. He seemed amazed and spellbound, watching me experience the satisfaction he had just given me. His lips fell to mine, light and soft. I felt like taffy.

"God, Kiera...God...that was..."

He dug in a little deeper and I closed my eyes. Surprisingly, the fire started resurfacing. I found his mouth, wondering if I could have that sensation with him again, but together this time. Our lips containing the soft groans we were making, I encouraged him to move his body at a speed that would satisfy him. He whimpered when he hit the right spot and I moaned softly, needing him even more than before.

His mouth falling open, he started to lower his head. My hand came up to his cheek, to make him stare at me. He clenched my hand in his as he closed his eyes. I watched the euphoria flood his features. Just as his hips paused, he cringed, almost looking pained. It passed immediately as a soft, but deep noise left his throat. He bit his lip to contain it, but the sound, mixed with the look of pure pleasure on his sculpted face, pushed me over the edge again.

Keeping my eyes open, so I could watch every second of his bliss, I felt my climax wash over me again. It wasn't as intense as the first time, more peaceful, more perfect. As his body collapsed against mine, I finally closed my eyes, letting the shared moment of ecstasy sweep me away.

Chapter 14 – Merry Christmas

I woke the next morning gloriously achy. As I stretched out my tight muscles, my hip hurt a bit from sleeping on the hard floor. My arm was mostly numb from partially lying on it. My womanly parts were also feeling the dull strain, renewed from weeks of being ignored by last night's powerful reconnection. But none of that truly bothered me, because a warm arm was flopped over my stomach.

I turned my head and snuggled into the warmth of Kellan's neck, missing the feeling of waking up next to him. His arm tightened around my waist and the words I'd missed even more brushed against my ear. "Mornin'."

He inhaled deeply and stretched out his muscles. I had to imagine that he was every bit as sore as I was, although, his man parts probably weren't. That was just a side effect for women…it was nice, though. A reminder.

I leaned in to kiss his neck. "Good morning, yourself." Popping my eyes all the way open, I propped myself up on my elbow. Smiling down at the half-dozing man beside me, I whispered, "Merry Christmas, Kellan."

He opened his eyes and reached up for my face. "Merry Christmas, Kiera." His hand threaded through my hair and wrapped around my neck. As he started pulling me down to his lips, my bedroom door opened. I froze, wide-eyed, suddenly remembering where I was.

"Kiera? Where are you?"

Hearing my sister's soft voice, I popped my head up. Her luxurious hair piled into an adorably cute ponytail on the top of her head, Anna laughed when she saw where I was hiding. Dressed in pink and green camouflage pajamas, she giggled as she laid herself down on my squeaky mattress. Propping her face into her hands and clicking her heels together, she looked over the edge of the bed to our love nest on the floor.

Smiling down at the two of us as I lowered myself back down to Kellan's arms, she laughed out, "Well, I was going to wish you a Merry Christmas and ask if you wanted to head downstairs with me, but I can see that you've already unwrapped your present." She smiled over at Kellan peering up at her with an amused grin. "Hey, Kellan, glad you finally made it."

He chuckled, squeezing me tight. "Hey, Anna. Thanks."

Pulling the blankets up Kellan's chest, hiding his tattoo as well as his marvelous pecs, since Anna was clearly enjoying the visual that she walked into this morning, I sighed at my sister. "What time is it?"

Anna swung her perfectly emerald eyes to me. "It's breakfast time…Mom's making eggs."

I sat up straight, clutching the sheet to my chest; it fell off Kellan a little in the process. "Breakfast…is Dad up?"

Anna clicked her heels together, smiling wickedly. "Yep." She pointed at Kellan. "And he'd better get out of here, before Dad realizes he's not on the couch."

I scrambled into action, pushing Kellan out of the blankets. He squirmed and fought me, obviously wanting to stay where he was. "Kiera, relax."

Shaking my head, I pushed him harder. "No, Anna's right, he's gonna kill you if you're up here."

Twisting his lips at me, Kellan raised an eyebrow. "What's he going to do, really? Ground you?"

Shoving his shoulder, I nodded. "Yes, right after he castrates you."

Sighing, Kellan stood up...not bothering to hide himself at all. My sister grinned at his nakedness and I slapped my hand over her eyes. Narrowing mine at Kellan, as I kept Anna from prying away my fingers, I watched him slip his clothes back on. Smirking at me, he muttered, "Fine, I'll sneak into the hallway so he'll think I was in the bathroom."

I shook my head. "No, you should sneak out the window. Make him think you went for a walk or something."

Zipping up his jeans, Kellan dropped his mouth open. Since he was mostly dressed, I stopped fighting with Anna to keep my hand over her eyes; she scowled when she noticed Kellan was no longer fully naked, then smiled that he was still shirtless. Holding his shirt in his hands, he pointed at the window with his thumb. "We're on the second story, Kiera."

Wrapping a sheet around me, I shook my head. "Please, he won't believe that you were just in the bathroom." I pointed out the window. "There's a store about a block from here that should still be open. You could pick up some milk...my mom would love you for that."

He shook his head, his hands on his hips. "My shoes and jacket are downstairs in the living room?"

Anna brightened. "No they aren't. I put them outside when I woke up."

I looked over at her, surprised. Anna shrugged as she giggled. "It's not the first time I've had to hide a boy, Kiera." She winked at me and I shook my head at the adventurous girl.

Kellan groaned, slipping on his shirt. Frowning, he muttered, "Damn it, I haven't snuck out of a woman's window since I was fifteen."

I rolled my eyes at him, but Anna giggled. "Kellan, I think you and I seriously need to swap some stories someday." He looked back at Anna with a crooked grin and she winked at him. I watched the adventurous pair with incredulity. Standing up, I shoved him towards the window.

Lamenting openly, he glanced out at the wintery landscape before him, the frozen trellis he would have to climb down. He looked back at me with a pitiful expression. "You're an adult, Kiera. He really would probably get over it quicker than you think."

I hadn't told Kellan how hard it had been to get Dad to concede to him staying on the couch, in the same building as me. "He was going to have you sleep in a tent, Kellan...in the backyard." I raised my eyebrow at him, my expression completely serious.

He started to laugh until he realized that I wasn't joking. "Fine," he leaned in to kiss my cheek, "but you owe me, big time."

I giggled as he pinched my butt. Anna giggled too. Saluting us with two fingers above his eyebrow, he ducked out the window. I held my breath as I watched him, hoping he didn't fall. When he was at the ledge of the roof, I whispered, "Be careful."

He looked up at me, a puff of air leaving his mouth as he shivered in his long-sleeved t-shirt. Anna came over to join me as I stared out the window and Kellan smirked at the two of us. Twisting his lip devilishly, he muttered, "You're lucky last night was completely worth this…"

I flushed and Anna let out a throaty laugh. As Kellan began descending, I quietly called his name. When he looked up at me, light snowflakes falling on his rosy cheeks, I smiled and said, "Pick up some eggnog, too."

He closed his eyes and shook his head in disbelief, continuing his retreat from my bedroom. Laughing at the look on his face, I silently closed the window. Shrugging out of my sheet burrito, I threw on some I-just-woke-up pajamas. Anna helped me put all of the covers back onto my bed. We were sitting on the edge of it, laughing over Kellan's sullen expression, when my door swung open. Smoothing my hair into a pony tail, I smiled as Dad poked his head in.

Staring at him warmly, I watched his light brown eyes scour my room for intruders. The thinning hair on his head was streaked with gray, and as I watched him frown at me, at my empty room, and then at my sister, I was pretty sure we were both to blame for the change in his hair color.

"Merry Christmas, Dad," I said brightly, hopping up to give him a hug.

Seeing my room with no trace of a boy in it, he relaxed and hugged me back. "Merry Christmas, sweetheart." Pulling apart from me, he did his best to contain a smile. "Did that Kellan fellow decide not to stay here, then? I see that he's not downstairs."

I frowned as best I could and looked back at Anna sitting on my squeaky mattress. "He's not? He was there last night when I went to bed?" I looked back at Dad, keeping my voice as even as I could. Fortunately, or unfortunately, the last year had made me a better liar than I'd ever wished to be.

Dad frowned, but Anna stood up and joined us at the door. "I ran into him this morning. He said he was going to run to the store and get some milk for Mom, since we're almost out." She tilted her head at Dad. "Wasn't that nice of him, Daddy?"

Dad twisted his lips, but had no argument against Anna. Shrugging, he mumbled, "Yeah, I guess…"

Smiling at each other, Anna and I shepherded our clueless Dad downstairs. I secretly thanked her when we got to the bottom. In my ear she whispered, "I heard you guys last night…no need to thank me, you needed that."

I flushed as we entered the kitchen.

Effortless

Mom was there, whisking a bowl of eggs into a yellow, frothy mess that matched the frilly bathrobe she was wearing over her flannel pajamas. Over the smell of greasy, crackling bacon was the undeniable aroma of cinnamon rolls. It made my mouth water. As my mom worked away on the breakfast, I came up beside her and rested my head on her shoulder. The comforting smells and sounds instantly brought me back to every Christmas morning I'd ever had with my family.

Mom's hair was still the same shade as Anna's and mine. It wasn't because of good genes that the aging process hadn't started for her. No, her secret weapon was a product whose tagline was —*Fight the good fight*. It always made me giggle when I saw the hair color box in her bathroom. The slogan was similar to something Denny would have come up with. Oddly, I paused a moment to wonder whether he was enjoying his Christmas day with Abby.

Squeezing my waist, Mom looked over her shoulder at Dad. He was sitting at the table reading the paper, while Anna gushed about how excited she was for us to open her present; she'd picked out the same thing for every member of our family. As Dad absentmindedly nodded at Anna, Mom looked back to me. Her green eyes, a gift she'd passed to Anna, sparkled as they met mine.

"Did you have a good night last night?" I flushed a bit, wondering if she knew what really happened. She did wake up before Dad...

Playing with the end of my ponytail, I tried a nonchalant shrug. "Yeah, it was nice to see Kellan again. I've missed him."

Mom smiled, returning to her cooking. With a knowing smile, she nodded. "Uh-huh." Biting my lip and praying to God that she hadn't heard us, too, I twisted to leave.

Mom looked back at me before I completely turned around. Frowning a little, she shook her head. "I'm sure he's a good boy, Kiera, and I'm sure you are deeply in love with him, but...not in the house, okay?"

Needing to block out the sudden image of my mother explaining the birds and the bees to me when I was thirteen, I briefly closed my eyes. Not able to answer, I only nodded and quickly walked over to my sister.

Anna smiled and wrapped her arm around me. Changing her topic of conversation, she started talking about a cute boy who frequented her work place. I wanted to frown at her, but I didn't. She and Griffin weren't exclusive and could date whomever they pleased. But really, I had to wonder about a guy who frequently dropped by Hooters. Sure, it wasn't a strip club or anything, but single guys dropped in for one reason and one reason alone...and it wasn't for the hot wings. And Anna deserved better than a horn dog like that.

Shaking my head, I rolled my eyes at myself. Anna was already involved with a horn dog. Well, at least I knew that particular dog, and he was pretty harmless. I mean, he wasn't some creepy stalker guy, and he wasn't violent. Compared to the potential rapists that Anna could be involved with, Griffin, with all of his gross, obnoxious behavior, was actually preferable. God, did I just defend Griffin?

I was distracted from my musings by a knock at the door. Anna gave me a tiny smile then stood up. "I'll get it."

Dad pointed at her, a frown back on his face. "Sit. I'll get it."

I was anxious, hoping Dad went easy on Kellan. It *was* Christmas and all, and even if we sent him away as a cover story, he was nice enough to go to the store to get the family some milk…and hopefully some eggnog, too.

Anna and I followed after Dad as we made our way to the front door. Adjusting the button-up pajama top that he was wearing and trying to stand as tall as he could, Dad prepared himself to open the door. I had to smile at the show; Dad was closer to Denny's height and Kellan was still going to tower over him. If he was going to try to intimidate Kellan through size, it wasn't going to work.

As Dad slowly opened the door, Mom came up behind us, wanting to join in on the welcome party. The winter wonderland behind Kellan made for the perfect backdrop as the door swung all the way in. His black leather jacket matched his black shirt and the contrast with the scenery made him impossible to miss. The movie star good looks didn't hurt either.

From behind me, I heard my mother quietly mutter, "Oh, my…"

I flushed as Anna giggled. Mom had seen pictures of Kellan, of course (I'd sent home more than a few care packages), but seeing him in person was something else. Dad, obviously not having heard his wife's reaction to my boyfriend, eyed Kellan up and down. Throwing on an effortless smile, Kellan extended his hand, the one not holding the plastic grocery bag. "Mr. Allen, it's very nice to finally meet you. I'm Kellan Kyle."

Dad sniffed a moment before taking the gorgeous boy's hand. He shook it for a long time while he silently judged to see if Kellan was worthy of me. I knew from experience that Kellan wouldn't pass Dad's test today. It took three months of almost daily interaction for Dad to not say Denny's name with a sneer. And until Denny had taken me away, Dad had really liked him.

"Uh-huh," was Dad's response to Kellan's introduction.

Mom sighed irritably and stepped around us. Maybe feeling that her husband wasn't being quite as hospitable as he could be on Christmas morning, she walked over to the door. Placing her hand on Dad's shoulder, she addressed Kellan. "It's nice to meet you, too, Kellan." Motioning into the warmth of the house, she added, "Please come in, it's freezing out there."

Kellan smiled at her as she forced Dad to step aside so he could enter. Glancing at me quickly, a wry smile touching his lips for a moment, Kellan muttered, "I know."

I looked away before I started laughing. When I looked back, Kellan was extending the bag to my mom; Dad had his hands on his hips, clearly not thrilled that another male was in his home, trying to sweep away his little girl. I didn't bother telling Dad that I'd been swept away long ago…

"Mrs. Allen, I noticed that you were low on milk so I got you some more." Mom smiled as she took the bag and Kellan looked over at me again, adding, "I got some eggnog, too, just in case anyone wanted some." He smirked at me as he turned back to my mom.

A flake of snow in his hair melted, dropping to his cheek and rolling down his skin. Every female in the house watched its progression. Snapping out of it first, my mom smiled and took the bag from him. "Thank you, Kellan. That was very thoughtful of you."

Shrugging, Kellan looked down at the floor, a soft smile on his lips. "It was the least I could do, since you're letting me stay for a few days."

Dad dropped his hands from his waist and twisted his head to stare at me. "A few days?"

I'd sort of failed to mention that when I asked about Kellan's staying. Honestly, I wasn't sure how long I'd get to have him for. My insides squirming at the thought of all the time we'd have together, I frowned at my father. "Dad!"

He moaned and shook his head, but didn't complain any further. I was sure I'd hear more later, but for the moment, he was being nice enough to not say anything around Kellan. My mom watched the showdown between Dad and me with curiosity, then encouraged Kellan to take off his jacket and make himself at home. I slung it up on the coat rack for him, bouncing a little as I took his hand. It was just so nice to have him near me again. I knew the next separation would be excruciating...but I'd deal with that when it happened.

Kellan smiled once he smelled the combination of coffee, cinnamon and bacon. Looking perfectly at ease with my family, he sat at the table across from Dad. While I made Kellan a cup of coffee, Dad eyed him like he was going to go mental at any moment, pull out a WMD or something. Kellan only smiled at him, asking if he was a Cincinnati Reds fan or a Cleveland Indians fan. Dad brightened, then stopped himself. Shrugging, he said the Reds were all right.

Mom and I both looked at each other and rolled our eyes. Dad loved the Cincinnati Reds; he was glued to the television whenever his favorite baseball team was on the air. It was well-known in the house that if you wanted anything from him, you waited until the Reds were winning to ask...and you didn't bother asking if they were losing.

I returned to the table just as Kellan started going into specifics of the game. I listened to his deep voice, enraptured. He knew more than I'd realized he did. Kellan had never struck me as the athletic type. That was Denny. Denny always watched sports highlights. He and Dad had bonded over a few amazing plays. But Kellan knew enough to keep up his end of the conversation and engaged Dad in dialogue until Mom and I set the plates of food down.

Pouring myself a huge glass of eggnog, I sat beside Kellan. He glanced over at my glass and smiled to himself. I squeezed his thigh under the table, thanking him for the treat he bought just for me. As we gazed at each other for a moment, I had to firmly resist the urge to lean up and kiss him. My father cleared his throat.

Kellan glanced up at him as Anna handed Kellan a plate of bacon. As Kellan took some, my dad pointed at him with the serving spoon. "So, Kiera tells us you are in a...band?"

Dad said it like it was a foreign word he was uncertain how to pronounce. His face held an equally confused expression. To Dad, bands were something you did as a teenager. Real men went to college, got degrees, and joined the stereotypical work force. He just didn't understand Kellan's life choices at all. I frowned as I looked across the table at him. He might understand better if he knew Kellan's history, knew just what music had helped him through, but that wasn't my story to tell. And it wasn't one Kellan told openly.

Passing the plate of bacon to me, Kellan gave me a warm smile. "Yes, sir. We're on tour right now. Our next show is on New Year's Eve in D.C."

My shoulders slumped a little at the news. Having a definite departure date kind of sucked. Dad brightened a little, though. Slopping a mess of eggs on his plate, he casually said, "Oh, so you'll be away a lot...on this tour-thing?"

Grabbing the plate of rolls from Anna, who eyed Dad with annoyance, Kellan quietly said, "Yes..." He grabbed a roll and handed the rest to me. Our fingers touched under the plate and Kellan stroked my thumb with his. The expression in his eyes screamed an apology—that he'd be leaving soon, that he'd be gone for so long, that we'd be separated again. Swallowing, I nodded at him encouragingly.

Digging into the plate of bacon, Dad smiled. "Oh, well, that's good that you're finding success." Kellan nodded at him, taking the eggs as they made their way around the table. As Dad loaded his fork with food, he asked, "So what do you boys call yourselves anyway?"

I cringed, knowing my dad wasn't going to like this. Anna laughed while Kellan looked down, seemingly unsure if he should say the name of his band to the man he was attempting to impress. Maybe understanding that lying would do no good right now, Kellan picked up his fork and muttered, "D-Bags."

Dad sputtered on the food he was attempting to swallow. Coughing a little, he leaned over his plate. "Excuse me?"

Clearing his throat, Kellan looked up at him. "Um, the band...we're named...D-Bags." He shrugged. "It's just...supposed to be funny." As Dad narrowed his eyes, clearly not amused, Kellan murmured, "We might change it...if we go mainstream."

Anna looked between the two men and laughed. Spunkily shaking her head, her high ponytail flipping around her face, she told Kellan, "You better not. I love that you're Douchebags."

Kellan bit his lip to hide his amusement while my mother gasped. "Anna!"

Teasingly shoving Kellan's shoulder back, Anna laughed again and dug into her food. Dad frowned at my sister, but said nothing more about the band's name. It was peaceful around the table as we all ate our breakfast. Mom's food was incredible and I nearly purred as I popped a gooey piece of cinnamon roll in my mouth. Kellan watched me eat it, a slightly naughty look in his eye. I smacked his leg under the table, warning him as quietly as I could to behave himself.

When he playfully grinned at me, popping a piece of roll into his mouth, I forced myself to look away. I'd suddenly envisioned licking cinnamon and sugar off his skin, and that was certainly not a thought I should be having on Christmas morning...at my parents' table. While Kellan chuckled, I met eyes with my dad. He was watching us with a furrowed brow. His eyes darted past me for a second, into the living room, and I held my breath, hoping he didn't piece anything together.

What he did say, though, made a cold wash of nerves go over me, and I suddenly would have preferred him asking about last night. "Kellan…is it true what they say about rock stars?"

Kellan finished eating his roll and looked around the table. Bunching his brows in confusion, he shook his head. "What do you mean?"

Dad paused to take a bite of his bacon while I tensed. There were so many different paths he could take this conversation down, and all of them were bad. "You know, about the women that follow the bands around, trying to…get to know them."

Anna dropped her fork and stared at Dad while Mom brightly exclaimed, "Would anyone like some more eggs?"

Kellan ignored her question, keeping his eyes locked on Dad's. "Some women are like that, yes, but it's a lot less than you would probably think--"

Dad cut him off, waving his bacon slice in the air. "But it is true, though, you do have women trying to seduce you? To lead you away from my daughter?"

Irritation surged in me. I hated our life being discussed so openly. "Dad!"

Dad ignored me and focused intently on Kellan. As Kellan unwaveringly met his eyes, I suddenly saw my dad's true fear with me dating a rock star. It wasn't really that he considered the job frivolous, or that there was an alarming potential for drug or alcohol abuse. It was that my dad didn't think Kellan could possibly be faithful to me. It was my own fears reflected back to me. Somehow, that made them seem all the more probable.

Beside me, Kellan whispered, "Yes."

I blinked and looked over at him, not expecting him to answer so honestly. It stung, too, knowing that he was getting offers. Even if he was rejecting them, it still hurt to know that they really were out there. My eyes started watering and Kellan purposely avoided looking at me.

Dad leaned forward in his chair and I looked back at him, begging my eyes not to tear. I did not want to cry in front of my parents. They would never trust Kellan if I didn't trust him. As Anna sputtered that none of this was Dad's business, Dad pointed the last of his bacon at Kellan. "Don't you think it would be better for Kiera then, if you paused the relationship while you were away…so she doesn't get hurt by your…admirers?"

Kellan shook his head. "I never…I don't…" He closed his eyes, taking a moment to collect himself. Just as I felt my eyes starting to pool over, Kellan opened his and looked over at me. "I love your daughter, and I'd never do anything to hurt her."

My mother stood up then, collecting Dad's plate. "Of course you wouldn't, dear. Martin's just being an ass."

Dad frowned at Mom and I blinked, staring up at her. Mom never swore, not even the mild ones. When Dad looked about to object, Mom gave him a glance—the glance. It was a pointed look that said so much. It was a full-on sentence in just a second of connection. She might as well have screamed—*You have said enough, and if you open your mouth again there will be hell to pay in this house for the next six months! It is Christmas morning and I will not let you make my baby girl cry while she is visiting us, for quite possibly the only time until next winter, by making her doubt the man that she is clearly head-over-heels in love with!*

Dad wisely said nothing.

When a strained quiet fell over the table, Mom looked around. "Should we open presents then?"

Kellan slapped on a smooth smile as he stood up. "Sounds wonderful, Mrs. Allen."

Mom smiled at him around her hands full of plates. "Caroline, dear."

Kellan nodded at her. "Caroline, thank you for breakfast. It was incredible." He motioned around the house with his hand. "Is there a bathroom…?"

"Oh, sure." Mom motioned upstairs with her one free pinky.

Kellan smiled and looked around the room as he excused himself. He seemed happy and unperturbed, but I saw his fingers go to the bridge of his nose as he turned the corner to head upstairs. I knew enough about him to know that the conversation had bothered him. He was taking a minute.

My eyes snapped back to Dad when Kellan was out of earshot. "Dad! What was that all about?"

Anna crossed her arms over her chest and glared at him. He looked between the two of us. For once, his face was almost sheepish. "I'm sorry if I stepped over the line there, Kiera." He leaned forward and pointed his finger to where I could hear water running upstairs. "But these are questions you need to ask yourself if you are going to be in a serious relationship with him. Is he on the same page? Does he really love you? Can he turn down woman after woman? If you take the relationship to the next level, will he soil your marriage bed?"

I flushed and looked down, too flustered to say anything. Anna spoke up in my silence. "He's a good guy, Dad. You don't even know him."

Her hands free now, Mom came up to rest her palms on my shoulders. "That could have been handled more privately, Martin."

Dad glanced up at her. "I'm just looking out for our daughter."

I peeked up at him then. "I can look out for myself, Dad." Glancing over my shoulder really fast, I leaned in and whispered, "I've had all of the doubts that you have, okay. I think about it. I worry about it." I shook my head. "But I love him. Shouldn't I give him the chance to fail before I condemn him?"

Dad's eyes widened as he sat back in his chair. A hand rubbed over his jaw as he softly smiled at me. Fatherly pride stretching over his face, he shook his head. "You always were too smart for your own good."

I relaxed back into Mom who was behind me and shook my head. "Not really…but I'm trying to be smarter." I bit my lip, not wanting to let too much truth about my vast failings slip out. My parents still didn't know the real reason Denny and I had broken up. They assumed he left the country for a job, and I was content to let them think that. "I'm in love with him, Dad. Pausing...isn't an option for me."

I heard a sniff from the doorway and looked back to see Kellan standing there, head down as he listened. He looked up and met my eye, a genuine, peaceful smile on his face. Dad sighed, maybe finally seeing that he really had lost his little girl. I stood up and walked over to Kellan. Cupping his cheeks that were slightly moist, like he splashed water on them, I searched his unique eyes. "Not being yours isn't an option anymore," I whispered.

He nodded and leaned down to kiss me. I let him, Dad be damned.

Twenty minutes later, you wouldn't even know the conversation had happened. Kellan let it slide off him and Dad looked a little chagrined that he had brought it up. He even stopped giving Kellan sullen, disapproving looks. He wasn't suddenly warm towards him or anything, but he did stop being the brutish, overprotective father.

Anna forgot about the incident the minute we stepped near the tree. Eating breakfast first was the most difficult part about Christmas for her. We'd only started doing that in the last couple of years, when the presents part of the holidays started taking a back seat to the family part of the holidays. But she was still a giddy little girl when it came time to rip open stuff.

Kellan sat beside me on the couch as she started distributing gifts. She handed everybody a similarly wrapped, flat square and made us all open them together. Kellan laughed as he looked around at all of us opening Anna's gift. I laughed when I saw what it was. We were all now proud owners of next year's Hooters calendar. I blinked as I stared at the three orange and white clad-vixens on the cover.

Dropping my jaw, I looked up at her. "You got the cover?"

Anna clapped and giggled, stomping her feet in her excitement. "Yes! I was hoping you didn't see one in the stores, I wanted to surprise you."

I stood up and gave her a hug, Mom and Dad and Kellan following suit. I knew she'd made the calendar for April, but the cover was a huge deal. Sitting back down, I flipped to her page. God, she was pretty. I immediately closed it. Kellan set his aside and grabbed my hand, leaning into me. Smiling over the fact that he didn't peek at her picture, I kissed his cheek.

The standard gifts went around the room—clothes, books, music, movies and games. The merriment in the air was palpable as we all laughed and enjoyed each other's company. Kellan silently watched the whole affair, his eyes soft and speculative. When it got near the end of the pile under the tree, Anna handed him a present from my parents. He blinked at the gift, surprised, like he hadn't been expecting to receive anything from them. Honestly, I was pretty surprised, too.

My dad was wrapped up in playing with a new, techy gadget, but Mom watched Kellan as he turned the present over and over. I elbowed him gently. "Open it."

He looked up at me, then at my mom. "You didn't have to…" He shrugged and Mom smiled.

"I know."

Swallowing, Kellan unwrapped the present. Inside a simple, white box, was a small scrapbook. Kellan smiled as he started to flip through the pages. I blinked as I looked over his shoulder. It was a book about the two of us, about our life together. There were pictures of just me, some taken when I was pretty young. There were pictures of Seattle—his house, the bar, the Space Needle. And then there were pictures of the two of us.

Most of those pictures were candid photographs taken without our knowledge. There was one of him staring at me at work. I had my back to him, helping a customer, and the look on his face was nearly reverent as he secretly watched me. There were others where we were smiling at each other, laughing at some private moment. A few were of us softly kissing each other. And the very last photo was a close-up of the two of us cuddling together, sleeping on my ugly, orange sofa. Even in sleep, Kellan had a soft smile on his face.

Anna giggled and I glanced up at her and Mom. As Kellan shook his head in disbelief, Mom quietly said, "Anna helped me put that together for you, Kellan. So you could take a piece of home with you on the road."

Kellan looked up at her, his eyes a little glossy. "Thank you…so much."

Mom nodded at him. Sniffing a little, he brightened and reached over the back of the couch to dig through his bag. "I have presents, too."

I smiled and tilted my head at him. Grinning, he dispersed gifts to Anna, a joint one for my mom and dad, and one for me. Grinning myself, I pointed to where I'd hidden one for him at the back of the Christmas tree. "Don't forget yours."

He smirked at me, grabbed it, then sat beside me again. As my family opened his presents, laughter and gratitude echoing around the room, Kellan and I stared at each other. "Together?" he whispered, lifting my gift in his hands.

I nodded, and we started tearing into each other's gifts at the same time. I watched him more than I opened mine, then laughed when I saw he was doing the same. Shaking my head, I stopped and pointed at the gift he was halfheartedly opening. "You first."

He frowned, then laughed. A few minutes later he was holding what I'd purchased for him. Kellan was hard to shop for; he didn't really need or want anything. But there were a few things he cared about, and I played on those when I started looking around for presents. First, he liked to write. He was constantly scribbling lyrics into spiral notebooks that he shoved into his dresser drawers. So I bought him some elegant journals, maybe for the lyrics that were keepers. He was also trying to be more involved with writing the music, so one of the journals was music sheets.

Second, Kellan liked the classics. Being stuck on a bus with noisy guys, I thought he might enjoy a reprieve, so I found an outstanding deal on a Discman, and burned all his favorite classic rock songs on CDs. The technology was outdated with digital downloads being all the rage now, but considering Kellan still had a tape player in his car, I figured it was about as far as I could push him in that area.

Third, Kellan liked sex. Not wanting to give him something that would embarrass me in front of my family, I had taken a picture of the moderately sexy outfit that was awaiting him when he came home. I'd picked it up right before heading out here, after he jokingly mentioned buying me something. For some reason, I'd known our style levels would be completely different, and if I was going to wear something…like that…I wanted to pick it out.

Finding the picture tucked in one of the journals, he glanced at me with a raised eyebrow. When I pointed to the cuffs in the very top corner of the picture, his grin turned heated. I flushed, knowing I would have to be very, very drunk to ever use them, but the look on his face was worth it.

The last thing I'd tucked into the box, I had picked up on a whim. It was a Hot Wheels car. And not just any Hot Wheels car, but a classic muscle car. I wasn't sure if it was a Chevelle, but it was close, and it was shiny black. Kellan's car was the last thing that Kellan really cared about and I bought the toy as a way to let him know that I was taking care of his baby.

When Kellan spotted it, he picked it up and stared at me. His mouth dropped open and he looked completely thrown. I creased my brows as I watched his eyes start to tear up again. He shook his head and muttered something that I swear was, "How did you know?"

I opened my mouth to ask him what he said, but he grabbed me, hugging me tight. "Thank you, Kiera…you don't know how much I love this, all of this." He pulled back to gaze at me, his heart in his eyes. "How much I love you."

I swallowed and nodded. Palming his toy, he pointed to the box in my hands. "Your turn."

Exhaling in a rush, I concentrated on the box in my fingertips. Biting my lip, I wondered what he could have gotten for me as I finished unwrapping the partly opened gift. Once I saw the shape of the box, my heart started thudding. It was a ring box. I paused, unsure if I should open this. Was he proposing? What would I say if he was? Honestly, a part of me thrilled over the idea of being his wife, but my dad had a good point. Kellan and I still had issues to work through before we could even think about heading down that path. I mean, we hadn't even gotten to the point where we could live together again. This step seemed too big.

Knowing he was watching me intently, and not wanting him to think I was doubting him in any way, I popped the box out and opened the lid. Inside were two silver bands, one clearly a man's, one a woman's; the woman's was elegantly lined with small diamonds. Confused, I scrunched my brows and looked up at him. He smiled, peering down at me.

Reaching down, he grabbed the man's ring. "They're promise rings," he whispered. Picking up the woman's, he lifted my right hand. Sliding it on my finger, he softly said, "You wear one." He slipped the man's on the ring finger of his right hand. "And I wear one." Smiling contently, he shook his head. "And we promise that no one comes between us. That we…belong to each other, and only each other."

As I stared at him, amazed and warmed, a tear rolled down my cheek. "I love it," I whispered, leaning over to kiss him.

We tenderly kissed on that couch for a long moment. We probably would have kissed longer, but a wadded-up piece of gift paper smacked me in the face. Frowning, I turned to glare at my sister. She grinned, giggling as she lifted a box of very expensive perfume...her favorite kind. "Thanks, Kellan, I love it."

He nodded at her, laughing lightly as he snuggled into my side. From the other couch, my dad cleared his throat and pointed at what Kellan had gotten for them. "Yes, thank you...Kellan."

Mom grinned as she hugged what looked like plane tickets in her hand. As I scrunched my face, trying to figure out where they were going, Kellan leaned down to my ear. "I got them tickets to Seattle, so they could see you graduate in June."

My mouth dropped open as I looked back at him. He grinned and laughed at the look on my face. "Kellan...you didn't have to..."

He shrugged. "I know, but your parents should see all of your hard work pay off, and tickets are expensive, so..." He shrugged again.

As the relaxed ambiance of a successful Christmas morning flowed throughout the room, I leaned into Kellan's body. Lacing our hands together, I watched where the rings lined up and smiled. Sighing at the physical representation of our commitment to each other, I noticed that Kellan was still fingering the toy car in his other hand.

Pulling back, I looked up at him. "When I gave you that toy, you said something. What was it?"

Kellan looked down at our hands, smiling to himself. Shaking his head, he murmured, "It's nothing."

I kissed his jaw. "Tell me anyway."

He looked over at me and then at the room full of the family that I loved. Anna was snuggling with Mom, thanking her for a cashmere set that probably cost my parents a small fortune. Dad was flipping through Anna's calendar, telling her that she looked very...pretty.

Absorbing the feeling in the room, Kellan shook his head. "This is so nice...so peaceful. Kind of idyllic." His voice low, almost inaudible, he whispered, "I keep waiting for the yelling to start." He glanced over at me and then looked down at our hands again. "It means so much to me that you let me...be a part of this." He looked back up at me, his face content. "I think this is my new favorite Christmas morning."

I smiled, jabbing him in the ribs. "Even though you had to climb down a trellis?" I whispered, careful to not let Dad hear me. "Even being...interrogated?" I said more seriously.

He smiled down on me and nodded. "Yep...still the best."

Knowing that he probably hadn't had too many bright spots in his childhood, I speculated at what memory had been his favorite up until this point.

When I asked him, he turned his head, his eyes getting a faraway look as he remembered. "I was five. It was Christmas Eve. My dad was angry at...something...I don't remember what, and he tossed me into a wall, broke my arm."

My eyes widened as Kellan's contented smile grew. This was a good memory?

Not reacting to my face, he glanced at his arm slung around me and ran our entwined fingers over a bone under his shirt. "It broke here." In my horror, I realized it was the exact same spot Denny had broken his arm.

Kellan shrugged, his face still serene. "They took me to the emergency room, my mom complaining the entire time that they would be late for a party. I don't know why I remember her saying that..." Looking over to the Christmas tree, Kellan shook his head. "Anyway, they checked me in, then left. I didn't see them again until Christmas night."

Leaning back on the couch, Kellan smiled wider as his story grew more and more awful. "There was this nurse there, and I guess she felt sorry for me or something, because I was all alone on Christmas morning." He looked over at the toy car in his hand, lifting it up to examine it closer. "She gave me a set of three Hot Wheels. A fire truck, a police car, and...a muscle car." He grinned as he met my eye. "Just like this one."

Shaking his head, he laughed a little. "I played with those cars all day..." Running the toy down my arm, he murmured, "But this one was my favorite. It was the only thing I wish I'd remembered to take to L.A. when I left home. But I forgot, and my parents...tossed it."

He met eyes with me again. "That Christmas was the best one I'd ever had, because I wasn't at home. That toy was the best gift I'd ever received, even better than my guitar I think, because the guitar was mainly a ploy from my parents to keep me out of their hair..." He lifted the car again. "This...was pure."

He swallowed, searching my eyes. "I thought I'd never see anything like that car again...how did you know to get me this?"

I shook my head, tears stinging the edges of my eyes. "It just...seemed like you."

Kellan frowned as he watched my eyes water and fill. "Hey, I didn't tell you that to make you feel sorry for me." He cupped my cheek. "I'm okay, Kiera." I nodded under his fingertips but a tear escaped me anyway. Brushing it aside with his thumb, he smiled at me. "I just wanted to let you know what it meant to me. To...thank you for letting me have this experience with you and your family. It means more than you'll ever really understand."

I shook my head. "No, I think I get it."

I kissed him lightly but my lip was trembling. Knowing I was going to start sobbing for him if I didn't change my thoughts, I shook my head and inhaled deep. "I could use some eggnog. You?"

Kellan smiled peacefully and shook his head. "No, I don't need anything."

I nodded, kissed his head, and hurried out of there. He didn't need or want my pity. He had dealt with his past a long time ago.

Brushing my fingers under my eyes, I ran into my mom in the kitchen. She smiled as she made another pot of coffee. "Kellan seems to be enjoying himself?"

Yes, more than she'd ever realize. I shook my head, forcing on the effortless smile that Kellan always wore. "Yeah, thank you so much for getting Dad to let him come. I know it was you, and I'm really…" I swallowed, his emotional story still with me, "I'm really grateful."

Mom frowned then came over to give me a hug. "Hey, it's all right. No need to get all blubbery."

I sighed at myself, hugging her back. "I know." Releasing her, I rested my head on her shoulder. She patted my arm then glanced down at the ring on my finger. She frowned for a moment and then looked back into the living room at Kellan.

Looking back with her, I could see that Anna had joined him on the couch and was flipping through her calendar with him. They were peering at something intently, Kellan laughing a bit and shaking his head. Watching the naturally beautiful pair, I sighed. Then I rubbed my ring with my thumb and smiled. He'd chosen me.

"Is that from Kellan?" my mom asked quietly.

I looked back at her and nodded. "Yeah, he got us both promise rings. Sweet, huh?"

She hesitated before responding. "Honey, I may disagree with how your father broached the subject, but I don't entirely disagree with him about Kellan." She shook her head, watching Kellan and Anna get into a playful wrapping paper fight. "He's so…attractive, Kiera, even more so in person than in his pictures." Looking back at me, she frowned. "That sort of thing gets noticed by women, and attractive men aren't always good with…one relationship. And even if he doesn't stray, it takes a special person to be able to handle all of the attention he'll receive. Are you sure you're that woman? Are you sure you want to date him?"

She looked back at Kellan and my sister, and I suddenly felt like what she was really saying was that Anna, my beautiful, provocative, spontaneous, easy-going sister, was a better match for him. Frowning, I crossed my arms over my chest. "Yes, I'm sure. I know what you guys think of me, but Kellan sees more, he loves me."

Mom took a step back and narrowed her eyes at me. "What are you talking about, Kiera?"

I stiffened, not really wanting to talk about the constant references that I'd heard, not wanting to talk about the major differences between Anna and me, differences that had been pointed out to me my entire childhood. Mom squeezed my shoulder when I didn't answer her. When she repeated her question, I sighed, and muttered, "You know…that Anna's the beautiful one and I'm…I'm the smart one."

Mom sighed and squeezed me tight. "Oh, Kiera, honey. I hope we never made you feel that way, it was never our intention." Pulling back, she looked me in the eye. "That's not what we think. We're always telling people about both of our beautiful daughters, and they always agree with us. You're every bit as attractive as your sister, Kiera. I think you're the only one that doesn't see it."

Looking back into the living room, Mom shook her head. "But Anna...relies on her looks. It's become how she defines herself. Sometimes I worry that her looks are all she'll have, and when those eventually fade..."

Smiling, she looked over at me and smoothed back my hair. "But you are beautiful and smart, and you'll do well with whatever life hands you." She leaned in to place a kiss on my forehead. "Your father and I are both very proud of the woman you're becoming." Sighing, she shook her head. "You're our baby...we don't want to see you hurt is all."

I smiled, looking back at Kellan. Anna was admiring his ring. He smiled at her and then looked up at me. Noticing me watching, he nodded a little, like he was telling me that everything would be okay. As Mom kissed my head and walked back into the living room, I heard Kellan's jacket ringing. Thinking maybe it was the guys wishing us a Merry Christmas, I walked over and plucked it out of his pocket. It was a text from a number I didn't recognize; the name just said 'private.' I was about to hit the read button when the phone was yanked from my hands.

Surprised, I looked over at Kellan standing beside me. Smiling, he glanced at the screen, hit a button, then tucked the phone in his pocket. Ice washed through me; he didn't even look at the message, like he was going to when he was alone. A downside to giving him a cell phone struck me as my curiosity piqued.

Ignoring the look on my face, he pointed over to Anna. "Want to play a game? Anna thinks she can beat me at Monopoly." He laughed a little and shook his head. I frowned. No, I didn't want to play a game, I wanted to know who had just texted him.

"Sure," I muttered. As he started leading me away, I started to wonder if maybe my parents were wiser than I wanted to believe. Before I could stop myself, I asked, "Who was that text from?"

Kellan effortlessly smiled back at me and shook his head. "It was just from Griffin." He leaned in and laughed. "Trust me, with the stuff he's been sending me lately, you don't want to see it."

I frowned, but nodded. It was a completely plausible story and he had just given us promise rings. He wouldn't do that if he wasn't living up to his end of the promise...right?

Chapter 15 – Unexpected

Kellan spent five more days with me. It felt like five months with how much time we spent together. I showed him everything my hometown had to offer while he was here. My old school, the street all the kids in the neighborhood used to play on, the café I frequented everyday for lunch my senior year of high school. Kellan acted like I was showing him around Disneyland, genuinely interested in seeing where I grew up.

For some reason, though, I shied away from all of the places that Denny and I had been together, places that were important to our relationship. The restaurant where we'd had our first date, this one particular espresso stand that we hit nearly every morning before classes, the book store that we used to go to on lazy, Sunday mornings.

Even though I avoided pointing it out to Kellan, there was so much of Denny in this city that it was nearly overwhelming at times. We had entered adulthood together here. In a way, we'd sort of grown up together here. Walking around the reminders brought Denny to the forefront of my mind, but I pushed him back.

I could speak with my longtime friend later. My boyfriend, the man who'd recently given me his heart in a band of silver, was my primary focus. Especially since I wasn't sure when I'd get to see him again, once his five days were up.

And once those five days were up, the time didn't feel like five months anymore. It suddenly felt more like five seconds. Walking him as far as I could through the airport, I felt the heaviness of our separation in my heart. My mom was right about our relationship in one respect—it was hard. Him leaving, going out on the road to places unknown with people unknown was taxing. It took a special person to be able to wear the weight of that strain. I wanted to be that person, I desperately wanted it. But I'd always liked consistency, and Kellan's life was no longer predictable. He was fluid now, carving a path that was as ever-changing as the weather. It knotted my stomach.

Bag slung over his shoulder, Kellan twisted to face me when it was time to part. Heart in his eyes, he rested his forehead against mine. "No goodbyes," he whispered.

I nodded, biting my lip as my eyes stubbornly stung. "I'll miss you."

He nodded against me, sighing softly. "I'll miss you more."

I grinned a little, shaking my head. "No, it doesn't work that way. It's always harder on the person being left than the person leaving…that's just a fact."

Pulling back, he cupped my cheek. "I'm not leaving you. I'll never leave you."

I swallowed, placing my hand over his. "I know," I whispered, hoping that what he'd just said was a fact.

He searched my eyes for long seconds, then he leaned in to kiss me. It was the softest, sweetest, most tender physical act we'd ever shared. I never wanted it to stop. I suddenly wished we were contestants in one of those kissing contests right then, the kind where the couple who was locked together the longest won some outrageous prize, just so the moment would have to continue for days.

But that wasn't what was happening, and eventually, the moment did end. He pulled away, slowly, reluctantly. Biting his lip, he sighed and brushed the tears from my cheeks; I only then realized I was crying. Engulfing me in a warm hug, he whispered in my ear, "I love you, just you…I promise."

I smiled as we pulled apart, reaching up to feel his face under my fingertips. "I promise, too," I whispered back.

He gave me a breathtaking smile then stepped back. Grabbing my hand, he kissed the back of it. Then he had to go, and I had to let him. I felt my heart squeeze as I watched his figure retreat. But then my eyes drifted down his body and words from Matt's neighbor drifted through my head. I smiled and shook my head. That spunky old lady was right…he did have a nice butt.

Anna and I spent New Year's Eve in Ohio. She went out with a group of her old friends, while I stayed home with my parents. I played a board game with them while I thought about Kellan singing his heart out on a stage somewhere. It had been forever since I'd heard him sing…I missed it.

New Year's Day saw Anna and I back on a plane, going home. Mom and Dad saw us both off at the gate. Mom sobbing while she hugged her girls, Dad telling us that we were welcome to come back any time we wanted, for however long we wanted. He even told me that Kellan could visit again sometime too, since he was a decent man and had obeyed the house rules.

I didn't tell Dad that Kellan and I had broken his rules on that very first night. I also didn't mention that every night after that, I'd snuck downstairs to cuddle with Kellan on the plastic-coated couch. But technically that hadn't been breaking the rules, since Dad's only stipulation was that Kellan couldn't come up to my room. He never said anything about me going down to him.

I also didn't mention that fact to Mom, since Kellan and I had caved once or twice on that couch, and she had specifically asked for that not to happen in her house. I couldn't help it, though. Sometimes my common sense flew right out the window when Kellan touched me. Okay, most of the time it did.

When our plane touched down on the west coast, my heart dropped a little. At least back in Ohio, I was geographically closer to where Kellan was, as he continued his tour by the east coast. Now that I was back at home, the country seemed so large. I cursed the vastness of it all.

Stepping into Pete's that night, since the work-free part of my winter vacation was over with, a cute, spirited blonde threw her arms around me and assaulted me with her embraces. "Kiera! You're back!" Pulling back, Jenny beamed up at me. "We missed you so much."

I laughed as I hugged her, warmed by her welcome. "I missed you guys, too." As we separated, a flash of sparkle around her neck caught my eye. Fingering the pendant against her skin, a gold heart with a diamond floating in the center of it, I smiled. "This is really pretty. Is it from Evan?"

Jenny picked it up and giggled. "Yeah." She pointed to the silver guitar I always wore tucked under my clothes. "Now we kind of match, right?"

I smiled and nodded, lightly tracing the shape of the guitar under my shirt. Jenny flicked a finger at the ring I was unconsciously showing her. A knowing smile on her face, she asked, "That from Kellan?"

She clearly already knew it was, so I looked down at it and nodded. She pulled my hand over to examine it. Shaking her head she told me, "Yeah, Evan told me about these. He was there when Kellan picked them out." She peeked up at me, her blue eyes bright. "Kellan wears one too, right?"

I nodded again, fingering the elegant band around my finger. "Yeah, his is plain silver. It's simple, it suits him…it's really nice."

My voice turned dreamy and Jenny smiled, dropping my hand. "That boy never ceases to surprise me," she murmured. "I honestly didn't think he had it in him to be so committed to one person." She shrugged, hugging me again. "Well, I'm glad it's you that he loves." Starting to walk away, she shook her head with relief. "If I had to constantly hang around some of the girls he's been with, I think I'd shoot myself." She smirked, then seemed to realize what she'd just said and stopped walking. "Oh, I didn't mean to bring up…you know…he's just…there were some that…"

She sighed and shrugged, looking really embarrassed. I forced myself to laugh and shrug my shoulders. "I know. I know what he was. It's okay, Jenny. Don't worry about it."

She relaxed a little, tossing out an apology before scampering off to work. I inhaled a deep breath and let the comment go. Kellan's past flings were no great secret. It almost seemed like there was a group of them that held weekly meetings to compare notes. Oh, he did that with you, too! How amazing for the both of us!

I smirked at myself, imagining Rita as the president of the club, Candy as the vice president, and Rain as the treasurer…mechanic girl could be the secretary. Rolling my eyes, I headed to the back room to start getting ready for work. Filling up that imaginary club's imaginary positions had been way too easy.

Before I knew it, I was back into my old routine. The school quarter started and I signed up for all new classes. As I was still going for my Bachelor of Art with a major in English, my classes were heavy on literature…and homework. I enrolled in a class that would certainly prove as challenging as my Critical Practices course— Studies in Expository Writing. Under my guidance counselor's advice, I also signed up for a course on the Theory and Practice of Teaching Writing. Her philosophy was that teaching others was, in itself, a great learning tool. I agreed with the concept, but the thought of standing in front of an audience presenting lectures made me want to pee my pants. I could do it if I had to, though. If Kellan had survived the challenges in his life, I could surely get through my far more trivial woes.

On the bright side, I now had Friday afternoons off. True, I'd mainly be studying, but a bright side was still a bright side. On top of that, my ethics class was over, and no more ethics meant no more Candy. Since her academic focus was not English, we no longer shared the same classes.

Cheyenne did, though. The outgoing woman slung her arm around me when she showed up in my poetry class. She briefly queried about my rock star boyfriend and then proceeded to chat profusely about her winter break. I listened eagerly, thankful that I had a life and connections outside of Kellan. That, for once, focusing on him wasn't all I had. Like Mom feared with Anna, I didn't want to rely on one thing for my happiness. That wasn't to say that Kellan didn't bring me the greatest joy, he did, but there were other pockets of contentment that I drew strength from, too.

This new school quarter might actually be the best one I've had here, and possibly the most challenging. One frigid February afternoon after poetry class, Cheyenne and I decided to rest our brains by ducking out for some much-needed coffee. The professor was explaining how different interpretations could completely alter the meaning of a poem. I had a difficult time wrapping my head around the flowery, poetic language, but Cheyenne was actually quite intuitive on the subject.

As we walked, I listened to her explanation of our latest assignment, enraptured. I finally felt like I understood the piece. Completely engrossed, I walked right into another person. I'd never actually collision-coursed into someone before, and my face turned about five shades of red. While Cheyenne giggled at my clumsiness, I quickly apologized to the stranger I had nearly steamrolled over.

He took a step back, steadying himself, and we both locked eyes on each other at the same time, each stammering apologies. "I'm sorr--"

I couldn't finish my sentence as I stared into a warm set of deep brown eyes. Brown eyes that I was certain I'd never stare into again. Feeling all the blood drain from my face, I whispered, "Denny?"

He inhaled a deep breath, holding it for a second before releasing it in a rush. With a soft smile, he quietly said, "Hi, Kiera."

Hearing his accent curl around my name in person gave me an ache in my stomach. I stared at him, shocked into momentary silence. Denny Harris. He looked the same as he had the last time I'd seen him over a year ago. The same, yet different, too. His dark hair was a bit longer than before, styled back away from his face in a way that made him seem older. The scruff along his jaw was thicker too. Nowhere near a beard, but heavier than he used to keep it. It aged him. In fact, everything about him seemed older, from the clearly more expensive clothes he wore, to the way he held himself with a bit more confidence. It was almost like he'd left Seattle a boy and returned a man.

"You look good," I finally whispered, my throat feeling painfully dry.

He smiled uncertainly, his eyes drifting over my body for a second. "So do you."

A tension built up as we stared at each other. It must have made Cheyenne uncomfortable; I know it was making me feel that way. I had just never expected to literally run into my ex on the street.

Placing her hand on my shoulder, she murmured, "I should go...I'll see you later, Kiera."

I nodded at her, never once taking my eyes from Denny. People hustled around us on the chilly sidewalk, but I ignored them. Denny couldn't really be standing before me, could he? After another long moment, when he started looking around, like he didn't know what to say, I sputtered, "You're back…in Seattle?"

He looked at me and smiled, and I felt stupidity flow right through me. Of course he was back…I was staring right at him. Bewildered, I added, "I mean, why are you back?" Closing my eyes, knowing I was sounding rude and flustered, I took a deep breath before I spoke again. Reopening them, I calmly told him, "I mean…it's good to see you."

He ran a hand through his hair, contemplating before answering. "It's good to see you, too."

Shaking my head at the impossibility of him being here, only one thought kept crashing around my head. Well, a second thought really, right behind the first one that I'd already rudely asked him. Thinking this one wasn't quite so rude, I allowed myself to ask it. "Why didn't you tell me you were coming?" Sixteen hour flights weren't exactly spur of the moment things after all, and Denny and I did talk on occasion, although, not since Kellan had left back in November.

Denny looked around the street, then over to the coffee shop Cheyenne and I had been heading towards. He motioned to it with his hand. "Do you want to go inside? Talk somewhere…warm." He shivered, and I smiled; he was acclimated to warmer weather now, especially this time of year.

After I nodded an agreement, we silently turned towards the shop. Walking beside him, a small part of me wanted to reach out and hold his hand. It was odd to feel that way after so much time apart, but it was still in me, somewhere. I didn't, though. I'd made a promise to be true to Kellan, a promise encircled around my finger. I wasn't about to break it.

Denny paused at the door, holding it open for me like the gentleman he was. I smiled and thanked him, and he looked away, a flush lightly coloring his tanned face. It seemed I wasn't the only one holding onto a lingering attraction. But I knew Denny wouldn't do anything about it, either. He was loyal to the person he was with. And he was with Abby now. As we moved to order our drinks, I idly wondered if she was in Seattle with him.

I ordered a latte; Denny ordered tea. I smiled at how familiar everything felt. Sitting at a quiet booth, we both sipped our steaming cups in silence. I was the one that broke it first. "So, do you need your car back?"

I cringed, feeling bad for asking him that right out of the gate, and for the fact that Anna had so "girlified" his vehicle that he probably wouldn't want it back. Denny smiled and shook his head. "No, the company got me a rental. You can keep it." He tilted his head and smiled warmly before returning to his mug.

I cleared my throat, tucking some hair behind my ears. "The company? So, you're here for work?"

Denny nodded, not looking up at me. "Yeah, they're expanding, opening branches in the U.S., in Seattle." He shrugged. "Since I know the area and have a lot of contacts here, they gave me the assignment." He looked back up at me. "I'll be running the office here."

A ghost of a smile formed on his lips as my mouth fell open. He was so young, still a few years from thirty, and he was in charge? I always knew he was brilliant, but...wow. "Oh, my God, Denny, that's...incredible. Congratulations."

His smile widened. "Thank you."

Shaking my head, still amazed, I murmured, "Abby must be so proud of you. Is she here?" I looked around like she was suddenly going to appear beside one of the tables.

Denny sighed softly and I looked back at him. Sadly peering into his cup, he shook his head. "No...she's still in Australia."

Recognizing the loss in his face, I put a hand on his arm. Even though I didn't want to feel it, there was something between us in that brief connection. Something warm and familiar, something that reminded me of being held, being comforted, being loved. I dropped my fingers when he snapped his eyes up to mine. His eyes reflected the same remembrance that I was feeling. In a whisper I told him, "I'm sorry the two of you didn't work out."

He furrowed his brows and shook his head. "No, we're still together. She just...she couldn't make it up yet." He frowned and looked back at the doors. "We work for the same company and they wouldn't let her out of her current assignment. She has to finish up with the client before she can fly out here. It's a long job...it may be months before she can make it."

He looked back at me. "Why would you assume we broke up?"

I froze, not exactly sure how to answer that. I just assumed that he was forced to choose between a girl and his dream job. I assumed that he, once again, chose the job over the girl. As he studied my face, his mouth dropped a little. "Because I took the Tucson job, right?"

I shrugged, still not wanting to say it. He sighed and reached across the table to grab my hand. "You know I'm sorry for that, Kiera. I think...I think that's really the only thing I regret with you." I looked up from our joined skin to lock eyes with him. He smiled a little. "Well, that and..." He nodded at my head and I cringed, not wanting to remember that either. Remorseful, he shook his head. "But Tucson...I should have called you. I should have talked to you first, before I just...took it."

I bit my lip, not wanting to start crying. I'd cried enough over Denny and I. His thumb idly stroked mine as he searched my face, his deep eyes looking soulfully apologetic. Knowing that I had way more to apologize for than he did, I smiled reassuringly. "Everything is okay now, Denny. You don't need to feel bad about that anymore."

He nodded, but didn't seem any less regretful. Searching his eyes, I again marveled at how odd it was to see him here, in my city, practically on my doorstep. Shaking my head, I asked again, "Why didn't you tell me you were coming?"

Denny looked away, not answering. Seeing his jaw tighten under the thicker hairline, I surmised what he didn't want to say. "You were hoping you wouldn't see me. You were hoping the city would be large enough that we'd never cross paths." He looked back to me, his expression weary. I shook my head. "I'm right, aren't I?"

Shrugging, he looked down at our hands. Somewhere in my questions, I had laced them together and we were now holding each other across the table. I didn't pull away. He didn't either. Instead, he shook his head and whispered, "Talking with you on the phone is one thing, but I wasn't… I didn't know if I could handle…seeing you." He looked up at me, his eyes glossy. "You're so…" His eyes drifted over my face and he didn't finish his thought.

Swallowing, he looked back at our hands. "I was just hoping that I could come back secretly and then we'd still have the long distance friendship thing. I wanted to avoid this…confusion."

He sighed and I finally released his hand. Patting the top of it, I pushed it back towards him. "There isn't any confusion, Denny." He looked up at me, and I smiled at him. "You're with Abby and you're happy with her, right?" Smiling softly, Denny nodded. I nodded too, ignoring the ever-so-slight pang I felt. "And I'm happy with Kellan."

His face flinched just fractionally, so swiftly that I would have missed it if I hadn't been looking for it. Not allowing myself to dwell on the guilt building, I smiled and shook my head. "So, if we're both happy, then there's no reason to fear a face-to-face friendship." My eyes stinging, I brokenly told him, "And I've missed that friendship…so much."

His eyes even glossier, he returned his hand to mine. "I have too, Kiera."

Pulling back his hand, he laughed a little and ran it through his hair. I laughed a little as well, the emotion releasing from me. We'd been friends for far too long to let this awkwardness permanently alter our relationship. If he was going to be here for a while, we'd find a way to move past it.

Smiling, I picked up my coffee and took a long sip. He did as well, his eyes flashing to the ring on my finger. He didn't react to seeing it, so I wasn't sure if he understood what it meant. People wore rings on their right hands, and it wasn't necessarily symbolic. I didn't intend to tell him what it meant, either. He'd probably find it morbidly funny that Kellan had given us a physical reminder to be faithful to one another. Looking at the gift through Denny's eyes, the tender exchange between us seemed a little…sad.

A thought struck me that made me frown. There was no way I could tell Kellan that Denny was in Seattle, not while Kellan was thousands of miles away. He'd flip out. He'd drop everything and come home. He was friends with Denny, considered him a brother, but there was way too much uncertainty between us…our rings were proof of that. And Denny was the one person on this earth that I *had* cheated on Kellan with.

That wasn't really what had happened; technically I was being unfaithful to Denny, not Kellan. But I'd made love to Kellan, told him that I was his…then slept with Denny one last time. Kellan knew about it…it ate at him. Denny was the one person Kellan would never trust me with. I just couldn't risk him throwing away his dream on an unfounded fear. I'd never hurt him like that again. Never. Not even if Kellan cheated on me, and I hated him. I'd end it with him before I ever touched another man. I would not be a "whore" again. I just couldn't live with the consequences.

Besides, that wasn't going to happen. Denny and I were no longer in love with each other, so Kellan had nothing to worry about. But I'd never be able to convince him. He'd possessively watch over me like an animal marking its territory, warding off other males. Kellan didn't share...he'd already told me that much.

Perhaps noticing my expression, Denny quietly asked, "Everything okay?"

I straightened my face. "Yeah, just thinking..." I bit my lip, wondering if I should confess my fears to Denny or not. Again, he'd probably find it morbidly funny. Deciding to put it a different way, I shrugged and asked, "Is Abby okay with you being here...with me?"

Denny immediately shook his head, lowering his mug from his mouth. "I'm not here with you."

I flushed and looked down. I hadn't expected words that harshly true to leave his mouth. I was used to flowers and poetry. I was used to sappy comments about me being his heart. He sighed. "That came out wrong. I just mean...I came here for the job." I looked back up at him, and he shrugged. "Abby knows what went down with you and me. She knows that I would never go back to you, Kiera."

He held my eye, not backing down from his coldly honest statement. I felt my lip quaver as so many emotions flooded me that I couldn't sort through them all. It was no great shock; he was bluntly saying exactly what I'd been thinking, but still...hearing it put so plainly... Yeah, it stung.

Frowning, he shook his head. "I'm sorry if that sounds...cold." He finally looked away from me, down to the cup cooling in his hands. "Sometimes the truth is cold." He peered up at me, and when he spoke again, his accent was thicker with emotion. "I still want your friendship, though. You're still important to me."

I nodded, swiping a stubborn tear away from my eye. "It's okay, you can be honest with me, Denny." I sighed, laughing a little. "I was sitting here, sort of thinking the same thing, anyway." His dark brows creased, and I laughed again. "Just that Kellan has nothing to worry about because you and I would never...go down that path again."

Denny laughed. Raising his mug, he extended it to me. "To never sleeping together again?" he teased, a sparkle in his eye.

Seeing my favorite goofy grin returning, I smiled and clinked his mug with mine. "To never having sex again." He raised an eyebrow at me and I quickly added, "With each other, I mean."

Laughing heartily, he sipped his tea as I downed my coffee. God, I was an idiot. Still chuckling, he relaxed back in his seat again. I smiled that the residual tension was finally melting away. I didn't think I could ever just be friends with Kellan again—hell, we couldn't manage to just be friends when we were friends—but Denny...the comfort there made it easy to slip into that role with each other.

As Denny smirked to himself, I worried my lip, thinking of Kellan again. Setting down my drink, I cleared my throat. Denny looked up at me. "Um, this is going to sound weird, but if you happen to talk to Kellan anytime soon...can you not tell him that you're here?"

Denny sighed, his shoulders slumping. "Kiera…"

I hastily interrupted his protest. "Please? Just…fail to mention it?"

Sighing, Denny leaned over the table. "Kiera, I don't want to tell you how to handle your relationship with him, but…you'll never last if you start lying to him."

I shook my head, leaning over as well. "And I won't lie…I just don't want to tell him right now."

Denny gave me a dry look, like he didn't see the difference in my statement. Honestly, I knew I was stretching the truth line, but Kellan would not react well to Denny being so close to me while he was gone. It was too similar to how we'd first gotten together.

Placing my hand over Denny's, I shook my head again. "I know this is big, and I will tell him," I pleaded. "I just need to figure out how to tell him without…scaring him."

Denny stared at me a moment, then his face softened in compassion. "All right, I won't tell him…but I won't lie either. If he asks me, I'll tell him." I started nodding immediately and Denny raised his eyebrows. "I'll tell him everything, Kiera…even this conversation."

I swallowed, then nodded. "That's fine…it won't come to that. I'll tell him first."

Resigned, he gazed out the window. "You better…I don't need him venting his frustrations on me."

He bit his lip as his voice trailed off. I flinched. That was exactly what Denny had done to Kellan, the night he'd beaten him to a bloody pulp. Holding his hand in both of mine, I whispered, "Thank you, Denny."

He nodded, looking back to me. Changing the subject, I shifted to his new job. He brightened instantly, and then it was just like it was years ago, when he was telling me about something he was really excited about. He'd been in town for about a month, since the first part of the year, living out of a four star hotel until he found a place to rent.

"Why don't you stay at Kellan's?" I asked before thinking it through.

He looked at me oddly, then shook his head. "No, I don't think that would be a good idea."

I cringed, nodding. No, probably not. The ghosts were there for me. For Denny, who, without warning, had had a heartbreaking situation explode in his face…those ghosts would be even harder to handle. I wouldn't blame him if he never wanted to set foot in Kellan's house again. It was kind of dumb for me to even ask. I was just trying to be practical, like Denny often was, and Kellan's place was completely empty right now. Vacant, patiently waiting for its owner's return, just like me.

After describing some of the campaigns he'd been involved with, including a feminine hygiene product that he could barely talk about with a straight face, I finally noticed the time on a clock behind him.

"Oh crap, I'm gonna be late." Denny glanced at the clock I was looking at and scrunched his face. It was a cute expression, and I laughed before I remembered why I really needed to go. Standing up, I collected my jacket and book bag. "We've been talking for longer than I realized. I'm gonna be late for work."

Denny nodded, standing and gathering his coat as well.

Pausing as I slipped mine on, I tilted my head at the door. "Do you want to come with me?" Shrugging, I added, "I could get you some dinner…just like old times."

He looked down, smiling softly. "Just like old times." When he looked back up, he shrugged, his goofy grin returning. "Sure…why not?"

Denny followed me to Pete's in his sleek, black, expensive-looking company car. It made me smile that he was doing so well. I'd always known that Denny would succeed in anything he tried. That was something I never worried about. And being in charge at his age… it would seem he was already going places.

Pulling into Kellan's unofficially reserved parking spot, I watched Denny pull up beside me. He was frowning as he stared at the Chevelle, maybe wondering where his Honda was. I'd probably have to mention at some point that Anna had nearly confiscated the vehicle from me. Hopefully he wasn't too bothered by the news.

But he didn't mention anything as he stood by his sporty car, waiting for me. It was so weird to see him here, like I'd fallen through a wormhole and been pulled back in time. Things were different, but they were also the same. As I stepped up to his side, we started walking to the doors. I felt a split-second of loss that he didn't hold his hand out for me. It wasn't that I wanted him to, or needed him to, more like I'd expected him to.

When you've been with someone for so long, you learn to anticipate their behavior, and in the past, Denny would have always smiled and extended a hand to me if we were walking together. It was a little jarring that he didn't, and I instantly stopped feeling like I was reliving the past.

The flaw with my impromptu plan became clear when we walked through the doors together—everyone's jaw dropped as they all stared at us. Rita, Kate, all the regulars…even Jenny looked taken aback. Not many of them knew about the Denny/Kellan triangle, but they knew that Denny was my ex and Kellan was my current.

The fact that Denny was conveniently back in town while Kellan was on tour was enough to cause a swirl of gossip in and of itself. By their expressions, the fact that Denny and I were suddenly hanging out at the bar together was even more scandalous. I'd probably have to have the "don't tell Kellan" speech with a few of my friends too. Just for now. I needed some time first, a plan to keep Kellan from overreacting.

Leaning over a little as he stood beside me, Denny murmured, "Is it just me, or is everyone staring at us?"

I sighed and rolled my eyes, looking up at him. "It's not just you...I guess it's been a slow week for news." I laughed. "We're now the hottest story in town."

He smirked at me. "Oh good, and I was worried that this would be awkward."

I laughed a little more and motioned for him to take a seat anywhere he wanted. Surprisingly, or maybe it was just an unconscious habit since he usually sat there, he chose the band's table.

I watched him for a moment before heading to the back to deposit my belongings. And in the process, I almost had my second collision of the day when Jenny stepped in front of me. Sidestepping just in time, I felt my heart skip a beat. I really hated running into people.

Jenny frowned as she glanced at Denny. She leaned into me. Speaking quietly, like she was afraid Denny could hear our conversation all the way across the room, she whispered, "What are you doing, Kiera?"

I looked over her face, a flame of irritation starting to flicker in me. Did everyone think I was incapable of just being friends with a guy? "Well, I thought I'd start my shift, since I am a few minutes late."

I tried to continue to the back, but Jenny grabbed my arm. "No, with him, what are you doing with him?"

I looked over at Denny. Leaning on his elbows over the table, he was looking around the bar, absorbing his surroundings. Maybe he'd missed the place? Seeing his friend back in the city, Sam started heading Denny's way. I heard his booming greeting as I twisted back to Jenny. "I ran into an old friend who is back in town. I invited him here to buy him dinner, because I've missed seeing him." Carefully unfurling her fingers from my arm, I added, "Why is that a problem?"

I knew why...and so did Jenny. Shaking her head, she murmured, "He's not just a friend, Kiera, he's your ex, the ex you and Kellan..."

She exhaled, and I bit my lip to hold back my comment. Yes, I knew exactly what Kellan and I had done to him. I didn't need it spelled out. Glancing at my promise ring, she changed what she was about to say. "Does Kellan know he's here? Are you going to...see him...while Kellan's away?"

I tilted my head, wondering if she'd really just asked if I was going to start carrying on with two men again. Shaking my head a little more harshly than was necessary, I snapped, "No!" She flinched a little at my reaction and exhaling, I made myself relax. I looped my arm around hers and started walking us to the back.

She relaxed against me as we walked, and in a more controlled voice I told her, "Yes, I'm going to probably hang out with him a few times while he's back in town." She raised her eyebrows at me and I quickly added, "No, I'm not 'seeing' him." I glanced down at the ring snug around my finger and smiled. "I'm Kellan's...and that's not going to change, but Denny is a friend, and I'm not just going to ignore that he's here."

We stepped into the hallway and Jenny nodded, looking contemplative. Shaking my head, I added, "I'm not going back down a road that ended...as badly as it did." I dropped my head. "I've learned my lesson, Jenny. I'm not that person anymore."

She patted my back as we stopped in front of the back room. "I know, Kiera. I guess I just didn't want to see you mess up a good thing." She ducked down to meet my eye. "And you and Kellan are a good thing."

I smiled and nodded. As she gave me a swift hug and prepared to leave, I grabbed her elbow. "Can you...when you talk to Evan, can you not mention that Denny's here?"

Her shoulders slumping, she gave me the exact same look Denny had earlier. "Kiera..."

"Kellan won't understand. He won't believe that nothing is going on. He will drop the tour and come home. He'll stay by my side until I'm done with school or Denny leaves, whichever comes first." I slowly shook my head. "He'll throw away everything, Jenny. His dreams...and Evan's."

Jenny sighed, holding my gaze. "You're going to tell him?"

I nodded. "Yes...as soon as I figure out how."

Closing her eyes, she shook her head. Opening them, she seemed resigned...and irritated. "I hate lying, Kiera, especially to Evan."

Releasing her elbow, I looked down. I hated lying too, but sometimes you had to fudge a little bit, to protect people. As Denny said, sometimes the truth was cold. Why inflict pain if you didn't have to? "I know, Jenny." I peeked back up at her. "Just don't mention it, if you can help it."

She pursed her lips, then nodded. Shaking her head a little, she walked away. I called out a thanks but she didn't look back at me. I sighed, hating this small deception already. It was necessary, though, for the time being.

Chapter 16 – Doubt

When I returned to the bar, Denny was still chatting with Sam, only now, Kate and a few regulars were with him. They were all laughing as they sat around talking, and I took a moment to just smile and absorb the fact that he was back. Watching his goofy grin and hearing him laugh brought back all of the good feelings from when we were together. It made me realize how much I'd missed him this past year. It would be hard on me when he left again. And it was pretty hard the first time.

As Kate squeezed his shoulders and gave him a hug, he looked over to where I was still standing, watching him. His goofy grin changed into a warm smile and he nodded a little at me. Face flushing a million degrees, I stopped reminiscing and headed towards the bar to get him a drink.

Rita eyed me speculatively as she poured a beer for him. In a voice loud enough for me to hear, she murmured, "When the cat's away…"

I grit my teeth. Snapping at Rita wouldn't do any good. She tended to think everyone was hooking up with everyone. She saw sordid behavior in just about anything. She'd even told me once that The Little Mermaid was darn near pornographic. I still had no idea why…

Pretending that I hadn't heard her, and that I couldn't clearly see the top of her bra under her deeply cut v-neck, I grabbed Denny's drink and headed to the band's table, well, what used to be the band's table.

The front doors squeaked open as I passed by, and I halfheartedly glanced over. Seeing someone who usually didn't come into the bar, I stopped. Rachel locked eyes with me immediately. Her tanned skin seemed to glow and her almond eyes sparkled. Lifting a laptop tucked under her arm, her long sheet of dark hair almost obscuring it, her wide smile widened. "Oh, hey, Kiera. I'm glad you're here tonight. I wanted to show you and Jenny something."

Seeing her roommate enter, Jenny walked over to us, curious. "Did you get it up and running?" she asked, pointing her finger to the machine Rachel was disentangling from her hair.

Nodding, she started walking back to Denny's table. Natural, I supposed, since her boyfriend generally sat in the same seat that Denny was now plopped in. Wondering what they were talking about, I watched with furrowed brows as Rachel set up the laptop across from Denny.

As Sam and the regulars left Denny and returned to their own evenings, Denny tilted his head at the newcomer at his table. "Hello," he said politely, not knowing who Rachel was.

She nervously tucked her hair behind her ears. Barely making eye contact with him, she turned on the computer. "Hi," she squeaked out. "Hope you don't mind if I borrow your table for a second."

Denny laughed at her shyness, glancing up at me with a small, knowing smile, like Rachel reminded him of me. "Not at all."

Lowering my eyes, I flicked my hand between Rachel and Denny. "Denny,

Rachel...Rachel, Denny." They both made brief contact and Rachel nodded her head a little at him. Wanting to laugh that Denny had a point, I added, "Rachel is Jenny's roommate and Matt's girlfriend." Looking back at Denny, I creased my brows. "Denny's...my ex." I shrugged.

Rachel's eyes flew up to Denny's. "You're the ex? *The* ex?"

She immediately flushed and looked down at her computer. Denny flushed as well, looking away. I bit my lip...I guess either Matt or Jenny had filled Rachel in on all the drama that was Kellan and I having an affair behind Denny's back. Great. I guessed I'd have to have the "don't tell Matt so he doesn't tell Kellan" speech with her, too.

More because I needed something to do with my hands than anything else, I handed Denny his beer. He immediately took a sip. Because I felt bad, I also gave him an apple flavored lollipop. He twisted his lips and shook his head, laughing as he took it. I wondered why until I realized what I'd given him...a sucker. And just when he was probably feeling like a giant sucker.

Sighing a little, I considered asking him what he wanted to eat, but Rachel spoke again before I could. Logging onto the Internet, she typed in a phrase. "Matt asked me to set this up, so I thought I'd do it while the boys were gone." She shook her head, her smile returning. "We just went live an hour ago, and people have already sent me stuff to post."

As the page she typed in loaded, my jaw dropped open. It was a D-Bag website. I shook my head as she scrolled through some of the different pages. Everything was on there—photos of the guys, a playlist of all their songs, their tour schedule, a short biography of the band members, and feedback from the fans.

I frowned when she clicked over Kellan's bio. At the bottom of his description was a photo of him on stage...shirtless. It was an older photo; I couldn't see any trace of his tattoo, just lean, toned, etched muscle. It was an incredibly hot shot. Whoever took it caught him running a hand back through his hair as he twisted towards the camera. His head was down, but his eyes were up, looking right at the photographer. With eyes that promised satisfaction, a soft, seductive smile played across his lips. I was fairly certain that the person who'd captured this moment probably got a very private performance later.

Wondering if these were Rachel's personal pictures, I crossed my arms over my chest. "Why's Kellan the only one half-naked?" Glancing over the photos of the other boys, all of them dressed normally, I frowned a little deeper.

Rachel looked back at me, her cheeks flushing. "Matt gave me these pictures. He's been collecting them from fans over the years." She pointed at Kellan's body, then clicked back to the homepage, where I finally noticed that his mostly bare image had also been seamlessly blended into a good chunk of the wallpaper. Shaking her head as she shifted her gaze from the screen back to me, she quietly said, "Matt told me to work with what they've got...to play up their best features."

Shrinking away from my gaze, she muttered, "Kellan's body is...one of their best features, even I'll admit that."

Sighing, I shook my head and rolled my eyes. Denny stood up and walked over to look at the screen. Chuckling a little, he nodded. "She has a point." Glancing over at me, he raised an eyebrow. "Marketing-wise, it's a solid strategy...sex sells."

Hating that the "sex" being sold revolved around my boyfriend, and sort of hating that my ex was the one defending it, I blurted to Rachel, "You said people were sending you stuff? What stuff?"

Rachel sat up straight and clapped her hands. "Oh, I'm so excited to show you this part." Giggling, maybe glad that I wasn't going to go off on her or anything, she moved the cursor to a section titled "Videos." I was confused. The band doesn't have any videos. At least, none that I'd ever seen.

Scrolling past a few, she settled on a thumbnail of the boys on stage. As she started playing the video, I laughed a little. It definitely wasn't a professionally edited video. It was an amateurish clip, something created by a fan on their cell phone. The picture was shaky and almost overpowered by the sound of nearby shrieking. It looked like it had been taken at a recent show and Rachel confirmed that the footage was dated a couple of weeks ago.

Jenny giggled and leaned in, her eyes focused on her man banging away on his drums. Rachel smiled happily as she watched Matt strumming his guitar so fast you could barely register his finger movements. My eyes stayed glued on Kellan. It seemed like a lifetime ago that I had watched him perform onstage. It had only been three months, halfway through our allotted separation, but it felt much, much longer.

Leaning back on a hip, I sighed again, but in contentment this time. Just as he did when he was here playing at Pete's, Kellan commanded the stage with his presence. He seemed completely comfortable, perfectly at home. It was still miraculous to me.

Unconsciously, I leaned into Denny's side. He straightened, and took a half-step away from me. I muttered an apology, but Denny wasn't looking at me. His eyes remained glued on Kellan, too. I had no idea how he felt, watching the man he'd lost me to thriving in his chosen profession.

Pushing the thought from my head, I returned my focus to Kellan strutting across the stage, belting out lyrics, and interacting with the crowd. He reached out for them, playfully held a hand to his ear, and gave them flirty smiles. I swear he even winked at a couple of people. I tried to ignore the twinge in my stomach.

When the song ended, I wanted to applaud with the crowd. They'd all done such a great job. Not that I was concerned that they wouldn't—the guys always did great—but it was nice to see that the constant traveling and the tiring, transient lifestyle, hadn't hampered their talent at all.

Just as I was about to ask Rachel how many more videos there were, and if I could borrow her computer over my dinner break, the cell camera focused in on Kellan. I stopped mid-sentence, to stare at his image, so close, yet so far away. Smiling to the crowd, he thanked them all, bowed and then blew out a kiss. He twisted to head off the stage. The person recording the footage followed his progress; apparently the fan found Kellan the most appealing one to watch.

Just as Kellan started to round a corner that led to a behind the scenes area, a woman darted out from around the corner first.

She startled me, showing up on the screen like that, but Kellan didn't react to her appearance at all. Like he knew she'd be there. He only gave her a breathtaking grin. I felt all of the blood draining from my body, as I watched Kellan playfully grab both of her elbows. Shaking his head, his face still showing nothing but joy, he animatedly said something to her.

The statuesque woman returned his smile and nodded, her face equally delighted. She wasn't what I had expected a band-following groupie to look like. She seemed high class, poised and elegant, with dark ebony hair in a loosely held back bun and designer clothes that screamed money. She had creamy, mocha skin with perfect bone structure beneath it and lips that were undeniably full and soft. She was…gorgeous. Model gorgeous. Celebrity gorgeous. Halle Berry gorgeous. Scrutinizing, I considered for a second if it really was Halle Berry. Wouldn't that just be my luck? If he'd hooked up with an A-list actress already.

Just as she twisted her face, and I saw enough of it to know that it wasn't the actress, Kellan leaned into her ear. I had no idea if he was telling her something, or if he was nibbling on it. And there was nothing more to see, since the video abruptly ended. I blinked as the screen returned to the tiny thumbnail of the band. Did I really just see what I thought I'd seen? I didn't want to believe it, but it looked…suspicious. There was also that odd text over Christmas that he wouldn't allow me to read. He said it was from Griffin. Was it?

Anger boiling in my stomach, I pointed to the computer. "Could you…play that last part again please?" I asked, my voice short and tight.

Rachel tucked her hair behind her ears repeatedly. "Kiera, I'm sorry. That one just came in…I was so excited to show you guys, I hadn't watched it all the way through yet."

Glaring at her, even though I didn't mean to, I snapped, "Play it again, Rachel." Calming myself, since I really didn't know what I was seeing, I added, "Please."

I felt Denny's hand on my shoulder, but I couldn't look at him. I was sure he wouldn't gloat, but I was also sure he wouldn't be that surprised, either. Maybe I'd been dreaming about having a monogamous relationship with Kellan. Maybe that just wasn't possible. Squeezing my eyes shut, I shook my head. No, I couldn't leap to conclusions without talking to him. I couldn't condemn him without letting him fail first. Isn't that what I convinced my dad?

Feeling another hand touch me, I opened my eyes at Jenny. Biting her lip, she shook her head. "I'm sure there's a perfectly logical explanation, Kiera. I'm sure that was nothing…really."

I felt my eyes sting as I nodded at her. Sure, it might be nothing, we really didn't know. But it was enough of something for each one of them to wonder about it. And that made my stomach start to churn.

Jenny went back to work, excitedly telling Kate all about Evan's performance, while I watched the clip again. Denny stayed by my side, not saying anything, but not making any move to walk away. I shook my head as I watched Kellan lean into the beauty again. Seeing it was riling up my stomach. I really should stop myself. I really shouldn't watch. But I felt frozen in place, staring at the screen over Rachel's shoulder.

After playing the clip again, Rachel attempted to navigate us to a different section of the website, possibly to distract me, but I was too deep in my jealous fit to just let it slide. My patience was wearing thin, and although I'd matured over the year, I still had a lot of room for growth; I grabbed the mouse from her and clicked the video again.

Sighing, she stood up and inched her way between Denny and I. "I'll just...give you a moment," she murmured, walking away from the table.

Biting my nails, I watched the clip again and again, obsessively considering what it all meant. He seemed very comfortable with a person that I didn't know. A person I'd certainly never heard him mention in all of his phone conversations. Just as I was replaying the moment where Kellan leaned into her for about the twentieth time, the laptop was snapped shut in my face.

Blinking, I looked up at Denny. Still standing behind me, he crossed his arms over his chest. "You're going to give yourself an ulcer, worrying about something that you have no proof to support." He raised his eyebrows. "Trust me...I know."

I flushed and averted my eyes but Denny quickly added, "And besides, you promised me dinner, and I'm starving." Peeking up at him, I managed to smile a little. Seeing my mood lift, he shook his head. "Do you think you could get me one of those world-famous burgers that you guys have?"

Biting my lip, I glanced at the closed laptop. I wanted to watch it again, but Denny was right, I had no proof that Kellan was doing anything wrong. I couldn't do anything but make myself angry as I watched a brief moment that I was probably taking out of context...hopefully. I'd have to wait and ask Kellan later, and I'd have to ask him in an indirect way that didn't sound like I was accusing him of sleeping with her. I'd have to bring it up subtly...and subtleness wasn't my strong point.

Letting the video go for now, I stood and placed my hand on Denny's shoulder. "Of course." I sighed. "I'm sorry it took so long."

Denny glanced down at the computer on the table. "Not a problem, Kiera...I understand," he whispered.

I'd like to say that I let the video go after that moment. I'd like to say it, but it wouldn't be true. I snagged the laptop from Rachel, telling her that I'd give it back tomorrow. Denny shook his head at me as he ate his dinner, but the sympathetic smile he gave me told me he understood. He stood to leave, promising to call tomorrow to see how I was doing. I marveled that he was still my caretaker, despite everything, despite being physically separated from me for a year. I gave him a swift hug, a hug that stirred a swirl of whispers around the bar. I told him to tell Abby hi for me. The smile on his face was the largest I'd seen all night, and I noticed him pulling his phone out of his pocket as he headed out to the parking lot. I figured he was going to call her right then and there.

After my shift, I went home and watched every clip available on the band's website. While I enjoyed seeing Kellan in action again, I also saw that woman two more times. From what I could make out by the background, the woman appeared in three different locations and in three different instances, like she really was following them as the band traveled from town to town.

My blood boiled and sleep evaded me that night. I watched the videos over and over, cell phone in hand, on the verge of calling Kellan and demanding an answer. My sister plodded into my room near dawn, crashing into the bed with me. Like Denny, she slammed shut the laptop, letting out an annoyed grunt.

I sighed, leaning back on the pillows, my hand squeezing tight around my phone. "What are you doing up?" I muttered.

Removing the computer from my lap, she replaced it with her head and glared up at me. "I could practically hear you fuming through the walls. What's going on?"

I shook my head. "Nothing." It had to be nothing...he'd promised.

Seeing my face, she sat up. "No it's not...what happened?" She glanced over to the computer, picking it up and opening it. "Something in here?" she asked, her silky locks falling over her shoulder.

I bit my lip and nodded, then shook my head. "Just a girl that keeps popping up in some fan footage of the band." I sighed as Anna navigated to the page I'd been staring at all night. "I just...don't know what it means."

When Anna looked up at me with furrowed brows, I sighed and showed her which video to play. She silently watched the video, then looked up at me and shook her head. "I don't know, Kiera." Glancing at the cell in my hand, she shrugged. "Why don't you just call and ask?"

A wistful sound escaped me as I stared at my phone. "I wish I could...but I don't want to be *that* girl." Sitting up, I locked my arms around my legs. "Plus, what would I say? I saw you touch a girl in a video...care to explain?"

Looking down I shook my head and remembered Denny's words. "I have no proof that he's cheating, just a short glimpse of...familiarity...with a girl that I don't know. That's not enough to start cornering him with questions." I peeked back up at her and smiled sadly. "I don't want to be the jealous girl back home who can't handle the fame of her guy. That's how couples like us break apart."

Sighing herself, she reached up to tuck some hair behind my ear. "Yeah, I suppose." Brightening, her face way too attractive for the insane hour, she exclaimed, "I could ask Griffin? I'm sure he knows who that girl is." She frowned right after she said it, like if Griffin knew her, then he knew her intimately.

Biting my lip, I shook my head. "No, any answers need to come from Kellan. I can't be the girl who uses his friends to spy on him, either." Closing my eyes, I pushed the computer away from the both of us. "No...I need to let this go. I need to trust him." I opened my eyes and shrugged. "That's the only way we're going to work, if we start trusting each other...and it's probably nothing anyway."

She nodded, agreeing with me. "Yeah, I'm sure. He's way too crazy in love to do anything as stupid as cheat on you."

I nodded, smiling softly. As Anna gave me a hug, a stray thought entered my brain and I asked Anna about it on a whim. "Hey, what's Griffin's cell number?"

She stared at me, her perfectly emerald eyes more than a little surprised that I'd want to know; Griffin and I didn't exactly talk. I generally avoided any conversation with him. I just couldn't get that weird text out of my head, not with this new information exposed to me.

"I just...I need...Kellan got this..." I sighed. "What's his number?"

She rattled it off instantly and I closed my eyes. The number on Kellan's phone was burned into my brain...and the number Anna just gave me wasn't it. The text wasn't from Griffin. Kellan had lied.

When I finally passed out from exhaustion, I had a terrible dream. I dreamt I kept running into women wearing the exact same promise ring Kellan gave me. Then, I kept finding notes tucked all over his house addressed to other girls. I even dreamt that he proposed to the Halle Berry doppelganger on national TV. And Denny was there, giving me sympathetic, supportive glances, as if he knew my pain, which only made me feel worse. When I started awake, I felt like I hadn't slept at all.

Irritated at myself for overacting—one plus one doesn't always equal two—I forced myself to shower and get ready for the day. I was instantly grateful that my class was in the afternoon; I'd have slept right through it if it wasn't. Leaving my hair damp and dripping, I shuffled out to the living room, where I could hear Anna watching cartoons while she slurped down a bowl of cereal.

Pushing all of the doubt out of my brain, I sat beside her, laying my wet head on her shoulder. She glanced over at me in-between spoonfuls, then nonchalantly said, "Do you remember when I came home and you and Kellan were seriously making out on the couch?"

I straightened, staring at her with wide eyes. "Yeah..." How could I have forgotten? I'd been mortified.

The "incident" had occurred during our period of abstinence. We weren't having sex yet, but we were definitely pushing the envelope. He'd been shirtless, jeans unbuttoned. I'd had a light tank top on, but he'd scrunched it all the way up my stomach. The memory of his lips on my belly assaulted me as I rewound back to that night.

His hands on my hips, pulling at the fabric of my shorts, like he wanted to tear them off. My fingers tangling in his hair, as I yanked his mouth back to mine. The moans I made as his lean body pressed against every square inch of me. Our breaths fast as we both considered how far to take the moment. We'd been taking it slow, together for more than two months, but we had still held back, wanting the moment to be perfect. And holding back with Kellan was hard.

As was his body, as he rhythmically pressed his hips into mine. I remembered momentarily losing control and grabbing his hand. I'd just needed him to touch me again. I'd led his fingers up my thigh, wanting him to feel the swollen ache that I had for him, wanting him to know that I needed him. It was the first time he'd touched me down there since the affair.

Understanding my directive, his hand had quickly darted under my clothing. When his thumb circled over my wet flesh, we both sucked in quick breaths, groaning. I can still clearly remember him dropping his head to my shoulder and huskily telling me that he missed feeling this…that he missed me.

Knowing just the right amount of pressure to use, knowing just the perfect pattern to follow, he'd had me on the brink of releasing. Wanting to please him, too, I ducked my hand into his open jeans.

And, of course, that had been when my sister had unexpectedly come home. It had been as close to being caught in the act as I'd ever been. It was also the last time Kellan and I ever took things that far in a public room.

Blushing horribly, I averted my eyes to the TV. Anna laughed huskily, slurping another bite of sugary green circles. "God, that was pretty hot. I did feel really bad for ruining your climax, though." I glared at her and she laughed again. "Remember? I told you I'd duck into my room for a few minutes if you wanted to finish."

As she laughed again, I blushed even more. When I'd finally noticed that she was home, I'd scrambled to get Kellan disentangled from me and get redressed. He'd chuckled, not bothered in the slightest, and had wanted to take Anna up on her outlandish offer. I made him go for a walk with me. Anything to douse the fire in my lower body.

Dropping my head into my hands, I shook it. "Why are you bringing that up?" I glared at her again. "Just to humiliate me?"

She smirked at my expression. "No." Dropping her spoon into her bowl, she leaned back on the ugly couch where the intimate moment had happened. "Do you remember what Kellan said?"

I creased my brows, trying to remember anything aside from the embarrassment. Seeing that I didn't, Anna smiled. "He said, 'Don't worry about it, Kiera. When we're old and gray, you'll look back at this moment and laugh. We'll tell our grandkids about it…and completely gross them out.'"

I looked down, finally remembering his words. Anna grabbed my chin, making me look back at her. My eyes felt misty when I did. "I brought it up to remind you that Kellan is thinking long-term with you. You're not just a girl he's seeing. You're THE girl. You're it for him. I see it in his eyes when he looks at you." She sighed, wistfully. "He's completely, madly, deeply in love with you, and he wants a lifetime with you…so stop stressing."

Relieved, I felt a weight lifting off of me. She was right. I was fearing the fear…everything was okay. Nodding at her, I was considering calling Kellan, just to tell him that I loved him, when there was a knock at the front door.

Anna ruffled my hair and diverted her attention back to the television while I got up to see who was here.

Opening the door, I was greeted by Denny's warm smile. It surprised me almost as much as bumping into him yesterday had. It was one thing to hang out for a little while last night, but it was another for him to just drop by. I guessed he missed our friendship just as much as I did.

"Hey, Kiera. I was going to call, but I thought I'd stop by instead, since I was in the area. You doing all right?" He tilted his head as his dark eyes searched my face.

Feeling better after talking to Anna, I shook my head and laughed a little. "Yeah, I'm fine. I overreacted last night." I flung my hand towards the offending laptop; I was definitely returning it today. "I flipped out over nothing."

He nodded and smiled, and I put my hand on his arm. "Thank you, for...being a friend. I can't think of too many guys who would have been as...supportive in the situation."

He looked down at my hand on his arm, then shrugged. "You and I have been through a lot, Kiera, and most of it was good." His eyes flashed back up to mine. "I don't want to see you in pain. I don't have a...vendetta against you." In a whisper that I almost didn't hear, he added, "You're my best friend, still, and I'd do anything for you, Kiera."

I swallowed, hating and loving the sentence he'd just said. Knowing I shouldn't, I reached up and gave him as friendly and platonic a hug as I could. He held me back, equally platonic, with a huge gap between our bodies. "You're my best friend, too, Denny. I know it may not seem like it sometimes...but you are."

Just as I was thinking that maybe that had been our problem all along, that we were more friends than lovers, an expletive sounded from the couch.

Denny and I released each other and twisted to look back at Anna. Her mouth agape, she stared at Denny in our doorway. With everything that had happened, I'd forgotten to tell her that he was back in town. She was looking at him like he just magically materialized into the room.

I stood aside and motioned for him to come in while she sputtered, "Denny? What the hell? Did I wake up three years ago?" She looked over to the window with a view of Lake Union. "God, we're not back home in Ohio, are we?" Her brow bunched into a perfectly adorable pout. "Because I cannot go through living with Mom and Dad again, Kiera."

Denny chuckled at her while I gave her a wry look. "No, Anna, you didn't time travel in your sleep. Denny's back in town for work."

Frowning, she eyed him with suspicion and unhappiness. Denny wasn't Anna's favorite person anymore, not since he'd beaten Kellan to a pulp and rattled my melon. I didn't think she'd ever forgive him for kicking me, even if it was an accident. I was the one that had stupidly used my body as a shield, and Denny wasn't exactly in his right mind at the time, either. But Anna couldn't get past the fact that he'd hurt people she cared about...even if we sort of deserved it.

"Hey, Denny...long time, no see." She said it with a very slight edge, like she preferred the "no see" part.

Denny looked away, guilt flooding his face. He knew how Anna felt about him; she'd bluntly pulled him aside and told him. My sister wasn't one to mince words. If she had a problem with you, you'd know it. "Hi, Anna."

Uncomfortable with the building tension, I twisted to Denny. "So, shouldn't you be at work or something?" I glanced at the dress shirt and the coordinating slacks he had on. He looked like he just stepped off the pages of a GQ magazine.

"I'm on a lunch break." Hands casually tucked in his pockets, he nodded his head at the door. "Care to join me?"

Seeing that I had just enough time to squeeze in lunch before class, I nodded and grabbed my bag from the table. Anna scowled at me, but didn't say anything in front of Denny. I mentally reminded myself to ask her to not mention anything about this to Griffin. I wasn't sure how often they communicated, but I didn't need that particular D-Bag mouthing off to Kellan about Denny. I would tell Kellan when the timing was right, and in a way that wouldn't be hurtful to him. I was sure Griffin wouldn't be so tactful.

Thinking of Griffin reminded me of Kellan's odd text, a text that he'd said was from Griffin, but I suppressed the thought as Denny led me to his company car. Kellan might or might not have fibbed. Perhaps Griffin had a new number that Anna didn't know about, or maybe he was sending gross pictures from Matt's phone. That seemed plausible.

Just as I was feeling better about the strange text, Denny stopped us in front of his sleek, two-door sports car. It looked like one of those cars that they always showed doing a revolution turn in the commercials, like real people drove that way.

I let out a low whistle as Denny popped the passenger's side open. "Now I see why you don't need your Honda back," I muttered, sliding onto the creamy, leather seat.

Denny softly laughed as he stepped in the driver's side. "Yeah, it's not bad." He started it, revving the engine. Giving me a crooked grin, he shrugged. "There are some perks to being in charge."

I laughed at his expression as he drove us along the roller coaster steep hills, happy that he was thriving too. At least I hadn't damaged the men in my life so badly that they'd never recover from it.

My bag rang as we headed out to a café that Denny frequented. I reached in and grabbed my phone, figuring it was probably Anna, about to give me a mouthful for heading out with Denny. I stared at the screen and hesitated, just for a second. Denny eyed me curiously as I answered it.

"Hello?"

"Hey, gorgeous…guess where I woke up today?"

I smiled as Kellan's sultry voice met my ear. "I have no idea." And I really didn't, I'd lost track of his exact location ages ago.

Kellan chuckled and I glanced over at Denny; his eyes were back on the road. It gave me a weird sort of guilt to be back in a situation that was eerily similar to last year. Different though, since Denny and I weren't doing anything inappropriate.

"Kansas…know what's in Kansas?"

I leaned back in my seat and shook my head. "No."

"Nothing," he dryly said. "Miles and miles of nothing." I laughed at his answer and he sighed. "God, I've missed your laugh. It's just not the same over the phone, you know."

Closing my eyes, I twirled a lock of hair around my finger, imagining that it was his. "I know…I've missed you, too." I heard Denny shift beside me, but I kept my eyes closed, biting my lip as a little more guilt flooded me.

Just as I was thinking of ways to tell Kellan that Denny was back, Kellan asked, "So, what have you been up to lately?"

I opened my eyes and tensed, wondering if someone had told him already. "Uh…just work and school. Did I tell you I started my new quarter last month? I have a poetry class now."

I rolled my eyes, hating that I'd chosen the most trivial fact to tell him. By his reaction, though, you would have thought I'd just told him I won the lottery. "Really? I like poetry…it's a lot like lyric writing. Less cursing though."

He chuckled again and I relaxed. If he knew about Denny, he probably wouldn't be joking. I glanced over at Denny, who was deliberately focusing his attention on the roads. Maybe he was uncomfortable. Maybe he was just giving me privacy. I wasn't sure. As I watched him, Kellan added, "So what are you up to today?"

I flushed, not wanting to lie, but not ready to tell him. "Nothing really…"

He sighed softly. "Well, I've just got endless driving in front of me…please tell me your life is more interesting than that. One of us needs a good story to tell."

I smirked, knowing his life was already more interesting and exciting than the average person's, even if it did involve endless driving. Biting my lip, I studied Denny again. "Well…I'm on my way to have lunch with a friend."

Denny looked over at me, raising a dark eyebrow and frowning slightly. He clearly wanted me to elaborate on the details to Kellan, but I couldn't. Not yet. Not over the phone. We needed to have this conversation in person.

Kellan brightly said, "Good. It's good that you're getting out, having a life."

I looked straight ahead and twisted my lips. "Of course I still have a life. Do you think my world revolves around you?"

I was obviously teasing, but Kellan paused a moment before answering. "No, no I don't think that at all." His voice was quiet, introspective, and I again wondered if he knew something. Maybe I should tell him over the phone anyway…

"You all right?" I asked quietly.

He inhaled a deep breath, taking a very long pause before answering. "Yeah, I'm fine." There was so much that he wasn't saying in his voice. Even though Kellan was good at it, I knew he was lying to me.

"Kellan…is there something you want to tell me?" My heart started pounding, the ice in my stomach so painful I nearly doubled over. That woman's face flashed in my mind, the look on his as he leaned in to whisper in her ear. The mysterious text number ran through my brain in a never-ending loop…

He sniffed and took another long moment. "It's nothing, Kiera…just the stress of the road. I'm sure you can imagine what life on a bus with Griffin is like." He chuckled, his voice back to light and happiness, but I didn't believe a word of it.

I bit my lip as I stared at Denny, now darting concerned glances in my direction. Kellan was withholding something from me, that much I could tell. I had no idea what or why, but I couldn't open up to him about Denny now. I just couldn't. "Okay, well…if something was going on, you know that you could tell me…right?"

He sighed softly. "Yeah, I know…" His voice trailed off, then brightened. "But really, nothing is up, aside from the fact that I miss you like crazy."

A sad smile touched my lips. "Yeah, me too." As we pulled into the parking area of the café, I sighed. "Hey, I'm here at the restaurant…I need to go. I'll call you later?"

"Yeah, okay." With a humorless chuckle he added, "I'll be here, on the road through nowhere, wishing Griffin didn't need to let The Hulk breathe quite so often."

I laughed, the levity easing the knot in my belly. "I love you, Kellan."

"I love you too, Kiera." He said it immediately, with no hesitation or trace of deceit. If anything else, he at least honestly meant it when he said it.

I hung up the phone as Denny shut off the car. Turning to me, he shook his head. "You didn't tell him I was here." It was a statement, not a question.

I sighed, fingering the contraption in my palm. "Not yet, it didn't feel right." I peeked up at him. "I will…soon. I promise."

He shook his head again but didn't comment any further. Just as he cracked open his door, his cell phone rang. He glanced back at me, a small smile on his lips. "Well, aren't we popular?" I smiled at his comment and watched as he checked the screen. The small smile on his face grew about a million times brighter. He looked up at me really quick. "It's Abby, I need to take this."

I nodded as he answered, "Hey, babe." Pushing open his door, he stepped out to the parking lot. Before closing his door, I heard him say, "No, you caught me heading out to lunch with Kiera…"

He shut the door and I didn't hear any more than that, but I marveled that he'd openly confessed that he was with me. I guessed they didn't have the same trust issues that Kellan and I had. That's what you get when your relationship starts by betraying someone—a never-ending well of doubt. If we could do it to someone, it could be done to us.

Giving Denny a private moment to catch up with his faraway girlfriend, I ran my fingers back through my mostly dry hair and stared at my phone. I wanted an explanation to magically appear on it, but it didn't. Sighing, I typed a message into it and pressed send.

I watched Denny through the window while I waited for a reply. He was leaning against the hood of the car, laughing at whatever conversation he and Abby were having. He seemed genuinely happy, his eyes practically glowing as he spoke to her. I wondered if he looked like that when he'd talked to me so long ago. I wondered if he tenderly made love to Abby before he left her. I was pretty sure he did...and it was probably a lot more romantic than getting sloshed and having sex in a bathroom at a party.

As I watched Denny run a hand back through his hair in a warm, familiar way, my phone buzzed in my hand. Pressing the screen, I read the message from Kellan. 'I love you too...more than anything. I can't wait to see you again...soon, hopefully.'

I repeated the sentiment, then opened my door to join Denny, since his conversation looked about over. Sighing peacefully, he nodded over to the café doors. "Sorry about that, she was getting ready for work and I didn't want to miss her." Looking down, he kicked at a rock as we walked along. "I make sure to talk to her as often as I can..."

He looked up at me from the corner of his eyes and a flash of guilt ran through me. I was the reason he kept in constant contact. My cheating spree with Kellan had started while he was away. The experience had made him all the more attentive to his current girl. I guessed something good had come out of the whole mess after all.

Not commenting, I only nodded as we made our way inside. Sitting down, I tried to keep the light smile on my face. "So, Abby...what's she like?"

He looked at me blankly before picking up a menu. "You don't really want to talk about this, do you?"

Watching him absentmindedly flip through the pages, I nodded. "Yes, I do actually." When he looked up at me, I shrugged. "We're friends, remember, and that means sharing our lives. She's obviously an important part. I saw your face while you were talking to her..."

With a reminiscent smile on his face, he looked over my shoulder. "She's...she's great. She's warm and sweet...loving."

He stared at the table, a small flush coloring his cheeks. I felt the same mild embarrassment, but I did my best to ignore it. We should be able to talk about the significant people in our lives. His fingers flicking over the menu pages, he exhaled softly. "I was really...broken when I got home. She helped me through it, made me smile again."

His warm brown eyes looked up at me and I clenched my stomach, willing my eyes not to water. I'd done that. I'd broken him. Smiling softly, he shook his head. "I think I love her, Kiera...really love her. I think she's the one," he whispered.

Then my eyes did water, and I couldn't possibly stop the reaction. I nodded as I swiped my fingers under my eyes. "Good, I'm glad, Denny."

And I was happy...and devastatingly sad too. It was hard, watching someone you'd loved once loving someone else, and loving them more than they ever loved you. But, really, that's exactly what I'd done to Denny with Kellan.

Denny's hand stretched across the table to rest on my arm. "I'm sorry if that hurts you. I just wanted to be *honest* with you." He stressed the word honest.

As I considered the multitude of things that I hadn't been honest about in my life, Denny squeezed my arm and asked, "What about you and Kellan? Are you guys really okay? Are you happy, Kiera?"

Knowing I was worrying about things with Kellan before their time, I smiled as effortlessly as I could. "Yeah, I am." I nodded, remembering all of the good times Kellan and I had shared. "I mean, being with him has its challenges...but...we're good."

I obliviously stroked the ring on my finger and Denny's eyes locked onto it. His dark depths glossier when he met my eyes again, he smiled effortlessly too. "Good, I'm glad, Kiera...I really am."

Chapter 17 – Boise

A month passed and nothing much changed in my life, even with Denny's return. I went to school, I went to work. I had coffee with Cheyenne while she attempted to explain poetry; it still didn't make much sense to me. I spoke to Kellan three or four times a day, more often if he was having a traveling day. Sometimes the calls were brief, sometimes they lasted for hours; our phone calls on Valentine's Day had been especially lengthy. Denny came around to the bar for dinner most nights, and we spent the time catching up on our year apart.

I also agreed to sign up for an advanced art course with Jenny and Kate on Saturday mornings…even though I was atrocious and the instructor humored me with every comment he made. I made a mental note to not repeat the six-week course with Jenny. Her talent was just way beyond my skills.

But as much as the good things stayed the same, the questionable things also remained the same. I avoided computers, too tempted to Google Kellan's name, too afraid of what I might discover. And I definitely didn't want to see anymore footage of him with Halle 2. I just couldn't handle seeing it again.

Yet, I never asked him about it when we talked. And I never told him about Denny's return to Seattle. My mouth locked up when I tried. Just the idea of Kellan cheating on me, terrified me.…so much so that I didn't want to give him that same fear. Especially when it wasn't warranted. Denny and I were only friends. Truly, just friends.

So, the nagging doubts continued to linger between us, and I allowed it, not ready to confess what I knew, too scared to hear what Kellan knew…

Getting home from class on a windy Thursday afternoon, I collapsed beside my sister on the sofa, grateful for a few hours of respite. I wasn't scheduled to work until tomorrow night, and I didn't have classes until Monday, so I was free to just be a couch potato.

Anna sighed, irritably tapping her foot as she flicked through the television channels. I tried to ignore her restlessness. She'd been increasingly agitated since the holidays. I suspected that she was peeved that Griffin hadn't asked to see her over the holidays. It upset her more than she was willing to let on. I suspected she missed him. Since they hadn't had any romantic rendezvous, she hadn't been with him, well, since the night of the going away party. And Anna, for some godforsaken reason, liked being with him.

Tossing the remote on the floor, she laid her head back on the orange monstrosity we were sitting on. "God, I'm so freaking bored." Popping her head up, she excitedly leaned forward. "Let's go to Boise."

I blinked at her. "What?"

Nodding, she leaned forward even more, her décolletage sweater showing off assets that I would never have. "Let's go to Boise. The guys are playing a show there tonight and it's the closest they're going to be to us until the end of the tour. So let's go to their concert!"

Playing on my sympathy, she gave me puppy dog eyes, and stuck out her full bottom lip. I shook my head. "Idaho? By tonight? It's almost five now...we don't have time to drive that far, Anna."

She sat up on her knees, really excited now. "So we'll hop a flight. It's probably only an hour or so by plane."

Disapprovingly, I raised my eyebrow. "We can't just 'hop on a plane' to see a concert, Anna."

Returning the gesture, she replied, "We can do anything we want, Kiera. Come on, live a little."

Sensing victory, she started pulling me up off the couch. "You're too focused, too structured. You need to let loose every once in a while. Besides, don't you want to see Kellan?"

Biting my lip, I stifled a sigh. I did want to see him, more than anything, but...there were conversations that we needed to have, conversations that I wasn't ready to have yet. I desperately missed him though...and I hadn't found any playful notes in a while to help keep the loneliness at bay...

Maybe seeing that she was starting to sell me on the idea, Anna dragged me to my room and started packing a bag for me. I cringed when she found the lacy lingerie that was part of Kellan's Christmas gift. I cringed further when she shoved it in my bag. Like I'd wear that on a tour bus. Sitting on the bed while she zipped the bag closed, I murmured, "I don't want him to think I'm checking up on him."

She paused. Anna knew I still had questions about the video. "You could finally ask him about the girl?" I shook my head and she twisted her lips, then shrugged. "Well, he'll be too busy screwing your brains out to care anyway."

I scoffed and threw a pillow at her, and she laughed. Then her face got serious. "I want to see Griffin, Kiera. I think I...I think I miss him." She sneered as if the idea was odd to her. It was a little odd to me, too, but then again, so was their entire relationship.

Caving, I exaggerated an annoyed sigh. "Fine, when's the flight?"

Anna squealed and clapped her hands before running to her room. "You won't regret this, Kiera! We're gonna have the best time!"

Hoping she was right, I grabbed my bag.

While the drive across Washington to the bottom of Idaho took around eight hours, it turned out that a flight there was under an hour. We made an early evening plane and touched down in Boise with time to spare. I hated handing over all of my hard-earned tip money for the ticket, but when I stepped out of the airport and smelled the same air that I knew Kellan was breathing, it was worth every penny.

Wanting to surprise the boys, we didn't call them on the way over. Actually, we didn't call anybody. It was the most impulsive thing I'd ever done, well, if you didn't count having spur-of-the-moment sex in an espresso stand impulsive. I tended to think of different adjectives when I thought about that night.

Rushing out to see Kellan when he didn't know I was coming was exciting, and my heart was racing when we hailed a cab. Calling Rachel to verify where the boys were playing, I instantly felt bad that we hadn't paused long enough to include Rachel and Jenny in our plans. They would've wanted to see their boyfriends too. But really, we'd barely made the flight with just the two of us, considering how strict airport security was now; the interesting collection of "toys" that Anna packed in her carry-on didn't help either.

By the time we found the place it was just about time for the show to start. I had no idea how we were going to get in to see a sold-out show. Although I was thrilled that the tour was going well, it made everything that much harder. I'd never needed a ticket to watch Kellan play before. I was used to just walking into work and having him there, singing, just for me. Or so it seemed sometimes.

Hoping we could find some scalpers, we got out of the cab at what looked like an old theater. It was massive, though, and people milled about outside, smoking or chatting on their phones. Light boxes along the entrance displayed the tour's posters, with our favorite band's name the last on the list of hot groups performing tonight.

On the marquee though, the D-Bags were right under the main attraction. It was as close to top billing as a small, relatively unknown band could get. Impressed by the sign, my heart swelled with pride for Kellan. He was actually doing it. He was actually becoming a rock star, right before my eyes. It blew my mind.

Just as I headed towards a group of meandering people, feeling like an idiot as I clutched my overnight bag, Anna grabbed my arm and jerked me towards the alley. I squeaked in surprise, then looked around the dark area she was leading us to. Not wanting to be mugged, I pulled back on her arm.

"Where are we going?"

Cocking her head at me, her hair perfectly pulled into a loose ponytail, she nodded at the alley where I was sure Jack the Ripper was hiding. "The back entrance is probably down there. We're going in."

I gave her a dry look. "They're not just going to let us in the back, Anna. We'll have to buy tickets, just like everybody else."

Rolling her eyes at me, she adjusted the ridiculously tight t-shirt she'd changed into before leaving the house. "Kiera, I've never bought a concert ticket in my life, and I'm not about to start now." Smiling in that seductive way that she and Kellan had down to a science, she smirked and headed towards the alley again. Her bag elegantly slung over her shoulder looked more like an overlarge purse than the duffel bag that mine resembled.

Hoping we survived this, I exhaled a quick breath and hurried to catch up to her. If we were going to die, I wanted us to die together.

Confidently strutting down the dark street, Anna looked completely comfortable with the situation. Wishing I had her guts, I tried to at least act like I did. Like she expected, we ran into a door being blocked by what could have been Sam's long lost brother. All muscle and rough demeanor, he narrowed his eyes at us as we approached.

"Keep walking," he muttered as we got close enough to hear.

Anna ran a finger along the deep v-neck of her shirt. "But we want to talk to you."

He frowned at her, then at me. "I just got rid of the last batch of you. Don't you girls have anything better to do than try and screw rock stars?"

I bristled at his words, both because that wasn't what we were doing, not really, and because there was a steady group of girls out there that tried to do exactly what he was saying. Sticking my chin up, I defiantly said, "We just want to see our boyfriends, and they happen to be in one of the bands. If you could let us by, we'd really appreciate it."

He smirked at me. "Wow, I've never heard that one before." Rolling his eyes, he added, "When are you girls gonna learn that the actual girlfriends get passes to the show. They don't come back here to see me." With a smirk he added, "Not that the actual girlfriends are around much…if you know what I mean."

He eyed my sister and me up and down, clearly undressing us, and my eyes narrowed at what he was implying—whores trumped girlfriends, by a long shot. Trying to ignore the heat in my stomach, I shook my head. "Our boyfriends don't know we're here…it's a surprise."

He smiled with one edge of his lip, his bulging biceps not moving from in front of his chest. "Yes, and when they see you out here after the show, it will certainly be a surprise."

My mouth dropped open in frustration but Anna shot me a look to keep me quiet. Sidling up to the man, she ran a finger along his arm. Licking her lip as slowly and seductively as she could, she throatily murmured, "There must be some way to get past this…" she squeezed his arm, then let her hand travel down his side, "…impressive body in our way."

Smirking at Anna, his eyes traveled to her chest and stayed there. She subtly straightened her shoulders, giving him the best view she could. One of his hands uncrossing, he brazenly reached out and cupped one of her breasts. I wanted to smack his smug face, but Anna held a warning finger behind her back, telling me not to.

As Anna wasn't wearing a bra, the man got a nice little nipple rub. It disgusted me, but Anna only smiled at him like he was complimenting her on her hair. Smiling that she wasn't moving, he dropped his hand and motioned to her shirt. "Show me, and I'll let you in."

I sputtered and mumbled a protest but Anna only shrugged and lifted her shirt for him. When she finally lowered the fabric back down into place, I could tell the bouncer was…pleased. If the dazed smile on his face wasn't a big enough clue, the bulge in his jeans was unmistakable.

I twisted my lips and looked away. "Dog," I muttered. I was pretty sure Sam never would have pulled crap like that.

Focusing on my sister, I watched her brush her fingers over the man's cheek. "Satisfied," she purred, biting her lip and glancing down at the evidence of his arousal.

"Definitely," he growled. "Whatever guy you land in there is one lucky bastard."

Anna smiled as he moved aside from the door. Rolling my eyes, I started to follow her, but the jerk blocked my path. "Nope, sorry, sweetheart." Leering at my chest, he shook his head. "You haven't paid the price of admission."

Dropping my bag, I immediately crossed my arms over my chest, covering my already covered body. "I am not flashing you!"

He shrugged, unperturbed. "Then you're not getting back there."

My mouth dropped open and I smacked him across the chest. He narrowed his eyes at me, and I stopped instantly, remembering that this was not a bouncer at Pete's that I was messing with. Lifting my chin, I spat out, "You're a pig."

Smirking, he winked at me. "Yeah, and you're still not getting back there until I see some tatas."

An exasperated noise fell out of my mouth as I looked up at Anna, waiting with one palm on the door. She shrugged and made a stripping motion with her hand. I cringed, not wanting to do this...but wanting to see Kellan.

My cheeks flaming so hot they hurt, I shook my head indignantly. "Go get Kellan Kyle! He's the lead singer of the D-Bags. He'll vouch for me, that I'm his girlfriend...and then you'll have to let me in!"

The man yawned, bored. "Listen, sweetheart. The musicians and I have a deal. I don't bother them, and they let me have a groupie or two. It works out great, and I'm not going to jeopardize that for you." He smiled again, in a creepy way that made my skin crawl. "Now strip...or go home."

Feeling tears sting my eyes, I glared at my sister. "I'm gonna kill you for this, Anna." Before she could answer, I twisted to the man and snarled, "The bra stays on!"

He rolled his eyes and shrugged and I closed mine. Wishing I could disappear, I fought against every instinct in my body and lifted my shirt for the repugnant man before me. I heard him chuckle as he muttered, "Ah, white cotton with a cute little flower in the middle. Aren't you a sweet thing?"

Just as his fingers came out to touch, I smacked his hand away and lowered my clothes, holding them tight around myself. Looking satisfied that I had done it, he motioned to the door where Anna was standing. Glaring at him, I picked up my bag and stiffly walked past him.

Grabbing my arm as I brushed against him, he leaned into me. "I love the innocent ones...they're the wildest in the sack." He nodded at the closed door. "I'll be around, once you're done with this Kellan guy, if you want to experience a real man." He ground his still-aroused body into my leg and I forced myself to not slap him.

Backing away, I straightened and muttered, "No, thank you." Then shoved Anna's back so she'd open the door and get us out of that damn alley. "You're so dead, Anna," I muttered again when she finally opened the heavy, steel door. The sound of the bouncer chuckling was mercifully muffled by the cacophony coming from inside the theater.

Anna was highly entertained by the whole thing. As we walked down the hall, she slung her arm over my shoulders and laughed out, "Oh, my God, I so thought you were going to deck that guy!" Biting my lip, I glared at her. She only laughed harder and squeezed me tight. Resting her head against mine, she merrily exclaimed, "Ah, relax, Kiera, no harm done, and now you're one step closer to Kellan."

She winked at me as I pushed her away. "I'll turn you into a vixen yet, sister," she giggled. I rolled my eyes at her but did smile a little. Well, Kellan wanted me to have a good story to tell him. I guessed now I did.

The music of the band on stage filtered around us as we aimlessly walked through corridors and open areas. There were tons of people about. Some worked at the venue, walking around with headsets and clipboards, some looked like security, which we purposely avoided since we weren't technically supposed to be here, some were from a local radio station, and some were clearly band members. But the majority were women, just like us. It helped us blend in, but I wasn't too thrilled with the girl-to-guy ratio that I was seeing.

Not knowing where our boys were in the lineup, or where they might be hanging out until it was their turn, we just kept searching. Anna flipped out when she spotted Justin and his band— Anna loved their music just as much as I did. She started heading his way but I grabbed her arm. "Don't, Anna!"

She glared back at me. "Don't you know who that is?"

I rolled my eyes and nodded. "Yeah, we met when the boys left."

Anna slung her arm around me, dragging me forward. "Perfect, then he'll tell you where Kellan is."

I felt heat in my cheeks that was nearly painful. Our introduction hadn't exactly been smooth...and...he'd been at the restaurant for Kellan's little erotic performance. Oh God, I could not look him in the eye after that!

"He won't remember me, Anna." Oh God, yeah, he probably would remember me now...

Anna giggled in my ear as we got closer to Justin, his smile wide as he talked with a couple of girls nearby. "Who could forget you, Kiera?"

I rolled my eyes at her and wanted to protest further, but Justin had turned his head and noticed us. His light blue eyes widened as he pointed a finger at me; I could see the spark of recognition in the pale depths. He did remember me, which meant he probably remembered overhearing the phone sex, too. Damn it. *I really hate you right now, Kellan Kyle.*

Tilting his blond head, he grinned crookedly and let out a short laugh. "Hey, aren't you...Kellan's girl?"

Biting my lip, I walked up to him. My knees were shaking, but I made myself say, "Yeah, my sister and I came out to see him...to surprise him." Not able to look Justin in the eye, I stared at the ink scrawled across his chest; I couldn't read it, but the lines were a nice distraction for my embarrassment.

Anna took over at my ineptitude. Thrusting her hand out and sliding as close to him as etiquette allowed, she purred, "Anna Allen, huge fan. 'Kick Me When I'm Down' has got to be my favorite song in the world."

I looked up at her and scowled. Of course she would remember a song title. Justin seemed pleased that she had, and that she wasn't wearing a bra. His eyes only quickly flashed over her breasts, not blatantly staring like the bouncer had, but he still checked her out as he shook her hand. "Nice to meet you, Anna."

His eyes burned a little as he watched her and I thought my sister might actually have a shot with him. Not surprising, really. My sister could have just about anybody, and she usually got whatever boy she set her sights on. Except Kellan.

But Anna didn't seem too interested in Justin. Instead, she waved her hand around the mammoth backstage area. "We're looking for the D-Bags. Have you seen Kellan and Griffin?"

Justin pursed his lips. He seemed disappointed that Anna didn't want to hang out with him. "Griffin?" By the way his lip twisted even more, I thought maybe Justin had met The Hulk, too. Pointing over his shoulder with his thumb, he shrugged. "Last I saw, they were drinking with some girls back there."

A knot in my stomach formed at hearing his words. Drinking with girls? I tried to put a lid on the knot growing, though. Drinking with girls didn't mean sleeping with girls. At least, not in Kellan's case.

Anna brightened and thanked him. We both said goodbye, and Justin seemed a little sad as Anna left his sight. I looked back before we turned a corner to another corridor and accidentally locked eyes with Justin. He suddenly looked amused. He chuckled and leaned over to a friend of his, pointing at me again. The friend stared at me, too, chuckling in the same way. Knowing that they were talking about Kellan faking jacking-off at their table, I clenched my fists and hurried after Anna as she pushed herself through a group of people. That was not the way I wanted a celebrity to remember me. In fact, I'd rather he didn't.

As we got to a large room filled with people, I felt like we'd stepped back into Pete's bar. It was smaller than the bar, but the alcohol was flowing, girls were giggling, and the music from the stage was being piped through some speakers, filling the room with noise. I suddenly felt like I should have a tray and a bag full of lollipops.

I looked around the clusters of people, but didn't see my D-Bag anywhere. Chairs and couches were sporadically tossed around the space, with small tables holding stacks of empty cups. I wasn't sure how long ago the show had started, but this party seemed in full swing already.

Girls clamored over boys I didn't know; I figured they were some of the other band's members. As I watched a girl lean up and tug on a boy's earlobe, I wondered if any of these guys had girls waiting back home. It made me nauseous to think about it. Anna grabbed my hand, leading us through the throngs, and my stomach tightened with every step.

Maybe coming here had been a bad idea. If I caught Kellan in the act with another girl...my heart might explode right then and there. I didn't think I could take it. While I'd always felt bad about Denny having seen our moment, I now had a newfound appreciation for his pain. No wonder he'd flown off the handle. I already wanted to as I watched boys openly flirting with loose girls, and I hadn't even found Kellan yet.

I found him a few moments later. He was standing with his back to me, luckily with no girls hanging on him, chuckling over something in front of him. Women next to me mimicked pinching his ass and giggled. Other women standing nearby looked ready to sling their drunken arms around him and kiss him. Ignoring them, I concentrated on the messy head of sandy-brown hair that I'd missed so much. As he leaned over to laughingly whisper something to the man beside him, who I finally realized was Griffin, my eyes fixed on the strong jaw line, the full lips speaking words through his smile.

He was so impossibly attractive, it was nearly unfair. But that wasn't all he was, and my heart swelled with the love I felt for him, love that had only been growing since we'd been forced apart.

Then I noticed what held his and Griffin's rapt attention.

As Anna sidestepped us around some girls that she couldn't plow through, I got a full shot of what Kellan and Griffin were watching and laughing about. Draped over the makeshift bar that someone had set up back here, a buxom, blonde bimbo was spread out. Wearing impractically tiny shorts and only a bra for a top, she was having shots of liquor poured over her while other, equally skanky women, sucked the liquid off. One girl even poured some in the blonde's mouth, then immediately dived in to retrieve it.

I watched them for a second, disgusted by the obvious ploy to get the rock star's attentions, then I twisted my head over to stare at Kellan. He was still watching them, chewing on his bottom lip as he twisted a bottle of beer in his hands. Narrowing my eyes, I stared at his jeans. I knew it was wrong, a guy couldn't help being aroused by beautiful girls acting overtly sexual, but I needed to know if he was getting turned on by this. I didn't see any telltale signs...yet.

I was still staring at his jeans when Anna finally pulled us close enough that Kellan and Griffin noticed. When the view of his hips went from a side angle to a front angle, my heart started beating ten times faster and I looked up to his face. Embarrassed that he'd caught me staring at his privates, I blushed.

He didn't look embarrassed, though, not that he would ever be embarrassed about me staring at his body. No, instead, he looked completely floored. Mouth wide open, he stared at me like he had just wished me into existence. Griffin, beside him, looked equally shocked as he stared at Anna.

Griffin, surprisingly, snapped out of it first. "Hell yeah!" he exclaimed, pushing past Kellan to scoop up a giggling Anna. His tongue was deep down her throat in seconds. A moment after that, her legs were around his waist and he was walking out of the room with her, bullying aside anyone who wasn't quick enough to move.

I blinked at how rapidly they got down to business, then twisted back to Kellan. Recovering slowly, he shook his head, a smile replacing his shocked expression. "You're here?" he said, stepping towards me.

I nodded, a smile on my own lips. I accidentally flicked a glance at the co-eds making out and Kellan followed my eyes. Knitting his brows, he looked back at me and shrugged. Looking a little sheepish, he grabbed my hand and pulled me into him. "Sorry about that." Running his other hand back through my hair, his eyes lovingly washed over my face. "Some girls will do anything to get noticed," he whispered.

Feeling the heat in my belly fading as those indigo eyes absorbed me, I nodded. I didn't point out that they'd succeeded in getting his attention. He'd definitely been invested until I walked up. But men were men...you couldn't expect them to not look at something like that. Even Denny would have watched.

Smiling warmly at me, he cupped my cheek; the heat of it traveled all the way down my body. "I can't believe you're here." He glanced around at where he was. "How did you get back here?"

I sighed morosely. "You would not believe what I had to do." I raised an eyebrow. "Make sure you say bye to Anna...because I'm killing her when we get home."

He chuckled at me, his smile glorious. "Ah, I can't wait to hear this story."

Biting my lip, I stepped closer to his body. "Maybe it could wait just a little bit?" I whispered, my eyes locking onto his mouth.

Understanding what I needed, his lips were instantly on mine. I wanted to groan and clutch him to me. It was the first part of March. It had been over two months since our last kiss, back in December...and I'd missed this so much. Kellan's arms wrapped around me, his hand cupping my cheek moving back to cradle my neck. My arms slipped up his chest, one continuing on to tangle in his hair. His tongue slid against mine, tasting me, teasing me. The chaos of the world slipped away as we melded together, and for a few long seconds, it was just the two of us in this packed room.

But then someone tapped Kellan's shoulder, and he grudgingly pulled away from me. Hiding a scowl, I looked over at who couldn't wait a few moments to have his attention. Thinking that maybe the buxom blonde on the counter was going to try something a little more aggressive, I fully expected to see her there. But when Halle 2's eyes met mine, I wished to God that it had been the blonde.

The actress's lookalike glanced at me, then focused on Kellan. "Kellan, I'm ready for you."

My mouth dropped open as wide as Kellan's had when he'd first noticed me here. Had she seriously just propositioned him right in front of me? Who the hell was this chick?

Expecting Kellan to stutter and stammer and flail about for a lie that made sense, I was a little surprised when he only nodded at her and said, "Okay, I'll need a minute, though."

The statuesque woman looked me up and down, shook her head a little, then smiled back at him. Placing a hand on his shoulder, she leaned in so he could hear her over the music and laughter in the room. "The conference room upstairs...when you're ready."

Kellan nodded, still smiling warmly at her. I wanted to punch the jackass in the face. She smirked at me, then turned and walked away. I just stood there, my arms falling from Kellan to hang loosely at my sides. That hadn't really just happened, had it? I dug my nails into my palms, trying to wake myself up. I was dreaming. This was just another nightmare about her...that was all.

But I didn't wake up, and Kellan twisted back around to face me. He didn't seem chagrined at all about being caught. Of course, he didn't know that I knew she was his stalker. He didn't know that I'd watched the videos, that I'd seen her hanging around, that I knew he knew her. As he watched my blank expression, he bit his lip, finally seeming nervous.

"I need to tell you something...can we talk?"

I briefly closed my eyes at those hated words, then nodded and turned away from him. I aimlessly walked towards the hallway that Anna and Griffin had disappeared in, not really knowing where I was going, just hoping that there was enough privacy back here so that I could murder him without attracting too much attention.

When we got to a spot where the crowd had thinned out, Kellan grabbed my elbow, making me stop. I wanted to pull away. I wanted to keep walking. If I kept walking, then I wouldn't have to hear him say that he'd fallen for someone else...and he was about to go have sex with her in a conference room. God, how tacky.

Bunching his brows as I stiffened in his arms, he asked, "Hey, are you...mad at me?"

Bristling, I stuck my chin out and threw my bag on the ground. "No, why would I be mad?" He shook his head and was about to answer, but I stupidly answered for him. "You're only about to dump me for the hot celebrity lookalike that's been stalking you for weeks. You're only about to go have sex with her on an office table. You're only about to crush me into a thousand pieces, and right after I exposed my chest to some jackass just to see you, too!"

He blinked and gaped at me as I started breathing heavy. I really hadn't meant to say any of that. I planned on letting him hang himself. "Wait, you think...?" He stopped and tilted his head. "You did what to come see me?"

Irritated, I shoved his chest away and started storming off...somewhere. Sighing, he grabbed my shoulders and turned me around. Backing me into a wall, he stared me down. "I am not dumping you. I am not about to have sex with her. And I am not going to crush you."

He gave me a minute to calm down. When I was breathing regularly, I searched his face. "Then what...is going on?"

Releasing my shoulders, he shook his head. "Well, what I was going to tell you, before you leapt to that wild conclusion, is..." he bit his lip, his face beaming underneath it, "...we got signed." He nodded his head upstairs. "That's Lana. She's a rep from the record company. She's been following the tour, examining the bands...and she wants to sign us to her label." He laughed a little, shaking his head. "We're going to have a record, Kiera, an actual, professional record...can you believe it?"

My mouth dropped open again as my eyes watered. My mind hadn't gone down that path at all. I'd automatically assumed the worst. I shoved his shoulders away from me. "Why didn't you tell me you were being scouted, jackass!"

He cringed away from me, frowning as I started smacking his chest. "Because I really didn't expect much. I didn't think she'd pick us...and..." His voice trailed off and I stopped hitting him. Sighing, he grabbed my hands and peeked up at me from under his lashes. "I didn't want to disappoint you...if she wasn't interested in us. I know you think I'm going to go all the way... I didn't want to let you down..."

He looked down, and I instantly felt like an idiot. Slinging my arms around him, I hugged him tight. "God, Kellan, I'd never be disappointed in you...ever." Pulling back, I cupped his cheeks, my eyes hazy with tears. "I'm so proud of you, of everything you do, and even if it ended right here, I'd be anything but disappointed in you."

He exhaled, seemingly relieved. Sniffling, he looked around the hall. "Well, I haven't even told the guys yet...I didn't want to jinx it, so we need to find them and get them upstairs to sign the legal stuff." He looked back at me, raising an eyebrow. "That's what's going down on the conference room table...not sex." He grabbed my hips, pulling me into him. "But if you want to, once everyone is gone...I'd never tell you no."

He chuckled and I grabbed his face, kissing him hard. I might take him up on that offer. I was just so relieved that he wasn't sleeping with her. And so very proud of him for what he was doing.

Pulling apart from me, he reached down and picked up my forgotten bag. "Come on, we've got to take care of this before it's our turn on stage." Holding his hand out for me, he smiled like a little boy. "They bumped us up the lineup; we play right under Justin's band now. Pretty cool, huh?"

Leaning into his side, I giggled and nodded. "That's amazing, Kellan."

Feeling better about a lot of things as we walked around the halls, looking for D-Bags, I considered all of the videos I've seen her in. That's why she was around so much, she was scoping out the band. And that's the reason why they seemed friendly. She was wooing him...in a way. Lana? Seemed like a respectable enough name, not that names really mean anything, but still...

As I processed this new information, Kellan smiled down at me. "Hey, what did you mean when you said she's been stalking me for weeks? How did you know about that?"

Biting my lip, I took tiny peeks at his face. "Uh, Rachel put up this website, and fans have posted videos of your shows. I've been watching you..." My voice trailed off and I had the weird sensation that *I* was the stalker, not the other way around.

"She finally got that up and running, huh? Well, that should make Matt happy." Releasing my hand, Kellan slung his arm around my shoulder. "So, you've been checking up on me?"

I stared up at his face, his eyes amused as he searched for his friends. "No…" His dark blue eyes swung down to mine, even more amused. I sighed. "Maybe…a little."

Tilting his head, he squeezed me tighter. "And was I being good?"

Uncertain how to respond, since I sort of thought he was diddling the record rep, I floundered, lost for words. Fortunately, Griffin and Anna reappeared from around a corner. I smiled at seeing them, which was a strange reaction for me to have at seeing Griffin. Anna had a dopey, satisfied look on her face while she adjusted her hair and clothes. I figured they'd already gone a round then…maybe two.

Slapping Griffin on the shoulder, Kellan filled him in on the situation. Griffin, over the moon by the news, took off in search of his cousin, who was apparently in a quiet space with Evan, working out a piece of music. The thought of them dedicating their free time to practice instead of flirting with the ample number of overzealous female fans, made me smile. Rachel was right, it was all about the music with Matt. Evan, too, in a way.

Kellan led us to an elevator blocked by a security guard. Backstage clearance didn't get you upstairs, apparently. With Anna giggling and clutching my arm, the three of us got waved past the guard after Kellan said a few words to him. He gave Kellan an approving look as the elevator doors closed behind us, like he thought Kellan was about to have a threesome with my sister and me. Ew.

While Anna reached into her bag to grab a sucker (and I did not want to know why), Kellan dropped my bag and wrapped his arms around me. Kissing me a little too passionately considering my sister was watching, he murmured, "I'm sorry I didn't tell you about this earlier…but I'm glad you're here."

Content, I ran my fingers through his hair. "I'm glad I'm here, too." All the stress of the previous weeks washed off of me as his mouth explored mine. I was just wishing we had some more privacy when the elevator stopped and the doors dinged open. Anna smiled at us around her lollipop before stepping out.

Kellan grabbed my bag again, as well as my hand. "So," he asked merrily as we exited, "anything you've been holding off on telling me?"

He laughed as he said it, so I was sure he didn't actually know anything. Anna frowned and gave me a pointed look. She obviously wanted me to tell him. And I would…I should. He should know Denny had reappeared in his absence. But just as I had to deal with the swarms of eager women downstairs, Kellan was going to have to trust me, too.

Inhaling deep, I was just about to tell him when his phone buzzed. Frowning slightly, he reached into his back pocket. He silenced it without looking at the number and placed it back in his pocket. Staring straight ahead, he proceeded to walk down the hall as if nothing happened. Counting off all of the people who I knew in Kellan's life, I wondered who had just called him. Lana was waiting in the room we were getting closer to, and the guys were all on their way up. It wasn't Griffin this time. Of course, I was almost certain it hadn't been Griffin last time.

All of the momentary good feelings that I felt about us faded as I watched him deliberately avoid eye contact with me. He was still hiding something, and I had no idea what…or who. Tears stinging my eyes, I shut my mouth and said absolutely nothing about Denny being in town.

Chapter 18 – Let it Go

I stared at my hands as we all sat around a large, oak table. Lana, the attractive rep from the record label, distributed contracts with a considerable amount of fine print. The boys silently read through them while Lana broke them down into layman's terms. I tuned her out, focusing instead on the music drifting up through the floor. They weren't even halfway through the show yet, so Kellan and the guys had more than enough time to consider this career-changing opportunity being presented to them.

When Lana finished speaking, Kellan glanced up at her, then looked over to Matt and Evan. "What do you guys think?" he asked quietly.

Having just heard about this deal for the first time, they both looked over at him with serious expressions. In unison, Matt's blond, spiky head and Evan's buzzed-cut, brown head, twisted to look at each other. They both smiled and turned back to Kellan. Matt nodded. "Yeah, we're in."

Kellan beamed at his band-brothers as Lana showed the boys where they needed to sign. From what I could decipher from the contracts, they seemed pretty fair; the boys weren't getting ripped off or anything. They still retained control over what songs they produced and released, so Kellan could continue to write his own material. Their profits from the first album would be mild, but their profits would exponentially increase with the next two; their contract was for three albums, with options for more if those were successful. I was sure they would be huge hits. I had yet to meet someone who disliked their music.

While Kellan nodded and smiled at his friends, I heard a disgruntled sound from Griffin's direction. Still feeling a little melancholy after Kellan's suspiciously ignored phone call, I looked over at Griffin, scowling at a piece of paper.

"Dude, Kell, did you read this? I don't believe this shit!"

Matt chuckled and murmured, "I don't believe that you can actually read…"

Griffin glared at him, but held up a memo from the stack of papers and thrust it out to Kellan. Kellan cast me a quick, nervous glance. "Yeah…I read it."

My curiosity beating out my common sense, I asked Griffin, "Read what?"

Griffin held the paper up to me, as if I could read the tiny font from the distance where he sat. "This says that we shouldn't have sex with all the girls hanging around, because chicks will try to screw us just to get knocked up! So we have to pay them to raise the kid! For eighteen years!"

He stared at me with a look of complete shock on his face, like that thought had never occurred to him before. I would have found it humorous, if I hadn't been in such a sour mood. I narrowed my eyes at Kellan. "They gave you a pamphlet on sleeping with fans?"

He shrugged and studied his papers. "It's just a warning…"

Lana spoke up, to clarify. "It's a standard precaution that we give to all of our rising celebrities. They will be targets to all sorts of different people, and we give them guidelines on how to best protect themselves from…being manipulated."

She smiled sweetly at me. "It's the company's way of protecting the asset. It's a very common practice nowadays." Laughing a little, she shrugged. "Athletes have to sit through a seminar about it." Leaning down to rifle through her suitcase, she murmured, "They never listen though…"

Griffin snorted and threw his pen down. "Well, what's the point of being a rock star if I can't bang the groupies?"

Rolling my eyes, I found myself muttering, "I thought it was supposed to be about the music?"

Griffin, unfortunately, heard my sullen comment and chose to respond to it. "No, no, I'm pretty sure it's the pussy."

Flushing, I leaned back and crossed my arms over my chest. Jackass. Kellan reached over and patted my thigh. I wanted to smack his hand away. Griffin's comment just cut a little too close to home. I heard my sister smack Griffin across the head and looked back to see him scowling at her and rubbing the sore spot.

"What?" he muttered. She rolled her eyes and shook her head as Matt laughed at his nimrod relative.

"Dude, it doesn't say you shouldn't have sex. It says you should always use protection." Matt rolled his eyes. "You can still sleep with them if you want, just wrap it up." Smirking, he shook his head. "And please do. The last thing the world needs is another you."

Griffin turned and glared at Matt. "Fuck you, man." Looking a little defeated, Griffin looked over at Kellan again. "Is that true? Do girls really do that?"

Squeezing my leg, Kellan shrugged. "Some."

Picking his pen back up, Griffin proceeded to sign his contract. "Well that's fucked up."

Kellan finished with his stack and handed his papers to Lana. She smiled warmly at him as she tucked them in her briefcase. It was a friendly smile that clearly indicated that she liked him on a personal level as well as a professional one. I wasn't exactly thrilled that they were friends, but I wasn't really surprised either. Kellan made friends wherever he went, even if he wasn't always aware of it. He seemed to think he was completely alone in the world, but he wasn't. Even without me, he had a wide circle of people who cared about him.

Kissing my cheek, he ran his lips up to my ear. Closing my eyes, I heard him whisper, "I still have forty-five minutes of free time…want to go somewhere more private?"

I could only nod as a flash of desire swept through me. I might still have doubts and insecurities about our relationship, I might still question whether he was being a little too friendly with Lana, or some zealot fan, and I might still want to rip his phone out of his pocket and read his secretive messages…but, ultimately, I loved him and I missed him, and I wanted to be alone with him.

Kellan stood up and told the guys he'd see them before the performance. Matt and Evan knowingly glanced at me, smiled, then nodded. Griffin continued to stare at his contract, looking horribly confused. Anna leaned over his shoulder. Her breasts pressed against his arm and he shifted his gaze to stare right down her cleavage. Then he didn't seem so confused. Then he didn't seem to care much about the contract at all.

Still gallantly holding my bag, Kellan led us out of the building through a secret, hidden exit. It let out right by their busses parked behind the building. Pushing open a bus door, Kellan smiled back at me and nodded to it. "Come on, let me show you where I live now."

I giggled a little as I clutched his hand. I'd never been on a tour bus before. Plush chairs arranged to face each other had small tables tucked between them. It reminded me of the inside of a train, and I smiled, remembering that my first train ride had been with Kellan...ages ago.

Kellan tossed my bag on an empty seat, and led me through a curtained off area. This part of the bus was windowless, and as the heavy curtain fell back into place, the only light that illuminated us was from the tiny LED lights imbedded in the bus floor.

Kellan turned to face me and wrapped his arms around my waist. It was quiet in here, our breathing the only sound not being absorbed by the heavy fabric doors. Leaning his head against mine, Kellan softly said, "Welcome to my bedroom."

My breath quickened as his lips inched closer to mine. "Your bedroom?" I whispered, my voice coming out a little husky. The anticipation of being with him made my body feel like Jell-O.

His lips angled away from my mouth to rub against my jaw. My eyes fluttered as his breath washed over my skin. "Mine and the other guys..." One of his hands slid down my backside as he trailed soft kisses down my neck. Breathing a little heavier, I tilted my head so he could explore farther down.

Murmuring as he went, his voice just as husky as mine, he continued describing his traveling home. "We're all packed into these cubbies, like sardines." He got to the base of my throat and moved over to lightly run his tongue up the center. I gasped, dropping my head back as my hands ran over his backside.

Making a deep, satisfied noise as he reached the top, his free hand grabbed my cheek. "It's not as spacious as your bed back home, but there's just enough room for two..."

He rested his face against mine, his lips so close we were nearly touching. It was hard to focus on anything other than those lips, but I made myself look over at what he was talking about. Lining the walls of this enclosed space were bunk beds; three beds per stack, with two stacks per wall. Each bed had its own privacy curtain. They looked exceedingly small and claustrophobic.

Kellan pointed to the bottom one in the stack we were leaning against. "That's mine," he whispered. "My home away from home, where I try to get some sleep with a bunch of snoring, smelly dudes around me." He chuckled a little, then sighed and brought his hand back to my face. Pulling back to look at me, his face gorgeous, highlighted by the soft gleam from the floor, his dark eyes searched mine. "Where I dream about you...where I miss you..."

His eyes watered a little as I watched him take me in, causing my own eyes to mist. "I miss you too, Kellan."

Then I couldn't hold off anymore, and my hand moved up to tangle into his hair, pulling his lips to mine. He groaned at my force, then passionately returned my kiss. The quiet space was quickly filled with fast breaths and noisy moans as we reconnected. Pushing me against the bunk bed frame, Kellan reached down to hitch my leg around his hip. I scratched my nails down his back as his body lined up with mine. Damn, maybe I'd just let him take me right here, pressed up against the beds.

Filling with need every second his mouth was on mine, I reached down and pushed up his shirt. He helped me halfway through, tossing his shirt somewhere over his shoulder. I dragged my fingers over the swirls of my name inked across his chest and he hissed in an erotic breath, whispering something that sounded like I love you, or I miss you, or maybe even I want you...I was too dazed to know for sure.

As he pushed his hips into mine, grinding the hardness of his ache over the softness of mine, I wrapped my arms around his head, pulling him to me. God I'd missed him. His lips attached to my neck, as his fingers worked their way up my shirt. When he had the material far enough, he pulled aside my bra and closed his hot mouth over a sensitive nipple. An overly sensitive nipple. A nipple that had obviously missed his caresses. Just his mouth sucking it brought me right to the edge of climaxing.

Knowing we were alone, I let out a long cry as his tongue threatened to push me over the edge. He moaned against my skin as he felt my body tensing for that glorious moment. Pulling back his hips, he used just one hand to quickly unbutton my jeans. I cried out, "Yes," as his fingers headed down for the spot that would definitely send me spiraling into bliss. As nice as his erotic notes and steamy phone calls had been, nothing compared to him physically touching me.

I was gripping his shoulders and panting with everything I had, waiting for his finger to slide against me...just once...when a flash of light entering the room nearly blinded me.

Kellan instantly removed his hand from my jeans and released my breast, helping me smooth the fabric back into place. Ice washed over me, killing my near-release, and I struggled to slow my breathing. Kellan's breath was fast too, as he stepped in front of me, shielding me from view even though he was much farther along in the undressing part than I was.

As we both stared at the person entering the sleeping area from the opposite direction, where the bathrooms presumably were, I quickly fastened my jeans. Holding on to Kellan's bare shoulders, I peeked over at a disheveled-looking rocker. He had crazy, going-everywhere hair—a poor imitation of Kellan's sexy mess, if you asked me. And with heavily lined eyes, corded bracelets all the way up his wrists, and skull rings on every darkly painted finger, he clearly didn't want to be mistaken for anything but a stereotypical musician. He really only needed, *I'm a rebel and you'll never understand me*, stamped to his forehead to spell it out any clearer.

Hoping this guy hadn't heard me nearly orgasm, and knowing there was no way he hadn't heard *all* of that, I turned beet red. The guy feigned surprise as he held the curtain open, still blinding us. "Hey, sorry, Kellan...didn't mean to...interrupt." He smirked at me as he stepped into the room. "Hey, cutie, what's up?"

I buried my head in Kellan's shoulder, wishing I could disappear. Now I was mortified to be around two of Kellan's tour mates. Wonderful.

Kellan shoved the guy's shoulder, trying to get him to leave the private area where we were attempting to have a moment. "Yeah, well, it happens, don't worry about it."

The man surrendered under Kellan's force and chuckled as he traipsed to the other side of the curtained off area. "Yeah, yeah, I'm leaving." Opening the curtains, he grinned back at Kellan. "Damn, man, I don't know how you manage to always score with the hottest chick." He eyed me up and down. "And two in one night, bro...I wish I had that kind of stamina."

I felt all of the blood drain from my face as I stared up at Kellan. He seemed paler, too. I vaguely heard the rocker say, "Hey, sweetie, I'm available, if you want to bang me next? I don't mind getting his seconds...again."

I was too dazed to respond. I was too dazed to do much of anything. In a couple of sentences, that man had just confirmed my biggest fear. Kellan was cheating on me...repeatedly. As I heard chuckling from the rocker leaving, I dropped my hands from Kellan's body. I didn't feel like touching him anymore. I watched as Kellan closed his eyes, swallowed, then reopened them. In slow motion, he twisted to face me.

I did it without thought or deliberation. I did it without realizing I'd done it. My hand reached out, on its own accord and smacked him across the cheek. The promise ring around my finger dug into his skin, cutting his jaw, and a tiny drop of blood appeared.

"You son of a bitch!" I snarled, backing away from him as far as I could in the cramped space.

He winced and rubbed his jaw. "Jesus, Kiera. Can I explain before you start whaling on me?"

His eyes flashed to mine, angry, but it was nothing compared to the anger and betrayal that I felt. "You can explain 'scoring the hottest chick?' You can explain 'two in one night?' You can explain him 'getting your seconds...again?'"

Sighing, Kellan ran his hand over his face. When he looked at me again, he seemed less angry. I wasn't. "Yes, Kiera. I can explain."

Poking my finger in his chiseled chest, I shoved him back a step. "Are you cheating on me?"

Grabbing my hand, he tried to lace ours together. "No, I'm not." He ducked down to meet my eyes, but I was so furious I couldn't look at him. "Hey, I'm not, Kiera. I've already told you that before...several times probably."

Inhaling a steadying breath, I tried to ask a question calmly. My voice warbled as I tried to control it. "Then what...was he talking about?"

Kellan grabbed my other hand, trying to pry loose my clenched fist. Maybe he realized that if I was going to strike him again, it wasn't going to be with an open palm. Funny, I never considered myself a violent person before Kellan. He just brought that out in me.

When relaxing my hands didn't seem to do anything, Kellan grabbed my cheeks, forcing me to look directly at him. My eyes started to water. I sniffed back the tears. I did not want to cry.

His brow creased as he searched my face. "He's lying, Kiera. He said that to get a rise out of you. He knows who you are, they all do. I flip through that photo book all the time…" He smiled softly and shook his head. "They all think you're beautiful…"

I batted his hands away. "Why would *he* lie?" I stressed "he," just so Kellan would know that I was much more inclined to believe him to be the liar.

Sighing, Kellan shook his head and kept his distance. "Because we were the last band to join the tour and we got bumped to the second in the lineup. Because Lana wanted to sign our band and not his." He shrugged. "Because he's a childish, immature asshole with a grudge against me, Kiera, and if making you doubt me got us fighting tonight instead of…" He sighed again and tossed his hands up. "Because this, right here, is what he wanted…his stupid form of payback for our band being better than his."

Watching the exasperated expression on his face, I softened a little. It sounded plausible but, most of Kellan's lies sounded plausible. I knew. Back when we'd been fooling around behind Denny's back, I was often well aware when Kellan was lying, and Kellan was good at it.

"Why should I believe you?" I whispered.

He tossed his hands up into the air again. "I haven't done anything wrong! Why shouldn't you believe me?"

Just then, as if fate was trying to screw with us even further, Kellan's phone chirped in his pocket; it was a text message. He closed his eyes, seemingly cursing the same fate I was. When he reopened them, he stared at me blankly.

I narrowed my eyes. "Do you need to get that?"

He shook his head. "No."

Clenching my jaw, closing my hands into fists, I seethed, "How do you know? It might be important?"

He let out a slow exhale before shaking his head. "You're important…that can wait."

My eyes watered again. "What can wait?" I whispered, not sure if his last statement was comforting or not.

He stepped towards me and tentatively cupped my cheek. "I'm not doing anything, baby. I love you. I'm being faithful to you." He held up his ring, his thumb stroking the metal. "I promised…I promise."

He dropped his forehead to mine. "We don't have much time together. Please, just let this go…"

"Let what go?" I whispered.

He sighed, then his lips lowered to mine. "I love you, Kiera...please believe in me."

I wanted to object, I wanted to scream at him to let me know what he was hiding, to tell me something that would renew my faith in him, but the words slipped out of my mind as his mouth softly moved over my skin.

Maybe I was being weak...maybe I just wasn't ready to know. For whatever reason...I let it go.

After a few calming moments, Kellan reached down and put his shirt back on and we laid down side by side on his bunk. There was a cubby built into the wall and I stared at the few belongings he kept near him—the journals I'd given him, his Discman, the photo book my mom and sister made for him, and the little toy car. Swallowing, wanting to believe him, I fingered the tiny, metal muscle car.

Kellan sighed and kissed my shoulder. "I love you..." he whispered.

Clutching the car, remembering the connection that we had, the way he'd opened up to me, let me into his life like no one else before me, not even his band mates, I looked over at him. "I love you, too..."

He smiled, his fingers tucking a strand of hair behind my ear before tracing the chain around my neck. Pulling the necklace out of my shirt, his thumb stroked the edge of the silver guitar; the diamond in the center of it gleamed, even in the faint light surrounding us.

Bunching his brows, the soft smile on his lips faded as he watched his fingers. "Kiera...I should tell you something..."

Hating the ice that instantly formed in my stomach, hating that I knew he was hiding things from me, I instantly recalled that I too, was hiding things from him. Guilt easing the knot burning through my insides, I whispered, "I should tell you something too..."

His eyes flashed up to mine, narrowing. "Tell me what?"

Swallowing, searching his perfect face, I stammered for a way to break his heart. I just knew that he'd react badly to the news that his rival was back in town. Not that Denny was really a rival anymore, but Kellan had never felt like he compared to him. Kellan seemed to think I'd be better off with Denny. If he knew Denny was back in my life, especially while he was away...it might end us.

Dreaded tears filling my vision, I considered Kellan's odd, secretive texts that he clearly didn't want to talk about, the searing doubt that one asshole rocker had so easily placed into my head, the videos of his friendly attitude towards Lana that seared me with jealousy, the looming dread in my belly over whatever he needed to tell me now....

Maybe we were already over, and I just didn't realize it yet?

"Um, well..."

As I started stumbling over something to say, somebody banged on the bus door and a familiar voice drifted to us from outside. "Kell? You and Kiera in there?"

Hearing Evan's jovial voice brought me back to a simpler time, when Kellan and I were only having a secret affair behind my boyfriend's back. Wow, I never thought I'd see the day when that horrid moment in my life would be considered the "good ole days."

Kellan sighed, then leaned over and shouted, "Yeah, we're in here."

Evan walked over to our section of the bus and I heard him clear his throat. "You, uh...dressed?"

Kellan chuckled a little while I blushed. "Yeah...what's up?"

"We're on in ten, so, you know, we should get ready."

Kellan blinked and sat up on his elbows. "Already? Damn..." He stood up, then looked back at me. "I'm sorry...it's our turn."

I nodded, swallowing. "I know." He extended his hand to me, uncertain whether or not I'd take it. Exhaling slowly, I stood up and grabbed his hand. Regardless of our issues, I still loved him...heart and soul.

Letting out a relieved sigh, he kissed the back of my hand, right over my promise ring. Cringing, I glanced at his face; he still had a scratch along his jaw where my ring had nicked him. Feeling remorse for hurting him, I leaned up and kissed his jaw. His eyes were glossy when they met mine again. Understanding my silent apology, he nodded.

"Come on...want to watch our show?"

With an exuberant smile on my face, I nodded eagerly and clasped his hand in both of mine. "Yeah, definitely." If there was one thing that could turn my mood around in a heartbeat, it was watching Kellan sing. And I'd missed that, too.

Outside the bus, we met up with Evan, who jovially slung his arm around me. I smiled, leaning into him. I wanted so badly to question him about Kellan's secret. I didn't, though. For one, he probably wouldn't tell me, since Kellan was his friend and sort of his boss; Evan wouldn't want to rock that boat if he could help it. Plus...Kellan had kept our affair from all of the guys, including Evan. Evan had been pretty surprised when he found out about us. I was pretty sure that whatever was going on with Kellan, all the guys were just as clueless as me. I had to trust that Kellan would tell me when he was ready, and that hopefully it wouldn't hurt...too much.

Walking back through their super-secret rock star entrance, we hurriedly proceeded towards the back of the stage. Justin waved as we passed by; his band was ending the show, immediately after the D-Bags played. I flushed as I timidly waved back. I didn't think I'd ever feel comfortable around him now.

Luckily we didn't see the rocker who had made the insinuations about Kellan. I'm sure I would have punched him if we had.

As we got to the waiting area beside the stage, I glanced up at the band acknowledging the hysterical crowd. Nerves flooded through me as Kellan released my hand and grabbed his guitar. I was getting anxious for him; the small part of the crowd that I could see looked massive to me, and the noise as the MC introduced

Kellan's band was ear splitting—a hundred times louder than Pete's. But Kellan looked calm as could be as he waited with a foot on a step, smiling at me.

Just as the crowd died down, he nodded at me, then turned and darted onstage. If the situation was reversed, I'd have been frozen on that step, unable to move. The rest of the guys followed him up there, and I watched, spellbound. Evan and Matt waved while Kellan and Griffin reached down to touch a few lucky fans in the front.

The roar of the crowd was thunderous and I swear a couple of girls that Kellan touched started crying. It was so…surreal. Even without a hit song playing endlessly on every radio station across the country, these girls knew who Kellan was, and who his band was. The guys had everything in place for stardom…including a contract with the same record label that had released Justin's album.

As I was ruminating about what that meant for us, my sister looped her arms around my waist. "Isn't this exciting, Kiera!"

I glanced over at the vivacious beauty, momentarily jealous over how simple her relationship with Griffin was. They both knew exactly what they were and weren't to each other. There was no deception, no lies, no jealousy, no…nothing. They gave each other what they needed, when they needed it, and moved on when they were done. In a way, it was a win-win situation. Although…it sounded a little empty, too.

Leaning back in her arms, I nodded. My stomach was surging with adrenaline as I watched Evan start the set. Then Matt kicked in, Kellan close behind him, and all of a sudden, I felt like we were back at Evan's loft, watching the boys rehearse. There was just a much larger audience watching this time.

I smiled wide as Kellan's voice filled the theater. He was so good at this. It was as effortless to him as breathing. I'd seen him sing drunk, depressed, with a cold, heck, I'd even seen him sing while battling stomach flu; he'd looked a little green that night, but his voice… That always sounded amazing.

So was his stage presence. Kellan was electrifying, and he knew how to energize a crowd. It was one of those things the repugnant rocker on the bus would never understand. Dressing the part won't turn you into a star—you either have that certain spark or you don't. And Kellan oozed it. Even if he had been only so-so on the attractive scale, he'd still have drawn every eye to him. He had a magnetic pull on people. He was just…special.

Since they shared the night with other bands, their set was shorter than usual, but the crowd seemed satisfied, nonetheless. I was somewhat relieved that Kellan didn't play the melancholy song, the one he wrote about me while we were apart. Even though he played it at Pete's, I didn't want the rest of the country singing along to "my song."

Instead, the D-bags played their biggest hits, the ones that the fans back home loved. Even though the night hadn't gone as planned, I was still glad that I'd impulsively flown out with my sister to see this. I knew I'd remember it forever.

Taking a final bow, Kellan shook his head, then leaned over and kissed the crying girl on the cheek. I blinked, a little surprised that he'd do that, but when the girl slumped back into her friends like she was fainting, I had to smile. I shook my

230

head at the oddness of it all while Anna adorably snorted.

Skipping down the stairs two steps at a time, Kellan scooped me into his arms. Obviously running on pure adrenaline, he spun me in a circle, laughing as I squealed. His arms wrapped firmly around my thighs as he held me up, and, leaning back, he looked at me. "What did you think?"

Sighing, I threaded my fingers back through his hair and rested my head against his. "I think it was perfect, Kellan."

Setting me down, he smiled warmly at me. The last band to perform swept past us and Kellan twisted to watch them bound to their microphones. Looking back at me, he smiled and raised an eyebrow. "Do you want to stay and watch your favorite band?"

Flushing, I glanced at Justin onstage for a microsecond before looking back at Kellan. "Second favorite," I said, shaking my head. Kellan laughed, and I wrapped my arms around his neck and laid my head on his shoulder. "I just want to be with you...wherever that is...," I whispered in his ear.

Nestling into my hair, he nodded and held me tight. "Okay," he murmured, before the sound was drowned out by the band onstage.

As the rest of the D-Bags dispersed, Evan and Matt excitedly talking about the deal they had just inked, Griffin with his hands all over Anna's body, Kellan and I stayed just where we were, holding each other, slightly swaying to the music around us. It was peaceful and I felt that familiar contentment again. If I could, I would have held him like this all night long. I would have held him like this forever.

But forever wasn't in the cards for us tonight and before I knew it, the show was over and the roadies were moving in to tear down the set. Kellan pulled me out of the way, towards the backstage area where a group of fans were hanging around, waiting for the band to appear.

Being the consummate professional that he was, Kellan stayed and signed autographs while I sat in the corner and waited. No one paid any attention to me, and I was fine with letting Kellan have the spotlight.

After a while, someone finally stepped in to clear out the room. The man stepped up to me with an imposing look on his face. "You too, missy...everybody out."

He grabbed my elbow and I instinctively pulled back. He didn't like that. "You can't stay, groupies gotta go."

I narrowed my eyes. "I'm not a groupie."

He rolled his eyes, like he heard that every night. Just as I was wondering how to convince yet another bouncer that I wasn't some trollop following the bands around, Kellan intervened. "Sorry, she's with me."

The bouncer shrugged and let me go. Kellan laced our hands together and led me back towards the secret exit. As we walked, he got a playful smile on his face. "That little incident reminds me...what exactly did you do to get backstage?"

I sighed, running my hand over my face. "You don't want to know."

He chuckled, twisting to walk backwards down the hall. "Now I definitely want to know." He raised an eyebrow at me expectantly.

Not able to resist the sultry look on his face, I murmured, "I flashed the guy at the door."

Kellan stopped in his tracks and I ran straight into him. "You what?" he said flatly.

Bunching my brows, I shook my head and took a step back. "He wouldn't let us through until Anna and I showed him our chests. I kept my bra on, though...Anna didn't."

Kellan clenched his jaw, his expression hardening. His face reminded me of the night he'd stopped that perv from fondling me, the night he was knifed in the ribs. "What did he look like?" His eyes scanned the hall behind me like he was searching for the guy.

I brought my hand up, focusing his gaze on me. "Hey, it's okay." I grimaced and added, "It was mortifying and humiliating, but he didn't hurt me or anything. He didn't even touch me." I didn't mention that he rubbed Anna a little. I also didn't mention that he offered to "do" me. The first of two unwanted invitations I'd had tonight...wasn't I popular all of a sudden?

Kellan exhaled, shaking his head. "Why would you do that? You could have called me...I would've let you in?"

I sighed, stroking his cheek. "I wanted to surprise you."

He narrowed his eyes. "You thought I was sleeping with Lana. Did you want to surprise me...or catch me?"

I bit my lip and shook my head. "I don't know," I whispered.

Shaking his head, Kellan turned around and forcefully pushed open the door to the exit. Dejected, I slowly followed him.

Chapter 19 – Okay

There was a flurry of activity in the parking lot when I got out there. Guys were loading the vans and busses, band members were hanging around, talking about the show. Even some stray fans were hanging around. I didn't see my sister and Griffin anywhere, but Evan had stopped Kellan halfway to the bus, and was handing him his guitar as they talked for a moment.

By the time I caught up to Kellan, he didn't seem peeved anymore. He smiled over at me and grabbed my hand. Evan clapped his shoulder and darted on the bus after Matt.

As all the other guys started loading onto the busses, I looked up at Kellan. "Are you leaving?"

He looked down at me and shrugged. "Yeah." He pointed over to a bright-eyed bus driver drinking a very large cup of coffee. "They rotate the drivers so someone is always ready to go. Since we can sleep in the busses, we don't stay in one place unless we've got another show nearby." He tilted his head at me. "Our next one's in Reno." Pausing, Kellan raised an eyebrow at me. "You could come with me? Catch a flight home from there?"

Slinging his guitar over his shoulder, he wrapped his arms around my waist. I did the same, smiling at the thought of a very long bus ride with him. Then I frowned, considering the logistics of it all, plus the roundtrip ticket burning a hole through my duffel bag. "I already have a ticket home, and it's from here…"

I shrugged, hating that I couldn't be as impulsive as my sister. She wouldn't think twice about hopping on a bus to destinations unknown. Kellan pursed his lips, thinking. "Well, what if I get you a ticket from Reno to here?" He leaned into me, grinning mischievously. "Then you could still use your ticket."

I leaned up and kissed his chin, glad that he wasn't too angry over my admission that I hadn't really trusted him. "I don't want you to spend your money on me, Kellan."

He leaned back and shrugged. "Who else am I going to spend it on?" Shaking his head, he added, "Besides, this would be for me." Pulling me close, he rested his head against mine. "I want some more time with you."

Sighing contently, I conceded. "All right, but only if Anna goes, too. I don't want to leave her alone here."

Kellan grinned and started leading me to the bus. "I'm sure she's attached to Griffin as we speak." I cringed, knowing that was probably correct…in every sense.

And sure enough, when we hopped back on the bus, the sounds of someone having a good time drifted back to us. I flushed instantly; Kellan only grinned and shook his head. As the sound of something vibrating mixed with clear sounds of approval, I closed my eyes, horrified, remembering all of the…toys…Anna had packed.

Leading me to an empty seat where he'd tossed my bag earlier, Kellan set his guitar down and nodded towards the curtained area. "I could go get my Discman, if you don't want to listen to them?"

I grabbed his arm, embarrassed for Anna, even though she probably wouldn't have cared if he walked in on them. "No!"

Chuckling, Kellan sat beside me at the table and grabbed my hand. "It's okay, they're probably in the back bedroom."

I looked over at him and frowned. "There's a back bedroom?" He didn't take me back there earlier?

Kellan grimaced. "Yeah...Griffin's kind of taken it over, though, so I figured you wouldn't want to...hang out in there."

Just the thought of doing anything remotely intimate near places Griffin...laid his body...in was disturbing. "Yeah, no thanks."

The driver hopped on the bus, taking a head count of his rock stars. Frowning at the lascivious sounds of pleasure coming from the back of the bus, the paunchy man sighed and said, "All right, which one's back there? I don't want to have to go look...again."

A cluster of boys shifted their attention from the back of the bus to glance up at the driver. Laughing, one of them replied, "It's just Griffin back there."

The bus driver rolled his eyes and shook his head. "Why am I not surprised?" Sighing, he headed to the driver's chair; it was plush, more suited for steering a sleek spacecraft than a bus. As he started the vehicle, the rumble of the engine helped to block out my sister's cries for more, but not nearly enough.

Hating that all of the boys were listening to her, their eyes staring through the heavy fabric like they'd all developed X-ray vision, I twisted to Kellan. He wasn't looking, but his head was down and he was smiling to himself. Hoping he wasn't visualizing what every other horny guy on the bus was probably imagining, I muttered, "Are you mad at me?"

Looking over at me, his small smile faded, and he shook his head. His finger came up to tuck a lock of hair behind my ear as he quietly said, "No, I'm not." Sighing, he searched my eyes. "I get it, Kiera. I get why you'd have doubts, I get why you'd question..." Closing his eyes for a second, he looked down at our hands resting between us. "I wish..."

Not finishing that, he looked back up at me. "It's okay, I get it, and I'm not mad."

I exhaled slowly and nodded. Then he put his arm around me and I cuddled into his side. He kissed my head and we stared out the window, watching the streetlights blur past as we made our way through the city.

Just as the gentle rocking of the vehicle started lulling me to sleep, a chorus of cheers erupted in the bus. Startled awake, I lifted my head off of Kellan's shoulder just in time to see Griffin bowing. He and Anna were apparently done with their romp and were finally out of hiding. As Griffin walked out of the back, he high-fived some guy in the closest seat.

Grossly enough, it was the same douche that had walked in on Kellan and me. The man sneered behind Griffin's back but immediately stopped at the sight of Anna walking out; his jaw nearly hit the floor. That made me smile for some reason…probably because I knew the jerk didn't have a chance with my sister. I may not understand her infatuation with Griffin, but she did have standards.

And Anna was someone every guy wanted, Kellan's female equivalent. Nearly every jaw dropped as the beauty walked past them. She looked like a movie star, fresh from filming a love scene, with her hair attractively messy and her makeup flawless. I had no idea how she pulled off looking so great after a session like that. If it were me, I'd look…less than great.

Anna smiled seductively at the crowd watching her; she even reached out to tousle one of the boy's hair. An idiotic smile was plastered on his face as she sashayed past. And they all leaned in to check out her ass. It made me roll my eyes, but I was used to that sort of thing. So was Anna…it didn't even faze her.

She followed where Griffin was heading, and that, unfortunately, was towards us. With a content sigh, he sat in the bench opposite us, grabbing my bag off the seat and unceremoniously tossing it on the table. Anna sat next to him, her smile equally satisfied. At the very least, they pleased each other. Hopefully this was enough to satisfy Anna for a while.

Griffin smiled over at me, then Kellan. "Bedroom's free, if you want it?"

I was already shaking my head when Kellan said, "We're good, thanks." No way was I giving this audience a performance like my sister just had…not stone cold sober anyway.

Kellan watched some of the guys retreating to their "rooms," and looked back at me. "You want to get some sleep? You look tired."

Griffin chuckled, clearly hearing dirty words in Kellan's innocent question. Then he reached over to Anna and cupped her braless breast. When he murmured to her, "I just can't get enough of these," and leaned down to kiss one through her shirt, I cringed and looked up at Kellan.

"Yes…please."

Threading her fingers through Griffin's hair, Anna laid her head back and closed her eyes, enjoying his attention. As Kellan and I stood up, she huskily said, "See you in the morning, sis." Peeking one eye open, she added, "Have fun."

I smirked at her, resisting the urge to smack Griffin off her chest. Pausing in my escape from them, I told her, "We're catching an early flight tomorrow to Boise, then back home."

She closed her eyes, nodding, not caring in the least how or if we got back home. I sighed as I walked away, wishing I could be that cavalier.

A few guys that were still awake whistled at Kellan and me retreating through the curtain, one even clapping his shoulder. Shaking my head, I hoped they weren't too disappointed that nothing was going to happen. Well, no, after seeing their faces watching my sister, I sort of hoped they were a little disappointed.

Some of the bunks were full, their occupants already snoring, as Kellan helped me get into his bottom bunk. I laughed a little as I got in. It kind of reminded me of summer camp. A really tight summer camp.

I lay on my side and pressed my back against the wall to give Kellan as much space as I could. He lay on his side too, facing me, tangling his legs with mine. Pulling up a thin blanket near our feet, we cuddled into each other as best we could. Lying so close on the pillow that our noses touched, we smiled at each other.

He gave me a soft kiss as he reached a hand back to thread it through my hair. My heart rate increased a little as the intimacy of the moment surged through me. I found his lips in the near-dark, wanting to just kiss him for a while.

Light and languid, our lips moved together like we'd never been apart. Pulling back for a second, Kellan whispered, "I've missed this…I've missed you."

I leaned back, studying his face in the soft light. "I've missed you, too…so much."

Just as my heart was swelling, staring at him as he stared at me, a voice above us said, "Less talking…more screwing."

A chuckle went around the room, and I flushed, remembering that we weren't as alone as it seemed. Kellan thumped the ceiling of his bed with his fist. "Shut it, Mark."

I buried my head in Kellan's chest, and he chuckled, rubbing my back. In my ear, he whispered, "I could finish what I started earlier…if you want to--"

His hand slinked down to my hip, rubbing over the back pocket, and a part of me instantly did want him to continue. I knew I'd never be quiet enough, though, not with how tightly packed together we were in this bus, and I really didn't need to be embarrassed around every band member on this tour.

Biting my lip, I sighed and reluctantly shook my head. Kellan smiled, his hand coming back up to brush my face. "Another time, then?"

I nodded and pulled his head down to me so we could at least kiss a little.

I had difficulty remembering where I was when I woke up. I wasn't even really sure if I was awake at all. As Kellan's arms were wrapped around me, my head resting on his chest, I felt like I was still dreaming. It wasn't an absurd thought—I dreamed of Kellan often. Running my hand over his pecs, I wondered when I'd wake up. Probably when I got to the good part, that's when it always happened.

Sighing, I kissed his chest, wishing that, for once, this dream would let us finish. Exhaling contently, his arms squeezed me tighter. "Mornin'," he breathed into my hair.

It sent a shiver down my back, and I smiled. Peeking up at him, I whispered, "Am I dreaming, or am I really waking up with you?"

He smiled down on me, adjusting himself so he could see me better. "You dream about waking up with me?"

I nodded, propping myself up to look over his body under the thin blanket. I frowned slightly. "You're usually naked in my dreams, though, so I must be awake."

Quietly laughing, he pulled me back to his chest. "You're usually naked in my dreams, too," he murmured, kissing my neck.

A thrill went through me, but it was halted by the sound of snoring, coughing, and the occasional...unseemly noises going on around us. Kellan frowned. "Sorry, smelly bus of boys...not exactly romantic."

I sighed and stroked his face. "It's better than nothing." His hand clenched over mine as we settled onto his pillows, facing each other. Remembering yesterday's emotional roller coaster, I rubbed my thumb over his. "Hey, you mentioned that you wanted to tell me something last night...what was it?" I whispered, not sure if I was ready to hear it.

Kellan looked down, then back up. "I..." He looked past me, at where his phone was tucked in his cubby. "I..." Frowning slightly, he searched my face for a moment, then smiling, he shrugged. "I didn't tell you the bad part about getting signed."

I blinked, not expecting the conversation to go in that direction, and also having a horrid feeling that he had just smoothly changed the subject. "What?" I whispered, lead forming in my stomach.

Looking down, he shook his head. "As soon as the tour ends in May, they want us in L.A., to record the album." He looked back up at me, his face apologetic. "In the meantime, the guys and I will be spending every free moment we have going through our songs, picking out the best ones...perfecting them." He shrugged. "We have to be ready when we get there..."

I sighed, my heart cracking a little. "You're basically telling me that you won't have any time to spend with me...for a while...aren't you?"

He swallowed, shaking his head. "I'm sorry...we need to do this, so I won't be able to visit, like I'd hoped. I'm sorry."

Now I swallowed. "It's okay...I understand." I looked down as I considered all of the moments together that we'd already missed, that we were going to miss...our first Valentine's Day as a couple had already passed, the flowers he'd sent me long wilted. Our anniversary was fast approaching, in a couple of weeks, mid-March. Kellan's birthday was in April, mine was in May. My graduation...

My eyes snapped up to his, watery. "Could you make it back in June?"

He nodded, cupping my cheek. "I'm not missing your graduation...no matter what. I don't care if I have to walk out on a recording session...I'm not missing it, Kiera."

I smiled and sighed, knowing that I'd at least get to see him then...three months from now. And after that...I supposed they would be touring again to promote the album. As a little bit of sadness washed over me, he held me close and rubbed my back. So quietly that I almost didn't hear him, he whispered, "And there was something you wanted to tell me?"

I stiffened, not wanting to say it. He'd never go to L.A. if he knew that Denny was back in my life. He'd flip out if he realized that Denny was the friend that I was frequently having lunch with. But, ultimately, I didn't want to tell Kellan about it…because, I knew, with everything in me, that he'd lied about what he wanted to tell me. I was sure that the bit about not coming home was true, and it probably was something that he wanted to mention, but I was also sure that it hadn't been on his mind last night. I was sure that his leaving had nothing to do with whoever was calling him.

I bit my lip, not sure what to tell him. Propping myself up to look at him, I shook my head. "I love you, Kellan, and you don't have anything to worry about when it comes to me, but I don't think I can tell you just yet."

Frowning, he sat up on his elbow. "What? Why not?"

Guilt sweeping over me, I shook my head. "You're just going to have to believe in me."

His mouth dropped open a little and he glanced at his phone really quick. His mouth closed and I knew that he understood. He knew that I was aware that he hadn't really told me anything. That what he had briefly wanted to tell me last night and what he had ended up telling me this morning were two entirely different things. My eyes watered as I waited for him to open up, to tell me the truth. His eyes glossier, he only stared at me.

Swallowing, he nodded. "Okay," he whispered, and it broke my heart.

Kellan and I cuddled a lot and kissed a great deal, but we didn't say much after that. I felt a gap between us, and I hated leaving him with a wedge there; it terrified me that it would only be driven deeper when we were apart. But he wasn't opening up to me, and I couldn't open up to him. There was no way around it but for one of us to cave, and I knew neither of us would…not in the short amount of time we had.

Sometime after I'd fallen asleep last night, Kellan had booked a flight for Anna and me. When the bus finally arrived at its destination, he arranged for a car to pick us all up later in the afternoon, just so we could spend as much time together as possible. Surprisingly, when it was time to go, Griffin also came to the airport to see us off. I wanted to take that as a good sign, but really, Griffin could've just wanted to get away for a moment.

Saying goodbye in the drop-off area, I searched Kellan's face, silently begging him to talk to me, and equally terrified that he would. Cupping my face, he kissed each cheek, then rested his head against mine. "Don't be mad about the flight," he murmured.

I gave him a sullen expression as I glanced at the departure board behind him. He'd bought us tickets straight back to Seattle, making my roundtrip ticket from Boise pretty much worthless. Indifferent to my expression, he smiled. "You have to work tonight. You don't want to have to mess around with a layover."

I sighed, knowing he was right. Shaking my head, I kissed him. "I know…thank you."

Kissing me back, he muttered, "Worth every penny."

Pulling back from him, ignoring Anna and Griffin molesting each other beside us, I tilted my head. "Kellan…?"

He raised his eyebrows, looking a little nervous and very reluctant. "Yeah?"

I almost put my hand out and asked for his phone. I wanted to. Especially when it had chirped this morning as we were eating breakfast. He'd ignored it, like he always did, and it drove me crazy, like it always did. But prying through his phone was not the kind of girlfriend that I wanted to be. I'd asked him to believe in me; I'd have to do the same.

Exhaling slowly as I shook my head, I whispered, "I'll miss you."

He smiled, looking relieved. "I'll miss you, too. I'll call you tonight, okay?"

I nodded, giving him a final kiss before heading to the gate. Kellan waved as I walked down the hall, dragging my sister with me. Twisting around as the boys disappeared, Anna giggled and leaned into my side. "See, Kiera, I told you that would be a blast!"

I contained the frustrated sigh I wanted to make. It had been many things, some good, some bad, but none of it I would refer to as a blast. Well, maybe the concert…that had been a lot of fun. And holding Kellan, kissing him, falling asleep with him, smelling his scent again…that had been fun, too.

Smiling up at her, I nodded. "Yeah, you were right. It was…a blast, Anna."

She giggled almost the entire way home.

My adventure with Anna to Boise left me a little melancholy, thinking about how long Kellan was going to be gone, wondering just what he was keeping from me, wondering how to tell him what I was keeping from him.

Denny, still being the attentive friend, noticed.

Sipping on a green beer, green in honor of St. Patrick's Day, Denny watched me during my shift, concern clear in his warm eyes. It had been two weeks since I'd left Kellan's side, two weeks without any clear answers from him on what he was doing. And Kellan didn't question me, either. He understood that if I was going to open my door for him, he'd have to do the same for me. And, he didn't seem ready to do that.

Sighing as I cleaned off an already-clean table, I felt Denny step up behind me. Looking back at him, dressed in his very debonair work clothes, I watched him look up to where Poetic Bliss was performing on the D-Bag's stage. "It's strange, isn't it? Having someone else play up there?"

I smiled and glanced up to the stage, watching Tuesday jam out a solo on her guitar. Tuesday…ridiculous name. "Yeah, it's definitely…odd."

"You all right, Kiera? You've seemed down since your trip. Something happen in Boise?" Denny looked back at me and raised his eyebrows, holding my gaze.

I bit my lip and looked down at the table. No one else had asked me about my mood. No one else had even noticed, not even Jenny. Of course, she'd missed the impromptu trip and was a little sullen about the whole thing. It surprised me a little, since Jenny was so easygoing about everything, but she missed Evan as much as I missed Kellan, so I understood her being a little snippy…even though I apologized for not inviting her every chance that I got.

"I don't know," I admitted. "Maybe..."

I looked back up at him, at his furrowed brows and the honest concern in his features. "You want to talk about it?" he asked softly, over the volume of the music.

Knowing I really didn't have anyone else to talk to, I nodded. "Want to come over after my shift?"

Denny smiled softly and nodded. "Sure. I'll meet you over there. I'm sure everything will be fine, Kiera." He patted my shoulder before turning and walking away.

I smiled at him, amazed by him, and watched as he headed over to chat with Sam, who was casually leaning against the far wall. I'd thought it before and I'd probably think it again: Abby was a very lucky lady to have Denny.

When I got home, Anna was surprisingly already in bed, so I quietly put on the kettle to make tea. I generally didn't like the stuff, but with a good dose of honey and a lot of milk in it, it wasn't so bad. Denny, however, loved it as much as I loved coffee, so I did it for him.

Ten minutes later, a small knock signaled Denny's arrival. Smiling at his timing, I unlocked the door and let him in. He gave me a brief, friendly hug, which I returned. Smelling the tea, he walked over to the small kitchen with a goofy grin on his face. "I was just having a craving." He leaned over the cup, inhaling the Earl Grey. "And my favorite, too." He faked a surprised expression. "How did you know?"

I shook my head at him, enjoying the way his accent formed phrases, tweaked syllables, made any plain word interesting. "You're such a dork," I muttered, laughing a little.

Straightening, he grabbed the cup that wasn't half milk. "That's why you love me," he said, starting to drink from it. Realizing what he'd said, he stopped and shook his head a little. "Well, I guess *loved* would be more accurate."

Denny's expression hardened a little on the word, and I leaned against the counter and sighed. He might seem fine, he might seem over what had happened between us, but he wasn't, not completely. I didn't blame him. Personally, I couldn't believe he was in my kitchen at all.

Knowing he didn't want any more apologies from me, I shrugged and said, "No, love is still accurate." Sipping his drink, he gave me a look that was both curious and guarded. Clarifying, I said, "You're my best friend, remember? And best friends love each other."

Setting the drink down, he smiled at me crookedly. "Yeah, I suppose." Frowning slightly, he shook his head and crossed his arms over his chest. "So, friend, what's going on with you?"

Watching my untouched cup cooling on the counter, I swallowed my pain and my pride. "How did you know I was cheating on you?" I whispered, my heart surging as the guilt hit me like a brick wall. I'd never wanted to ask him that question, but it was suddenly relevant.

I couldn't look at him, but I heard his expression in his silence. I could easily picture his contemplative eyes, slightly filled with pain but also concern. Finally, his accent filled the room, thicker, like it sometimes was when he was hurting. "You think Kellan's cheating on you?"

I glanced up at him, only mildly surprised. My question hadn't been all that hard to draw conclusions from…and Denny was brilliant. "I don't know…maybe? How did you know? What did I do to make you first start to think it?"

I swallowed again, hating what I was making him say to me, what I was making him talk about. Swallowing, he looked down at his cup. "Uh, I don't know how to answer that, Kiera." He looked up, his dark eyes a little darker. "It was more a feeling than facts. You were…distant, secretive, like you were holding something back, something you wanted to tell me…but couldn't."

My eyes watered, catching the similarities. Denny sighed. "He is cheating on you, isn't he?"

Not able to answer, I only shrugged as a tear dropped to my cheek. Denny watched it fall, but stayed where he was. "I'm sorry, Kiera. I'm not surprised, but I am sorry."

I blinked and straightened. "You thought he would cheat on me?"

Uncrossing his arms, Denny ran a hand back through his hair. Looking uncomfortable, he sighed. "Look, I know you love him, but I've known him a long time, and he's not…" He looked at the ceiling for a second and closed his eyes. Reopening them, he met my eye again. "I like Kellan, I do, but he's not cut out for a relationship with just one person. That's never been his style, Kiera. I'm sorry this is happening now, but honestly, I'm more surprised that it didn't happen sooner."

My jaw dropped as I stared at him. I felt like he had just punched a hole through my heart. It was one thing to silently have those fears, it was another for one of Kellan's friends to confirm them. And even though Denny had good reason to make me hate Kellan, playing that sort of mind game wasn't his style. He wouldn't have said it if he didn't believe it. Of course, Denny didn't know Kellan as well as I did. Denny only knew a small chunk of Kellan's past.

Walking over to me, he grabbed my hand. "I'm sorry to have to say that to you, I really am, but you should understand who you're involved with. And Kellan…doesn't know how to be faithful, Kiera. He just doesn't."

More tears building, I quickly swiped them away. "You don't know him like I do, Denny. You don't know what he's been through, the pain he fights, how much he's been tortured. You think he just got beat up as a kid, but it's so much worse than that…"

I shut my mouth, not wanting to spill any more of Kellan's secrets; they weren't mine to spill. Denny bunched his brows at me and frowned. "A bad childhood doesn't make up for being a…for screwing around on people. You can come from a brutal background and still be a decent person. It doesn't give you a free pass to hurt people."

I sighed and looked down. "I know…I'm just saying that there's more to Kellan's story than you know."

"Like what?" he whispered.

I looked up at him but shook my head. "It's not for me to say. I'm sorry."

Denny nodded, his eyes looking a little sad as he realized just how close Kellan and I really were. "Well then, maybe I'm wrong." Exhaling, he shook his head. "But if you think he's cheating on you, Kiera…then he probably is."

I felt another tear slide down my cheek and Denny brushed it off. "I'm sorry," he whispered. I nodded and he added, "Did you tell Kellan about me being back in town?"

Sighing, I shook my head and stared over at the card table. A vase full of bright red roses dressed up the space, the week-old bouquet still in its full glory. Kellan's anniversary present to me. He'd had them delivered to Pete's, but feeling ill, I'd gone home early. I didn't get them until the following night. We'd missed each other on the celebration of our year together, and it felt horribly symbolic.

Denny leaned over to meet my eye. "Why didn't you tell him? And don't tell me that it was because you were sparing his feelings. That may be part of it, but what's the real reason you didn't tell him?"

I stared at Denny, wishing I could just walk away from this painful conversation. Knowing I couldn't, I shrugged and whispered, "He's hiding something from me, and if he was going to hide something from me…then I wanted to hide something from him."

A sob escaped me as I admitted that, and Denny wrapped his arms around me, finally. I held him close as my tears of fear and frustration took me over. Hating myself for feeling what I felt, for admitting it to Denny, I took a moment to completely fall apart. Denny only held me, not commenting as he rubbed my back. I could only imagine that he was thanking fate that his new relationship wasn't so complicated.

When I could breathe again, Denny released me and freshened our tea. Moving to sit on the couch, I told him everything I worried about—the fans, the exotic record rep who could probably pose for all of the major fashion magazines, the weird texts and phone calls that Kellan hid from me, the fact that Kellan had known I was holding something back…and that he'd let it go because he didn't want to divulge his own secrets.

Denny listened, not really commenting on Kellan's behavior. He also didn't try to dissuade my fears with false hope. Once he heard all of the facts, he never once told me it was nothing, or it would be okay, or I was overreacting. He only listened and nodded, and I suddenly realized why people gave each other unfounded reassurance. Not hearing, "It's probably nothing," from the person you were divulging your fears to made those fears seem completely warranted, even if you didn't have enough proof to back them up.

When I had nothing more to say, Denny picked at a seam in the couch, maybe wondering what to say as well. I watched him, feeling empty and tired inside. Then he spotted something and leaned into the ugly, orange sofa. Using both hands, he pried something out of a hole in the fabric, a hole I barely registered anymore.

When he pulled out a piece of paper, my heart stubbornly skipped a beat. It was one last love note from Kellan, a remnant of the game he'd left for me when he first went away what felt like a lifetime ago now.

Denny opened it while my eyes watered. He read over it for a moment before he handed it to me. In a soft voice, he said, "I think this was meant for you."

Hands shaking, I reached out for the paper. Blinking away the water forming in my eyes so I could read it, I held my breath.

> I hid this one in the hopes that you would find it long after I'm gone. I hope you find this months from now, when I'm still out there, on the road, away from you. I can't imagine what the time apart has done to us. I'm hoping we're closer. I'm hoping we're more in love than ever. I'm hoping that when I come back, you'll move in with me. In all honesty, I'm hoping that when I come back you'll agree to marry me someday. Because that's what I want, what I dream about. You, mine, for the rest of my life. I hope you feel the same...because I don't know what I would do without you. I love you so much. But, if for some reason we're not closer, if something has come between us, please, I'm begging you...don't give up on me. Stay. Stay with me. Work it out with me. Just don't leave me...please.
>
> I love you, always,
>
> Kellan

Chapter 20 – Oh, My God

After Denny left, I went to bed with that note clutched in my fingers. I knew Kellan wrote it back in the fall, before things had shifted between us, but it did comfort me. He'd known, even back then, that something might distance us while he was on the road. He'd known and begged me in advance not to leave him. And I didn't want to. I wanted him. I wanted the life he'd mapped out on paper. I just wanted to trust him, too.

My phone rang by my bed early the next morning. Still clutching the letter in my slow-to-respond fingers, I fumbled with the noisy contraption and managed to hit the answer button just before it switched to voicemail.

A warm voice filled my ear. "Happy Anniversary."

I smiled and rolled onto my back, imagining the dark blue eyes that accompanied the voice. "You don't have to keep telling me that every time you call, Kellan."

He sighed, the soft sound almost overshadowed by the squeak of a mattress compressing. "I know, but I still feel really bad that I missed it, that I couldn't fly out to you. A year together is a big deal, and I really wanted to see you…but stuff kept coming up…"

I bit my lip. He'd mentioned before that it was things for the new album that had come up. Just when he thought he could get away, the record execs came at him with a new contract amendment for him to sign. The company wanted to formally approve every song before they would consent to having it recorded. Kellan wasn't thrilled with the fact that a corporation had final say over his music, but making an album was expensive, and the studio had to ensure that they got the best bang for their buck. Fiscally it made sense, but it also made the recording process that much more complicated. Especially since they wanted all of the songs signed off on before the group came out to L.A. in May. That didn't give Kellan and the guys a whole lot of time.

I understood all of that…but I had really wanted to spend my anniversary with my boyfriend, not a bottle of Nyquil. "You had good reason, Kellan. I understand. Besides, I was pretty sick anyway, and you did send me flowers."

I smiled, thinking of them in the other room, but Kellan sighed again. "Yeah, flowers you didn't get on time. I'm really sorry about that. I was sure I'd find you at Pete's on a Saturday night."

Now I sighed. "It's okay, Kellan, it's not a big deal."

"It is to me, Kiera. I'm really sorry it's turned out this way. I'll make it up to you…someday…I promise."

Shifting to my side, I laid my head on my arm. Silence passed between Kellan and me. The moment began to fill with tension as I thought of all of the obstacles between us, physical and emotional ones. Squeezing my hand holding the paper, I whispered, "I found your letter last night, the one in the couch."

Silence, then a mattress squeaking as he adjusted his position as well.

"Oh…and?"

I heard the uncertainty in his voice, like he thought he went too far, openly admitting that he wanted to marry me. Maybe he thought I didn't want that for us. Maybe he thought I was still hoping to marry Denny one day, since that had been our unofficial plan. "You really see that future for us?"

"Yeah, I do, Kiera…all the time. Do…do you?"

"Yeah." Remembering the fears I'd confessed to Denny last night, fears that Denny had solidified in me with his silence, a thought began to override my answer. With my head screaming at me, *If you think he's cheating on you, Kiera, then he probably is*, I quickly added, "Maybe…someday."

As Kellan absorbed my seemingly lukewarm response, the awkward silence on the line grew even bigger. Hating the tension that was forming in my stomach, I whispered, "I miss you."

His response came in a rush. "I miss you, too. I know we saw each other a couple of weeks ago, but it wasn't enough, not nearly enough… I really miss you."

Hearing the melancholy in his voice, I scrunched my brows and bit my lip. "Kellan? You…okay?"

My heart started beating faster as I waited for his answer. Even though he only paused for a few seconds, it seemed like an eternity. "Yeah…just exhausted. I never realized how…taxing this would be. Always on the road, always away from home, always having to deal with…people. I know it's early for you and you probably want to go back to sleep, but could you stay on the line for a bit? I'm feeling… I just want to listen to you breathe for a while."

Sympathy for him rushing through me, I wished I could put my arms around him, squeeze him tight…kiss him. "I don't have anywhere to be but right here with you, Kellan."

I heard rustling sounds as he exhaled contently. "Good, I love you, Kiera. It seems like forever since I've held you, since I've made love to you."

I flushed a little, then remembered it had been a while…since Christmas Eve actually. "It has been forever, Kellan." Hoping and praying that my last time had also been Kellan's last time, I swallowed. In the silence I heard another squeak of a mattress. "Where are you?" I asked, ice prickling my skin that maybe he was calling from a hotel room…and not his.

He let out a sensual noise of contentment. "On the bus, in the back bedroom. All the guys are gone, so I snagged Griffin's bed." He laughed a little. "I just couldn't spend another moment in that tiny bunk."

Picturing him somewhere that Griffin did…Griffin-type things in, I grimaced. Then, picturing him sleepily sprawled out on a bed, I smiled. A rush of desire tingled me and I whispered, "So…you're alone? Completely alone?"

"Yeah…why?"

Dropping his letter to my bed, I covered my eyes with my hands. God, I could not ask him to be intimate with me over the phone, I just couldn't. But, we were drifting further and further apart...I felt it. And maybe a moment of reconnection was exactly what we needed right now.

Flaming hot to the touch in my embarrassment, I squeaked out, "I want to... Will you...?"

As my throat dried up and speech became impossible, Kellan quietly asked, "What, Kiera?"

Keeping my eyes tightly closed, I shifted onto my back and pretended that I was Anna. She'd have no problems asking Griffin to have sex over the phone. Oh, God, I really wished I hadn't just had that thought. Sighing at myself, I forced the words to come out. "I feel like we're drifting, Kellan, and I just want to feel closer to you. I--"

Kellan cut me off. "I'm sorry, Kiera. I feel like that's my fault. I just...I...I should... We should talk about... God, this is hard..."

My eyes watering, I shook my head. No, I didn't want him to break my heart right now. I wanted him to make me feel better. I wanted him to make me feel like we were completely in sync, completely in love, and completely devoted to each other. I wanted to feel worshipped again, even if it was just for this one moment.

"No, don't, Kellan. I don't want to talk right now. I just want you to make me feel good..."

His end went silent, then, "Kiera, are you asking me to...do you want me to make love to you?"

I groaned a little as his words went straight through my body. I knew that I was using sex as a diversion, like he sometimes did. I knew that I was sidestepping our issues, and I also knew that if I pushed right now, really pushed, I could probably get some honesty out of him. But...I wasn't ready to hear his sins. And it had been so long, and I'd missed him...so much. If we could just pretend...

"Yes," I whispered, my voice husky. "Make me feel it, Kellan...make me feel like your wife..."

"Oh, God, Kiera...I want you so much..."

I ran my hand over my body, over the places he liked to touch. My breath quicker, I whispered, "I don't know what to do, Kellan."

He groaned in my ear, the sound sending a jolting ache right through me. Keeping my eyes tightly closed, I found that I could easily imagine that my hand was his. Especially with his voice in my ear, guiding me. "Take your shirt off, baby. I need to run my tongue over those beautiful breasts..."

It was a half an hour later before he finally let me have the explosion my body was craving. He'd kept me on the edge, tantalizing me by telling me exactly where to go, what to touch. And he always said that he was doing it, so I didn't feel stupid or self-conscious. Although, I stopped caring about that about five minutes into it. Really, I stopped caring about that when he started touching himself. And his voice when he came... God, it was still ringing in my ears.

Panting into the phone, it took me a minute to register that he was talking to me. "Hey, you still there?"

He chuckled a little and I felt that embarrassment start to slide back in. I pushed it away, though. "Yeah, sorry." I laughed a little too. "I got a little distracted there."

He purred in my ear—a delicious sound. "Yes, I know. God, that was incredible, Kiera…you were incredible."

Not feeling like I really did anything special, I murmured, "Are you sure that was okay? That was definitely a first for me…"

He sighed and laughed. "Uh, considering I haven't come that hard on my own in a long time…yeah, that was perfect. And…a first for me, too."

That startled me so much, I sat up in bed. "You've never had phone sex before?"

I flushed at asking him that so bluntly, but he only chuckled at my response. "No…why do you sound so surprised?"

I sucked on my lip, remembering the heated words he'd used to stoke my body, remembering him urging me to do whatever felt good. At the time, it had all seemed so natural coming out of his mouth that I'd have believed he got paid professionally to do it. He probably could. Being an overly sexual person did have its bright spots.

"Because you were amazing…"

"Amazing, reall--?" He cut off what he was saying and swore.

I bunched my brows. "Kellan? Everything all right?"

Sounding like he was moving in a hurry, he murmured, "Yeah, it's just…the guys came back. I have to go…clean up. Sorry."

A flood of heat rushed to my cheeks, picturing what he probably looked like right now. I wrapped the blankets around my bare body, feeling embarrassed at just the thought of being walked in on in that position. "Oh, okay, I love you."

Chuckling, he told me that he loved me, too, then disconnected the phone. I set it down on my nightstand and stretched out under my covers, remembering him moaning my name. For the time being, I felt completely content and relaxed, and I hoped the feeling would last.

It surprisingly lasted for a while. I felt on cloud nine as I floated through my days. Cheyenne noticed it, asking me during poetry class if it had anything to do with the rose that I was twirling in my fingers. I smiled and nodded at the perky woman. I had no idea how Kellan had managed to pull it off, but every day since our heated moment on the phone, I'd been approached by complete strangers and handed a single red rose. Sometimes it happened here at school, sometimes at work. Once at Starbucks. It was almost like Kellan wanted to make sure that he didn't miss me again.

It was only the Wednesday after our phone call, and I already had a vase of fourteen roses at home. If he kept up this pace, I'd have to buy more vases. And I'd probably have to move out. My sister was being a bear lately and rolled her eyes at every romantic gesture Kellan made. She even snipped that the flowers were stinking up the apartment. Really? How was that even possible?

I tried not to gloat about it, since she seemed pretty irritated at Griffin's lack of...everything, but I hoped her mood improved soon. If it didn't, maybe I'd go shack up with Denny?

He'd finally found a place to live and it was...impressive. It was a house in a secluded residential area on Queen Anne Hill. The places up there are pretty nice, and Denny had an amazing view of the city. My jaw had dropped when he showed me around.

After class today, I was going to go help him pick out furniture. He had a keen sense of style when it came to decorating (I'd always thought it went hand in hand with advertising). I think he invited me along just to make sure I was okay.

He hadn't said anything about my mood improvement since the night I cried in his arms, the night he found Kellan's love letter, but Denny watched me like a hawk, waiting for me to break down again. I felt bad that I had caved in front of him, admitted my fears to him, so I overcompensated my joyousness around him, probably making it seem disingenuous. As a result, he called me a lot and invited me out a lot.

I didn't mind. I enjoyed spending time with Denny...I always had.

Winter quarter was ending and today was the last day of my poetry class. I gave Cheyenne a hug and thanked her for helping me through it. I was certain I never would have figured out the flowery language without her help.

"No problem, Kiera. Maybe for our last quarter, we can still get together and study over coffee?"

Knowing my spring quarter was as challenging as the previous one had been, I exhaled with a long sigh. "Yeah, definitely." As I waved goodbye to the boisterous blonde, she gave me a warm smile. It was an overly affectionate smile and it made me frown. The smile seemed...a little too fond.

Waving goodbye to my other classmates, I hoped that Cheyenne hadn't taken a liking to me. I wasn't sure if she was interested in boys or girls; things like that don't usually come up in casual conversations. Although, when we talked about Kellan, she often mentioned an ex she'd had years ago in high school. I was pretty sure that had been a guy. At any rate, I didn't want to hurt yet another person in my life.

But then again, maybe I was reading too much into it. Cheyenne was friendly with just about everybody in class. It wasn't like I was a drop-dead beauty that everybody lusted after. No, that was Kellan...not me.

Laughing at myself, I headed out to the parking area where Denny had arranged to meet me. Knowing we were shopping together today, I had left Kellan's "baby" safely parked at my apartment, with firm instructions to my sister not to take it for a test drive. Looking sullen and tired, she only shrugged and muttered, "Whatever."

Stepping out of his car as I arrived, Denny cocked his head at me. "What's so funny?"

Still giggling over the idea of yet another person being enamored with me, I shook my head. "Just realizing that I think way too much of myself."

Pursing his lips, Denny shook his head and rolled his eyes. It was an adorable expression and I grinned. "Right, your self-esteem is just...obnoxious." He gave me his charming, goofy grin. "You should really work on your modesty."

I smacked his shoulder, laughing as I opened his car door. Sliding into his creamy, luxurious seats, eagerly anticipating the warming sensation of the heater installed in them, I looked over at Denny as he got in his side. He eyed the flower in my hand as he started the car. "That from Kellan?"

He raised a dark eyebrow at me as I set the flower on the dash. "Yeah," I said, a little dreamily.

"Everything...all right then?"

Hearing his concern, I looked back at him, his dark eyes now concentrating on the road. "I guess. I mean, we haven't talked yet, but I feel like we've taken a step closer together."

Not looking me, Denny said, "But you haven't talked yet, so nothing's really changed."

I sighed, twisting to look out the window. "No, no, I guess it hasn't. I don't really want to talk about it though, Denny."

He sighed a little, then softly said, "Okay, Kiera. It's your relationship, not mine."

Looking back over at him, I cocked my head. "Speaking of yours...any word on Abby coming over?"

He visibly brightened as he looked back at me. "Yeah, her assignment is wrapping up soon. She thinks she could make it out here by the end of April."

Denny's eyes filled with a warmth that I had only seen in reference to me. It hurt a little, seeing it in connection to another woman, but strangely enough, it also made me feel good, too. Denny was a part of my life, and I loved him. I wanted to see him happy and she was the reason for his happiness. Placing my hand on his knee, I gave him a soft smile. "I'm glad, Denny. I'm sure you've missed her."

I instantly wondered if he'd had heated conversations on the phone with her. Probably not. That wasn't Denny's style. But then again, it wasn't my style either...and I'd done it. If Abby was anything like Kellan, I supposed she could have opened Denny up to all sorts of new experiences. In some ways, Denny and I were too alike. The two of us being with people whose personalities were different than ours was probably a good thing. Opposites attract and all.

Denny looked down at my hand on his knee, then up to me. He gave me a quick smile, but minutely pulled his leg away. I understood and immediately removed my hand. Some things felt too familiar. Some lines shouldn't be crossed anymore. And being so alike, we both understood that.

Walking through every furniture store downtown, we finally decided on the perfect living room and dining room sets. We even selected a bedroom set. And yes, picking out a bed with your ex boyfriend, knowing that he'll be using it with his current girlfriend…is weird.

We both had uncomfortable expressions on our faces when the salesman made us sit on a mattress together. But then, when we were lying on our backs, pondering this awkward situation we were in, we'd both looked at each other and started laughing. It was so bizarre, it had crossed into the realm of amusing.

Laughing on that plastic-coated mattress with Denny, I couldn't help but wonder what Kellan would say if he knew where I was and what I was doing. If he could see us, see that there was only friendship between us now, he might accept it. But to tell him about this over the phone…with no visual to go with the explanation, would sound bad, especially since Denny had been here for several months now. The longer he stayed, the harder it was to explain.

Settling on a relatively firm queen-sized mattress, we picked out the furniture to go with it. Denny decided on a beautiful sleigh bed that Abby was sure to love. Running his hand over the back of it, Denny told me about Abby's romantic notion of going on a sleigh ride in the dead of winter. Bundling up together under heavy blankets while a couple of beautiful horses pulled you through banks of pristine snow, light flakes dropping on your hair, sounded pretty amazing to me too. I hoped she thought of that when she saw this bed…and having that thought was weird too.

It was getting late when I finally returned to my apartment. After making the preparations for all of his new stuff to be delivered, Denny had taken me out for a celebratory dinner. His topic of conversation was all about Abby and how excited he was to show her their new place.

I smiled politely, happy that he was happy, but felt a small twinge of pain at the thought of his home being called "theirs." It didn't bother me as much as I'd have once thought, though. Probably because Kellan sometimes called his place "ours," and that always brought a smile to my face. I wanted Abby to have the same good feelings, even though we'd never met.

Walking through my door around ten o'clock that night, I was pretty surprised to find my sister pacing the living room. For one, she was rarely upset enough to pace, and two, I was pretty sure she should be at work.

Pointing at her as I set my bag on the table, I started to ask why she wasn't at Hooters. She didn't even let me get the first word of my question out though. Twisting to me, hands on her hips, she spat out, "There you are. Where have you been? I've been calling you forever."

Glancing at my bag, I realized my phone must have died. I hope Kellan hadn't tried to call. "Uh, I was out with Denny. Why?"

When I looked back at her, she was glaring at me. "I don't know why you hang out with him." I started to defend him when she shook her head and raised her hands, interrupting me. "Look, I don't really care about you and Denny." Stepping up to me, she grabbed my forearms. Eyes wide, she frantically sputtered, "I'm late, Kiera."

Furrowing my brows, I shook my head. "Okay, well the Honda is here...you could have left for work anytime?" I said, confused. Anna and I hadn't fought over the car since Kellan left me the Chevelle. And honestly, it was parked right outside, too, if she really needed to leave.

Dropping her head back, she gave me an exasperated groan. "God, Kiera, not that kind of late!" Her head snapped back up as her eyes widened. Voice trembling, she slowly repeated, "I'm l-a-t-e."

She glanced at her stomach and my eyes grew to saucers. "Oh, my God, you're pregnant!"

Shushing me, she looked around our empty apartment. Like she didn't want the dust bunnies to hear, she murmured, "I don't know...but I'm freaking out."

Mouth agape, I asked her all the questions floating around my head. "How late? When was your last period? How far along are you? Who was the last guy you were with?" Pausing a second, I raised an eyebrow at her. "Do you know who the father is?"

Glaring at me, she dropped my arms and started smacking me. "Yes! I know who the father is...bitch."

Attempting to block her hits, I backed up a step. "Sorry. Jesus, Anna." Successfully stepping out of her range, I held my hands up. "Don't kill me for saying this, but you don't always stick to just one guy."

Her lip trembled and her perfectly green eyes filled with tears. Dropping her head into her hands, she started to cry. Feeling bad, I quickly put my arms around her and held her to me. Between sobs she got out, "I know...but I've...only been with one lately...and...oh God, Kiera..."

She looked back up at me, her face desolate. "It's Griffin's..."

Now my face was desolate. "Oh, my God, I was afraid you were going to say that..." If there was one person on this earth that should never procreate...it was Griffin. But he had, and now my sister was possibly carrying his seed.

Clutching her arms, I grabbed my bag and pulled her towards the door. "Come on, we have to get you a test."

Surprisingly, she jerked on my arm. She was shaking her head as I looked back at her, her face looking genuinely terrified. "I can't..."

Running my hand down her arm as soothingly as I could, I whispered, "You have to know, Anna. Either way, you have to know."

She still looked spooked, but she didn't argue, so I very gently pulled her forward. I felt like I was breaking in a wild mare that was going to bolt at any sudden movement, or sharp sound. I finally got the freaked-out Anna into Kellan's car.

But just as I turned the ignition, she opened the door and bolted. Pursing my lips at her through the window, I shook my head. "Get back in the car, Anna."

She slammed the door shut and shook her head. "You do it; I'll wait upstairs." Disappointed at her reluctance to face reality, I nodded and backed the car out of the lot. Hopefully, she'd still be home when I got back. Anna could avoid responsibility with the best of them. I had no idea what she'd do if the stick turned blue.

At the drugstore, I picked up every kind of test, including the ones that detected early pregnancies. If Griffin was the father, then it had to have happened in Boise, and that was just a few weeks ago. It seemed too early for her to test positive, but then, I wasn't an expert on the subject. I'd leave that up to EPT.

Wishing my sister was here to buy these, wishing the person at the register tonight was a girl and not a twenty-something guy, I set down my basket full of pregnancy tests, muttering, "They're for my sister…"

The man smirked at me but said nothing. I was sure he thought I was lying. Oddly enough, I felt the urge to cover up, even though I was already wearing a thick jacket. I don't know, but buying pregnancy tests was sort of like buying condoms. It was a flashing neon sign hovering above you that screamed—*I'm having sex!* Well, I supposed the tests screamed—*I had sex!*

I hoped I didn't run into anyone I knew…

Luckily, I didn't, and I got out of there with bright red cheeks and most of my pride intact. When I returned to the apartment, my sister was still there. I found her huddled on the couch, under a blanket, shaking like she'd just watched a horror movie. Sighing at her, I handed her the paper bag. She wouldn't take it. Instead, she dropped her head in her hands and started crying again.

Sinking down to my knees, I put the bag out of sight behind me and brushed her silky hair behind her ears. "Hey, it will be okay, sis." In what I thought was a hopeful voice I added, "I mean, you're probably not pregnant. Don't you use the pill?" I'd used it diligently ever since Denny and I had started getting serious. I just assumed Anna did the same.

She looked up at me, her face forlorn. "Most days…"

I suppressed the rant I wanted to give her. You can't go around "sowing your wild oats" so carelessly. But, she was freaking out, and the last thing she needed was a lecture from me. Smiling instead, I patted her leg. "Do you want me to help you?"

Rolling her eyes, she glared at the bag I was hiding with my body. "No, thank you. I can pee all by myself."

Sighing, I watched as she stood up, grabbed the bag, and stormed out of the room. I tried to imagine the free-spirited vixen pregnant…but I couldn't.

She came out of the bathroom a few minutes later, holding five sticks in one hand. She stared at them, horrified, like they were going to start calling her Mommy at any moment. "Okay, now what?"

Walking up to her, I eyed the freshly wet sticks…they were blank. "Well, I think you have to wait a few minutes, Anna."

She looked up at me, her cheeks flushed. "I have to wait? I have to sit here and wait to see if my life is over or not?"

"Anna, your life doesn't have to be over if you are preg--"

She put her finger up to my mouth, silencing me. "Don't say the p-word. It's bad luck." I rolled my eyes at her, hoping she'd washed that finger, but chose not to comment on her ridiculous superstition.

Running her hand through her hair, Anna continued to stare at the sticks in her other palm. "I need a drink," she muttered.

As she started to head towards the kitchen, I grabbed her arm. "Anna, you can't drink, not if you're preg--" She glared at me for nearly saying the dreaded p-word again and I quickly changed it to, "not if you're with child."

I smiled at my turn-of-phrase; Anna frowned. "Damn it! This sucks already."

Forcefully taking the sticks from her, I made her sit on the couch. Her eyes locked on the test sticks in my hand. I almost felt like I could hypnotize her into a trance by waving those sticks. I wished I could, since every ten seconds she asked, "Anything?"

Glancing at the sticks, I responded with, "No, be patient."

After the tenth query I noticed a change. When I didn't answer her immediately, Anna stood up. I held her back with a hand, trying to remember if, on this particular brand, two dashes was a good thing…because I was definitely seeing two.

"What? What's the verdict?" she asked, agitated as she grabbed my hand keeping her back.

"I don't know yet, Anna."

Narrowing my eyes, hoping that I was remembering the directions wrong, I looked for the one that used plain English to spell out your fate. As the words blossomed to life right in front of my eyes, I almost felt like crying.

My sister was near frantic with worry when I looked up at her. In the loudest voice I could muster, I whispered, "You're pregnant…they're positive."

Her eyes widened and glossed over. Dropping my arm, she quietly asked, "All of them?" like somehow, if just one said no, it would negate the rest.

I glanced at them again, then up to her. All of the ones without words were similar—two dashes, a dash and a plus sign, one even had a smiley face. Adding that to the one that joyfully pronounced PREGNANT and it could only mean one thing.

I nodded and gave her a sad smile. "All of them. Congratulations, Anna, you're gonna have a baby."

She started sobbing…and not from happiness.

When Anna gathered herself, she seemed convinced that she could change the outcome of technology. "No!" Grabbing the sticks, she started marching her way to the bathroom. On the way, she screamed, "No fucking way! These are wrong. I am NOT pregnant!"

I gingerly followed behind the angry-at-fate woman, trying to help her without getting my head torn off. After she slammed the bathroom door shut, I timidly knocked on it. "Anna? What are you doing?"

Her voice trembling with fear and rage, she yelled, "I'm taking the rest of them! Because they're wrong! There's no way that fucker knocked me up! None!"

I sighed, not wanting to tell her that it was possible. Griffin may be an idiot, but his sperm could still swim...apparently. Very quietly, I asked, "Are you sure it was Griffin?"

I cringed after I asked, knowing the temperamental woman would probably throttle me for kind of calling her a slut for a second time. The door cracked open and twin emerald eyes blazed at me. "Yes...I'm...sure."

She slammed the door shut again and I winced. "Okay, just checking..."

After a long period of silence, I slowly opened the door. Anna had laid every test along the perimeter of the small sink. They were all various colors and styles, and the screens showed various symbols or words, but the results were the same on every single one of them.

Confirmed by a dozen different tests...Anna was pregnant.

She looked back up at me, teary eyed, her anger sapped. "What do I do, Kiera?"

I stepped into the room and hugged the lost woman. She seemed completely thrown, and I'd never seen my sister thrown. She tended to roll with whatever life gave her, breezing from place to place, man to man, job to job. A child though...that was a permanent responsibility that she couldn't escape from.

"You'll do the best you can, Anna, and I'll help you as much as I can."

I pulled back to look at her and she broke away from me, taking a step back in the small room. Shaking her head, she sputtered, "No, I can't do this, Kiera. I'm not you. I'm not responsible or reliable or even that smart." She tossed her hands up in the air. "I work at Hooters for fuck's sake. All I have is nice hair and a great rack. What the hell do I have to offer a kid?"

Sighing, I put my hand on her arm. "You'll do better than you think, and I know you, you'll love that baby...so much. And what more does a baby need, but love?"

Tears ran down her cheeks, and she shook her head again. "I can't do this...I don't want to. I don't want kids, I've never wanted kids." She ran her hands back through her hair, groaning. "Oh, my God...Dad! He's going to kill me. Mom...she'll never look at me the same..."

Sniffling, she covered her face for a second and I patted her arm. "They'll...come around, Anna. They'll be proud grandparents, and you and Griffin--"

She dropped her hands, her jaw following. "Griffin...oh, my God. Griffin is going to be a father!" She said it like she had just now realized what his role in all of this was going to be.

I rubbed her arm supportively. "Yeah, that's kind of how it works, Anna."

Shaking her head, her face still in disbelief, she said, "Griffin can't be a dad,

Kiera. He just can't." She pointed out the bathroom window to where our boys were miles and miles away from us. "He blows pot into puppies' faces, Kiera! Can you picture him around a child?"

I cringed. Nope, not in a million years. I tried to switch it to a placating smile, but Anna noticed my expression. In some attempt to reassure her, I said, "Well, you'll have me, Kellan, Evan, and Matt, especially Matt, since he's family. They'll...keep Griffin in check."

Sighing, she closed the toilet seat and sat on it. "Griffin...he'll think I did this on purpose, like those groupies they were warned about." She looked up at me, fresh tears in her eyes. "He'll never want to be with me again."

Tears in my own eyes, I shook my head. "Anna, he won't..." I closed my mouth. No, Anna was right. That's exactly what he would think. Shaking my head, I shrugged. "I'm sorry."

I swallowed back the tears threatening to spill over as sympathy washed through me. Whatever was between her and Griffin, it was clear that Anna genuinely did like him, maybe love him. I wasn't sure, but I knew it was over now, and I knew how much an ending relationship hurt.

Watching my struggling emotions, Anna suddenly stood up. "I'm gonna be sick..." I moved to hug her, thinking her pain was emotional, but she held one hand out to me and one to her mouth. "No, I'm really gonna be sick."

Turning around, she quickly opened the lid and proceeded to throw up in the toilet. Holding her hair back, I rubbed her shoulder while she rested her head on her arm. She sniffled a few times, breathing heavily, then, her anger seemed to resurface.

Shooting up to her feet, she wiped her mouth with a towel. As I gave her whatever words of encouragement I could think of, she grabbed the paper bag from the drug store and started shoving all of the tests inside of it. Crumpling up the bag, she stormed out of the bathroom.

Curious which way the emotional woman was going to swing now, I followed her out. Oddly enough, she stormed into my room. "Anna...now what are you doing?"

Opening one of my dresser drawers, she shoved the bag inside and closed it. Glaring, she looked back at me. "No, this isn't happening. This is just some weird dream that I'm going to wake up from any minute."

Dropping my mouth open, I pointed at the bag in my drawer. "You're not dreaming, Anna. That did happen, and you need to deal with it now."

She gave me a blank look as she started to walk out of the room. "I don't know what you're talking about, Kiera."

I grabbed her shoulders as she walked past me. She didn't look at me. "You can't just wish this away, Anna. It's going to happen to you whether you want to acknowledge it or not."

Her face completely emotionless, she finally turned to look at me. "No,

Kiera…it doesn't have to happen."

All of the blood drained from my face, from my body. Did she mean…? I couldn't believe my sister would contemplate that. I knew she was freaking out, I knew she was distraught, but…I couldn't believe she'd even consider…ending the pregnancy. "Anna…you can't…"

She jerked away from me, a trace of emotion back on her features. "I don't know yet, Kiera, okay. I just…I need to let this sink in for a few days, all right?"

I nodded at her, swallowing. Thinking was a good thing. Head down, she started to leave my room. At the door she stopped and looked back. "Don't tell anyone about this, Kiera, please? Not Mom or Dad, not Jenny, not Kellan or Denny…no one."

I sighed and took a step towards her. "Anna, you don't have to do this alone."

She shook her head and held her hand out to stop me. "Please? If I decide to have an abor… If I decide to stop this, I don't want any of them to ever know. Ever. Please? I haven't told Kellan about your little secret! And I totally covered for you when you were in the hospital after the Denny-Kellan fiasco, made up some stupid story about your appendix bursting when Dad got the bill…you owe me this."

Her voice wavered so bad, it betrayed how much this decision was eating at her. I knew my sister wasn't a cold person that could end a life on a whim, but I knew the idea of bringing a baby into the world scared the crap out of her, especially with her weird situation with Griffin. Hoping she'd come around if I gave her space and silence, I nodded. "All right, I promise you I will not say a word…to anyone."

She nodded and turned to leave, and I grabbed her arm. "But you have to tell me…before you do it." Tears dripping down my cheeks now, I shook my head. "If you decide not to keep it, you tell me before…not after, okay?"

Her eyes watered, tears slowly leaving them and trailing down her splotchy cheeks. Pulling her into a hug, I added, "That's my niece or nephew in there. You have to at least give me one last chance to talk you out of it. And if I can't…you have to let me go with you…to hold your hand."

When I pulled back, tears were streaming down her face and she nodded, hiccupping back a sob. My own face as wet as hers, I cupped her cheeks. "I love you, Anna. I know you'll do…what's best."

She nodded, turned, and left.

Chapter 21 – Hope

The following weeks were all about my sister. We spent my spring break holed up in the apartment. I tried to convince her to see a doctor. She told me no, threw up in the bathroom, and then cried in her bed for hours.

I sat with her and stroked her hair. I pointed to her Hooters calendar on the wall, reminding her how beautiful she was, and that this was her month to shine. It was April now, and her gorgeous face was proudly featured for the world to see. She complained that she felt bloated and fat already, and her tight outfit was getting tighter every day; she tore down the calendar and shoved it in her nightstand.

I hoped her job wouldn't influence her decision on whether or not to keep the baby. She was the only girl in her restaurant selected for the calendar, and she was kind of top dog there because of it. I wasn't sure if they'd allow her to continue her duties as a waitress once she started showing. I'd never seen a pregnant girl in an opaque tank top and super-tight boy shorts. But I knew that legally she had rights, and if she ever used her job as an excuse to terminate the baby, I'd bombard her with a list of them.

I walked on eggshells whenever Anna was near, trying to not add to her anxieties. It didn't take much to stress her out, either. I didn't entirely blame her for being on edge. Her situation was scary and daunting, and being flooded with mood-altering hormones didn't help. I did, however, tell her to back off when she rudely barked at me that the smell of coffee made her want to hurl, and I needed to stop bringing it into the house.

She cried when I snapped at her, and I instantly felt bad and stopped making coffee in the mornings. I guessed I could suffer through a few days of caffeine withdrawal to help her. Especially if it helped to convince her that she could be a mom. And I knew she could. Under all the carefree playfulness was a woman with a great well of love in her. She might not have found the right man to share it with yet, but I knew it was there.

I even invited her to another one of Jenny's six week long art courses. Why I kept signing up for these classes with her, I did not know. Pity, I guessed, since I still felt awful about the Boise trip.

Anna grudgingly came along, sulking and morose the entire time she sat beside me. Jenny raised an eyebrow and watched the generally bubbly and happy Anna with curiosity but made no comment about it. Maybe she figured Griffin had been an ass to her. And…he definitely had been an ass, he just wasn't aware of it yet.

Nobody was. Anna still wouldn't allow me to tell anyone, not even Denny, who noticed her mood right away. He'd come over to take me to the movies, and Anna hadn't given him her usual dirty look. She barely even glanced at him as she muttered, "Have a good time. One of us should…"

She was always saying morbid things like that. It was as if she'd just received word that she had a fatal disease and only had nine months to live. I assured her repeatedly that she had a great support system in place and she could still have a life after a child, but I was pretty sure she didn't believe me. She was still pregnant, though, seven weeks according to an online due date calendar. I kept my fingers crossed that I would be holding my niece or nephew by the end of November.

Looking a little green, Anna watched the teacher explain the object of today's lesson. Anna groaned loudly, when she saw what is was. Today we were drawing…children.

Rolling my eyes, I cursed fate. Why couldn't today be an abstract art day? Anna seemed to agree with me, and partially stood from her stool, in a motion to leave.

Her perfect pony tail swishing along her back, Kate tilted her head and asked Anna, "You all right? You look like you're going to be ill."

Anna's eyes widened, but she regained her composure, sat back down, and picked up her pencil. As two adorable ten-year-old kids sat to model for us, Anna sighed and muttered, "I'm fine." Relieved, I thanked fate that our model was not a sleeping infant. That would have driven poor Anna over the edge.

Jenny was well into her project when the rest of us finally started. I sighed as I watched her flawlessly draw out the basic shape of a human head. Mine looked like Mr. Potato-Head. I still couldn't quite get the hang of realism…and this was my umpteenth class.

Jenny smiled at me when I sighed morosely. "You'll get there, Kiera," she said warmly, any trace of a fight lingering between us gone.

Jenny didn't hold grudges for long, which was a good thing. It helped that during my break, she had taken a trip to visit Evan. She called to invite me to take the trip to Texas with her and Rachel, but I couldn't leave Anna, not in the condition she was in. Hating that I was missing out on an opportunity to spend a week with Kellan, I gave Jenny a vague excuse for why I couldn't go. I don't think Jenny understood my reasoning, but any resentment she felt towards me had faded by the time she returned.

Sighing again, I erased part of the line I had just drawn. "I don't know why I keep coming to these classes with you. I'll never be good at this." Jenny laughed a little, and I joined in with her. "I guess I'm trying to be well-rounded."

Giggling, Jenny pointed at my misshapen person. "Well, I think you need the practice, cuz that looks oblong to me."

I smacked her on the shoulder, then watched, amazed, as she went back to her incredibly lifelike drawing. I was terrible at this, and Kate was okay, but Jenny…she was amazing.

By the end of the session, I had created something that could possibly pass for a mammal. That beat my sister's stick figure. Kate's attempt was good, if not a little disproportionate. Jenny's portrait however, was breathtaking. She'd decided to turn the children into infants.

I wasn't sure if Jenny was just having an, I-love-my-man-and-I-want-to-have-his-kids-someday moment, or if she'd maybe, subconsciously, picked up on something, but the infants she had turned the models into were perfect.

"Wow, Jenny…wow." It was all I could think to say.

A scraping noise on the other side of me brought my attention back around to Anna. She'd scooted her chair away from her easel and was staring at Jenny's picture with her jaw dropped. One hand was resting on her stomach as her eyes slowly became glossier.

I put my hand on her thigh right as Jenny asked, "You okay, Anna?"

My sister nodded, not looking up at the artist. "Yeah, that's just…really good, Jenny."

The perky blonde beamed at Anna's awed face. "Thanks! I'm glad you like it so much. Do you want it?"

Anna finally glanced up at her, teary eyed. "You'd give it to me?"

Jenny shrugged, tearing it off the paper stand. "Yeah, I was just goofing around." Rolling it up, she handed it to Anna. "Here, since it moves you so much, you should have it."

Anna took it with trembling fingers. I thought she might break down into a sobbing, hysterical, hormonal mess, but swallowing a few times, she managed to wrangle in her mood and smile at Jenny. "Thank you, I really like it."

Leaning close to my sister, I quietly asked her if she was okay.

She nodded. "Yeah." Looking me in the eyes, she jerked her thumb over her shoulder. "I'm not feeling so hot. I think I'm going to go home and crash."

I nodded at her and patted her shoulder. As she left, Kate wrinkled her brows together, her topaz eyes seeming a little confused. "Is your sister…all right?"

Thinking about the look on her face as she'd stared at Jenny's infants, I smiled. "Yeah, yeah I think she'll be just fine."

Since none of us had anything to do until work later tonight, we headed over to one of my favorite coffee spots. Since Anna was banning the substance from our home, I had to buy it elsewhere. It was a heck of a lot more expensive, but as a fulltime student with a fulltime job, smart or not, I needed all the help I could get.

Kate, Jenny and I chose a back booth, as we planned on hanging out for a while. Rachel also joined us after Jenny texted her, and our party of four quickly turned into a gossip session about boys. Kate especially stoked the conversation, wanting to hear all about our love lives, since hers was currently nonexistent.

Introspectively, I thought about my situation. I thought about Kellan and the secrets he was keeping from me. He'd almost revealed them a couple of times, and that last time, before our intimate session over the phone, he'd been choked up over how to do it.

His words flew through my brain as Rachel quietly admitted that Matt was an excellent kisser.

God, this is hard…

Kellan's words mixed with Denny's warning in my brain, and ice formed in my stomach.

If you think he's cheating on you, Kiera…then he probably is…

Finally getting a chance to think about it, now that the stress of my sister's pregnancy was momentarily on the back burner, I considered all of the conversations I'd recently had with Kellan. Although he always sounded glad to talk to me, and was always eager to try to turn me on, he also seemed...worn, exhausted, like he was carrying a weight with him.

I didn't know what that meant, but my intuition told me that it wasn't good. My heart told me he'd fallen for someone else, and he didn't know how to tell me. I understood how it could happen...it had happened to me after all, but it killed me to think that he was stringing me along, biding his time to rip my heart out. Like Denny must have thought at some point, it would just be easier if Kellan told me...better to know than constantly wonder.

Feeling a well of despair start to creep up on me, I stared at my creamy coffee and ignored the conversations flowing around me. A chin on my shoulder brought me back to the present. Tilting her head at me, Jenny asked, "You all right? You sort of look like your sister did earlier."

I glanced at Rachel and Kate, the pair deep in conversation over who Kate could start seeing. Looking back at Jenny, I worried my lip and considered what I should say to her. She'd just seen the guys. Did she notice anything? Did Evan say anything?

Curiosity burning holes in my stomach, I finally asked, "When you were out visiting the boys...how was Kellan?"

Jenny blinked, not expecting my question. "Uh, fine, I guess. Why?"

Looking back down, I shrugged. "I don't know. I just feel like he...wants to tell me something..."

"Maybe you're just deferring your own guilt?"

I looked back at her and she raised a pale eyebrow. "You know, because you haven't told him about Denny being in town...right?" Shaking her head, she added, "I'm guessing that he knows nothing about how much time the two of you spend together."

I sighed, shaking my head. "No, I haven't told him yet, but I will, I just..." My eyes watered, and Jenny's disapproving scowl faded. "I need to know what he's hiding first," I whispered.

Jenny's face softened as she put an arm around me. "Hey, it's okay, Kiera. I mean, I didn't notice anything suspicious, and Evan would have told me if Kellan was...doing anything wrong."

I swallowed, discreetly wiping my eyes. Glancing at the pair across from us, still deep in their own conversation, I muttered, "Kellan's good at hiding things if he needs to...Evan had no idea about the two of us, remember?"

Sighing, Jenny pulled me into her shoulder. "Yeah, but Kellan is so in love with you...he wouldn't cheat on you." She whispered it, but I felt like the words crashed around the room.

I cringed, swallowing back more tears. I really didn't want to break down in front of Kate and Rachel. I didn't want to discuss this with a table of people. Really, I wanted to push it back to the far corner of my brain where I didn't have to think about it…that would be wonderful.

Trying to cheer me up, Jenny spunkily said, "Besides, I only ever saw him on his phone, talking to you. Would he talk to you so much if he was cheating on you?"

All of the color drained from my face. "He was on the phone? A lot?"

Furrowing her brows, she nodded. "Yeah…with you…right?"

I slowly shook my head. My sister had been such a mess the week that Jenny and Rachel were in Texas that I barely had time to answer my phone, let alone talk to Kellan. In fact, the only times I *had* talked to him were really late at night, after Anna finally passed out from exhaustion. Jenny would have surely been asleep as well during those conversations, so whoever she'd seen him on the phone with…was not me.

Clutching her arm, I leaned forward intently. "What was he saying on the phone? Did he sound…happy, in love?"

My voice broke on the word and Jenny's pale eyes glossed over. Shaking her head, she murmured, "I thought he was talking to you…"

In near hysterics, I tugged on her arm. "What did he say?"

She swallowed, shaking her head. "I don't…I wasn't paying attention, but…he…" She swallowed again, her eyes nearly to the brim now with sympathetic tears. "He was laughing…he seemed…happy."

Feeling like I was going to start hyperventilating, I stood up. Jenny started to stand with me, but I held my hand up. "I just…need a minute."

I quickly dashed to the bathroom, hoping Jenny and the others would let me fall apart alone. She'd practically confirmed my greatest fear. Kellan was involved with someone else, someone who made him laugh. And I bet she was gorgeous, too…

My hand was over my mouth and I was holding in the sobs as I sank against the cool, tile wall. Letting myself slide down it, I sat on the floor and dropped my head into my hands. How could he do this to me? Was it payback, for all the times I'd hurt him? Was it the universe getting even with me for being so awful to Denny? Or was Kellan really just the sex addict that Candy said he was, and this was inevitable?

Maybe Kellan found that going months without physically being with a woman was impossible, and caved. It happened all the time, so I didn't know why it surprised me. Maybe because I expected more from Kellan. Maybe I expected too much.

Sobbing uncontrollably, I let every doubt in my body leech out through my tears.

"Kiera? You okay?"

I glanced up to see a blonde in the doorway staring down at me. It wasn't the blonde I was expecting, though. It wasn't Jenny…it was my friend from school, Cheyenne. Wiping my eyes, I quickly muttered, "It's nothing," and started to stand.

She came up to me and helped me up. "You sure? You look devastated." Her eyes widened. "Did something bad happen? Is everything okay?"

Feeling a little strange, since my relationship with Cheyenne was mainly academic, I shrugged and repeated, "It's nothing, I'm fine."

Squaring my shoulders, she looked me in the eye. "It's not fine and you're not okay." Softening her face, she said, "I know we haven't known each other all that long, Kiera, but you can talk to me."

Smiling at her gesture, eased by the warmth in her mild accent, I leaned back into the wall and swiped my eyes dry. "It's just…Kellan. I think he's seeing someone else." My gut felt torn in half, just admitting it to someone.

Cheyenne's arms immediately wrapped around me. "Oh, God, Kiera, I'm so sorry." She pulled back to look at me, her face warm and open. "I know you really like him, are you sure?"

I shrugged, sighing. "No, I'm not sure of anything right now…except men suck." I sniffled and smiled a bit, but Cheyenne twisted her lip at me.

Stepping back, she threaded her fingers through her hair. She almost seemed nervous and I cocked an eyebrow at her. Swallowing, she looked around the empty bathroom. "Okay, I know I'm going to sound like an idiot, but, I think you're really great and smart and funny, and I know you like guys, but I was wondering if…"

My eyes widened as I listened to her. Was she saying she…dug me? Was I not so far off in thinking that she liked me? Wondering how to let her down easily, since I had zero experience in that, I took a step forward. "Oh, um, Cheyenne, I think you're great, too, and I like you--"

She visibly brightened and I stammered for a way to change what I'd just said. "No, I mean I like you, like you…not…like you, like you…like you…"

Yeah, even I was lost by my explanation, but Cheyenne didn't seem to care anymore. I said I liked her, and that was enough. Smiling ear-to-ear, she exclaimed, "Oh, I like you too!" Then she grabbed my face.

I didn't even know how to react. There is just no course on what to do or say in this situation, at least, none that I'd ever taken…but maybe I should.

She brought her lips down to mine, pressing us firmly together before softly moving against me. I had just enough time to think, *huh, that's different*, before I pushed her shoulders back. Her eyes were wide as she stared at me. I thought she looked mortified at herself, and I couldn't help but feel bad for her. Being rejected was no easy thing.

Stammering, she stepped back from me. "Sorry, oh God, I'm sorry. I thought you…I'm sorry."

Sighing that I was misleading to even my own sex, I shook my head. "No, I'm sorry. I didn't mean to make you think…" Exhaling, I switched to blunt honesty. "I'm not attracted to girls, Cheyenne. No offense or anything, but I like men…even philandering ones."

I sighed sadly as she flushed bright red. "Of course, I knew that…I really did. You have a boyfriend and you love him. I was just…caught up in the moment, and I've really liked you for a while and…" She closed her eyes and dropped her head back. "God, I'm an idiot."

Chuckling at how similar we were, I shook my head. "No, you're not, and it's fine, Cheyenne…really."

Groaning, she looked back down at me. "So, do you never want to see me again?"

I blinked, tilting my head. "Why would you think that?"

She flung her hands at where our moment just happened. "Because I totally took advantage of you." She gave me a sad smile. "Because I like you."

I looked down, shaking my head again. "Of course, I still want to see you," I looked up, "as a friend and schoolmate, but that's all we'll ever be…I'm sorry."

Her eyes watered but she smiled. "I know. I've always known it wouldn't happen. I guess I just…hoped."

I nodded at her, not knowing what else to say. Maybe having had enough embarrassment for one day, she grabbed the door handle. "Well, I should go." She pulled open the door, then raised an eyebrow at me. "We're still studying next week…right?"

Containing a sigh, I smiled. "Sure, yeah." I knew from now on I would have to be more careful around the girl. I didn't want to hurt her in any way. But, you can't help who you fall for. I knew that from experience.

As she walked away, I considered one good thing from the encounter— she'd stunned me out of my moment of agony, that was for sure. And I could now cross "being kissed by a girl" off my bucket list.

I was still stunned when I got home after my shift at the bar. I hadn't mentioned the kiss to the girls at the table, and really, when I returned all they had cared about was why I left. Jenny hadn't told them about our conversation, and I thanked her for that later.

I wondered whether Cheyenne would be a problem at school now, a new one to replace Candy, since her path had finally deviated from mine. In fact, last I heard, Candy was pregnant. It seemed to be going around these days.

My thought was reaffirmed when I opened my bedroom door to find a pregnant girl sitting on my bed. I was surprised that Anna was still up. She'd started going to bed pretty early lately.

Face sad but serene, she looked over at me as I sat beside her. "I've decided."

"And?" I held my breath, waiting for her answer.

She looked over my face for long seconds that felt like an eternity. Lifting one corner of her lip, she finally said, "I don't know if I'm going to keep this baby or not…but I won't kill it." She shrugged, looking down at her hands in her lap. "I can't," she whispered, her palm moving to rest on her abdomen.

My eyes watering, I threw my arms around her. "I'm so glad, Anna."

She nodded as she held me back, and I stroked her hair soothingly, like Mom used to do when we were little and frightened. "It will be okay, Anna. I'm here. I'll help you with everything."

She smiled at me when we pulled apart. "I made an appointment with the doctor for next week. Could you go with me?"

Nodding, I pulled her in tight again. "Of course, of course I'll go with you." Pulling back again, I raised my eyebrows. "Can I tell people? Kellan? Jenny?"

Anna immediately shook her head. "No, not yet." I frowned at her and she sighed, slumping. "Look, I don't know if I want to raise a baby, Kiera, and I don't want a million people giving me their opinions right now." She looked up at me, her bright jade eyes determined. "I want this to be my choice, and I want to make it before the world condemns me for it."

Sighing, I stroked her hair. "Yeah, okay…I won't say anything." She was silent a moment and I added, "Don't you think Griffin should know? Shouldn't he have a say?"

She stared at her hands, not able to look at me. "I know you won't approve of this, Kiera, but if I decide to give it up for adoption…" she looked back up at me, "Griffin will never know that he was the father. I'll never admit to it, and I'll deny it if anyone says otherwise."

Seeing the firm decision in her eyes, I shook my head. "Why, Anna? Why wouldn't you want him to know?"

Looking away, she shrugged. "It's just the way it has to be, Kiera." Looking back up, she shrugged. "If I do keep it…I'll tell him, okay?"

I nodded, hoping I could talk her out of this one. My feelings about Griffin aside, he had a right to know that he had a son or daughter in the world. I wasn't sure what he'd do with the information, but I felt he should know.

Perhaps noticing the inner turmoil in my eyes, Anna narrowed hers. "I'm serious about this, Kiera. You can't tell anyone."

Sighing, I shrugged. "I won't…I promise."

Satisfied with my response, she stood and left me alone in my room, my head swirling with the drama that seemed to gravitate towards me, like I was some pain-filled planet, pulling angst around me.

But my sister's mood lightened some, and the stress around the house eased. The following week I did meet with Cheyenne, and invited her over to work on our assignments. She was taking an advanced poetry class in her last quarter and I was taking an advanced expository writing class. It was tough. Along with my other classes, I was also working on getting three letters of recommendation and a critical-writing sample for my degree requirements.

Even though I enjoyed school, it was exhausting, and I was ready for it to end...in a month and a half.

Equally swamped with her own workload, Cheyenne commiserated with me. Laughing, we joked about the poetry paper I'd turned in last quarter that really barely classified as college-level material. Sitting across from me at my rickety card table, our books and papers spread between us, Cheyenne sighed and leaned back in her chair.

I started working on my paper when she spoke. "Hey, sorry about...kissing you last week, you know?"

Glancing up at her, a flush filling my cheeks, I shook my head. "Don't worry about it."

She bit her lip and looked down, getting back to work on her own stuff. "Yeah, well, thank you for not freaking out and refusing to ever talk to me again...that would have really sucked."

I laughed a little at her comment, then shook my head. "I've done so many impulsive things that I've regretted later..." I sighed. "I completely understand and I wouldn't make you feel bad about it."

"You? Impulsive?" She giggled a little. "Do tell." Throwing a pencil at her, I frowned at her amused expression. It sort of reminded me of Kellan's.

My sister bounded into the room a couple of seconds later, dressed in sweatpants and a baggy shirt. She wasn't huge or anything yet, but she was trying to hide the slight bump she had. I had no idea how she planned on explaining it to her work when she got larger. Her plan for now was letting them all see her constantly eating, so she could blame any chubbiness on over-snacking. Yeah, that might work...for the first few months.

Sucking on a lollipop, that I knew was actually something she found at a store called a "Pregger Pop," to help with the nausea, she widened her eyes at me. "You got kissed, Kiera? I'm so telling Kellan."

I narrowed my eyes at her, silently telling her that she owed it to me to not say a word, and she flushed, quickly saying, "Or not."

Cheyenne started looking a little uncomfortable, and I glared at my sister, wishing she had just a little more tact. The poor girl felt bad enough as it was, she didn't need Anna rubbing salt in her wounds.

Looking properly chagrined, Anna put a hand on Cheyenne's shoulder. "Hey, don't worry about it...everybody kisses Kiera."

I smacked Anna's arm but Cheyenne giggled and playfully responded with, "Yeah, well that's because she's so cute."

They both started laughing as I shook my head. Was embarrassing me everyone's favorite pastime? Seeing my expression, Anna leaned over and kissed my head. While I was happy that she was in better spirits, I wasn't thrilled that she was teasing me again.

She smiled down at me, then frowned a little. "Hey, it's time to go to my...thing."

She shrugged and I knew what she meant—her first doctor's appointment.

Inhaling deep, I nodded and started packing up my stuff. Cheyenne took the hint and started packing up hers, too. Walking us down to the parking lot, Cheyenne smiled at Kellan's car as I opened it. "That car is hot...see you later, Kiera," she drawled.

I laughed at her comment and nodded goodbye to her. Yeah, the car was pretty hot, and pretty fun to drive, too. I'd never tell Kellan, but I'd taken more than a few long drives in it.

Anna got quieter on the ride over, playing with the zipper of her light jacket. I smiled over at her reassuringly. It reminded me of how I'd looked and felt when she drove me against my will to see Kellan, over a year ago. I had been so apprehensive that night, the night we reunited, unsure if he'd want to see me, unsure if I'd be able to see him, but it had all worked out for the best, and I was sure this would too.

When we pulled up to the doctor's office, Anna let out a long, unsteady exhale. I put my hand on her shoulder. "Hey, I'm right here, Anna."

She smiled at me, nodding . "All right, let's do this."

"This" turned out to be a little boring. It mainly involved waiting and filling out paperwork. Anna seemed uncomfortable surrounded by all of the pregnant women in the lobby and focused on her issue of Cosmo instead. I looked around at all of the burgeoning bellies and tried to picture my sister, or myself, in that state. Life was so chaotic right now, it was hard to imagine having a baby in the middle of it. Feeling sympathetic, I grabbed Anna's hand while we waited.

Once in the office, the waiting continued. Anna stared, horrified, at a diagram posted on the wall of a baby inside a womb. "Oh, my God, Kiera, look at the size of it!" She looked back at me, her beautiful eyes as wide as saucers. "How the hell is *that* head supposed to come out of *this* hole?"

She pointed down at herself and I hushed her for her very loud comment. "I don't know, Anna, but women do it every day so it must work...somehow."

Closing her eyes, she leaned against my shoulder. "Yeah, and it's going to hurt like fucking hell."

I bumped her shoulder with mine. "Do you think you could tone down the language, you are carrying an impressionable embryo after all?"

She rolled her eyes at me. "It can't hear me, it doesn't have ears yet." Her eyes widened a bit. "Or does it?" Looking down at her stomach, she murmured, "Sorry kid...Mommy's got a potty mouth."

I bit back my grin, amused that she'd referenced herself as a mom. She'd never done that before. I wisely didn't comment on it, though, not with Anna being in such a fragile state.

I hopped off the table as soon as the doctor came in and Anna immediately grabbed my hand, forcing me to stand next to her. We answered dozens of questions with her and then she brought out a machine that looked like it was used in torture chambers...or sold in sex shops. Anna eyed the doctor curiously. "Uh, where does that go?"

The doctor held up a phallic-shaped wand connected to a portable computer. "You're too early for a traditional ultrasound, so we'll have to take an internal one." She smiled as she warmed up the machine. "Ready to see your baby's heartbeat?"

Anna sat up on her elbows, the paper lining beneath her rustling. "You can see that already?"

The doctor nodded and, curious, Anna let her do whatever she wanted with the odd machine. Moments later, my sister received her first glimpse of her child. Surrounded in a sea of black, a tiny gray speck blinked at us repeatedly, like it was saying hello in Morse code. Anna's jaw dropped. "Is that...?"

The doctor nodded, pointing at the speck we could clearly see. "Yep, that's the heart, strong and steady...perfectly normal."

My eyes welled up with tears watching it, and Anna squeezed my hand. When I looked down at her she had one hand on her stomach and tears in her own eyes. "Oh, my God, Kiera..." She looked back at me, wide-eyed. "There's something alive in me!"

I chuckled at her response and gave her a quick hug. "Yeah, I know, Anna." Leaning down, I kissed her head. "And it's going to be beautiful, just like its Mom."

She laughed and a tear rolled down her cheek. It was the first happy tear I'd seen from Anna lately, and seeing it gave me hope.

Chapter 22 – Don't Lie

Anna's effervescent personality returned after her doctor's visit. I spotted her looking at baby clothes when I took her shopping one afternoon, and eyeing infants in strollers as we passed them by. I even found a "What to Expect When You're Expecting" book in the kitchen. Of course, I discovered it in the freezer, so I figured something in there had freaked Anna out. When we were kids she would hide the scary books. When I was nine, she hid Stephen King's *It* in my sock drawer.

She wasn't quite at the acceptance level yet, but cruising into her ninth week, she was getting there. And I was still the only person who knew about her pregnancy. I had a feeling she'd hold off as long as she could from divulging the news. It wouldn't surprise me if she decided to tell our parents by showing up at their doorstep Christmas morning with the baby in tow. Assuming she kept it, of course.

I didn't like to think about the possibility that she wouldn't, but thinking about her dilemma helped detract me from my own worries. My conversations with Kellan of late had been quiet. Since Jenny's confession that he was actively engaging someone else on the phone, I didn't know what to think. Sure, he could be talking with just about anybody, from a record label representative to a friend back in Seattle, but my heart told me that wasn't it. My heart told me it was a girl.

But he didn't act like he loved me any less when we talked. He didn't act cold or distant. He acted like he was still completely in love with me. He huskily told me how much he loved me and that he wished he could be with me. We even made love again, over the phone. It wasn't the same as being with him, but it did help to keep me feeling close, even if I wasn't sure if we were.

And, needless to say, I hadn't told him about Denny. It seemed pointless now, since Denny had been back for so long. I wasn't sure what was going to happen when Kellan's tour ended and he went to L.A. to work on his album, but I was certain about what was going to happen with Denny and me.

Nothing…nothing was going to happen.

Even if Kellan and I broke up today, and God, I hoped not, nothing would happen between Denny and me. The feeling just wasn't there anymore. Nothing more than friendship and fond memories remained. Even Denny's lingering bitterness over our breakup had dwindled.

We were just…comfortable friends again.

So when he came into Pete's one Wednesday evening on the verge of tears, I was naturally concerned for my friend. Ignoring my duties for a moment, I sat beside him at a table. Handing him a beer, I quietly asked, "You okay?"

Wrapping his fingers around his bottle, he shook his head. "No, no, I'm not."

I frowned at seeing his normally jovial dark eyes looking so sad and soulful. Gently placing my hand on his arm, I peered around to look up into his face. "You want to talk about it?"

Sniffing, he looked up at me. His eyes searched mine for a moment.

Scratching the hair along his jaw, he sighed. "Yeah, actually, I think I do. Can I come over after your shift?"

I smiled, patting his arm. "Of course. I'll see you there."

He nodded, his smile still sad, and I leaned over on a whim and kissed his cheek. His smile softened as he looked up at me, and I grinned, happy that I could ease his heart, even just a little. Scuffing up his longer-than-I-was-used-to hair, I stood and left him to his drinking.

Jenny was frowning at me as I stepped up to her. "I saw that." She raised an eyebrow. "Anything going on?"

Knowing that she meant if anything was going on between Denny and me in a more than friendly way, I dryly told her, "No, nothing like that is going on." I frowned and looked back at Denny. "He's sad, and I was trying to cheer him up."

She looked over at where Denny was staring at his bottle. "Hmmm, yeah, he does seem sad." Twisting to head over to him, she stopped and quietly added, "I know things are…strained, with you and Kellan, but don't do anything…rash…by 'cheering' Denny up a little too well."

I gave her a wry smile. "I wasn't going to, Jenny, but thank you for that."

She smiled as she sucked on an apple lollipop. "No problem."

I shook my head at her as she bounced over to Denny and wrapped her arms around him. He gave her a small smile. It brightened a little when Jenny stuck a sucker in his palm. Wondering what was going on with my ex, wondering what was going on with my current, I finished my shift in self-contemplation.

I came home to an empty apartment and a note from Anna saying that she was spending the night at a friend's house. I smiled at seeing it. It was yet another sign that she was returning to the bubbly personality that I knew and loved. I also hoped that by "friend," she meant a girl. The last thing Anna needed right now was to drag another guy into the mix. She had enough complications.

As I was setting my bag down there was a knock on the door. Sighing softly, I walked over and opened it. Denny's glum face peered back at me. His dark eyes made darker by the slight circles of exhaustion underneath them, he looked worn.

Frowning, I motioned for him to come in. Still dressed in his work attire, he loosened his tie after slinging his jacket over a kitchen chair. Running a hand back through his hair, he twisted to face me. "Thanks for letting me come by, Kiera…I didn't know who else to talk to."

His accent thickened as he spoke and I stepped up to him, curious. "What's going on, Denny?"

Shaking his head, he closed his eyes. "It's nothing, really…nothing I should be worrying you about."

Cupping his cheek, I made him look at me. "It's bothering you, so you should talk to me about it. I'm your friend, Denny. Regardless of everything, I'm still your friend."

Sighing, he gave me a lopsided grin. "Yeah…I know." Glancing over to my ugly orange couch, he tilted his dark head. "Can we sit?"

Exhaling slowly, I nodded. "You want something to drink?" He shook his head and started walking over to the couch, so I followed him. Once he sat, he leaned over his knees. My heart surged a little at his posture and mannerisms; it reminded me of another conversation we'd had on a couch. A conversation that was difficult for the both of us.

Shaking off the awful memory of Denny asking me if I was happy being with him, I put my hand on his knee. "It's okay…what is it?"

He glanced up at me, his eyes sad. "It's Abby…"

My heart filled with lead as I considered all of the things that could have happened between them that would make him look so sad. Did she leave him? Cheat on him? Did another woman betray him? Him, the most loving, wonderful man I'd probably ever met? It seemed ridiculous to me, and my heart instantly hardened against this woman who'd caused him such pain.

And yes, I didn't miss the irony of feeling that way, considering I'd caused him more pain than anyone.

"Oh, are you two…over?"

He gave me a quizzical look, then shook his head. "No, she just…had a problem with her work visa. She can't make it over here yet. It's going to be a few more weeks until they get everything straightened out." He sighed, looking down at his hands. "We've been apart for so long, I just wanted…" When he looked back at me, his eyes were moist. "I wanted to see her."

My heart softened as I realized that she hadn't hurt him, not intentionally. He just missed her. No, I was the only one that had caused him pain. Abby, she was everything he deserved to have. Putting my arm on his leg, I grabbed his hand. He looked down at our fingers, but didn't make a move to disentangle us.

"I'm so sorry, Denny. I know how excited you were for her to see your new place."

Closing his eyes, he nodded. "Yeah, she was supposed to be here this weekend. I was going to have everything ready…make her a great meal, fill the house with her favorite flowers, light all the candles…"

He looked over at me, his face apologetic for describing his romantic intentions. It knotted my stomach only fractionally, and I gave him a warm, encouraging smile. Slumping in sadness, he quietly added, "I just want her here."

Rubbing his thumb against mine, he stared at me for a long time. When he finally spoke, his voice was quiet, his accent thick. "I think I hated you after you cheated on me…for a long time actually." My heart sunk and my eyes welled as he continued to stare me down. Shaking his head, he said, "But I think I should thank you now."

My jaw dropped as my eyes went wide. "Thank me? God, Denny…why? I was horrible to you."

He smiled, looking at our hands. "Yes, yes you were." Peeking up at me, he gave me a goofy grin. "But I'd have never gone back home if you hadn't hurt me so much. And if I'd never gone home, I'd never have met Abby." Looking past me, his smile widened as he thought of his lover, wherever she was. "And she…is a miracle to me."

Oddly, that sentence didn't hurt me as much as it would have a few months ago. It actually made me smile, and we both grinned at each other goofily. "I'm glad you're happy Denny, that's all I ever wanted for you."

He nodded at me, then frowned. "Well, I'd be happier if I could get her here…"

Leaning in, I felt comfortable enough to give my friend a hug, knowing neither one of us would be hurt by it. He laughed a little and returned the hug. Letting go of my hand so he could get both arms around me, he squeezed me tight. I chuckled as I held him, delighted that I could still comfort him.

Pulling back, I told him, "If it makes you feel any better, I got kissed by a girl a couple of weeks ago."

Giving me a playfully devilish grin, he leaned his head against mine. "You have my complete attention. Let's talk about the kiss."

I was giggling when I heard the door open. Wondering why Anna had decided to come back, I loosened my arms and looked over at the door. I stopped giggling when I saw who was standing there. I think I stopped breathing. Denny immediately dropped his arms from around me as a cold voice filled the room.

"I felt bad for missing our anniversary. We had a short break in the schedule, and even though Matt's irked at me for taking off, I just had to come out and see you."

My jaw dropped to see Kellan standing just inside my apartment door. Eyes narrowed, his midnight blue depths stared at Denny and me like he wanted to set us on fire. "I wanted to surprise you." His jaw tight, he spat out, "Are you surprised…? Because I know I am."

I instantly scooted away from Denny and stood up. Knowing how bad that moment looked, I held my hands up to Kellan. "I can explain."

Walking into the room, Kellan slammed my door shut behind him. He pointed at us with a hand holding a bouquet of flowers; they vibrated as his hand shook. "You can explain?" he yelled. "Explain what exactly? The fact that he is sitting in your living room and not thousands of miles away, or the fact that you had your hands all over each other!"

Tossing the flowers to the floor, he strode into the living room. I immediately put my hands on Kellan's chest, afraid of him and Denny getting too close together—afraid of a confrontation. Glaring down at me, Kellan pushed his body against my hands and seethed, "I'm listening…start explaining!"

My throat completely closed up on me as Denny slowly rose from the couch. "Kiera…I told you to tell him…" Denny murmured.

Kellan's eyes snapped over to his. "Tell me what? Tell me about the kiss? Is that what I heard you say?" His eyes flashed back to mine, cold, enraged. "Is that what you need to tell me, Kiera…or is there more?"

Shaking my head, tears blurred my vision. "No, Kellan, he didn't kiss me."

Kellan's eyes narrowed and he pushed me from him. "Then you kissed him?"

I swallowed, wishing this was just a horrid dream. I should have told him, I should have told him on that very first day I ran into Denny. "No, Kellan, I didn't kiss anybody…"

Kellan walked up to me, pressing me back with his body until my legs pressed against the couch. Even knowing that he was extremely mad, even filled with guilt and fear for our relationship, his proximity excited me. My rough breath matching his, I resisted the urge to touch him as he leaned down and snapped, "But someone kissed you? Who?"

Denny stepped up to Kellan, placing a hand on his arm. "Kellan…relax, mate."

Kellan snapped his head to Denny and shoved him back, hard. "Don't fucking call me mate! Why the hell are you with *my* girl?"

The possessive accent on the word was so clear it seemed to ring in the air. I put a calming hand on Kellan's chest but he ignored it, focusing on Denny instead. Stumbling back a step, Denny managed to catch himself before falling. Slowly straightening, he glared at Kellan. "Right…*your* girl."

Kellan sniffed, his jaw flexing hard, along with his fist. Sensing a fight about to erupt, I grabbed Kellan's face and made him look at me. "A girl at school kissed me! Okay?"

Kellan blinked, his expression relaxing. "A girl?" Scrunching his brows, he searched my face. "Really?"

Sighing, I shrugged. "Yes, a girl. Denny and I haven't done anything wrong. You stepped into a situation that was easy to take out of context." Stroking his cheek as I watched his face relax, I murmured, "But I didn't kiss her back. I haven't kissed anyone…but you."

His dark blue eyes searched mine for what felt like an eternity, then he gave me a small, crooked smile. "You got kissed by a girl, and I missed it?"

Shaking my head, I thumped his chest with my hand. Clearing his throat, Denny took the small moment of levity to make his escape. "I'll let you two work this out."

Maybe remembering that Denny was here, Kellan shifted his attention back to him. "What are you doing here?" he asked, slightly calmer than before.

Denny sighed, shaking his head. "Look, I don't want to be involved with this. I'm here for work, nothing more. I told her to tell you way back in February that I was here, but she was scared to…" He sighed, looking uncomfortable. "But that's between the two of you and I don't want to be here to watch you discuss it."

Kellan straightened, then nodded at Denny, apparently respecting his honesty. Denny inched by him, never breaking eye contact. Once clear of him, Denny looked back at me. "Thanks for listening, Kiera. I'll call you tomorrow."

He glanced back up at Kellan, then twisted to get his jacket and quietly left the apartment. Exhaling the knot of tension, grateful that at least another blowout hadn't happened, I waited for Kellan to turn back around and face me. When he did, his face was tight again.

"He'll call you tomorrow? What? Are you guys...buddies now?"

Shaking my head, knowing I had messed up once again, I trailed my hand down his chest. His stomach tightened as my fingers drifted over his abs, but his face showed nothing but irritation. "Yes, we are...and I'm sorry I didn't tell you he was here." I shrugged. "I didn't know how you'd react."

Bringing his hands to his hips, his jaw tightened. "You didn't know how I'd react, or how you'd react?"

His finger came out to touch my chest. "Maybe you thought you'd start back up again." He leaned into me, his face furious again, and his lips so close it was tantalizing. "Maybe you were hoping for it to start back up again?"

I tried to push him back from me, but only ended up pushing myself down onto the couch. Kellan stood before me, seething in anger as he stared down at me. Even though I hated the situation as I looked up at him, he'd been gone for so long that I was momentarily blown away by how attractive he was, especially when he was angry.

Licking my lips, I murmured, "Nothing happened, Kellan, and I didn't want anything to happen. Denny and I are just friends...I promise."

He studied my reaction, then leaned down and pulled me back to my feet. Every part of my body pressed against him when I was standing again. After so many months apart, it made me ache to touch him again, to be with him, to think about making love to him. I knew that it was a weird thing to feel when he was so angry at me, but I couldn't help feeling it. His hand firmly holding my backside didn't help either. I was nearly panting at him as he stared down at me.

"Don't lie to me, Kiera," he slowly enunciated, his lips coming down to hover right in front of mine.

My heart racing, I shook my head. "I'm not, Kellan...I swear. I never touched him like that. I gave him a hug because he's sad his girlfriend is stuck back in Australia, but there's never been more than friendship between us while you've been gone...I promise."

I leaned towards him while I spoke, my body unconsciously pressing into his. My hands drifted to his chest and I could feel his heart racing too. He lowered his head to mine. "Kiera...don't, don't lie to me...please."

I groaned as his other hand shifted to my waist, his fingers on my bottom squeezing. "I'm not, Kellan..." My fingers heading up to thread in his hair, I whimpered into his parted lips. "Please...believe me..."

His lips parted more as he breathed on me. His hand slowly slid up my chest and he closed his eyes and groaned when his palm ran over my breast. I hissed in a breath, clutching him tight. "Kellan, please…take me…"

He groaned, crashing his lips the short distance down to mine. I moaned between our mouths as his tongue slid into mine, possessively claiming me. I loved it and tightened my fingers in his hair. His hands shifted to grab my thighs, lifting me up to carry me. I clenched my legs around his waist. Our breaths frantic, our mouths furious, he turned us around and started walking us to my room.

I couldn't have cared less about anything but feeling more of that hardness pressed against my abdomen. I tried to rub against it while we walked, and Kellan whimpered, leaning against the wall as he stumbled in his step. "God, I want you so bad…"

I mumbled something back that was along the same lines, then found his mouth again. I'd missed his mouth for weeks, I couldn't miss another second.

He set me down and slammed my bedroom door in almost one movement. Then our frantic kissing shifted to frantic stripping. I ripped his jacket off, he ripped my shirt off. My bra was practically torn in half as he jerked it off of me, his mouth instantly suckling. It sent a jolt straight through me and I cried out, fiddling with my pants. Pausing, he jerked those off, then worked on the rest of his clothes.

I was drenched with need by the time he was pushing me onto the bed. Our mouths still attacking each other, he moved over the top of me. Breathing heavy, he paused his body against my entrance. Writhing beneath him, I cried out for him to do it, for him to take me. Tightening his jaw, he plunged into me, taking me hard, like he really did want to claim me.

Pushing hard and fast against each other, we were both climaxing in no time. Legs clamped tight against him, I shook as the explosion hit me. He shook as his body poured into mine. Slightly sweaty, we rode out the intensity, moaning after each level passed through us.

When it was over, he sagged against me. I panted, my hand covering my eyes as I recovered. Slowly pulling out, he shifted to my side. "I'm sorry, that's not how I wanted our first time after so long to be…"

I twisted to look at him as he moved to his back and stared at the ceiling. After a long moment of silence, I asked, "Do you believe me? About Denny?"

He sniffed and didn't look at me. But then sighing, he finally looked down and met my eye. "Yeah, I believe you." He didn't look happy at believing me, but at least he believed me. I nodded, then leaned over to kiss him.

We lightly kissed and when I broke away, I whispered, "I'm glad you're here. I've missed you…"

He smiled, warmth in it for the first time since his surprise appearance. "I've missed you, too…if you couldn't tell." He laughed a little and indicated his naked body with his hand.

I bit my lip as I examined the expanse of flesh before me, then gave him another quick kiss. I'm gonna brush my teeth and get ready for bed. I'll be right back." I sat up, then looked back at him. "You won't leave, right?"

He shook his head. "I'll be here, Kiera."

I smiled, quickly stood and rummaged through my drawer to pull on pajamas, then dashed out of the room. I felt Kellan's eyes on me as I left. Feeling dazed, nervous, euphoric and guilty, I hurried to finish up in the bathroom.

After brushing my teeth, I leaned against the counter and took a long, calming breath. That was too close to being something horrible. And even though Kellan had said he was fine with it, that he believed me, he didn't really seem that way. He seemed…hurt. And I swore I would never hurt him again. That promise had been one of my New Year's resolutions.

But I had hurt him. By not telling him the truth from the beginning, by concealing a fact that I knew would bother him, I'd hurt him again. And just when I was starting to believe I didn't suck.

Closing my eyes, I pushed out the look on his face when he'd caught me. He'd been so mad… And even though he'd said he was surprised, he hadn't really looked surprised. He'd looked resigned, like he knew I'd eventually cheat on him.

My eyes popped back open when I heard a door slam. My head snapped around when I registered that it was my bedroom door being viciously shut. Throwing open the bathroom door, I stepped out into the hall to see Kellan's back walking…no, storming away from me.

"Kellan? What are you doing?"

He ignored me. The only reaction he gave that he even heard me was his hands at his sides squeezing into fists. Completely dressed again, he headed to my book bag and started rummaging inside it. Pulling his hand out, I saw the flash of his car keys in them. Shoving the keys in his jacket pocket, he started heading for the front door. He was leaving? The very thought got my feet moving and I scampered down the hallway.

I managed to get to the door first, standing in front of it so he couldn't escape me, not without an explanation. "Are you leaving?"

He stood in front of me, staring right through me as his jaw tightened. I think if I had been anyone else, he'd have grabbed me and thrown me to the floor, physically removing me from his path. His eyes were narrow, his breath heavy. He was pissed…again.

Leaning back into the door, I shook my head at his complete lack of a response to my question. "Why? Because of Denny? I already told you nothing--"

His eyes snapped up to mine, cutting me off as effectively as shouting. In a tight, cold voice, he sneered, "Nothing? You must think I'm an idiot." Narrowing his eyes even more, he shook his head. "I may not be as 'brilliant' as Denny, but I'm not stupid, Kiera."

He put his hand on my arm and harshly tugged me. "Now, get out of my way!"

I resisted his pull and shook my head again. "Not until you talk to me. Why are you so pissed?"

His mouth dropped open and he took a step back. "Are you fucking kidding me?" Frustrated, he took another step back, bringing his hands up to run them through his hair.

Feeling confident that maybe he would yell at me instead of just making a run for it, I slightly moved away from the door. "Okay, I should have told you about Denny, I know that, but we didn't do anything!"

Kellan closed his eyes, his body shaking a little as pure anger flooded through him. Keeping them rigidly squeezed tight, he slowly said, "I need to get away from you. Please move, so I don't do something really stupid."

Then *I* did something really stupid. I grabbed his face, making him look at me. Touching him forced him over what slim edge he was holding on his control. He knocked my hands away and pushed my shoulders back, until I bumped into the door. Seething, he attempted to dial down his temper as he stared at me.

Ignoring that his fingers were digging into my arms, I shook my head. "No, talk to me!"

Clamping his jaw shut, he shook his head and took a step back. That brought my temper to the surface. He was hiding something from me. He was keeping secrets from me. How dare he get mad at me for not mentioning Denny, when he was outright lying to me! At least my secret didn't involve cheating. Kellan's, I was sure, did.

Anger bursting to life in my chest, I shoved his body away from me. "You son of a bitch! No, you don't get to run away from me. You're always trying to run away from me!" I shoved his chest again and he took a step back. "But not this time. This time...you will talk to me! We talk things out, remember?"

He batted my hands away and successfully grabbed the doorknob behind me. Twisting it, he managed to partly open it. With my shoulder, I body slammed the door closed. Glaring at me, he left his hand on the knob. "I've got nothing to say to you. Get out of my way!"

Anger and hurt mixed in my heart, turning into tears in my eyes, clouding my vision. I sniffed them back, refusing to cry. "Nothing to say? After everything you've done to me?"

His eyes widened in disbelief. God, he was such a good actor. "Me? What I've done to you?" His face hardening back up, he stepped into my body. "You're fucking your ex and I'm the bad guy? Is that how you want to play this, Kiera?"

I shoved him away from me, hard. His hand dislodged from the doorknob and I moved to stand in front of it. My own hands clenched into fists now, I shook my head. "I...am...not...sleeping with Denny! And yes, you--"

Just as I was about to accuse him of everything I feared, he reached down and pulled me away from the door. Arms looped around my waist, he twisted his body and plopped me down on the other side of him. Once free of me, he opened the door again.

Seeing that he really was going to leave, I grabbed his arm with both of mine and tugged with everything I had. His head snapped back to mine, his eyes enraged.

"Let me go, Kiera. I'm done. I don't want to be here anymore."

Feeling those tears heavier than before, moments from falling, I snapped, "You weren't done with me ten minutes ago, when you were screwing my brains out!"

Pain flashed over his face and his own eyes moistened. "That…was a mistake."

I swallowed repeatedly, not believing this was really happening. "You said you believed me," I whispered.

Sniffing, he shook his head. "And you said you wouldn't lie to me. Goodbye, Kiera."

I was so startled at hearing him say those words, I dropped his arm. The tears I couldn't hold back anymore splashing on my cheeks, I whispered, "You said there weren't any goodbyes between us…"

Closing his eyes, he dropped his head. When he lifted it back up, a tear rolled down his cheek. "I said a lot of things that weren't true…"

Ice twisting my stomach, making my breathing shallow, I heard myself asking a question that I didn't give my body permission to ask. "Are you breaking up with me?"

His glistening eyes searched my face. Another tear rolled down his skin and I wanted to wipe it away. I wanted to hold his head to me and tell him that he didn't have to be angry, that nothing happened with Denny, that I'd been faithful to him…that I loved him, more than anything. I couldn't, though. I couldn't move.

His eyes drifted down my body then snapped back up to mine. He inhaled deep, then whispered, "Yes, I am."

I heard the sob escape me, even though I didn't give myself permission for that, either. Kellan immediately turned from my grief and disappeared through the front door. As wracking sobs went through me, I stood, frozen in place. Then I heard the roar of his car starting in the distance, and I sank to my knees, burying my face in my hands.

That didn't just happen, did it? He didn't just come home unexpectedly, make love to me, then dump me…did he? As the sound of his car grew fainter and fainter, the sounds of my sobs grew louder and louder. Oh God…yes, that did just happen.

I lost him…I finally lost him.

Chapter 23 – Nothing to Lose

I'm not sure how long I stayed on that floor, contemplating the drastic shift my life had just taken. Before this tour had started, I was sure that Kellan and I were soul mates, destined to be together forever. While I feared that he'd finally wake up and realize that he could do so much better than me, I also clung to the belief that he'd never stray, because I was the first person he'd ever let into his heart. I believed that sealed us, cemented us together. But maybe, all it did was brand his body. Maybe my name tattooed across his chest was enough, a symbolic representation of how I'd opened him, freed him to love himself…and others.

And now that we were over, I was sure he would love again. I was sure that he'd get back on the road, banging groupies left and right until he got over his heartbreak, and then he'd find her. She'd be sweet, maybe shy, and she'd have complete faith in him. Because their relationship didn't start like ours did.

We'd started out with a betrayal. We both watched each other lie to a loved one. We both watched each other sleep with other people, all the while being in love with one another. Desperately in love. Watching that sort of betrayal, being a part of it…soured you.

We both knew what we were capable of. Maybe we had doomed ourselves from the very beginning. Maybe I was the one that did it. When Denny came back from Tucson, I should have told him what had happened while he was away. It would have ended us, but we were already over. It would have been a clean break, an honest break. Maybe then, Kellan and I would've had a chance.

Staring at my bedroom ceiling, sleep impossible, I clutched my cell phone, waiting for Kellan to call me and tell me that he didn't mean it, that he didn't break up with me. He didn't call though, and I knew that he'd soon be rejoining his band…and I'd never see him again.

Biting my lip, I debated if I should break down and call him. What would I say? What could I say? I could only plead my innocence, but Kellan didn't seem to believe me. He had for a brief moment, but then…whatever faith he'd had in me vanished. And I really wasn't sure why.

Running my hands back through my hair, I considered calling Anna and asking her to come home. She was staying at a friend's house, finally feeling happy enough to rejoin her social circle. I didn't really want to drag her back down with my depression. Maybe I could call Jenny?

Just as I was considering punching in her numbers, my phone chirped with a text message notice. Hoping against hope that Kellan was talking to me, I scanned the screen.

I sighed. It was from Denny, not Kellan. Biting my lip, I opened the message. 'Just checking on you…everything okay?'

Not sure if anything would be okay again, I texted back, 'No…Kellan broke up with me.'

At least, I think that's what I wrote. I couldn't see past the tears to be sure. By Denny's answer, it must have been.

'I'll be there in five.'

I wanted to object, to tell him that he didn't have to give up a night's sleep for me, since he did have to go to work in a few hours. But I didn't respond, because I really didn't want to be alone.

Sniffling into my pillow, I waited for the hole in my heart to stop stabbing me with pain. I waited to not feel like my life was over. That's all I felt, though...that everything was over. Every happiness I was ever going to have in my life, I'd already had. Every joy, I'd already felt. I thought of every time Kellan and I had spent together. If I had known that it would end so abruptly, maybe I would have cherished each moment a little more.

But then I realized...I had. I'd always cataloged every second with him. Memorized every feature about him, every word he said, every place he touched. I'd known. Some scared, insecure part of me had known that we wouldn't make it...so I'd savored my time with him. My sobs started back up.

My bedroom door cracked open a while later and a soft sigh met my ear. I sat up on an elbow as Denny stood in my door frame. In my grief, I must've forgotten to lock the front door after Kellan left. Then again, even if I was thinking straight, I don't think I could have locked the door behind him. I could never shut Kellan out like that.

Denny looked tired as he watched me, his dark eyes sympathetic. Smiling softly, he sat on the edge of my bed, the bed Kellan and I had just made love in. "I'm so sorry, Kiera...I really am."

I nodded and threw my arms around Denny. He sighed into my hair as he rubbed my back. As I held him close, I waited to feel...something...for him. I didn't, though. Even in my grief, even knowing Kellan and I were over, I felt nothing for him, just an overwhelming need for his friendship.

Relieved that I felt that way, I squeezed him tighter. "He's gone, Denny. He said he was done. He said goodbye...and he meant it."

Denny sighed again, returning my firm hug. "Is this because of me...or because of what Kellan's been hiding from you?"

I blinked and pulled back to look at him. Denny shrugged. "Maybe he feels guilty for what he's done. Maybe he wanted an out...and you gave him one?"

I sniffled and wiped my face off on a blanket. "I don't know...he won't talk to me." Anger crept into me at the thought that maybe all of that argument was more about Kellan's guilt over his whore, and not at all about him catching Denny and I together.

Tightening my jaw, I spat out, "He told me that he believed me about you and I being just friends. He had sex with me. Then he dumped me! Who does that?"

I flushed over explaining what had happened with Kellan so bluntly to Denny, but he only sighed and shook his head. "I don't know, Kiera...I'm sorry."

As Denny's eyes flashed over my face, concerned, I saw the same friendship that I felt for him reflected back at me. That was all there was between us on his end, too. Abby had his heart, and she would probably never do to him what Kellan just did to me. And why did he do it? If Kellan didn't trust me, if he didn't believe me, why didn't he just break up with me? Why have sex with me first? One final romp? God, that…pissed me off.

Pushing back from Denny, I scrunched my brows. "Can you do me a huge favor?"

He nodded, his expression confused but eager to help. "Yeah, of course, anything."

Unraveling myself from my blankets, I stood. "I need a ride, and Anna has the car."

Denny tentatively stood, eyeing me warily as I threw a sweatshirt over the tank top of my pajamas. "Um, a ride where, Kiera?" His accent slid over my name as his question came out slowly and cautiously.

Sliding my feet into some slip-on shoes, I twirled my hair up into a loose ponytail. "A ride to Kellan's."

Denny sighed, apparently fearing that was where I'd wanted to go. "Kiera, maybe you should just let this one go…?"

Standing straight, I glared at him. "I can't…let him go, Denny. I love him, and if he's going to leave me, then I want to know why. I'm going to find out the truth." Grabbing Denny's arm, I started pulling him out the door. "Even if I have to beat it out of him…" I muttered.

Denny sighed again.

He was silent on the drive over to Kellan's, probably wondering how to talk me out of this conversation I was about to have. I hoped I'd have the strength to have it, but really, I didn't have anything to lose. Kellan and I were over, what could he possibly say to me now that would hurt worse than that?

I just hoped he was home. He could have gone straight back to the airport, trying to catch an immediate flight back to…wherever his band was. I just prayed that he'd needed a minute to collect himself. Hopefully the end of our relationship was enough to give him pause, to need a moment alone.

Relief washed over me to see his car in the driveway when we pulled up. He was here. At least he was still here. Then my nerves crept up. He was here…and we'd have to have the talk we'd held off on for so long. It tightened my stomach and I immediately wanted to go home. Instead, I opened my door.

Denny opened his door too and I paused, shaking my head. "No, it will only make it worse if you come in." Sighing, I said, "Thank you for doing this…but you can go home now."

His dark brows bunched as he looked over my face. "Kiera, I don't think…"

I placed my hand on his arm. "I'll be fine, Denny, and you've done enough. More than enough." Smiling, I tilted my head at him. "Go home, get some sleep while you can…" Smiling wider, I added, "Or go call Abby and tell her how grateful you are to have her. I know she'll love to hear it." I laughed, feeling no humor.

Denny smiled and looked down. "Yeah, maybe I'll do that." Peeking back up at me, his eyes narrowed. "You call me…when this is over." He raised his eyebrow and waited until I responded.

I sighed, sadness washing over me. "Yeah…I will." Leaning over, I kissed his cheek. "Thank you, friend."

He smiled as I pushed open the door of his sporty rental. "Anytime…mate."

I grinned at the nickname he'd never used on me before, then stood and waited in front of the car. Waving as he backed away, I quietly thanked him again. I couldn't see his response through the glass, but I was sure he was shaking his head at me, wishing me well, but thinking I was crazy for coming here.

Turning back to Kellan's house, I started to agree with him. Maybe I was crazy for coming here, especially since Kellan was quite clear about the fact that things between us were no more, but I had to know. He knew what I'd been hiding…I had to know what he was hiding.

Exhaling shakily, I stepped up to his front door. Not wanting to use my key, since technically I shouldn't anymore, I quietly knocked on it. I didn't expect him to hear me, so I was preparing to knock even harder when the door cracked open.

Kellan's cool eyes stared at me through the crack, then he rolled them and shut the door in my face. Not expecting that, I blinked and stared at the heavy wood in my vision. Did he seriously just slam the door on me?

Irritation beating back my nerves, I opened the door. Surprisingly, it was unlocked. Kellan's back was the first thing I noticed—his back walking away from me again. After stepping in, I slammed the door behind me. He flinched and twisted to look at me.

Sighing, he ran a hand through his shaggy hair. "I'm not doing this, Kiera. I'm not having this conversation again…we're over."

He twisted around again and I grabbed his arm. "No, we're not, Kellan! Not until you tell me the truth."

He twisted to face me, his eyes dark with fury. "You first!"

I sighed, releasing his arm. Throwing my hands in the air, I sputtered, "I did! I told you the truth about Denny. Nothing happened! Goddamn it, why don't you believe that anymore? Or did you ever really believe me? Was that a lie just to have sex with me one last time?"

His face paled as his jaw dropped. "You think I knew that I was going to break up with you before I slept with you? You think I'd even touch you, if I knew what I know now!" His eyes flashed down my body again and I flushed, furious.

"And what the hell do you think you know!"

His face disgusted, he backed away from me. "You still can't be honest, can you?" Gritting his teeth, he lifted his chin defiantly. "I saw, Kiera. I saw the tests…the positive tests." His face darkening, he took a step towards me. "You shoved them in *my* drawer, with *my* clothes, just so I'd find them! Did you really think I'd stick around once I did?"

My jaw dropping, I took a step back. "What are you talking about?"

My nerves tingled as I started piecing together what he was so angry about. He didn't let me puzzle it out for long, though. His hands flinging to my body, he yelled, "I know you're fucking pregnant, Kiera, so stop acting like you're fucking innocent!"

I was speechless as I stared at him. I could clearly remember Anna, in her denial stage, shoving a paper bag full of positive pregnancy tests into my dresser drawer...Kellan's dresser drawer. He must have wanted to put on some clean clothes after our romp. He must have opened the drawer and seen them...and assumed they were mine.

And of course he would assume that. Why wouldn't he? They were in my room, in the drawer I'd set aside for him. God, did he really think I'd ever tell him something that serious in that way? How cold did he think I was?

I shook my head and his eyes sharpened dangerously. "Don't even try to deny it now. Not now, now that you know I know. Admit it, Kiera. Admit the truth...for once in your life." His face softened and I saw the sorrow in his eyes. He thought I was pregnant. He thought Denny got me pregnant while he was gone...

I shook my head again, stepping up to him. "Kellan, no, Denny and I didn't-_"

He cut me off, shoving me back from where I'd tried to touch him. "Don't, Kiera. Don't give me another half-truth. You lied about Denny being here!" I shook my head and he added, "No, Kiera, a lie of omission is still a lie!" He leaned into me. "You should know that better than anyone," he whispered.

I flushed and swallowed, wanting to assure him that I wasn't the one who was pregnant, but not knowing how to at this point. He wouldn't believe anything I said right now. Having no idea what to say, I found myself whispering, "I've only been with you..."

He curled his lips into a sneer. "Until today, we haven't had sex since December," his eyes rested on my stomach, "and I intimately know that you're not showing yet, so you're not four or five months along." His hate-filled eyes flashed up to mine. "I'm not stupid, Kiera...I know the kid isn't mine."

I swallowed and tried to tell him that I wasn't pregnant, but he didn't let me speak. Bringing his face right into mine, he seethed, "If you're still going to try denying that you slept with Denny, then go ahead, Kiera...tell me the only thing you can. Tell me you were raped." His eyes flashed, the anger in them powerful enough to make my knees start shaking. "I dare you," he added.

My jaw dropped at where he was taking the conversation. Anger surged through me and my hand came out to smack him. I was inches from his face when I stopped my hand. I couldn't blame him for saying that to me, thinking what he thought. It was his history coming around to bite me in the ass. His mom had done it to his dad, and his dad had hated Kellan for it, in utero.

S.C. Stephens

Kellan didn't even flinch from my near-strike. He only continued staring me down. I dropped my hand and Kellan smirked at me. Shaking his head, he quietly said, "You can leave now."

My eyes tearing up, I whispered, "You're so wrong…"

Turning away from me, he started walking into the living room. "Am I?" he tossed over his shoulder.

Balling my hands into fists, I started to follow him. "Yes, you are completely off on this one. I didn't sleep with Denny, I didn't sleep with anyone. I'm not the one who—"

His jacket, hanging on a hook near me, chirped, signaling a new text message. Remembering why I had really come here—to get the truth from him, the hypocrite—I made a beeline for his coat. His eyes widened as he realized what I was doing.

"Kiera, no!"

He moved towards me fast, but I was much faster. I had the phone retrieved and the message displayed before he got anywhere near me. Shaking my head, I read the text aloud to him. "Call me. I need to see you." My voice shook in my own sudden anger.

Kellan's face was pale as he looked at the phone and my eyes, like he was afraid of what I might do. His hand shaking, he extended it to me. "Please, give it back, Kiera."

Gripping it tighter, my body shaking as his secret started bubbling to the surface, I shook my head. "No, no I think I'll text the hussy back." I started to type in a message, but Kellan…flipped out.

Running to my side, he snatched the phone away and shoved my shoulder. He pushed me into the jacket hooks and a flash of pain went through me as I scraped against one. I winced and rubbed my arm. Kellan's eyes softened apologetically, but he clenched the phone to himself in relief.

Shaking my head, tears in my eyes, I snapped, "Who's the liar now, Kellan!"

He shook his head, his face still pale. "This is different. This isn't about you and me."

I put my hands on my hips, confused. "Then tell me the truth. What are you hiding?"

His eyes flashed to my body, hardening up again. "It doesn't concern you, and I don't have to tell you anything anymore."

Stubborn, angry tears leaking down my cheeks, I threw my hands in the air. "Fine, keep your fucking secrets, Kellan." He blinked at my seldom used swear, then gritted his teeth.

Knowing nothing good would happen if I stayed, I twisted back to the front door. He didn't stop me from opening it. The cool night air refreshing my face, I paused as I stared out into the empty night. Feeling just as empty inside, I tossed over my shoulder, "And just so you know, I'm not pregnant, asshole. Anna is. Griffin knocked her up in Boise and she's freaking out about it."

With those words, I stepped outside, slamming the door shut behind me.

I was halfway across the street, having no idea where I was going, since I didn't feel like going anywhere, when Kellan opened his front door. "Kiera, wait!" He yelled at me to stop, but I didn't. We were over. I didn't have to listen to him anymore...and I was pretty pissed off.

I was on the other side of the street when he finally caught up to me. Breathing heavier, he jerked my arm to make me stop. A slight wind whipped around the light lounge pants I was wearing, but I barely felt the chill. I had way too much adrenaline in me.

His gorgeous face looking like I'd just told him that pigs had started flying, he stared at me open-mouthed. "Anna? Anna's pregnant?"

I jerked my arm away from him, raising my chin. "Yes." My answer was crisp, as clipped as I could make the sound.

He flinched at my tone, then tenderly tried to put his hand on my arm. I pulled away, not letting him touch me. "Why didn't you tell me?" he whispered.

I sighed, feeling the tug of love in my soul as his sad eyes flicked over my face. I wanted to forgive him for everything, but I couldn't. I didn't trust him. "Anna made me promise not to say anything." Hanging my head, I added, "She's not sure if she's going...to keep it."

Kellan's body straightened in my vision. I peeked up at his face, the light wind ruffling his hair. His eyes were cautious. "She's not...she's not going to...?"

He swallowed, not finishing his question. I shook my head, understanding it. "No, she's going through with the pregnancy, she's just not sure about...adoption." I sighed again, hoping my sister didn't go that route. Even being half-Griffin, I wanted to know my niece or nephew. It wasn't my choice, though, and I'd support her, no matter what she decided.

Kellan let out an exhale. "Oh, good, I'd hate for..."

He trailed off and bit his lip and I watched his contemplative eyes. Kellan could have been an aborted baby, his mom had had reason enough. I supposed he had strong feelings on the subject. I wondered how he felt about adoption, since that might have been an easier childhood for him. Then I hardened my heart again. It didn't matter what he thought...not anymore.

Just as Kellan rolled his eyes and muttered, "Damn Griffin...I'm gonna kill him..." I twisted to keep walking down the street to nowhere.

Kellan didn't let me get five paces before grabbing my arm again. "Wait...please." I reluctantly looked back at him and he shrugged. "I'm sorry, Kiera...please don't walk away."

Pain and anger stinging my eyes, I removed his hand from mine. "You basically called me a whore and said you never wanted to see me again. Why shouldn't I walk away?"

Hanging his head, he shrugged. "I didn't know." He peeked up at me. "I thought... Seeing Denny here...and then...those tests..." He swallowed and closed his eyes. "I just thought...I thought what happened to my dad was happening to me. I thought you had another man's baby in you. I was just...angry. I've never felt that ill..." He opened his eyes and tilted his head. "I'm so sorry that I didn't believe you."

I nodded, understanding how he'd come to the conclusion he had. His face relaxed at seeing me acknowledge his apology. He started to wrap his arms around me, and I stiffened, pushing him back. He scrunched his brows together and I lifted my hand, showing him the ring encircling my finger.

"I kept my promise...I was faithful." I jerked my thumb back at the house, where his phone was safely tucked away. "Were you?"

His eyes looked back to the house, and he bit his lip. Looking back to me, his eyes latched onto the metal around my finger, then down to the matching ring on his hand. "Kiera...it's not what you think."

I grabbed his cheek, forcing him to look at me. "I don't know what to think, because you won't talk to me. What does that text mean?" I whispered.

His cheek was cool in the night breeze, but seemed even cooler as he stared at me with fear in his eyes. "I can't...I don't think I can..."

He stammered for more to say, and I shook my head, angrily. "You have to tell me now, Kellan, because this is tearing us apart." I pointed down the road, to the stop sign that indicated the end of his street. "Tell me now...or I keep walking, and we really do end this."

He shook his head, tears in his eyes. "Please, don't leave me."

Even though his face made me want to cave, even though I wanted nothing more than to throw my arms around him, kiss him, beg him to take me upstairs and make love to me again, but slowly this time, I forced myself to hold firm on my ultimatum. It was now or never.

I raised my eyebrows, waiting. He swallowed, then scrubbed his eyes. "Ugh, Goddamn it..." he muttered. Closing his eyes, he took a few deep breaths. When he opened them again, he seemed...resigned. "Okay, I'll tell you." He looked around the empty street. "But not here, all right...let's go back inside..."

I exhaled a shaky breath, resigned as well. Whatever this was between us was finally going to come out in the open...and I wasn't entirely thrilled about it. Kellan took my hand and led me back to his house. He kept his head down the entire way and I watched a shiver go through him. I figured it wasn't from the light breeze either.

Back inside, he indicated his lumpy couch as he gently shut the door. It was the first time in a while that a door closed quietly around us. As I sat down, he started pacing in front of me. It spiked my nerves, and I wanted him to sit down. He seemed to need the release of movement, though, so I kept silent.

Shifting back and forth, he nervously wiped his palms on his jeans. It was odd to see him this way; Kellan was rarely nervous. Glancing at me at every turn in his pacing, he still didn't speak. Thinking he wasn't going to be able to, I tried starting the conversation. "Who was that on the phone?"

He stopped and brought his fingers to the bridge of his nose. "Ugh, I can't...start there, Kiera."

I bit my lip, nodding and waiting for him to start where he could. Sighing, he stopped moving and stood in front of me. Running his hand down his face, his expression so worn I thought he might drop at any moment, he shook his head. "Back in December, a girl came up to me backstage."

I felt my stomach tighten as he paused. So it *was* about a girl? I wish I could say I was shocked...but I wasn't. Seeing my expression, Kellan slumped a little. "She told me..."

As Kellan stopped to swallow, a sudden burst of insight hit me. It was so obvious. I didn't know why I hadn't thought of it sooner. Dread and sadness filled me as I completely understood. "She told you that you have a child...right? Sometime in your life, you weren't safe...and now, somewhere out there, you've got a kid."

Tears filled my eyes as my vision of a future with Kellan irrevocably shifted. He'd never shut out a child, and I'd have to share a piece of him with another woman...forever. Sadness that I wasn't the one to have his firstborn nearly overwhelmed me, and a lone tear rolled down my cheek.

Seeing it, he squatted in front of me. Cupping my cheek, he shook his head. "No, Kiera...that's not it at all." Sighing, he rested his head against mine. "There isn't a miniature version of me out there anywhere, Kiera...okay?"

Swiping my fingers under my eyes, I scrunched my brows, even more lost than before. "Then what is it, Kellan? Because I really don't understand."

He sat back on his heels, his head down. "I know you don't. And I know it seems like I'm hiding an affair..." Looking up at me, he shrugged. "Do you really not see, knowing what you know about me, what might make me...lie to you?"

Pain flashed through me that he'd just openly admitted to lying. More tears running down my face, I shook my head. He exhaled, looking a little defeated that he'd have to tell me, since I couldn't guess it. Closing his eyes, he whispered, "She told me that she wanted me to meet...her father."

When he opened his eyes, they were moist. I blinked, surprised. "Father? That's...odd."

Kellan smiled sadly, shaking his head. "Yeah, well, she seems to think that...he might be my father, too."

He said it so quietly that it took me a moment to register the words. When I did, my mouth dropped open. "Your father, too? So she's your...?" I blinked, my mind still processing. "Wait, your father? Your biological father? Is he? Is she...your sister?"

"Yes, she showed me an old picture of him and even if the resemblance didn't make it painfully obvious...I'd seen the same picture before. Mom showed it to me once..." Kellan swallowed, his eyes brimming with tears as he held my gaze. "And I can't, Kiera, I just can't see him...I can't do it."

I was so floored I had nothing to say. I stared at him in complete shock. Every scenario that I'd ever dreamt up about Kellan's secret revolved around him keeping the truth from me because of guilt, because of a girl. I'd never once imagined that he was hiding things from me out of pain, because he couldn't deal with the situation.

I couldn't imagine anything more life-changing for Kellan than contact from the man who'd spawned him. Spawned him, then, abandoned him. He'd left Kellan to a fate that no child should have to endure. I couldn't imagine what Kellan was feeling right now—confused, hurt? Or possibly, he wasn't feeling anything yet. Maybe he was suffering a case of denial that rivaled my sister's.

Wondering if that was why he didn't just tell me from the beginning, I leaned over and cupped his cheeks. His eyes flashed between mine, like he was a wounded animal in a trap that he desperately wanted to run from.

"Why didn't you ever say anything to me?"

He immediately started shaking his head. "I know you. You'd want me to meet with him. You'd want me to have some…bonding family moment with him…and I…I can't, Kiera."

Sighing, I stroked his cheek with my thumb. "He's your family, Kellan…"

Kellan shot to his feet. "No, no, he's nothing to me!" Running his hands back through his hair, he started looking around his home, his parents' home. "He left me. He took off and abandoned me. He let me grow up with…*those*…people." His body started shaking, his jaw clenching. "He wanted nothing to do with me…so I want nothing to do with him…"

His voice cracked in his anger, and I stood. Stepping into his trembling body, I ran my hand up his chest, to his jaw. The strong muscles there were still clamped tight as Kellan looked anywhere but directly at me. "He didn't know what situation he was leaving you in. How could he? Maybe he thought he was doing you a favor by stepping away, by not permanently breaking up the family he'd already…damaged."

Kellan's eyes snapped down to mine. "A favor? My dad used to whip me with his belt when he got angry. He'd hit me so hard that I had to sleep on my stomach for days afterwards. And I learned early on that running away from him would only make it worse when he did catch me. So I had to stand there, like a dog, and let him beat me. How is that…a favor?"

Kellan's eyes watered as he told me a horror that he'd never divulged before. I swallowed the lump in my throat and shook my head. "He didn't know…maybe you should see him so you can tell him, so you can finally talk about this stuff with someone."

He brushed past me, shaking his head. "I don't need to talk about it, Kiera. I'm fine." He looked back at me as he resumed his pacing. "And I don't need to see him…ever." He raised his chin. "Besides, I do have family. I have one aunt who despises me as much as my mom did. But I don't care. I don't need them. I'm fine on my own."

Knowing Kellan hated being on his own, hated being alone, I shook my head and stepped in front of him, breaking his cycle of movement. "That's just it, you aren't on your own anymore. You have family members out there that want to get to know you." He started to look away from me and I ducked down to meet his eye. "You have a sister, Kellan...don't you want to know her?"

Sighing, he paused and looked over my shoulder. "Hailey told me I have a brother, too..."

I smiled at how his family was getting bigger and bigger. He'd been alone for so long, maybe this was a good thing, not the nightmare he seemed to think it was. "Hailey? Is that your sister?"

Kellan nodded, then looked back down at me. Shrugging, he said, "I gave her my cell number once she told me who she was, and we've kept in contact." He smiled a little, then a short laugh escaped him. "She's pretty funny. Pretty smart, too. We've been talking a lot lately...she's a good kid."

My eyes widened as a puzzle piece fell into place. "That's who Jenny saw you talking to when she was visiting Evan? Your sister, right?"

Bunching his brows at me, he shook his head. "Jenny? In Texas?" He looked away, puzzled, then looked back, an answer in his eyes. "Is that why you thought I was cheating on you? Because Jenny saw me laughing on the phone with someone else?"

I slowly nodded. Pointing to his jacket on the hooks by the front door, I frowned. "Plus all of the mysterious texts you wouldn't let me see. You have to admit that was kind of suspicious."

Hurt at how he'd tried to shut me out of his life crept into my voice, and sighing, Kellan cupped my cheeks. "I'm sorry...I never meant for any of this to hurt you. I just wasn't ready..." He hung his head and swallowed. "I wanted to tell you, so many times...but I couldn't make myself say the words."

Looking back up at me, he shrugged. "It was like, if I told you...it was real...and I wanted to pretend that it wasn't." He closed his eyes and shook his head. "I just wanted to ignore it...ignore him..." His voice hardening, it started to warble with emotion. "But Hailey gave him my number, and he texts me every day...every goddamn day..."

Opening his eyes, he dropped my cheeks and pinched the bridge of his nose. "Every day he sends me messages, and every day I ignore him." Sighing, he raised his head up to the ceiling. "And I'm getting so tired of it all...I just want him to leave me alone."

Leveling his head, he exhaled wearily. "I even thought about changing my number, so he wouldn't have it anymore, but...I wanted to still be able to talk to you. And I couldn't exactly tell you why I wanted to change it, without...telling you why I wanted to change it." He shrugged. "So I get painful texts everyday that I try to forget about."

Kellan sighed again, and I saw the weariness in his expression. The torment was getting to him. I supposed I could understand why he wanted to hide from his dad. Why, out of spite or hatred, he never wanted to see him, but I couldn't believe he'd let the torture chip away at him like this. As I stared at the weary man before me, I tried to picture the energetic man who'd begun this fateful tour. They were nearly two different people now.

He sniffed and scrubbed his eyes, clearly fighting against breaking down and I rubbed his shoulder. "This is killing you, Kellan, don't you see that?"

He gave me a wry glance, like he thought I was overreacting, but he didn't see the threadbare person that he'd become in just a matter of months. "No, it is. It's eating at you...I can see it now. Have you talked with anyone about this? The guys? Evan? Have you been dealing with this alone...all this time?"

Slumping, he headed over to sit on the couch. "Who would I tell, Kiera? Everyone thinks my dad died with my mom." Looking up at me, he shrugged. "You're the only one I've ever been able to tell about my dad...not being my real dad." He swallowed. "I just can't get the words out around other people." Tilting his head, he gave me sad eyes. "Just you..."

Sitting beside him, I put my hand on his knee. "But your real dad contacting you...? You had to keep that from me?"

He looked away. "I didn't want to, and I did try to tell you a couple of times..." He looked back. "It was just too hard...too fresh." Lowering his head, he whispered, "I'm sorry if I hurt you..."

Cradling his head to my body, I felt the tears escape my eyes. "It's okay...I get it." As he exhaled and wrapped his arms around me, I whispered, "Christmas Day...was that text really from Griffin?"

Kellan stiffened in my arms, then pulled back. His eyes glossy, he shook his head. "No...that was from him." Cupping my cheek, his deep blue eyes searched mine. "I'm so sorry I lied...I just didn't want you to ask...I wasn't ready."

I nodded, more tears sliding down my skin. "All those texts...?"

"Were from him, I promise." Leaning his head into mine, he gave me a soft kiss. "They were all from him. I'll let you look at them if you want, if you don't believe me, but that's all I've been hiding...I promise." He kissed me again. "I promise..."

Letting all of my fear and doubt melt away from me, I melded my lips to his. "I believe you," I whispered. And I did.

His fingers on my cheek wrapped around to my neck, drawing me into the kiss we were sharing. I'd been so sure that we'd never have this intimacy again, I savored the sweet taste of him, the intoxicating smell of him. But even as our mouths started shifting the conversation into a different one, a more physical one, I felt his body trembling with the residual torment he was feeling.

Separating from his touch for a second, I pulled back to search his face. Passion was there, as it always was when we were together, but pain, too. "You need to see him, Kellan. You need to put this chapter behind you, so you can move forward."

He shook his head, leaning in to kiss me, to distract himself with the only thing he really knew how to block pain with—sex. I forced myself to push him back, even though a part of me wanted to cave. "You need to," I reiterated.

His eyes narrowing, he clamped his mouth shut. Inhaling deeply, he shook his head again. "This is exactly why I didn't want to tell you." I started to object, to reason with him that talking with the man who'd created him, then abandoned him, would help Kellan heal, but he didn't let me get out two words of my speech.

Mouth set in a firm line, eyes hardened and resolute, he again shook his head. "No, you can save all of your logical reasons and philosophical viewpoints. I will never see that man. Got it?"

Then he stood up and walked away, shutting the door on the conversation so hard that I felt my head rattle. Kellan wasn't ready and I didn't think he ever would be.

Chapter 24 – Trying Again

I gave Kellan a few moments of peace to collect himself, and then I went searching for him. I found him in his room, sitting on his bed, staring at the wall. I didn't know what he was thinking, what he was feeling. His face was blank, expressionless, and I thought that maybe he was just trying to not feel anything.

Leaning against his door frame, I stared at him for long seconds. He didn't acknowledge my presence, just kept staring at the wall. Containing a sigh, I whispered, "Can I come in?"

He inhaled and looked over at me. Nodding, he twisted back to stare at the wall. Glancing at the spot he was staring at, I noticed something I hadn't before. There was a circular section of the wall where the plaster was smooth, not textured like the rest of the wall. It was fist-sized. I bit my lip, hating the thought of Kellan hurting himself by punching a hole in the wall. It hadn't happened while I lived here, so it must have been from before…maybe right after his parents died.

Sitting beside him on the bed, I laid my head on his shoulder. He didn't do anything at first, then he sighed and laid his head on mine.

"I'm sorry if that was harsh, Kiera. I'm just…don't push me on this one, okay?"

Knowing this was exactly why he'd kept this secret from me in the first place, I nodded on his shoulder. "All right, Kellan."

We stayed quietly resting against each other for several minutes. I listened to his even breath, so long absent from my ear. I placed my hand over his heart, just to feel the steady beat. Closing my eyes, I whispered, "How long do you have? Until you have to go back?" I knew he'd left abruptly, just to surprise me, and I also knew he was incredibly busy prepping the new album. I had to imagine that I didn't have very long with him.

He confirmed that with one long sigh. "I have a flight in the morning, well, in a few hours."

I felt the tears prick my eyes. It was almost crueler that he came back just to leave again. But not really. We'd needed this break. We'd needed these conversations. Clutching his shirt under my fingertips, I wished things were different. I wished he could stay here with me.

"I wish you didn't have to go…"

He lifted his head off mine and I peeked up at him. Shaking his head, he bunched his brows. "Do you still want to be with me?" he whispered, looking afraid of my answer.

Blinking, I pulled back to search his face. "Of course." My hand reached up to brush his cheek. "I'm in love with you. Of course, I still want to be with you."

He smiled and looked down. "I know I'm not the easiest person to love…I thought maybe you'd had enough…"

Was he joking? I watched his eyes, downcast, sullen, and realized he wasn't. He really didn't see anything of value in himself to love. And why would he, when the people he'd loved the most, and I truly believed he had loved his parents, despite their cruelties, were incapable of giving him an ounce of love in return? Sometimes family was the cruelest form of love there was, for no one could hurt you more than the people who created you.

Forcing his head up, making him look at me, I gave him a warm smile. "Loving you, Kellan, is so easy, it's effortless." His smile matched mine, then I frowned and sighed. "Trusting you...that's the hard part."

He sighed, his eyes dropping. "We messed up, didn't we?"

"What do you mean?"

Peeking back up at me, he shrugged. "How we got together, the lies, the betrayals...we doomed ourselves before we even started." He shook his head. "We love each other so much...and we don't trust each other at all."

Hearing fears that I often felt being spoken out loud by him made my eyes water and my stomach tighten. Was it even possible to stay together? Maybe we shouldn't. Love...wasn't always enough. And love without trust...was that even love? Maybe lust was all we had.

Imagining not being with him anymore, imagining ending things right here made me hyperventilate. We couldn't end...we just couldn't. We did love each other. It wasn't just lust. I loved him so much it nearly brought me to my knees.

I wrapped my arms around him as my breaths came in sharp pulls. "Don't leave me," I begged, when I found the air to speak.

Kellan wrapped his arms around me just as tight. Voice cracking, he murmured, "I won't...I'm yours, Kiera, for as long as you want me."

Pulling back, I cupped his face. "Forever, I want you forever."

Gazing at me, a tear finally fell down his cheek and over my fingers. "I want that too, Kiera."

I brought my lips to his, needing to feel the love behind our intense connection, not just the fire. It swept through me instantly, growing in my chest until it was nearly painful. Silently, our lips and the occasional sniffle the only sound, we undressed each other.

When he laid me back on his sheets, his eyes swept down the length of my body. The heat his gaze usually gave me wasn't there. I still wanted him, intensely, but what was burning through my body, through my soul, was the need to connect with him. To comfort him. To show him that someone in the world cared about him. I wanted to give myself to him in a way that left me completely bare and open. And I wanted him to do the same for me.

Cupping his cheek, I urged him on top of me. Our gazes locked as I wrapped my legs around him. When he slowly slid into me, we both opened our mouths, but neither one of us closed our eyes. He searched my face as we silently began to move together. I felt tears stinging as I whispered, "I love you, Kellan...only you."

His eyes watered and he briefly closed his eyes. Opening them he murmured, "And I only love you…I will only ever love you."

He lowered his head to kiss me, our bodies still moving slow and steady. When I felt the buildup of my love for him coming to an apex, I grabbed his hand and squeezed it tight. He squeezed me back just as hard. Slowing our pace instead of increasing it, I started to shake with the impending release.

Kellan grabbed my cheek, sucking in a breath as he quickly kissed me. "I love you. God, I love you so much…"

He let out a quick exhale, his body shuddering as he came. I squeezed him tight as the intensity washed through me. I babbled some incoherent phrase about loving him more than life itself, and cinched my body around him as the joy flooded every muscle, every nerve, every cell in my body.

Tingling with good feelings, we slumped against each other. Wordlessly, Kellan repositioned us and curled into my body. Kissing my hair, he whispered, "I promise I won't keep anything from you again."

I nodded and kissed him back, the tears re-stinging my eyes. "And I promise that I won't keep anything from you either."

He nodded and we clung to each other. We'd try again. It was all we could do.

I woke up to my favorite thing in the world, a steaming cup of coffee, practically under my nose. Kellan was squatting by my side of the bed, holding it out to me, a content smile on his face, and I reconsidered what my favorite thing in the world was. Smiling, I ignored the cup and reached out for him.

"Hey," I whispered, my lips lightly brushing his.

"Mornin'," he whispered back.

I giggled at the word I'd missed so much, then carefully grabbed the cup in his hand. "You are a Godsend," I murmured, taking a sip.

Chuckling, he ran a hand back through my hair. "You and coffee…"

I flushed as I pulled the cup away. Fighting back remnants of sleep, since I really hadn't gotten much the night before, I glanced at his clock. "What time is your flight?"

I looked back at him and he smiled wider. "I have to go soon." It was only then that I noticed that he was already wearing his jacket, and his hair was slightly damp around the edges from a recent shower. Wow, I guessed I had been exceptionally tired. Breaking up will do that to you.

I sat up, sloshing a bit of coffee over my mug. "Well, I'll get ready. I'll come with you."

Rescuing my cup from my frantic hands, Kellan set it on the nightstand and shook his head at me. "No, I want you to stay here and relax." I frowned at him and he smiled. "Every separation between us seems to be long and dramatic, like we're never going to see each other again." He ran the back of his knuckle over my cheek. "It's like we're…savoring every moment because we both think it might be the last."

I bit my lip and nodded; I'd had those same thoughts. Kellan grinned, seeing my agreement. "So, let's break out of that cycle." Inhaling deep, he sat up straighter. "Goodbye, sweetheart. I have to go to work."

Grinning at him, I shrugged. "See ya."

Laughing at me, he shook his head and leaned in for a kiss. "Keep the bed warm for me," he murmured against my mouth. I was giggling when he pulled away. "I'll call you when I land."

I nodded. As if on cue, his phone in his jacket chirped. I glanced at his pocket and raised an eyebrow. Kellan rolled his eyes and sighed. Pulling his phone out, he glanced at the number. "That would be my father with his morning message." He raised an eyebrow at me. "There will be an afternoon and an evening one, I'm sure."

He hit the end button without even reading it. I frowned. "Don't you even read them?"

Sniffling, he put his phone back in his pocket. "No. I never read them, and I never respond." Lowering his head, he glanced up at me. "That's why I freaked out when you were going to. I don't want him to be...encouraged." He looked up at me. "I want him to stop."

I bit my lip, hard, wanting to object but knowing that Kellan wasn't going to budge on the matter and he'd get mad if I started in on him again. I nodded, then a question slipped out before I could stop it. "What does your sister think about you ignoring him?"

Kellan sighed and moved to sit on the bed beside me. "She thinks I'm being stubborn. She doesn't understand why I'm hurting him by refusing to..." He stopped talking and pulled his phone back out. "She asks me to give him a chance, every time I talk to her."

"Wise girl," I muttered.

Kellan heard me and lifted an eyebrow. Not wanting to start an argument, I held out my hand for the phone. "Can I read it?" Kellan narrowed his eyes and I quickly added, "I won't respond," I shrugged, "but I feel like someone should at least read them."

Kellan pondered it for a moment, then slowly gave me his phone. I wanted to jump for joy at the level of trust he'd just shown me. Maybe there was hope for us yet. Not wanting to betray that trust, I held the phone in one hand, found my way to his inbox and opened the missed message. Then I held the phone in my palm, all of my text-writing digits away from the device.

I perused the messages Kellan had refused to read, and tears stung my eyes. 'Please, talk to me today. There's so much I need to tell you.'

Biting my lip, I flipped to another. 'I know you're angry, but please don't shut me out.'

And another. 'I can be a part of your life, if you let me. Please call me.'

I flipped to a few more and they were all similar—I need to talk to you, please call me, I want to explain—and even one, near the end of the saved messages on Kellan's phone, that read, 'I regret leaving. Let me make it up to you…son.'

I had to wipe away a tear at that one. It was the message dated Christmas morning. If Kellan had just let me read it…all these months of secrets and held-back truths wouldn't have happened. Things between Kellan and I wouldn't have been nearly as strained.

Seeing my reaction, Kellan whispered, "What…what did he say?"

Sighing, I shook my head and handed him the phone. He didn't look at it as he put it in his pocket. "He just wants a chance to explain. He wants to get to know you." I placed my hand on his cheek. "He regrets leaving you, Kellan."

Kellan's eyes misted, and he nodded. Swallowing a couple of times, he stood up. "I should get going."

Staring up at him, at the moody, gorgeous, soulful man that he was, I smiled and hoped he'd let his father in…one day. Appearing deep in thought, Kellan was halfway through the door when I called his name. He looked back at me sprawled on his bed, naked under the light sheet that was wrapped around my torso, and smiled contently.

"I just wanted to wish you luck on the end of your tour, and tell you…" I bit my lip and he smiled wider. Seeing the happiness, even under his current confusion, I giggled. "I'll be here when you get back." I motioned with my eyes to indicate his house.

His line of sight followed mine and he beamed at me. Taking a step back into the room, he asked, "You're moving back in with me?"

I nodded, giggling more as I wrapped my arms around my knees. I had sort of decided that the moment he left, but recent events…solidified the decision. He shook his head at me, then took off his jacket. I stared at him, confused, as he stripped his shirt off and then started unbuttoning his jeans.

"What are you doing? I thought you had to go?"

Grinning at me, he crawled over the edge of the bed, making me lie back as his body hovered over mine. "I've got five minutes."

His mouth was over mine and I giggled under his lips. "Five?" I asked breathily as his fingers started to explore me.

Kicking off his shoes, he muttered, "Okay, fifteen then." Shoving off his jeans, he quickly darted under the sheet with me. I giggled as his warm, hard body collided with mine. And as silent as we were last night, we made up for it this morning.

He ended up running nearly a half hour behind…but it was worth it.

I stayed in Kellan's bed for who knows how long after he left the house. I was stretched out, envisioning where I could put all of my stuff, when I heard Kellan's phone ringing downstairs. Remembering that my cell was back at home, I thought that maybe Kellan's flight had touched down already and he was trying to let me know that he was okay.

Wrapping his sheet around myself burrito-style, I dashed down to his kitchen. Hoping I made it in time, I breathlessly picked up the receiver. "Hello?" I panted.

"Kiera...you okay?"

A familiar accent warmed my heart, and I smiled. "Hey, Denny. Yeah, I'm good."

A long pause. "Are you sure?"

Remembering my goodbye kiss to Kellan, I sighed. "Yeah, I'm sure."

He laughed a little, and I figured he was probably shaking his head at me. Denny was probably thinking, once again, that he was glad his relationship wasn't so complicated. I sometimes wished mine wasn't either; the fiery heat in our relationship sometimes burned us both. But I wouldn't change the love Kellan and I had for each other for anything. I'd already had the solid, comfortable relationship, and it wasn't enough. Complicated or not, Kellan and I needed each other.

As Denny chuckled, I sighed and added, "Kellan and I had a chance to talk about everything last night...it was a good talk. We're...back together, with no more secrets."

"Good, I'm glad to hear it. And I'm a little surprised. I sort of felt like I was dropping you off in the middle of a war zone." He chuckled again, and I pictured him running his hand over his jaw. "I was pretty worried about you this morning, especially when you didn't answer my texts. When I realized you probably left your cell at home, I thought I'd try you here."

"Oh, yeah, I guess I kind of ran out of there last night..." I paused to bite my lip. "Hey, Denny, thank you so much for being there for me. It meant a lot. It means a lot to me that you still...care. After everything, you still care."

A soft sigh met my ear. "I'll always care about you, Kiera. We may not be together anymore but I'm still the one you can call when you're...lost...all right?"

I smiled, wrapping the phone cord around my finger. "Yeah...same here, Denny. You can always talk to me."

"I know." His voice, so warm and soothing, sounded completely stress free. He really was okay. We both were. Denny's voice switched to inquisitiveness as he asked, "Is Kellan there? Maybe I should talk to him, now that things are calmer."

I shook my head, sighing a little. "No, he left early this morning. He had to catch a flight right back."

Denny exhaled, sounding a little relieved. Maybe he didn't really think Kellan had calmed down, at least not when it came to him. He probably figured he would get yelled at again if he spoke to Kellan. Pretty brave of him to even call here. "Quick trip," he muttered.

I nodded. "Yeah, he's a busy guy." I smiled when I said it, thinking of all of the upcoming adventures in Kellan's life. Adventures that maybe we would share.

Hearing the contentment in my voice, Denny's accent thickened as he asked, "Are you guys really okay now? After just one talk?"

I paused, considering. "It will take more than one talk, but," I shrugged, "we are talking and we'll never stop. We both want this, and we're gonna fight for it."

Even though Denny couldn't see it, I set my jaw and lifted my chin at my hopeful declaration. Denny sounded impressed, and I imagined him smiling and shaking his head. "You have changed...you've grown." Quietly laughing, I knew he was giving me his trademark, goofy grin. "Maturity sounds good on you."

I pursed my lips, wishing he was here so I could smack him for his comment, then I laughed with him, thinking maybe I wasn't so mature after all. "Yeah, well, I should get going if I want to make it to class on time." I sighed dramatically, remembering that I had obligations and couldn't lounge in Kellan's bed all day, even if I really wanted to. "Some of us still need to work on graduating."

I grinned ear-to-ear that I was so close to being done with the pressures and stress of academics. That only left me the pressures of what I was going to do with the rest of my life...but, like every college graduate, I'd deal with that later.

Chuckling at my comment, Denny agreed with me and wished me luck.

We said goodbye to each other and I hung up the phone. After taking a long, hot shower, I dressed in some spare clothes that I kept at Kellan's place. Sticking my fingers into the pockets of my jeans, I felt something in the bottom of one. Shaking my head, I retrieved a tiny scrap of notebook paper. On it, in Kellan's surprisingly neat handwriting, was one last note.

Remember today, that I love you.

Smiling like an idiot, I shoved the memento back in my pocket, and finished getting ready for school.

So much had happened in the past few hours that doing something as mundane as a writing class felt sort of odd. My secret about Denny was out. Kellan's secret about his dad was out. I was going to try to trust him with the assortment of floozies that seemed to hover around him, and he was going to trust me with my friendship with Denny.

It was sort of...epic...for us, and a huge step in the right direction. Maybe it was too soon, but I felt good about our future. No, I felt great about it.

Skipping a little as I made my way to the door, I stopped and grabbed the Chevelle keys. Kellan had tossed them on the half-moon table that we often used as a catch-all for our car keys when we'd lived together, ages ago.

I locked up Kellan's home, started his car, and made my way back to my place to collect my schoolwork. Well, it was my place for now. I'd have to tell Anna that she now had a spare room for the baby. I wasn't sure if that would make her decision about keeping the baby any easier or not. She'd have more space, but she'd also be on her own. Sort of. I'd never let her be truly alone.

She was in the kitchen when I entered. Having mustered her bravery, she was again reading through the pregnancy book. I could only presume from the small smile on her face and a hand on her belly that she wasn't reading anything frightening.

I smiled at her. "Hey, sis."

She glanced up from her book, small tears in her eyes. "Hey, Kiera. Did you know that the baby is about the size of a grape, and she's already forming fingers and toes?"

Walking up to glance at the book she was reading, I contained a smile. "She?" I asked casually, catching the feminine pronoun.

Swishing her hand in the air, she raised an eyebrow at me. "Yeah, I'm having a girl." She shook her head. "There's just no way I'd put another Griffin on this earth."

I let my smile show through, amused that she thought she had any say on the matter. I did hope she was right though; a mini-Griffin was not a pleasant thought. The firmness of her statement also made me happy. She'd said *I'm having a girl.* She personalized the pregnancy in a way that she hadn't before. She was bonding with the baby growing in her belly. That was definitely a good thing.

Not saying anything that might sway her one way or the other, I grabbed my bag off of the dining room table. I felt my sister's eyes watching me, and I knew I had a sappy smile on my face. I hadn't felt this good about my relationship with Kellan in a long time.

Setting her book down, Anna crossed her arms over her chest...her engorged chest. "Are you just now getting home? Where were you last night?" She narrowed her eyes, like she was sure I was with Denny.

Smiling at whose arms I'd been wrapped in, I shrugged. "I stayed at Kellan's."

She blinked. "Oh...alone?"

Smiling wider, I shook my head. "No..."

I trailed off, remembering Kellan's fingers on my body, his lips on my neck. Anna took my satisfied expression to mean one thing—she smacked me upside the head. "Damn it, Kiera. You hooked up with Denny, didn't you?"

Rubbing my skull, I frowned and considered smacking her back. The baby in her belly was the only thing that stayed my hand. "No, I did not, thank you very much." As she frowned at me, her full lips forming a perfect pout, I rolled my eyes and clarified. "Kellan flew in last night to surprise me. I spent the night with him."

I flushed after saying it, our heated night fresh in my brain. Anna blinked again. "Oh...oh!" She gave me a hug. "Oh, I'm so relieved. I was going to kill you if you'd gotten yourself stuck in another love triangle." Rolling her eyes, she shook her head. "Especially if it was the same love triangle." Smirking, she added, "If you're gonna be an idiot...at least branch out."

That time I did smack her, just on the arm, though.

Thinking of Kellan, and everything we had discussed, I felt heat entering my cheeks. There was one part of last night that Anna wasn't going to like, one part that I sort of hadn't meant to tell Kellan, but I'd had to, to defend myself.

As I bit my lip, Anna scrunched her brow. "What?" she asked cautiously.

S.C. Stephens

"Don't be mad…"

She instantly got mad. Tossing her hands in the air, she screeched, "You told him! Kellan is Griffin's best friend, and you told him? Kiera!"

I stepped back from her harsh tone, then scrunched my own brows. "Kellan is Griffin's best friend? Really?" Kellan had always seemed…tolerant of his bassist, at best.

Anna dropped her head into her hands. "Goddamn it, Kiera, you promised."

Feeling bad, I put my hand on her shoulder. "I'm sorry, I had to."

She glared at me between her fingers. "You had to?"

Sighing, I removed my hand from her body. "Kellan found the bag of tests…" Remembering his face when he'd broken up with me, I frowned. "He thought I was pregnant…"

Anna immediately stopped her pissy attitude, her hands covering her mouth as she gasped. "Oh God, Kiera…I'm sorry. I didn't think…I'm so sorry." I smiled feebly at her and she touched my shoulder, her face now only showing concern. "Are you guys okay? Are you still…together?" she whispered.

Thinking of his grin when he'd said goodbye, I nodded. "Yeah, we…talked it out." Talked, accused, cried, yelled…made love.

Exhaling in relief, she smiled. "Oh good, I'd hate to think that I…" Her face hardened back up as she remembered her situation. "He won't say anything to Griffin, right? You told him not to, right?"

I tilted my head, trying to remember if I'd ever told Kellan, specifically, to not say anything to the soon-to-be dad. "Um, well, things were a little intense and I don't think I actually…"

She shoved my shoulder back. "Kiera?"

Frowning at her shifting moods, I shook my head. "I told him you were considering adoption, so I'm sure he won't mention anything to Griffin until you've decided."

Her mouth dropped open and a hand subconsciously rested on her belly. "You told him I was thinking of giving her up? Why would you tell him that?"

Interested by her reaction, I said, "He needed to know why I didn't tell him about the pregnancy right away." I shook my head. "There was too much tension between us and I couldn't lie. I'm sorry, I had to tell him the truth."

She nodded, then sat in a folding chair by the table. Tears immediately started filling her eyes. "So now Kellan thinks I'm awful, huh? Giving up my baby…"

She swallowed, choking back a sob and I squatted in front of her. Holding her hands, I shook my head. "No, no of course not. Kellan…understands." I wasn't sure if that was the case, but I couldn't say anything else to Anna, since she was on the verge of losing it.

She nodded a few times as tears started trickling from her eyes. Then, like a pendulum, her mood moved in the opposite direction. It happened so fast, I nearly got whiplash. Standing up, her face was instantly fiery. "You need to call Kellan and make him keep his mouth shut!"

Her wild movement made me lose balance and I toppled to the floor. "What?"

Rummaging through my bag, Anna found my phone and flung it at me. "Call him! Do whatever you have to do!" She indicated my body with her finger. "Do that heavy breathing and moaning thing that I hear through the walls all the time—whatever you have to do!" She pointed at me, adding, "But make sure he keeps his big mouth shut!"

My mouth dropped wide open. Oh, my God! She'd heard the phone sex? Jesus, I'd be so happy when I was out of here. I flicked open the phone and dialed Kellan's number. It rang a few times, then, "Hey, this is Kellan. I'm probably onstage or making out with my girl. Leave me a message and I'll get back to you... if I feel like it."

I smiled at hearing the message that I begged him repeatedly to change. "Hey, Kellan, it's me. Um, Anna's flipping out about you telling Griffin..." Anna glared at me and I sputtered out, "Just call me back, okay?"

Shutting the phone, I shook my head. "He's traveling back to the band. He's probably in the air, or just about to land somewhere."

She sighed grumpily and I stood up, wondering if I should try to comfort her or run from her. Figuring her mood couldn't possibly swing much further today, I thought I'd take a chance and tell her the good news. Grabbing my bag, since I did need to head out to school, I started backing away from her.

"I'll try him later today, all right?" Anna nodded, her arms re-crossing over her chest. Knowing it was now or never, I quickly added, "I should probably tell you, so you have lots of time to make arrangements, but...I'm moving back in with Kellan."

I waited just long enough to see her jaw drop, then I yanked on the door and quickly made my escape. I thought I heard cursing as I fled down the hall.

Kellan called me back just as I shut off his car in the school parking lot. Watching my schoolmates shuffle about, on their way to their respective classes, I couldn't help but wonder if their lives were as melodramatic as mine.

A light splattering of April rain hit my windshield, making circular shapes that coalesced into long streams. Flowers were in bloom along the berms that I could see from the solitude of my car, petals open in welcome to the moisture. When I'd first arrived in Seattle, I hated the drizzle, preferring warmth and dryness, but I had so many nice memories in the rain that I'd come to embrace it just as much as the locals.

The cell phone propped against my ear filled with Kellan's warm laugh. His sound, combined with the light ting of drops hitting the roof, brought an image of Kellan into my mind—wet, hair slicked around his eyes, drops trailing across his lips...

"Hey, I just landed. Miss me already?"

S.C. Stephens

My image of him insanely erotic, I laughed, huskily. "Always."

"You said your sister was freaking out?"

I sighed, running a hand through my hair. "Yeah, she's just afraid of Griffin finding out...before she's ready to tell him."

Kellan sighed as well. "I wouldn't...that's not my secret to share."

I smiled at his comment. It meant that he understood my reason for withholding the information from him. "Well, I think she will tell him, and I think she's going to keep it...or her, I should say, since Anna is convinced she's having a girl."

Kellan chuckled. "Let's hope so. I think a baby girl to dote on is just what Griffin needs."

"Would you want a baby girl one day?" I asked, then cringed. I hadn't meant to ask him about kids yet. One step at a time, Kiera.

He was quiet for a moment, then responded, "Yeah...a girl, or a boy, would be fine, but...yeah, I do want kids."

I giggled, softly. "Me, too," I whispered. A comfortable silence passed between us, and knowing I really had to go to class, I sighed. "I should go...are we good?"

Kellan gave me a soft laugh. "I didn't convince you of that before I left? Really? You...sounded convinced." I felt the heat burn my cheeks as echoes of my...conviction...reverberated in my head. Before I could answer, Kellan said, "Yeah, Kiera...I think we're better than we've ever been, actually."

Smiling, I asked, "Even with Denny being back in town?" I hated to bring it up, but I needed to. Kellan and I couldn't hide from the hard conversations anymore. And Denny didn't need to be a hard conversation.

Kellan sighed; the sound was full of contentment. "Yeah, even with Denny in town. I don't know, Kiera, but Denny just doesn't worry me anymore. Maybe...maybe I really do trust you."

I exhaled, feeling the weight sliding off of my shoulders. "Oh, I'm so glad to hear you say that, Kellan, because there really is nothing there. No one...no one compares to you, Kellan. No one even comes close."

He groaned. "God, you're making me wish we were back in my bed when you say stuff like that." I giggled and flushed with heat, the good kind this time. Chuckling, he added, "I feel the same way, Kiera. No one comes close to you in my eyes...no one."

I closed my eyes, warmed beyond all doubt by his words, by his heart. "I love you. I'll see you in a few weeks."

"Okay, I love you too."

Chapter 25 – No Doubts

Maybe it was the removal of the doubt in our relationship, but the next few weeks flew by. Before I knew it, it was the end of May and Kellan's tour was over. The boys all returned to Seattle for a celebratory weekend before they embarked on their L.A. adventure to record their album. I was pretty surprised when Kellan called to say he was coming home. When he'd first told me about the album, he made it sound as if he would be going straight there. I was even more surprised, and mortified, when he told me Justin and his band were coming up with them. Apparently the two groups had really hit it off on the road. Not too surprising. Kellan was easy to get along with, for guys and for girls.

It was a Thursday night and I was talking with Jenny and Kate at the counter when they all strolled in. I flinched when I heard the front doors bang open. My eyes immediately snapped over to them, and excitement flooded every part of me.

Griffin burst through the doors, just like he used to when the D-Bags were a fixture here. Seeing him standing like a king before his court, wasn't what spiked my heart, though. No, it was knowing who would walk in a few steps after the egomaniac.

As the noise in the bar abated, Griffin exclaimed, "Your master has returned…you may worship me now."

Guffaws rang through the bar and the buzz of chatter started up again as the crowd welcomed the returning rockers. Griffin was harshly shoved forward by Matt. Scowling at his cousin, Matt raised his hand in greeting to echoes of his name being shouted around the room. He then immediately proceeded towards their old table in a deliberate effort to escape the spotlight.

Griffin frowned at Matt, at least until he found a table of coeds to pester. Evan stepped through the swinging front doors with Kellan, the two of them smiling, mid-laugh. The crowd boisterously cheered once all four band members were in their midst again. Kellan glanced around the room, acknowledging them with a hand wave and a nod. Evan shook his head, like he still couldn't wrap his head around the whole thing. Then the gentle man spotted his girl.

The heavily tatted rocker with gauges in his ears and a new piercing through his eyebrow, melted when Jenny jumped into his arms. There were squeals, giggles and lots of laughter as the two of them reunited.

I was giggling too as I left Kate by the bar to flood my man with affection (before the other girls around beat me to it). He was striding my way, his grin as wide as mine. When we met up, he grabbed my cheeks and pulled my mouth to his. His scent hit me just seconds before his warm lips touched mine. He held me to him as his mouth moved in sync with mine, his tongue just slipping in to brush against me. My fingers reached up to tangle into his tousled mess, twisting into the thick, light brown strands.

As his hands threaded back though my hair, his body inching forward to press against the length of mine, I slowly recalled that we were in a very public place. I didn't stop kissing him, though. I even managed to ignore the catcalls and whistles as people watched us. It was only when Kellan's hands started drifting down my body to squeeze my bottom that I pulled away.

Smiling breathlessly, I raised an eyebrow in warning. Equally breathless, he shrugged, like he just couldn't help himself. Giggling, I gave him a soft, public-friendly kiss.

"You're here," I breathed.

He matched my gentle kiss. "There was nowhere else I wanted to be."

Knowing that he had so much to do in the next few weeks, preparing his band's very first album, I shook my head and smiled. Maybe seeing that our intimate moment was over, bar regulars started approaching Kellan, congratulating him on the band's success. He shook hands, smiled, and made small talk as if he'd never left.

Smiling to myself, I left him to it. Kellan was getting a bear hug from Sam when the front doors reopened. As I was standing directly in front of them as they started reopening, I hastily stepped back to avoid getting smacked. Seeing who had just entered the bar, I wanted to freeze in place or run and hide. Knowing that I was overreacting, and that people were just people, despite their celebrity status, I slapped on a smile and approached the second set of rock stars entering the bar.

"Hello, Justin. It's good to see you again." Scanning the five twenty-something guys standing before me, smiling as they looked around the bar, I asked, "Can I get you guys something to drink?"

Justin's pale eyes met mine, and he nodded. "Yeah, we'll take a pitcher of whatever you've got on tap. Thanks, Kiera." He tapped me on the shoulder as he walked by.

Immensely proud of myself for sounding more like an adult and less like an adolescent schoolgirl, I watched the two bands meet up. Kellan and Justin shook hands and sat near each other at the band's favorite table. The rest of the guys spread out near the table, talking to fans or to each other. Even with Justin's band there, it was so natural to see the D-Bags here, and yet unnatural at the same time, since they'd been away for so long. I loved having them back.

I repeated the order to Rita, who was staring at Kellan and Justin like they were both sitting at the table completely naked. Some things never change. As I waited for her to make the guy's drinks blind, since she wouldn't take her eyes off of the group, I felt someone approach me.

Grabbing my arm, Kate pulled me over to her. "Do you know who that is with Kellan, Kiera?"

Smiling at her overwhelmed face, I nodded. "Yeah, I've met him a few times...he's nice."

Her topaz eyes widened as far as they could go. Staring at the pitcher that Rita was slowly putting on my tray, she stammered, "You have to introduce me...seriously."

I nodded at the tray, indicating with my head for her to take it. "No problem, follow me."

I grabbed Kellan's bottle, since he preferred his beer bottled, while Kate followed along with the pitcher and glasses. With a confidence that surprised even myself, I led Kate back to the rockers and introduced her to the visiting band. She was as much of a nervous, babbling wreck as I'd been when I first met them. It made me smile as I sat on Kellan's lap, completely comfortable.

An hour or two later, everyone in the bar was content, and the laughter and conversations were flowing as freely as the drinks. Someone played some fast songs on the jukebox and a group of girls grabbed Justin and his band mates to dance with them. It didn't take Rita long to ditch her duties at the bar to join them for a song or two. The grinding that the over-tanned, over-bleached, middle-aged, married woman did with that rock star was horribly embarrassing. Kellan was right—some women really would do anything for attention.

Kellan and I were taking a moment to twirl around at the edge of the crowd when I felt a tap on my shoulder. Seeing Griffin standing there, I instantly felt a ball of ice in my stomach. He wasn't trying to cut in, was he?

Sniffing, a disgruntled Griffin looked around the bar. "Hey, where's your sister?"

Holding Kellan's hand, I bit my lip. Once Anna had learned that the guys were coming up for a few days before heading to Los Angeles, she freaked out. She was showing now, and she couldn't easily conceal the pregnancy from Griffin. And since she still hadn't told him, she didn't want to see him. She'd hopped a flight back home. Yeah, she'd rather tell our parents, than her boyfriend.

Kellan glanced down at me and raised an eyebrow. I knew he wanted Griffin to know, but we had both agreed that Anna had to tell him. To Griffin, I shrugged and said, "Sorry, she had to go back east for a few days, to see our parents."

Griffin frowned, then tucked his chin-length hair behind his ears. "Really? Now?" He shook his head, his light eyes confused. "I told her we were coming up this weekend. She couldn't wait?"

I sighed, hating that I couldn't tell him. "Sorry, family thing." Griffin rolled his eyes, seemingly disappointed that his f-buddy, as he referred to Anna, wasn't available. Hating that he sort of used my sister, even if she was completely willing, I muttered, "Well, I'm sure you could find someone else to...hang out with this weekend."

Griffin shrugged, still looking forlorn. "Yeah, sure...but Anna's the best, though. She knows just what I like." His sullen expression took in the clumps of girls around the bar. "These girls, they're all too...giddy. It can be annoying...sometimes."

Surprised that those words would ever cross Griffin's lips, I said words that I never, ever thought would cross mine. "You could hang out with Kellan and me?"

I instantly wanted to take the words back. Kellan snapped his head to me, equally surprised by my invitation. His brow furrowing, he minutely shook his head. I clearly heard the question he wasn't asking—*Why the hell would you invite Griffin into our weekend? Are you crazy?*

I bit my lip, thinking maybe I was. Griffin, though, scowled at Kellan. "Nah, no thanks." Lightly smacking Kellan in the chest, he muttered, "I'd rather be alone than hang out with this jack-off."

Kellan blinked, his gorgeous face looking genuinely perplexed. "What did I do to you?"

Griffin narrowed his eyes, his thin lips tightening. "Jersey...those two hot girls?"

I raised an eyebrow but didn't allow myself to overreact to the statement. Everything Griffin said had to be taken with a grain of salt. Besides, Kellan wouldn't do anything to hurt me. That, I finally believed.

Kellan bit his lip, looking like he was struggling to not laugh in Griffin's face. "Uh, Griff...I was doing you a favor."

"Save it, man." Griffin poked him in the chest. "You were just jealous 'cuz you were doing the monogamous thing. Whatever. You didn't need to cock-block me! And right when things were getting interesting!"

A small laugh escaped Kellan. "Griffin..."

Shaking his head, Griffin turned and walked away. To his back, Kellan laughed out, "I tried to tell you...those weren't girls, dude." Griffin raised a middle finger in the air and Kellan laughed harder. Shaking his head, he looked back at me. "Maybe I should have just let him figure it out for himself?"

Laughing at the idiot that was about to have a child with my idiot sister, I shook my head. Kellan gave me a warm smile, wrapping his arms back around my waist. "Monogamous thing?" I asked, tilting my head.

He smiled wider, resting his head against mine. "Yeah, see, I told you I was being good."

Giggling, I gave him a soft kiss. "I know you were." Sighing, I shook my head. "Who knew I'd ever find a conversation with Griffin comforting?"

Grinning crookedly in a way that made me wish my shift was over, Kellan murmured, "Life's little mysteries."

Threading my hand back through the perfect mess of hair, a style that only Kellan could successfully pull off, I sighed. I searched his face as his eyes searched mine. The rare shade of his deep blue eyes, the perfect arch of his brow, the slant of his nose, the seductive curve of his lips, the strong angle of his jaw, his height, the lean cut of his body—physically, he was the epitome of what the ideal man would look like. But his heart, his soul, his pain, his humor, his music...that's what ultimately made me ache for him.

I wanted to give him everything. I wanted to give him the world. I couldn't, though. I didn't have that kind of power. But there was one thing I could do...one thing that I could help him with. And I knew it was something he wanted, even if he fought against it.

I had done something this morning. Something that I knew he wasn't going to like. But I had to do it. And I also had to tell him that I did it, even if it made him really angry.

Clearing my throat, I glanced around the bar full of witnesses. Well, at least he couldn't kill me after I told him. "Um, Kellan, since we're doing the honesty-at-all-costs policy, I have something to confess."

He grinned at me, his hands around my waist tightening. "Rob a bank while I was gone?"

Smirking at him, I shook my head. "No."

He leaned in, raising an eyebrow. "A sex shop?"

Flushing, I looked away. "No, I didn't rob anyone." Laughing, I looked back at where he was still giving me a devilish smile, probably still envisioning me in a sex shop. My cheeks heating, I smacked his chest and spat out, "Stop picturing me...where you're picturing me."

Laughing, he kissed my cheek. "Okay, what is it?"

Feeling seriousness fall around me, I bit my lip. "Okay, it's going to make you mad, but hear me out before you start yelling."

The smile immediately fell from his face and he narrowed his eyes. "What did you do?" he asked cautiously.

Swallowing, I started tracing the letters of my name on his shirt. Following the tattooed lines hidden beneath the fabric, I subtly reminded him that he loved me...just in case he forgot in about three seconds. "I invited your dad and his family to my graduation party at Pete's."

Kellan instantly pushed me away from him, frowning. "You what? Kiera, I told you I didn't want any contact with him. Why would you do that?"

Sighing, I stepped back up to him. "Because you need them, Kellan."

He immediately started shaking his head, but I cut off his objection. "No, you don't believe that you do...but you do, Kellan." Putting my hand back on his chest, I shook my head. "I've heard you talk about your sister. You care about her. And your brother? You've never even met him...don't you want to?"

I raised my eyebrows and waited for a second. Almost imperceptibly, Kellan nodded and feeling victorious, I continued. "And your dad...how do you know what you'll feel towards him, if you never give him a chance?" Putting my other hand on his cheek, I stroked my thumb over the smooth skin. "You could be missing out on something really good...because you're scared."

He looked down. "Kiera..."

I lifted his head, making him look at me. "I saw you on Christmas morning, Kellan. You wanted that bond, that family bond...and you can have it. You just have to be brave." I smiled that me, the one most pervious to nerves, was telling him, the one who rarely seemed to be self-conscious, to be brave. Smiling wider, I added, "You are a smart, handsome, rock star with a girlfriend who adores you. You have nothing to fear...ever."

He grinned at hearing variants of his words being repeated back to him. Gazing at me with adoration, he shook his head. "When did you get so wise?"

Smirking, I shrugged. "I am a college graduate, you know."

Kellan smirked right back. "Not yet."

Laughing, relieved that he wasn't too angry, I slung my arms around his neck. "Close enough."

His face a picture of puzzlement, he asked, "How did you get my dad's number anyway?"

I gave him a blank look. "Are you kidding, that number's been burned into my brain since December."

Sheepishly, he grimaced and looked down. "Yeah, sorry about that."

Leaning up, I kissed him. "It's okay…I get it now."

Noticing bar patrons starting to check their empty glasses, I figured I'd probably had a long enough break and should get back to work. Grabbing Kellan's hand, I pulled him with me back to the bar. Since Rita was still dirty-dancing with Justin, maybe Kellan could be the bartender?

Joking around, I asked Kellan if he wouldn't mind taking over for Rita. His eyes lit up, as he immediately hopped up on the bar and scooted around to the other side. By the elated expression on his face you'd think I had just given him the keys to the kingdom as he stared at all of the bar supplies. I wondered if he knew how to make anything? Well, he had helped me study for this job, back when I first arrived, so he must have picked up a thing or two.

Grinning at the adorable image of Kellan tying a half-apron around his waist, I shook my head. He was going to get so many tips. It was a good thing we pooled all of them at the end of the night. As I started helping my thirsty customers, Pete came out of his office to investigate.

The weary senior looked over the bustling activity of the bar on a night that was usually quiet and smiled. Seeing his bartender on the floor with the rock stars, he frowned, then his silver head looked back at the bar. I knew Pete liked Kellan, since they'd had a working relationship for years, but I wasn't sure if he'd be okay with Kellan serving his customers. But Kellan was already attracting attention in his newfound position. A line was forming at the bar as Kellan smiled and flirted his way through the orders.

I smiled, impressed by him. There really wasn't much Kellan couldn't do well, and serving drinks was no exception. I could easily picture an alternate life for Kellan, one where he wasn't a near famous rock star. I could easily picture him here, working alongside me, serving drinks every night. It was an intriguing idea, but I knew that Kellan's heart lay with music. The path he was on was the right one for him.

I watched him flip a bottle into the air "Cocktail" style, then watched as he nearly missed catching it. He eventually juggled the bottle into submission, just preventing it from crashing to the floor. The girls screamed and clapped, and Kellan, always the showman, bowed dramatically.

Pete shook his head, but I saw a small smile on his face as he watched the bills being tucked into the register. I figured he was fine with Kellan doing just about whatever he wanted to after that.

Kellan met my eye, laughing a little at the attention he was receiving. I laughed at him, then blew him a kiss. I would place my order later...at his place...our place, since I had moved my stuff in last weekend.

Just as I was remembering Jenny, Kate and Cheyenne helping me carry box after box into Kellan's house—my sister only "supervising" since she'd suddenly embraced her condition, claiming she was supporting a life, so she couldn't manhandle cardboard—a familiar face walked into the bar.

I smiled widely at seeing Denny stroll in. He was a regular now, since he usually stopped in a couple of times a week for dinner. He'd been mysteriously absent this week though; I hadn't even received a phone call from him. As I noticed him holding hands with someone entering the bar a step behind him, I suddenly understood why he'd dropped off the face of the earth.

I waved at Denny and his girlfriend, Abby, who must have finally made it over from Australia. Denny slung his arm around her waist and beamed with pride. Happy beyond belief for him, I motioned to a free table in my section. Nodding at me, he led her that way.

Turning back to a trio of college girls at one of my tables, I handed them a second round of margaritas. Straightening, I quickly told them, "There you go. Enjoy, and let me know if you need anything else."

One of the girls had her eyes glued on Kellan as she sipped on her straw. "Can we get *him* to go?" she slurred as her friends at the table giggled.

I glanced over at Kellan, still behind the bar. He'd noticed Denny's entrance too and was staring at Denny while he filled a mug with ale. I couldn't read Kellan's expression, so I didn't know whether he was okay with my friendship with Denny or not. But Kellan could see Denny's companion too, and if he still had any qualms about the matter, seeing the blonde on Denny's arm should have squelched them.

Looking back to my customers, I shook my head. "Sorry, no...he belongs to me." They all stared at me, shocked, and I felt a flutter in my stomach that I had just confessed such a personal detail to complete strangers. I tended to deflect attention from myself, and now I had the table's complete attention. I felt the warmth of embarrassment as they stared at me, but my immediate surge of love for Kellan flattened it.

Smiling, I lifted my promise ring and flicked it with my thumb. "He's off the market."

They all stared at my ring, then over at Kellan. Finally, the drunken one slurred, "Well, damn..." She looked up at me and smiled. "Nice catch."

Rolling my eyes, I giggled. Yeah, Kellan was a nice catch. It wasn't always easy being with him, but, it was always worth it. I was very lucky. Excusing myself, I headed over to see him. He pulled his eyes from Denny as I moved closer to him.

Deliberately keeping my back towards Denny, just so Kellan would know what he should already know—that I was his and his alone—I leaned across the bar. With a crooked grin, Kellan leaned towards me. My eyes lingered on his deep red shirt, his glorious chest impossible to hide underneath the fabric. Lazily, I let my gaze wander up to his eyes, drinking him in just as eagerly as the college girls had slung back their margaritas.

His gaze was fond and peaceful when our eyes locked. Nodding his head over my shoulder, he told me, "I should go say hi. The last time we saw each other, I wasn't exactly...nice."

We both grimaced. Yeah, that was not the best reunion after such a long separation. But it could have been so much worse. If Kellan was a little angrier, if Denny had done a little more to provoke him, Denny could've ended up with the broken arm this time.

Looking back at Denny seated at a table with Abby, I nodded. "Yeah, I should talk to him, too. I haven't had a chance to meet Abby yet."

Denny glanced up at the bar and frowned. With a word to Abby he started to stand, like he wanted to come over and talk to us, too. I supposed there were a few things that we *all* needed to discuss. Abby glanced up at me, smiled briefly, then put her hand on Denny's arm. He looked over at her and sat back down.

I twisted back to Kellan, just as someone pinched his butt. He had been so preoccupied with Denny and Abby that he hadn't noticed Rita sidling up behind him. He started at the unexpected contact, and side-stepped away from her. Rita, still giddy from her illicit dancing with Justin, wrapped her arms around his waist.

"I knew I'd get you back behind this bar again, sweetheart," she purred, her voice coarse from way too many cigarettes.

I flushed at her reference to their one night stand, then surprisingly laughed. Kellan was trying to disengage himself from her, but every time he moved one hand away, she moved the other one right back. The frustration on his face made me giggle and he narrowed his eyes at my enjoyment over his predicament. When Rita laid her head on his chest and contently closed her eyes, Kellan sighed. I shook my head at him and gave him a, *Hey, buddy, you reap what you sow*, expression.

Noticing my look, he smiled. There was a time when another woman snuggling on him would have left me in a jealous tizzy. I guessed I finally trusted him, too. Gathering himself, Kellan firmly grabbed Rita's shoulders and shoved her back.

Her eyes flashed open at the unexpected movement and she stared at him with her mouth agape. Hunching down to look her in the eye, Kellan quietly said, "I know we had a thing once, but that was years ago and I've moved on, we've both moved on." His eyes flashed down to her wedding ring. "But I'm with Kiera now, and your constant flirting isn't appropriate. Neither is your gossiping about things we did together. I would appreciate it, if in the future, both of those things would stop...please."

Rita blinked at him as he released her shoulders. I blinked at him, astonished. Kellan had never told anyone to back off like that before. Not that I'd ever heard, anyway. She didn't say another word as he scooted around the bar to meet me on my side. Untying his apron, he handed it to a still-stunned Rita. "Thank you, Rita, it was fun."

I had no idea if Kellan meant filling in for her at the bar, or the one time they'd shared together, but his tone clearly implied that both things were over. Rita took the fabric from him, her face glum. I felt a little bad watching her, but this had been a long time coming. Rita had always harbored a desire to sleep with him again, and that was never going to happen. Not while he was with me. And I planned on him being with me for a long, long time.

Warmed that he'd stood up for our relationship, I grabbed his hand and started to lead him towards Denny. That was when we nearly collided. Denny, with Abby in hand, had finally decided to come up and talk to us too. We both laughed at each other as Denny and I stumbled, trying to avoid the impact. Recovering, Denny smiled and put his arm around Abby's waist. "Kiera, Kellan, this is my girlfriend, Abby."

As Abby extended her hand to me, I subtly checked her out. She was adorably cute, with full pouty lips and twin dimples when she smiled. With her long blonde hair and pale gray eyes, she was almost the opposite of me, appearance-wise. But we were similar in build and stature so I felt on equal footing as we shook hands.

"Hello, Kiera, it's nice to finally meet you."

Her accent was just as charming as Denny's. I instantly wondered if Denny and Abby found each other's accents endearing. Or maybe, since they sounded so alike, they didn't hear it at all. Seemed a shame if they didn't notice that marvelous inflection.

I watched her absorbing my features as carefully as I was absorbing hers. Her eyes took in my plain jeans and red Pete's shirt as I took in her cute tailored gray skirt and suit jacket. I couldn't help thinking that if our roles were reversed, I would be so wary and suspicious of her. Regardless of how much she trusted Denny, he'd been alone with his ex for months, an ex that he once considered marrying. That had to strain even the strongest relationship. It was one of the reasons why I never told Kellan that Denny was home. But Abby only gave me a warm, carefree smile. She completely trusted Denny. That made me trust her. If she had complete confidence in him being faithful, then she had to have complete faith in herself that she would never cheat on him, either.

"You too, Abby. Denny talks about you all the time." Denny flushed a little after my statement, and I grinned at him.

He could be such a sap, and after recovering from the shock that Abby's arrival would be delayed for a few more weeks, he had started opening up to me about her when we got together. And he gushed about her whenever he did. Denny had a point when he said that our disastrous breakup was a blessing in disguise—he was madly in love with the woman standing next to him, and I was immensely happy for him.

When Abby and I broke apart, Kellan extended his hand. "It's nice to meet you, Abby." Abby, surprisingly, didn't eye Kellan with the open appeal that most women blatantly did. Sure, her eyes flicked over his face, but that was about all the notice she took of his appearance. And with her, I had a feeling that she wasn't ignoring his looks out of respect for Denny or me. With her, I more felt that she just wasn't interested.

As she tentatively took Kellan's hand, she looked back at Denny. This must have been a weird moment for her, shaking hands with the man who came between her boyfriend and the ex-love of his life. I couldn't imagine what she was feeling, except perhaps grateful that she'd never hurt Denny like I did. I was grateful for that, too.

Denny nodded slightly, and Abby looked back at Kellan. "It's nice to meet you, too, Kellan. Denny says…good things about you."

Kellan's mouth dropped open in surprise as their hands separated. Bunching his brows, he shook his head at Denny. "You do? Why? I was an asshole to you…"

Kellan seemed genuinely bemused at why Denny gave him the time of day, let alone spoke well of him. Denny stared at the floor for a second, before looking back up at the person he was once very close to. "And I nearly killed you." Denny sighed, running a hand through his hair. "In the end…whose crime was greater?"

Kellan shook his head and looked away. Feeling a tension building, I put my hand on Kellan's stomach. He looked down on me before shifting his attention back to Denny. "I still took something that wasn't mine. Even if you feel guilty for the fight…you really shouldn't ever talk to me again."

Kellan's eyes drifted to his boots, unable to keep Denny's gaze. Guilt flooded me, and I lowered my head as well. Happy ending or not, Kellan and I were jerks.

Denny, surprisingly, started laughing. Kellan and I both looked up at him. Grinning, he squeezed Abby tight and looked between the two of us. "You should see the looks on your faces right now." His accent curled around the words as he gave us a goofy grin.

Kellan and I glanced at each other, equally perplexed, and Denny laughed a little more. Clapping Kellan's shoulder, he shook his head. "Look, I know your life was hard, and I realize that Kiera must have been a…salve…for you." He raised his eyebrows. "I get it. I didn't like it, but I get it."

Kellan gave him a small smile and Denny shifted his attention back to me. "And you…" He bit his lip and sighed. "I know I put my job first." I shook my head and Denny cut me off. "No, I did, Kiera." He pointed to the ground. "I was coming to Seattle, with or without you. I was going to Tucson, with or without you. And, I may have panicked and rushed back to Seattle when I thought I'd lost you, but…my head was still on my job…not you."

Swallowing, he shook his head. "And I'm so sorry for that. And I don't blame you anymore for falling for someone who gave you the attention you wanted, the attention you deserved."

I swallowed and nodded, slight tears in my eyes. A silence built up around our foursome. Finally, Abby was the one who broke it. "Oh, my God, will the three of you just hug already?"

We all looked over at her and grinned. Wiping my eyes, I stepped up to Denny, giving him a warm, friendly hug. He wrapped his arms around me, and we both muttered apologies. Kellan sighed, then circled his arms over the both of us.

Nestled in the safety of the two men who'd nearly torn me asunder, I felt a piece of myself healing. I felt the guilt slowly leaving. We were all fine. We had all survived. And surprisingly, we were all still friends.

As the three of us pulled apart, Kellan and I embraced. Smiling, he kissed my head. Abby cuddled with Denny and I smiled over at her, pleased that Denny had found someone as warm, caring, and trusting as she appeared to be.

Kellan pointed back at Denny and Abby's table being taken over by a group of boys that looked barely legal. "Someone nabbed your seats." Running a hand back through his hair, Kellan shrugged. "The band's table has a couple of spots open...if you guys want to join us?"

Denny and Abby glanced at each other for a second, then Denny nodded. "Yeah, sounds nice...mate."

Kellan smiled, gave me another kiss on the head, then clapped Denny's back. As they started walking back to where Matt and Evan were talking with each other, all smiles over being back home, I heard Kellan lean down and mutter, "Hey, sorry for being an ass a few weeks ago. That was a...misunderstanding."

Smiling up at him, Denny clapped his back. "Don't worry about it. I'm used to you being an ass."

Abby giggled as she clung to Denny's hand. Kellan shook his head, but eventually laughed. The sight of them bonding again brought tears to my eyes. I really hadn't thought they'd ever get their friendship back on track. It took a pretty big person to see past the pain and betrayal. But Denny...was a pretty big person.

Denny and Abby left an hour or so later. Arms entwined around each other, they were the picture of merriment. I smiled and waved as they disappeared out the doors to head back to the home that I had helped Denny prepare for her. I wondered if he had filled the house with flowers on the day of her arrival as he'd said he would. Being the sap he was, I figured he did.

Justin and Kellan's bands closed out the bar. In fact, Jenny and I practically forced most of the boys to leave. Justin, in particular, seemed happy to stay until morning. It was so typical of a guy his age that I instantly felt even more relaxed around him. He was just another drunk guy, like all the other drunk guys I'd ever known. And as Matt and Griffin had to physically help him into Griffin's van, I wondered why I had ever been nervous around him.

My own D-Bag was the last to leave. Sitting on the edge of the bar, Kellan chatted with the weary bar owner as I cleaned up the mess everyone had left behind. Clapping Kellan on the shoulder, Pete thanked him again for lining up the new band. And Rain's band was really starting to bring in the crowds—guys and girls alike. From what Cheyenne confessed to me one afternoon, her crush had now moved on to Poetic Bliss's drummer, Meadow. I was relieved that she was no longer crushing on me anymore, and also that she hadn't fallen for Tuesday. I'd never be able to keep a straight face during any conversations about her.

When I finished wiping the spills and refilling the salt shakers, I smacked Kellan's thigh and wished Pete a goodnight. Pete waved us off and grumbled something about me not letting Kellan tend bar anymore, since he technically didn't work here. By the way he said it, though, it was clear that he'd hire him instantly if Kellan showed interest.

Waving goodbye to Pete, Kellan ignored his comment and any implied offers of employment. He had a job, one that was about to explode on him. Holding my fingers tightly in his, Kellan hummed a song as he walked us to his car.

Loving the peace in his voice, the merriment in his eyes, I leaned into his side. His eyes brightened when we approached his "baby." As promised, I had taken good care of her. I used only the best gas when filling her up and even waxed her the other day, in preparation for Kellan's homecoming. The orange lot lights cast a glow over the car as it shined beneath them.

Running his hand over the polished black metal, Kellan gave me a boyish grin. "Thanks for not wrecking her."

Kissing his jaw, I murmured, "I know what she means to you...I was good to her." Releasing Kellan, I started walking around to the other side. "I only got her up over a hundred that one time."

Kellan's jaw dropped as his eyes flashed down to inspect the Chevelle more closely. Shaking my head at him, I got into the passenger's side. Kellan was frowning at me when he got into his preferred spot—behind the steering wheel. "Not funny," he muttered.

I grinned and leaned over to kiss him but he pulled back. As I frowned, he smiled. "Happy Birthday, Kiera."

I was about to correct him, tell him that it wasn't my birthday yet, when I realized that it was. It was just a few hours into it, but technically, it was now my birthday. "Thank you, you're the first one to say it."

Smirking, he leaned into me. "I know, I planned it that way."

His lips were on mine then, soft and teasing as he moved against me. His tongue slid along my lip and I shuddered, delighting in the sensation. Cupping my cheek, he angled his mouth to fully enclose me. My breath heavier, I parted my lips to let him in. I groaned when his tongue brushed against mine. It had been weeks since our last physical encounter. My body was burning for him to touch me.

Inhaling his wondrous aroma, I pulled back from his mouth. His lips parted, his eyes blazing, he stared at me intently, like he wanted to devour me. God...I wanted him to.

"Take me home, Kellan." Placing my hand on his thigh, I leaned over to breathe in his ear, "Take me to our home."

He groaned. Biting his lip, he closed his eyes for a second and stopped moving, stopped breathing. Pulling back, I tilted my head at him. "Kellan? Are...you okay?"

Peeking an eye open at me, he smiled around where he was still biting his lip; the grin was impossibly attractive. Nodding, he said, "Yeah, I just needed a minute."

Giggling, I leaned back in to kiss him.

He drove us back to his place faster than he'd ever driven us before. Kissing as we walked through our front door, he stripped off his jacket and blindly threw it towards the hook. I heard it land on the floor. He kicked the door closed with his boot, then grabbed the backs of my thighs and lifted me up. As his lips traveled up my neck, he murmured, "Hmmm, which room should we christen first?"

I giggled, dropping my head to the side so he could fully explore the sensitive skin. "We've never done much in the laundry room?"

He instantly started heading for the hallway that went past the kitchen and into the small space where his washer and dryer were. I squirmed and laughed, rubbing against him in the process. "I was joking! Bed, Kellan..." I cupped his cheeks and softly kissed him. "I want to explore you in a bed."

Giving me a look filled with love and wonder, he swung us around and started heading upstairs. I kissed his neck as we walked. He rubbed circles into my thighs with his thumbs. He set me down once we were before the three doors on the second floor of his house—two bedrooms, one bathroom. All three doors were wide open. A rarity, since the room I had shared with Denny was usually kept firmly shut. I'd cleaned it out, though, while Kellan was away.

Pulling on his arm, I decided to take a second to show him. He frowned at me, then followed. As we stepped into the doorway, I leaned back and let him look in. He smiled when he saw it. I'd finally removed Joey's furniture—the bed, dresser, nightstand—all of it. I figured that if Kellan's ex-roommate/ex-fling hadn't returned in nearly two years to collect it, she wasn't going to. It held too many awful memories, anyway. I wanted it gone, to cleanse our home.

What I filled it with wasn't what you'd expect in a second bedroom. There wasn't a bed, a wardrobe holding winter clothes, or a TV. There was, however, a bookcase crammed full of Kellan's notebooks, my old futon, folded into a couch, and Kellan's first guitar; it was now a nostalgic piece of art hanging from the wall. I had also added a small desk under the window framed by warm curtains. In the corner, a CD player rested on an old coffee table with Kellan's favorite discs scattered around it. It was the perfect place for him to relax and dream up new masterpieces for his band.

Shaking his head, Kellan murmured, "Is this for me?"

Placing my hands on his chest, I nodded. "Yeah, since you don't need to have a roommate anymore, I thought I would give you a better use for the spare room." Placing a kiss on his strong jaw, I added, "It's all for you, for your art."

He smiled peacefully at me and I frowned and jerked my thumb over my shoulder. "Except the closet. I needed somewhere to put my clothes." And I also hoped that I could one day tuck a playpen in there. If Anna decided to keep her baby, I wanted to be ready.

Laughing, Kellan squeezed me tight. "It's perfect, thank you."

Pulling away, he frowned at me. "Wait, it's your birthday. Shouldn't I be doing something for you?"

I smiled at his pout. "Well, we missed celebrating your birthday last month, so you can think of this as a belated birthday present." Biting my lip, I nodded over to the other bedroom door. "But there is one thing you can do for me." I started pulling him across the hall.

Grinning, he eyed my body up and down, making me tingle all over. "Yeah? And that would be...?"

Once he was inside our room, I closed the door behind him and pressed him up against it. His mouth dropped open as I melded my slight curves into his body. With our hips flush together, I could feel his response. Mentally picturing the way he would tease me, I ran my nose along his jaw. He swallowed and his hands clenched my hips, pulling me into his rigid ache.

Dropping his head back as I reached his chin, he gasped when I quickly leaned up and flicked my tongue along his upper lip. Breath heavier, he moaned my name. "Kiera..."

Squirming against his body, I trailed my mouth up his jaw. I had to stand on my tippy toes, to reach his ear. I quickly darted my tongue inside and he hissed in a sharp breath. I felt invincible in his arms, like I could do anything wrapped in the warmth of his love. Kellan had always lifted me up, encouraged me to feel like the person he saw when he looked at me. And sheltered in his arms, I was starting to feel that way.

Knowing it was something that would normally have me huddled in a corner, mortified, I whispered something to him that I finally felt confident enough to whisper. It implied how much I trusted him, how safe I felt with him, and even though it seemed dirty, it wasn't. It was beautiful and honest.

"I put some handcuffs under your pillow...if you want to use them on me."

His eyes were huge when I pulled away from him. He'd joked, he'd teased, but I don't think he'd ever thought I would actually concede. Honestly, I was surprised myself. But I...trusted him and I loved him. And I knew he would never hurt or debase me. He would only make me feel loved and comforted...and satisfied. Besides, it was one more thing I could cross off my bucket list.

My, how I'd grown since meeting Kellan.

Kellan's eyes softened as he understood just what I was offering him. Gently kissing me, he murmured, "I love you, Kiera. Happy Birthday." I nodded, eagerly finding his lips again.

Chapter 26 – New Beginnings

Kellan and the guys had to leave Monday morning for Los Angeles. We all met at Pete's for a proper send off. Lana, the record label rep, showed up in a sleek stretch limo to transport them to the airport. Griffin was over the moon as he opened the door and peeked inside. Smiling back at Kellan, he exclaimed, "They've got champagne in here, Kell!"

Kellan shook his head at Griffin and twisted to look at me. "I still can't believe he's gonna be a dad," he whispered, rolling his eyes.

"You and me both," I sighed.

Anna was still at my parents'. I called her and tried to convince her to come home early, to see Griffin off, but she refused. Then Dad seized the phone and started chastising me for not informing them the minute I'd discovered Anna was pregnant. I tried to tell him that I was bound to secrecy, but he didn't much care about sibling pacts, not when the health and well-being of his child was at stake. Once he got the lecture out of his system, Mom came on the line and they both spent over an hour cautioning me on the ramifications of following in my sister's footsteps.

I repeatedly told them that I was taking precautions, but that only made them push the virtues of abstinence until marriage. They even grudgingly accepted the idea of Kellan as my potential spouse. Since I was lounging in bed with Kellan when the conversation was taking place, it had all seemed kind of humorous and absurd to me. And I probably shouldn't have, but I chose that moment to break the news that I had moved back in with Kellan. I swear I could still hear the disappointed groans.

As Griffin hopped out of the limo, Matt and Evan took a casual peek inside. On cloud nine, Griffin sauntered up to Kellan, tossing an arm over his shoulder. "This is gonna rock, man. Can you believe it? Chicks, money, mansions...there's nothing we won't be able to get."

Frowning, Kellan raised an eyebrow at his bassist. "Making a record doesn't mean you're automatically going to hit it big, Griffin. We'll probably still be nobodies...just nobodies with a label hounding us to pay back the recording costs."

Griffin snorted and ran his hand back through his pale hair. "Nah, won't happen. We've got something none of those other guys got."

Morbidly curious, I asked, "And what's that?"

Giving me a sly grin, Griffin thumped Kellan on the chest. "Him."

Kellan shook his head and looked down as Griffin strolled off to smack his cousin on the back of the head. Leaning into Kellan's side, the warm, spring air clean and refreshing, I smiled up at him. "He's right." Closing my eyes, I muttered, "And I can't believe I just agreed with Griffin."

Kellan chuckled and I opened my eyes to find him gazing at me. "You're both ridiculous," he whispered, leaning in to kiss my cheek.

Holding Kellan tight, I watched Evan scoop Jenny into a huge hug. Matt wrapped his arms around Rachel in a reserved manner, but the love being exchanged in the smaller gesture was clear. Griffin looked around for someone to hug, but the only people here, besides Lana, who was already slipping back into the car as she waited for her talents to wrap things up, were already coupled. Griffin glumly looked around for a moment, then got into the car by himself. Again, I wished Anna was here for him. Oddly enough, they kind of worked together.

After the couples broke apart, I gave Matt a brief hug. He smiled and returned the hug, then someone grappled me from behind. I squealed in surprise as Evan lifted me up, nearly plopping me over his shoulder. Kellan laughed at his friend and turned to wrap his arms around Jenny as Evan set me down. The two longtime friends shared a few words that I couldn't hear, then hugged briefly. After that, Kellan gave Rachel a one-armed hug while Jenny patted Matt's back.

Then the boys waved and climbed into their limousine to chase their rising star. And, like Griffin, I was certain they'd catch it. Kellan was too talented and attractive. His fame was fated, and all I could do was hold his hand and tell him that he was worthy of it.

I had tears in my eyes as I watched the limousine pull away. But they weren't tears of worry or sadness this time. No, I was immensely proud of him. How many people got an opportunity like this and actually went for it? I had to believe that it was a small number of people that chose to reach for their dreams, regardless of how impossible they seemed.

And once Kellan was safely tucked away in a recording studio, laying down the tracks that would soon be searing the souls of fans across the globe, I turned my attentions back to my dreams, my goals. I was graduating in a few weeks from college, and I finally knew what I wanted to do with my life.

I wanted to write. I wanted to be an author, with my name on the cover of a story that I had created. I wanted it more than anything.

I discovered that all of the time I had spent writing my assignments had opened up something in me. I enjoyed the tranquil moments when I could let my thoughts pour out onto the page instead of keeping them bottled inside. After Kellan and I had had an honest discussion about how badly we'd messed up our relationship by starting it with a betrayal…I'd started writing about it. At first, I was just jotting down notes during coffee with Cheyenne or Jenny. But eventually, I became immersed in it.

I started reliving the past as I wrote. It was like watching a movie in my head, one that I wished I could stop sometimes, as parts of it were exceedingly painful. But it was therapeutic, too. I didn't hold back any details either. It was an emotional, soul-bearing roller coaster ride of everything that had transpired between Kellan and I. Our slow build up, our passionate releases, our attempt to suppress what we felt for each other behind a wall of friendship, our heated fights—I wrote it all down.

I figured I would come out of the story as the villain, hated, reviled for betraying a man as good as Denny. Maybe it could've been different, if Denny had been the cold, abusive or jealous type, but he wasn't. Denny was a great man, so I knew that I'd come out as the heartless one. But that was okay. I had done it, and I had to live with the consequences. Besides, that wasn't who I was anymore. Being with Kellan had matured me. I'd learned a great deal about myself, and the person I wanted to become. I was still struggling through my insecurities, and knew I might have to push myself to overcome them, but I *would* get there.

The confident woman who shook her booty for her boyfriend, while dancing around in the kitchen eating pizza—she was in here somewhere, and she was ready to come out.

Time flew by as I prepared myself for life after higher education. With work and finals and my sister's return to Seattle, I barely had time to sleep. But somehow, I managed to pull it off, and before I could comprehend it, the middle of June was upon me…and I was about to become a University of Washington graduate.

As promised, Kellan flew back from Los Angeles to attend my commencement. Sitting on our bed, he distracted me with small talk about his album while I searched through my dresser for something suitable to wear. As I listened to Kellan going over the technical aspects of recording, I felt butterflies of excitement stir in my belly. I'd done it. It was hard work, and it had taken a toll on me, but I had made it through academia. And now I had to be put on display.

That was definitely the downside to graduating. But oddly, I was looking forward to it. Maybe because I knew Kellan, Anna, and my parents were going to be there. Even Denny said he'd come. Everyone I considered family would be in the audience, cheering me on. I found a lot of strength in that.

Holding up a pair of black slacks and a gray button-up shirt, I wondered if it screamed "graduate." A voice in my doorway drew my attention.

"No, not that one." Anna stood leaning against the frame, shaking her head. She took a step into the room and extended her hand to me. "Here, wear this." Sighing, she rolled her eyes. "Lord knows I won't be wearing it for a while."

Taking the small scrap of fabric from her, I smiled down at her protruding belly. Anna was sixteen weeks along, almost halfway to her November due date. In another month, she'd be able to find out if her prediction was correct, if she was having a girl or not. Her bulge was unmistakable now, and utterly adorable on her. She'd grown to embrace her new curves, no longer hiding them behind baggy sweats and shirts. The pale pink fabric of her maternity shirt clung to her hormonally enlarged chest and belly before meeting back up with her hips. It was as seductive as a mom-to-be could dress.

Her friends at work were surprisingly supportive when Anna finally spilled the news about her pregnancy. Her manager gave her a larger-sized Hooters uniform, and told her that her pregnancy wasn't a problem; girls working for the restaurant chain got pregnant all the time. Even though I had told Anna that they wouldn't, that legally they couldn't, Anna seemed relieved that they weren't firing her.

Anna felt even more relieved when the manager confessed that she'd had the same fears when she'd gotten pregnant as a waitress. Then the level-headed woman started showing my sister the ropes behind the scenes. Anna, surprisingly, loved it. And she was good at it, too. I think it gave her confidence, having something to fall back on that didn't rely on her looks. Not that my sister really needed that much help in the confidence department.

Smiling at the image of my devil-may-care sister trying her hand at responsibility, I unfolded the outfit she'd just handed me. It was a short, tight little black dress, the kind that was perfect for almost every occasion. I held it up to my body and pursed my lips. Anna dressed a lot more provocatively than I did, and I suspected a lot of skin would be showing.

Kellan, still lying on our bed, murmured his approval. "That…is perfect."

I glanced over at him. His midnight blue eyes were staring at my cleavage. The neck line was a low-cut square and would rest just above where it needed to. I highly doubted I would be able to wear a bra with it. Anna chuckled and I turned to watch her rub her stomach. She gave me a warm smile. "You'll be beautiful, sis."

I inhaled and stood up just a little straighter. I felt beautiful already, just being near the people who loved me. And even though the dress made me cringe, I would wear it, and wear it proudly. Because, today was a day for bravery. And I had role models of that bravery all around me. Anna was brave everyday as she accepted her pregnancy. And just last week…she had bought a crib. I helped her put it up in my old room and she'd cried when it was completed. I had faith that her bravery would extend to keeping the baby…and someday telling Griffin about it.

And Kellan was brave. Not for recording an album in L.A. No, I don't think that even fazed him. Kellan was brave, because he was coming to Pete's with me, to celebrate my graduation…and his dad would be in attendance. I'd already received a text from him confirming that he'd landed in Seattle. Kellan's face didn't show his turmoil as he smiled charmingly at me, but he was freaking out.

And Kellan was also brave…because he was letting my parents stay with us.

From across the hall, I heard my father's heavy footsteps as he walked over to stand beside Anna. Resting a hand on her shoulder, he looked into the room and frowned at the provocative dress I was holding to my body. Then, he forced the frown into a small smile. "Very beautiful, sweetheart. Your mother and I are very proud of you…even if you're graduating here in Washington and not at our Alma Mater."

Dad sighed at my school choice, and Anna rested her head on his shoulder. He rubbed her arm and held her tight. The surprise pregnancy had been quite a shock to my parents—according to Anna, Dad had cried—but after the shock had worn off they immediately turned into the loving, supportive people that I knew they would be. They even offered Anna free room and board if she wanted to move back to Ohio. She'd refused, deciding to stay here. Maybe it was because of Griffin, maybe me, or maybe Anna finally felt…home.

"Thank you, Daddy."

They were all staring at me now, and I felt heat start to creep into my cheeks. Then I laughed the embarrassment away. "Can I…change now?" I asked my dad and sister.

Anna giggled and backed away, pulling on Dad's arm. "Come on, Dad, let's go get something to eat…I'm starving."

Dad frowned and resisted Anna's pull. He looked over at Kellan, still comfortably lying on our bed. "Kellan, son, you want to give me a hand with...something?" Dad asked awkwardly.

I shook my head, seeing right through Dad's painful attempt to get Kellan out of the room so I could change in private. Poor guy. He was still struggling with his baby girl being all grown up. He must have known, since Kellan and I shared this bedroom, that Kellan had seen me naked before. Hell, Kellan had tied me to his headboard and stroked a feather over every bare inch of skin on me before...not that my dad needed to know that.

Grinning at my dad, Kellan stood up. "Sure, no problem."

He paused to kiss my head before leaving and I whispered a thank you for humoring my father. Maybe Dad realized the respect Kellan was showing him, for he clapped him on the shoulder as they left the room together. I couldn't contain my smile when I overheard Dad talking to him about baseball. Dad was making an effort to bond with Kellan, and that meant a lot to me.

Kellan drove us to school when I was ready to go. I smoothed my tight dress over my thighs, played with the guitar-shaped pendant around my neck, and twisted the promise ring on my finger. I couldn't stop fidgeting. Nervous, excited energy was flowing through my body. When I started the cycle of movement over again, Kellan grabbed my hand, calming me with his silent support. It worked, too.

Once there, my mother started bawling. It made me sniffle, watching the older version of my sister and me cry, but I managed to keep it all together as I hugged her. Dad shuffled her off, and Anna gave me a swift hug. The baby kicked just as our stomachs connected, and I stared down at it.

"Did you feel that?"

Anna laughed at my question and rubbed her side. "The little gymnast? Yeah, I feel that constantly." Contently smiling, she shook her perfect head of dark brown hair. "I'm just grateful that she's moved away from my bladder."

Kellan chuckled at Anna, slinging an arm around my waist. Anna gave me a quick kiss on the cheek then wobbled off after Mom and Dad. As always, Kellan stayed by my side and walked me to where I needed to go. My eyes on the expanse of thigh my dress was showing, I leaned into his side. "I love how you take care of me," I told him.

Looking down at me, he cocked an eyebrow. "You don't think I'm...clingy? Always needing to be near you?"

I laughed and looked up at him. "No...I think you got that part just right."

He gave me a crooked grin, then glancing up, stopped me. Wondering why, I looked up, too. A springy redhead, who had given me no end of grief during my time here, was standing a few feet in front of us. Candy. Kellan's...ex-fling. Her back was to us as she talked with a small group of friends, her two spies among them. I considered going around the woman, but she started turning in our direction and I blinked in surprise. Her belly was swollen with life, and she was much larger than my sister. She really was pregnant.

Kellan raised an eyebrow at seeing her condition but didn't comment on it. When Candy noticed us watching her, she did a double take. I sighed when she disengaged herself from her friends and started heading our way. So much for closing out the school year with never seeing her again. Oh well. Maybe we could finally get that introduction that we'd never had.

Kellan watched her impassively as she approached us. Candy lowered her eyes and looked a little glum. Before I could say anything to her, she started speaking to me. "Hey, I just wanted to apologize...for all the crap I used to give to you about Kellan."

She peeked up at me, then over at him. Her freckled cheeks flushed with color as Kellan knitted his brows. Shaking her head, she shrugged. "I guess I wanted attention." She looked down again. "I was pretty ignored in my high school, and being with you, gave me a certain amount of...clout...here." Her sad eyes looked back up at him. "Sorry. That was pretty shallow of me."

Kellan gave her a half-smile and shook his head. "It doesn't matter." His eyes drifted down her belly, then over to me. "We're not those people anymore, Candy." He looked back at her. "Don't worry about it."

I smiled that he had finally remembered her name. Candy nodded, then, rubbing her stomach, walked away. I was curious about who the father was, but didn't ask. Rumor had it that it was our ethics professor. Our married ethics professor. But, as I knew, rumors could be wrong. Then again, they could also be right.

Shaking off the drama that, for once, didn't involve me, I clutched Kellan's hand and went to find the one girl I did want to introduce him to. Cheyenne was just coming out of the bathroom when she spotted me. She squealed and gave me a huge hug, forcefully yanking me from Kellan.

"Kiera, can you believe it! We did it!" Her slight southern drawl thickened in her excitement. Then her pale eyes seemed to notice that I wasn't alone. She eyed Kellan, then gave him a cute smile that made her eyes sparkle. "You must be the boyfriend?"

Kellan nodded and extended his hand. "Kellan."

Shaking his hand, she muttered to me, "Now I can see why you're straight. I think he'd make anybody reconsider their orientation."

Hearing her, Kellan raised an eyebrow. Then he got a devilish smile and locked gazes with me. I knew he'd just figured out that Cheyenne was the girl who kissed me. Rolling my eyes at the hopelessly attractive smile on his face, I shoved his shoulder back. "Why don't you go have a seat with my parents?"

Grinning, Kellan looked between Cheyenne and I. "You sure? Are you...good...here?"

He chuckled a little, his lips curving seductively. Rolling my eyes again, I forcefully turned him around and made him walk away from us. He looked back at us before disappearing around a corner—the grin there was decidedly inappropriate. Men.

Cheyenne laughed a little as she turned back to me. "Kellan seems…nice."

I shook my head. "Nice…really isn't the best word to describe him." Amazing, hot, sexy, soulful, talented, deep, playful, moody, loving, and at times, considerate, yes…but nice? Well, okay, maybe it did suit him.

The ceremony was a blur to me. I was so energized and emotional, I only recalled segments of it. Seeing my family in the stands—my mom crying, my dad secretly wiping his eyes, Anna whistling with her fingers, and Denny and Kellan beaming at me as they sat side by side. I vaguely remembered the speeches and music. I recalled my name being announced and the ear-splitting noise from my cheering section. And then, it was over and we were back in Kellan's car, driving off to Pete's.

Mom, Dad, and Anna piled out of the car once Kellan parked it, eager to start on the celebration. I watched my sister hug Jenny and Kate in the parking lot, Cheyenne meeting up with them a couple of seconds later. Once my parents and friends disappeared through the front doors, I unfastened my seat belt, ready to join them.

"Coming?" I asked, cracking the car door.

Kellan hadn't moved since stopping the car; his hands were still glued to the steering wheel. His eyes riveted to the image of the bar in his rearview mirror, he muttered, "I'll be there in a sec."

Pale, he looked like he might start the car and drive off once I left. Closing my door, I twisted back around to him. "Hey, you okay?"

He reluctantly pulled his gaze from the mirror to look at me. Eyes wide, he whispered, "I don't think I can do this, Kiera."

I put my hand on his cheek and held his gaze. "Yes, you can. You can do anything." He shook his head and I pressed my lips to his. He didn't kiss me back at first. Too scared or freaked out about facing his biological father, his lips were rigid against mine. Using everything he'd taught me over the years, I teased, licked and sucked his mouth into submission. Within moments, he was kissing me back heartily, his earlier trepidation gone.

When he clutched my cheek and looked about ready to lay me down on his front seat, I pushed his chest away from me. Eyes burning into mine, he breathed raggedly. I bit my lip at the sight of this insanely erotic, yet deeply sensitive man. "Come on, people are waiting for us. Let's go say hello."

He shook his head a little as I opened my door. His eyes clearer, he frowned at me. "You turned me on…that's cheating."

Laughing, I got out of the car. When he popped up on the other side of it, I shook my head. "When do I ever not turn you on?"

Smiling at me acknowledging my attractiveness, he closed his door. "Well, finally you understand the problem that has plagued me from day one."

Holding my hand out to him, I waited for him to join me. "Yes, I do." When our hands met up, I leaned over to nibble on his ear. "And I'll fix your little problem later, I promise."

He gave me a provocative grin as he pulled me towards the bar. "Let's get this over with then."

Kellan tensed and held his breath as he stepped through the double doors. Only seeing the usual suspects, and not an older version of himself, he instantly relaxed. As the crowd assembled near the doors cheered for me, my cheeks blossomed with heat. I held my head high, though, proud of my accomplishment, and accepted the praise and accolades from my friends, family and coworkers.

As it was a Saturday afternoon, the day crew was on shift. Troy smiled at Kellan as we walked past the bar, and Kellan smiled back. As long as the person who fancied him was respectful to me, Kellan was always cordial with them, even the guys. Hun and Sweetie, the gray-haired waitresses that owned this place during daylight hours shuffled around, bringing everyone sodas and water. And Sal, Pete's business partner and the daytime cook, stepped out with plates and plates of food. Everybody was celebrating.

I looked around the sea of familiar faces in the warm, familiar bar. The cream-colored walls were just as cheery as when I had first stepped inside here. The oak floor just as worn. A few more bar signs dotted the walls and windows, but overall, it looked exactly the same. Although, the instruments that now held a place of honor on the darkened stage were a bright pink, a deep purple and an electric teal. One even had Hello Kitty stickers on it. But Jenny's portrait of our boys was behind the feminine instruments, keeping the band's place in the bar, even if it was a smaller place now.

Friends and study mates came up to me, giving me warm, congratulatory hugs. I returned them and gave the graduates my well wishes. Cheyenne gave me a hug, followed by Meadow. The uniquely named woman was playing the bar later tonight with her band, but by the way she was holding Cheyenne's hand, it was clear that she was here for her. I grinned at the schoolmate who saved my butt on numerous occasions when it came to poetry, and her lyrical girlfriend. Meadow's hair was the color of a deep sunset, her eyes as dark as Denny's, but the small smile on her lips exactly matched Cheyenne's, and it thrilled me that the sweet woman had found love after all.

As Kellan hopped up to the bar to get our table some drinks, Denny and Abby stepped through the doors. Kellan greeted them first, clapping Denny on the shoulder as he pointed back at me. Making sure my parents were comfortably seated, I jumped up to toss my arms around Denny.

He was all grins as I pulled away. "I did it, Denny!"

Tilting his dark head, he gave me a lopsided grin. "Did you ever think you wouldn't?"

My grin matching his, I nodded. "Yeah, there were times when school was just about the last thing on my mind."

Denny and I both turned to look over at Kellan talking to Troy at the bar. Smirking, Denny twisted back to me. "Yeah, I know." Just when I was feeling a bit of guilt seep into me, he laughed. "It's a miracle you graduated."

His humor cooling my feelings, I thumped him on the chest. "Quiet, you."

Laughing at me, he slung his arms around Abby and kissed her head. Then Abby gave me a brief hug and congratulated me. I shook my head at the warm...forgiving...pair and made room for them at the table with my parents. My mom looked between Denny, Kellan, and me with a very confused face. She must have pieced together what had really happened between the three of us, and was probably wondering how we could all still be friends. I wondered that too sometimes... I was very blessed.

As Kellan brought the table sodas, I tried to make sure my sister was as comfortable as could be. I even found a pillow in the back room for her to lean against, since bar chairs aren't notorious for being comfortable.

Just as she was giggling and thanking me, the doors burst open with loud fanfare.

Jaw dropping, I spun to watch Griffin and the rest of the D-Bags step inside. I hadn't realized that they'd come back with Kellan. I was touched, but then I remembered that they had just as much reason to return as Kellan did.

Evan's eyes locked onto Jenny a split-second before she jumped into his arms and showered him with kisses. Matt shook his head at Evan and looked back at Rachel walking through the door behind him. The Latin-Asian beauty tenderly grabbed the blond guitarist's hand as they quietly screamed their affection in one simple glance. All of the D-Bags' hearts resided in Seattle. Even Griffin's...if he ever stopped to think about it.

As it was, he was looking around the packed bar for someone...for Anna. She stiffened in her chair and her face went sheet white. She still hadn't told him that she was pregnant. She hadn't told Matt or Evan either, and she made every person who saw her condition promise to not tell Griffin. She wanted to be the one to tell him, even though it terrified her.

And now...the time was upon her. He was here, she was here, and with her tight, clingy, outfit, even Griffin wouldn't miss the fact that she was clearly expecting.

She stood up quicker than I'd seen her move in ages, since she liked to play up the helpless pregnant role. Breathing faster than normal, her eyes darted around the room, looking for an escape. Kellan walked up to greet his band mates as I grabbed Anna's arms, holding her in place.

"Let me go, Kiera," she snarled.

I shook my head. "No, you have to tell him, Anna. He has a right to know."

She grit her teeth and glared at me, but it was too late for her to escape—Kellan was bringing the boys to the table. With our parents watching the exchange between us curiously, I let her go. She started shaking as Griffin approached her.

At first, Griffin didn't notice. A crooked grin on his face, he walked up to her and nonchalantly shoved his tongue down her throat. Anna made a slight noise and her knees seemed to buckle a little. My stomach turned at the sight. Dad looked about ready to clock Griffin.

Evan and Matt behind Griffin were staring at Anna wide-eyed. Clearly, they noticed what Griffin didn't. They both looked up at me. I waved a greeting, then nodded at their unasked questions. Yes, she was really pregnant. Yes, the jackass kissing her was the father. Both of their mouths dropped open as they looked back at Griffin.

Finished mauling Anna, he wrapped his arms around her. That's when he seemed to notice that there was more of her to hug. Looking down, his light brows furrowed in confusion. "Uh, Anna?" Stepping back from her, he poked a finger into her stomach. "What happened to you?"

Anna batted his hand away, her lips tightening in a classic, hormonal mood swing. "You happened to me…ass hat."

Griffin twisted his lips, like he didn't understand. Matt smacked him over the head. "Dude, I told you to wrap it up! Don't you ever listen to me?"

Griffin sneered at his cousin behind him. "What the fuck are you talking about?"

I cringed at Griffin being so crude in front of my father. Dad, his face pale as he realized just who his grandchild's other half was, stood up. His thinning hair seemingly graying by the second, he poked Griffin in the shoulder. Annoyed, Griffin twisted back around.

Lifting his chin, our dad calmly told the bassist, "You will watch your language around my daughter, especially when she's carrying your child." He raised his eyebrow to Griffin, to drive that point home, in case Griffin was still confused.

Griffin shook his head, then finally the light turned on. His eyes widening, he stared at Anna's stomach in absolute horror. "You're pregnant?"

Anna smirked and rolled her eyes. "God, I hope our daughter somehow gets Kiera's smarts…otherwise she's doomed."

Griffin's face softened as he looked up into Anna's eyes. "Daughter? We're gonna have a girl?"

A slight smile crept into his face and Anna's eyes moistened. She shook her head. "I don't know yet, I just feel like…I feel like we made a girl."

His face more serious than I'd ever seen it, Griffin slowly put his hand on Anna's stomach. Her eyes welled so much I doubted she could even see the father of her baby anymore. Surprisingly, Griffin's eyes were a little moist too, as he ran his thumb over the bump. I hoped and prayed the baby took this opportunity to kick, so he would feel it.

Everyone around us was silent as Griffin stared at Anna's belly. Then, so soft I almost missed it, Griffin murmured, "A girl…I'm gonna have a little girl?"

Tears dripping down her cheeks now, Anna whispered, "I don't know if I'm keeping her."

My mother took a step forward at hearing Anna admit that; she hadn't admitted it to anyone but me. Dad grabbed Mom's arm, though, stopping her as he watched Griffin intently. Mom bit her lip, looking like she wanted to start in on a four-hour speech. It was her first grandbaby, after all.

Griffin snapped his head up. "What? You can't give away my kid?" He looked around the bar until he found Kellan, watching from behind Matt and Evan. "She can't do that, right, Kell? Don't I have a say?"

I swallowed the lump in my throat at the look on Griffin's face. I'd never seen him look so…panicked. It was like he was just offered something he really wanted, and then had it snatched away. He looked terrified.

Kellan started to answer him, but Anna brought her fingers to Griffin's cheek, forcing his eyes back to hers. Griffin was shaking when she spoke. "I won't…if you want to keep her…if you want to do this with me…I won't give her up."

I held my breath, waiting for his answer. I noticed my mom and dad clenching hands as they waited, too. We all wanted this baby, but it wasn't our choice. Apparently…it was Griffin's.

He swallowed, then looked down at her stomach again. After what seemed like an eternity, he looked back up at her. "Can we name her after my grandma?"

Anna started to sob, then nodded and threw her arms around his neck. Griffin smiled, inhaling a deep breath as he held her back. The rest of the band members glanced at each other, smiling. Through my own tears and sobs, I heard Matt lean down to Rachel by his side. "One of us should probably tell her that Grandma's name was Myrtle."

I laughed through my sobs, grateful that at least Griffin would have his more sensible band mates to help raise this baby. Thank God for that.

I turned away from the happy couple when I heard Griffin murmur, "Can we still screw when you're like this?" I noticed a group of people who had quietly entered the bar during that dramatic moment. My jaw dropped as I stared.

An older, middle-aged man was standing awkwardly by the bar. Dressed in a nice, black, collared shirt and khaki slacks, he seemed like he could be heading out to one of the golf clubs around the area. Lean and muscular with a head full of thick, sandy brown hair, he was one of those men that you knew would age well. He'd still be attractive at sixty. But that wasn't what stole my breath. It was that he was a spitting image of Kellan. Or rather, Kellan was a spitting image of him. The resemblance was…unmistakable. The jaw, the nose, the brows…everything…right down to the midnight blue eyes.

I was staring at Kellan's father, his natural father.

The man noticed me staring and nodded, lifting his hand in a small wave. I waved back, then noticed the two kids by his side. Well, one was a kid, the other was probably just a few years younger than me. The girl, Hailey, was Kellan's sister. She had the same light brown hair and dark blue eyes that Kellan and his father had. Seeing her father wave at me, she waved, too. A grin broke out on her face when she noticed her half-brother. The grin was so similar to Kellan's, I blinked.

Beside her was a young boy, possibly ten. Like the rest of Kellan's family, he had light hair and blue eyes, although his were a more traditional pale blue. He was staring at Kellan's back with a look of awe on his face. I had a feeling he'd heard a lot about his older brother lately. He clearly already idolized him.

My eyes slowly swung to Kellan's. He was having a conversation with Evan, most likely about making sure to keep a close eye on Griffin around his future child. He hadn't noticed his family yet. Feeling my eyes on him, he lifted his gaze to mine. Not able to change my shocked expression, I watched Kellan frown. Then he seemed to realize what I'd be so shocked about, and his face paled.

He closed his eyes, willing himself not to turn around. I quickly worked my way around the people congratulating Griffin and Anna. Making my way to him, I cupped his cheeks. "Kellan...it's time."

He shook his head, his eyes still closed. "I can't, Kiera." Peeking his eyes open, he cringed. "Ask them to come back later...I just can't right now."

I shook my head, brushing my thumbs over his cheeks. "You can do this, Kellan...I know you can."

He exhaled a shaky breath, then slowly started to turn his head. His breath was faster when he finally spotted the man who'd created him. Taking a step back, he reached down and clenched my hand, hard. His whole body started to tremble as he stared over at the three people who had turned his life upside down. Kellan's father lifted his hand, then let it fall when Kellan didn't react.

Kellan snapped his head back to me. "I can't...I can't do this...please, let's just go." Turning to me, he grabbed my arms. "I'll go anywhere you want to go. Let's just sneak out the back and we can do anything you want to do..."

Inhaling a deep breath, I stared Kellan down. He stopped rambling about all of the places we could go and all of the things we could do, and stared back at me. When he was calmer, he whispered, "I'm scared..."

I nodded, tears in my eyes. "I know...but I'm here, and I'll help you. Besides, what's the worst thing that could happen?"

He swallowed and murmured something that sounded like, "I could care." Closing his eyes, he nodded. He took a minute before facing his father. When he did, he seemed stronger. In fact, his strength seemed to grow with each step he took towards the man. I wasn't sure if he was drawing the courage from me, but I hoped so, since he constantly gave me courage.

When he was almost toe to toe with the man, he stopped. Kellan's father smiled; it was a sad one. "Hello, son," he whispered.

Kellan stiffened, clenching my hand as he nodded, but he didn't say anything. A tension built up as father and son stared at each other. Their appearance was so incredibly alike that I had to imagine every person in this bar now knew that the man who'd died in a car accident a few years ago wasn't genetically related to Kellan. This man before him now...clearly was.

Just as I wondered how to get one of the two silently brooding men to speak, Hailey stepped forward. She sighed as she looked between her half-brother and her father, then put a hand on Kellan's arm. Kellan looked down on her and his entire posture relaxed; I could feel the blood returning to my fingertips.

Putting her hand on her other brother's shoulder, she introduced him to Kellan. "Kellan, this is Riley. Ry, this is our older brother...Kellan."

Riley, still dazed, extended his hand to Kellan. "Wow, I watched some of your shows online. You're...really good. I just started playing the guitar, but I hope I'm as good as you some day." He gave Kellan a charming, awkward smile, and Kellan laughed a little.

Reaching out to scruff his hair, he murmured, "Maybe I can teach you a thing or two one day."

Watching Kellan start to bond with the family he'd never had, I felt the tears stinging my eyes and closing my throat. I choked them back as Kellan's dad cleared his throat. It was obviously affecting him, too.

Kellan timidly looked back up at him, and Hailey, seeing the beginning of a serious conversation, started leading Riley over to the pool tables. "Come on, Ry, let's give them a minute." I thought to do the same, but Kellan's death grip returned when I tried to pull my hand away. Resting my other hand on his arm, I gave him what support I could as his father began to speak.

"Look, I know you're mad at me...for walking out on you, and I don't blame you, but I was young and foolish and I hope you can give me a chance to make--"

Kellan cut the older version of himself off with one sharp question. "Do you know what they did to me?"

His father bunched his brows. "Who? Your parents?"

Kellan nodded, his jaw tight. "Did you know what they would do...how they would raise me...when you left? Did you know what sort of people they were?"

Again, his father blinked. "John and Susan? What are you talking about?" His eyes narrowed as he eyed Kellan cautiously.

Kellan cringed at hearing his parents' names spoken, then he took a step towards his father. When he answered his father's question, his voice, his jaw...his entire body was tight. "Did you know that you left me with people who would viciously abuse me...day in, day out?" His voice shaking, he quietly spat out, "Did...you...know?"

His father's face paled as he finally understood what Kellan was telling him, what Kellan had experienced growing up in that hellhole. By the tears in his eyes and the horror on his face, I didn't think he knew. Sometimes people who you thought you knew really well turned out to be people who you didn't know at all. That seemed to be the case here.

"Kellan...no...I had no idea. I thought..." He swallowed, his eyes misting. "I thought I was leaving you to a happy home, happier than I could have given you back then." As Kellan trembled, his father put his hand on his arm. "I know you won't understand, but I was a mess back then. I didn't know what I was doing. I got caught up in something with your mother that..." he sighed, "was a horrible mistake."

Quickly, he amended with, "Not that you were a mistake, just, the situation..."

Kellan sighed, softening as he looked down on me. "Yeah, I think I get that part." He held his eyes to mine and I could see the guilt in them, for what he had done to Denny with me. If Kellan had gotten me pregnant back then...I wondered just what he would have done. Tried to raise the baby with me? Or left the baby with the person who he believed was the more responsible parent, in our case, Denny?

I honestly didn't know what Kellan would have done. He didn't seem to know either, and the idea that he might have made the same choice, softened him towards his father some. Kellan nodded at his dad, and exhaling with relief that Kellan somewhat understood, his dad smiled; the smile was just as beautiful as Kellan's.

"I tried to see you once, you know. When you were about Riley's age."

Kellan blinked and stared up at him. "No, Mom never mentioned that you..."

His father lowered his eyes. "Yeah, she told me that you didn't know about me, that you believed John was your father." He looked back up at Kellan. "Was that true?"

Kellan shook his head. "No, I've always known that I was a bastard child."

His father flinched at his harsh description then shook his head. "She convinced me that I'd hurt you, by showing up in your life. That it was better if I stayed away...so I did."

Swallowing the emotion building, Kellan's father shook his head again. "She was manipulating me because I hurt her. I never should have listened to her. I should have tried harder to see you...I'm so sorry."

Kellan looked away and I watched a tear fall from the corner of his eye as he closed them. "I never knew you even thought about me," Kellan whispered, his voice still trembling.

His dad put his hand on his arm. "Of course I did. What father could forget about his son, his firstborn?" When Kellan looked back at him, the weary man sighed. "I stayed away for the wrong reasons, thinking I was protecting you by letting you believe the lie, even after their deaths." He choked up on the word death and cleared his throat. "But I'm here now, and I'd like to get to know you."

Slapping on a casual smile, the same smile Kellan could wear, practically on cue, he extended his hand to Kellan. "Hello. My name is Gavin Carter, and I'm your father."

Kellan grinned, then shook his head as he dropped my hand to grab his father's. "I'm Kellan Kyle...and I guess I'm your son."

Laughing as they shook hands, Gavin said, "It's nice to finally meet you, Kellan."

Kellan nodded. "Yeah...you too."

I was already holding back the sniffles when Gavin laid his other hand over their clasped ones. "I don't want to push you, but you have a home with us in Pennsylvania, Kellan. Whenever you're ready, you're always welcome there."

I wiped the tears off my cheeks as Kellan sniffed and nodded. Clasping his shoulder, Gavin said, "Can I buy you a beer?"

Kellan looked back at me, but I grinned and nodded. He needed this. He needed them. Even if he liked to think that he was fine on his own, a piece of Kellan had been missing from birth. He'd filled it with music, he'd filled it with sex, and he'd even filled it with me. But what he needed was what he was now being offered—a family.

Kissing his cheek, I left him to begin the bonding process. I was still wiping my eyes as I walked back to the table where my parents were having a deep conversation with Griffin and Anna; from what I could tell, they were trying to sell the couple on the idea of getting married. Griffin was giving them a blank expression, and I figured his mind was more on what he could do to Anna's body once he got her home. I was immediately grateful that I no longer lived with Anna.

Denny came up to me as I approached the group. Inquisitive eyes on Kellan, he asked, "Everything all right? What was that about?"

Looking over at the father and son, I smiled. "Everything's great, really great."

When I looked back to Denny, he was frowning, staring at Gavin like he was trying to place him. I could tell the minute he did. His dark eyes wider, he snapped his head back to me. "Is that man...? Is he...related to Kellan?"

I nodded, biting my lip. "That's his dad, his real dad."

Denny closed his eyes as years of understanding seemed to flood his features. "God...that explains...a lot." Opening his eyes, he bunched his brows, concerned. "Is Kellan...all right?"

I smiled that Denny still cared about Kellan, too. "Yeah, I think he'll be just fine."

Looping my arm through Denny's I looked around at all of the people in my life—Evan and Jenny cuddling together on a chair, Matt and Rachel talking quietly in a corner, Anna and Griffin giggling while my parents mentioned that it was never too late to give abstinence a try. Rita walked in and sheepishly waved her hand to me in a polite greeting. Kate was showing Abby a text message she'd received from Justin, who had apparently taken a fancy to her. Kellan's siblings were laughing, playing pool together as their long-lost brother caught up with his dad. And Kellan...was actually laughing as he clinked his beer bottle against his father's.

"I think we'll all be fine, Denny," I said, smiling up at the first love of my life who had somehow morphed into the best friend of my life.

Smiling down at me, Denny nodded and gave me my favorite goofy grin. "I think you might be right."

When the evening started winding down, people slowly filtering out of the bar for more private conclusions to their nights, Kellan and I slow danced together near the edge of the stage. Poetic Bliss had just wrapped up their set, and the vibrant girls were loitering around the stage, chatting with their growing fan base. Kellan and I ignored them all and continued dancing to a non-existent beat.

His arms wrapped around my waist, Kellan smiled as he stared down at me. His dad had left some time ago, but they were meeting for breakfast in the morning. It warmed my heart that Kellan was giving him a chance. Everyone deserved at least one chance.

Tilting his shaggy head, Kellan gave me a crooked smile. "So, graduate...what's next?"

I inhaled deep and smiled. "Anything...everything."

Leaning down, he pressed his lips to mine. I cherished the warmth and love that I felt in the connection. His hand reached up to curl around my neck, as he deepened the moment between us. I felt the familiar fire start to burn in me, more intense than ever before, strengthened by the trust and commitment we were forging daily.

Separating our lips, Kellan rested his head against mine. "I have to go back soon, to finish the album."

I sighed and stroked his cheek. "I know," I whispered.

"And after that...will be another tour...to promote the album." He lifted the edge of his lip in a sad smile.

I kissed the corner of his mouth, making his smile widen. "It will be okay...we'll find a way to stay close, just like we have the past few weeks."

Kellan nodded, his face subdued as he thought about how often we would be apart from each other. He hated being separated as much as I did, and for the same reasons I did—we missed each other. While Denny might be my best friend, Kellan was my soul mate, and being apart was...painful.

We silently danced together while people moved around our lightly swaying bodies. Over Kellan's shoulder, I watched Evan and Jenny walking out the doors arm in arm, Matt and Rachel close behind them. Anna and Griffin had left not too long after their reunion. What they were doing now, I didn't want to think about. The only couple still here was Denny and Abby. They were laughing at the bar together, looking perfectly content in their own little world.

Sighing, I rested my head against Kellan's chest, thankful that at least I had tonight with him. Kissing my head, he whispered in my hair, "Come with me."

Pulling back, I scrunched my brows. "What? Go with you...where?"

I looked at the front doors, thinking maybe he was ready to go home. Hopefully, by the time we got there, my parents would be asleep. They'd left several hours ago, so the chances were good. The chances were also good that my dad, ever over-protective, was waiting up for me to come home.

Kellan chuckled and shook his head. Tucking a strand of hair behind my ear, he murmured, "So cute..." Peeking up at his amused eyes, I frowned. He smiled even wider. "Come on tour with me. Hell, come to L.A. with me."

Blinking, I shook my head. "But, my…" I paused, realizing that the tether that had kept me in Seattle was gone. I didn't have to stay here. Sure, I didn't want to abandon my sister here, but if I wanted to take extended visits somewhere…I could.

Seeing me start to realize that, Kellan wrapped his arms around my waist. "You're done with school now. You can do whatever you want."

I frowned. "Shouldn't I have higher aspirations than being a groupie?"

Kellan laughed and shook his head. "You're not a groupie if I invite you to come with us." Ducking down, he met my eye. "When are you ever going to have another chance like this, Kiera? You have the rest of your life to find a job…or never find one. That would be fine with me."

I twisted my lips. "My parents will be so proud."

Kellan shrugged. "Blame it on me. They hate me, anyway."

Smiling, I shook my head. "They don't hate you…that much."

Kellan gave me a soft kiss, then sighed. "I don't care what you do, Kiera, I just want you with me." He pulled back. "And besides, don't you want to be a writer? Aren't you writing a book about us, about our life together?"

I raised an eyebrow at him, not realizing that he'd known that. I hadn't been hiding it…I just wasn't ready to show him yet. He grinned and smiled, then shrugged. "Jenny mentioned it…and I'd love to read it, when you're done."

Biting my lip, I wrinkled my nose. Parts of it were painful for me; they'd be especially painful to Kellan. But…open and honest, that was our policy. I nodded. "When it's ready."

Smiling, he dipped me. I laughed as he pulled me back up. "Well, writing is something that can be done anywhere, and to be the best writer you can be, you'll need to do a lot of research." He shrugged. "What better research could you have than traveling across the nation with me…and Griffin?"

I cringed at that, then chuckled. Squeezing me tight, Kellan rested his head against mine again. "You could come back as often as you wanted, Kiera, to visit Anna…your friends, but I'd like us to do this together this time."

Tightening my arms around his neck, I gave him a soft kiss. "Okay, let's do it."

His lips spread into a grin underneath mine, but then he frowned. "There's only one problem, though."

I frowned. "What's that?"

Sighing, he hung his head. "They don't let girlfriends tour on the bus with the band anymore…"

"Oh…" My body sagged as the exciting and scary prospect of life on a tour bus with a bunch of rowdy boys popped. It seemed like a strange rule to me, but, maybe that was another record label thing…to protect their assets, or something. Was I going to have to follow them around in Griffin's Vanagon?

Just as I was wondering why Kellan had suggested a plan that couldn't happen, he started chuckling. Watching his lips twist into an impish grin, I frowned. What was he up to now?

Shrugging, he added, "They only let the wives come with."

My jaw dropped to my chest. Kellan lifted my chin with his finger, smirking as he closed my mouth. "Wife?" I whispered. Was he serious? Was he really proposing to me?

Grinning, he ran his finger along my jaw. "We've gone about as slow as I can go, Kiera. I love you. I'm sure that I want my life to always have you in it." Shrugging, he shook his head. "Are you sure about me?"

Staring into the deep azure eyes that could carry me away for hours, I nodded. "Yes, I'm sure," I whispered, no doubt in my body about my statement.

He grinned, then kissed me. I tried to deepen the kiss, but he pulled back. Removing my hands from around his neck, he grabbed my right one. I furrowed my brow as I watched him remove the promise ring encircling one of my fingers. Smiling wider than I'd ever seen him, he slipped the ring onto my left finger. Then he mimicked the action with his ring.

Lifting my left hand with his left hand, he beamed at me. "There, now we're married."

Tears in my eyes, I shook my head at him. "I'm pretty sure it doesn't work like that, Kellan."

He shrugged. "Semantics." Smiling softly, he placed my left hand over his heart, and his left hand over my heart. "We're married…you're my wife." He nodded, staring at me intently.

The tears streaming down my cheeks now, I nodded back. "And you're my husband…"

Exhaling with relief, he grabbed my face, sealing the deal with a heart-stopping kiss. I knew that our marriage wasn't legitimate, but that was all a legal technicality that we could change whenever we wanted. In our hearts, we were married, and in the end, that's the part of a marriage that matters the most.

After we finally pulled apart, both of us crying at this point, I waved Denny and Abby over. I had to tell somebody that I had just gotten married. Abby teared up when I showed her our "wedding" rings, and hugged us both. Denny shook his head, containing an amused smile since he knew our "marriage" was symbolic, at best. But then he gave Kellan a hug.

"Congratulations, mate." Clapping him on the back, he laughed a little. "I'm glad I could be here for it."

Kellan laughed and looked at the ground. "Yeah, me too. It seems…" he looked back up at Denny, "appropriate."

Smiling, Denny nodded. Then he gave me a hug. I had to wipe my face on a napkin Abby handed me, I was crying so hard. In my ear, he whispered, "I'll admit, I'm surprised you guys made it," he pulled back to look at me, "but I'm happy that you did."

"Thank you…so much."

I started sobbing again and Kellan wrapped his arms around me. Grinning, he rocked me back and forth. "Should we go home and celebrate?" He wiggled his eyebrows suggestively and I laughed, Abby laughed too.

Shaking my head, I told him, "No…we're going to go rent the best hotel room in the city." Kellan lifted one eyebrow, and I giggled. "I am not spending my wedding night in the room right next door to my parents."

Kellan laughed and nodded, and I hoped my dad didn't kill my new husband when we came back home tomorrow. Or my mom…she was going to be pissed that she'd missed this. Although, I was sure I could talk Kellan into a formal ceremony, just to please her. Personally, I didn't need it. Our quiet moment on the dance floor of the bar where we'd first laid eyes on each other…was perfect.

Kellan started pulling us away, then looked back at Denny and Abby starting to slow dance on the empty floor. I watched them for a second, happy for them, happy for me. Kellan chuckled, then called out, "I could probably scrounge up a couple of rings if you guys want to get married, too?"

I thumped Kellan in the chest, and Denny laughed. Abby raised an eyebrow. "Oh, no, I'm not getting married in a bar. I'm getting the whole shebang." Denny looked back over to her and she lifted her other eyebrow, almost daring him to tell her otherwise. Wisely, Denny didn't say anything, only smiled and hugged her tight.

Kellan laughed, then shook his head. Grabbing my hand, he pulled us from the bar into a future that seemed chock full of possibilities. We were young…we were in love…and we were about to go off into the unknown and make a treasure-trove of stories that we could tell our children about someday. But I embraced the sea of change before me, because there was one thing that wouldn't be changing, and it was the most important thing of all.

Kellan was mine and I was his…forever.

The End

S.C. Stephens is an independent author and publisher who enjoys spending every free moment she has writing stories that are packed with emotion and heavy on romance. She wrote Thoughtless, her first attempt at a full length novel, in 2009. Since then she has written several other novels, and plans to have them all released as ebooks in the near future.

The Thoughtless Series:
Thoughtless
Effortless

Collision Course

The Conversion Trilogy:
Conversion
Bloodlines
'Til Death

It's All Relative

Not a Chance

You can contact S.C. Stephens at:
ThoughtlessRomantic@gmail.com

Made in the USA
Lexington, KY
15 July 2012